Carol Margaret Tetlow

Too Close For Comfort

with best wishes

Carol Tetlow

Éditions
DÉDICACES

Contents

Acknowledgements

Thank you Guy Boulianne, again, for being the publisher who believes in my work, for always being there and to all your team who work so tirelessly.

This novel is dedicated to Helen Norris, my proof reader. Really good friends are hard to come by but you are one of them and you have been there every step of the way. Thank you a million times.

Thank you to Bill, definitely the most long–suffering husband, but also the best.

Finally, thank you to all my readers, my followers on social media and my website. Please keep reading my books!

Follow me at www.carolmtetlow.co.uk
On Facebook at www.facebook.com/carol.goodman.
On Twitter @caroltetlow.

1

'Coffee,' called Nigel.

Ellie, with a certain degree of relief as she was glad of an excuse for a break, sat back on her heels and looked around her at the disarray of cardboard boxes, carrier bags and crumpled newspaper.

'I never realised how much stuff I'd managed to acquire,' she moaned as Nigel came into the room, a mug in each hand and an unopened packet of biscuits wedged under his arm.

'It's certainly going to take you a while to unpack and get straight. But, look at it this way, it's your house and you can take as long as you want.'

He handed Ellie one of the mugs and she took it gingerly, quickly putting it down on the floor and shaking her hot fingers. Moving in was wonderful despite the chaos, she decided, feeling her excitement hugging her, reminding her that this was her home.

When Ellie had first gone to university to study medicine, she had spent the first two years living in a hall of residence. She was grateful for this as it had afforded her the chance to make friendships with people on different courses, kept her well fed with regular if rather stodgy meals and given her the warm environment that was conducive to work. By the end of that time, the need to be more independent had taken a firm hold and she moved out, together with a group of three girls who she believed to be friends, into a dismal, terraced house gloomily decorated in dark paint that was peeling off the damp walls. The carpets were threadbare and the exposed floorboards decidedly dodgy in parts. The staircase had to be negotiated with care, as it was prone to uttering ominous-sounding creaks and whines if you ran up too quickly.

Ellie's parents, normally able to maintain a tactful silence when she did something they did not really approve of, could barely stifle their horror when shown her bedroom. Gagging on the foisty atmosphere, they tried to hold their breath as they took in the sight of the sagging mattress, stained with goodness only knew what and, if they weren't mistaken, that was surely a pile of mice droppings near the unused fireplace which now homed a particularly unreliable-looking electric heater.

The initial thrill of house sharing did not last long. Ellie, perhaps unusually for a student, liked order in her domestic life. She also liked to be comfortable and warm. Whilst bearable in the early autumn, as the trees discarded their leaves and colder weather set in, Ellie found herself spending increasing amounts of time in the library, unable to bear sitting in her room wearing so many jumpers that her arm movements were impeded and still needing an eiderdown around her as she huddled in front of the fire which proved to be as impotent as it looked.

Sadly her housemates did not share her love for neatness and as it became apparent to them that Ellie was a stickler for washing up, tidying and general cleaning, they left more and more for her to do, thinking nothing of leaving the cracked sink piled high with dirty pans and plates encrusted with dried fried egg and the worktops littered with crumbs, smears of jam and the cheapest margarine that the local shop had on offer.

What friendship there ever had been was long gone when Ellie, a year later, looked to improve her lot and managed to get a room in a top-floor flat in a huge Victorian house on a tree-lined avenue, within walking distance of the hospital where she was now working on the wards and also the town centre. Again, cold as a freezer in the winter, it had the slight advantage of one communal room with a good fire, which they all used to study in. Sharing with two other medical students from her year was a further bonus as they were all working similarly so that they could encourage and commiserate with each other and then throw fantastic parties when the exams were over.

Finals behind them, they passed the flat on to three people from the year below them and moved into hospital accommodation for their first jobs as qualified doctors. While this appealed slightly more to Ellie, as she was free from the cold and had her own bed and sitting rooms, she hated having to patter down the corridor to the communal bathrooms and toilets. Admittedly, the jobs she did were far busier than she had anticipated they would be, so in fact she spent very little time awake in her own room, the usual pattern of events being that when she was on call, it was rare for her even to see her own bed, let alone lie on it and then, when she had a free night, she would collapse gratefully between the sheets as early as she could do to catch up with some much needed rest.

After her year of house jobs, Ellie started training to be a general practitioner. She stayed at the same hospital to do two six-month posts, the first in Accident and Emergency, the second in obstetrics and gynaecology and then spent six months working in a local practice. Deciding that it was time for a move, she applied for a job in Medicine for the Elderly at Harrogate Hospital, the town where her parents lived, thinking it would be nice to be nearer to them but having no intention whatsoever of moving back in with them. It was her father Keith who had suggested that she buy her own house, rather than rent and the idea appealed so much to Ellie that she spent all her free weekends back with her parents house-hunting and leaving them strict instructions for them to continue the search when she had to go back to work.

Number 26, Swaledale Crescent was a small, semi-detached house, with a neat gravelled area at the front and a rather bigger garden at the back which was mostly lawned but edged by immaculately laid out borders. The house itself had been well cared for and needed little work to be done apart from some simple decorating to bring colour schemes more up to date and in line with Ellie's own personal preferences. Twenty minutes drive from her parents' house yet only ten minutes stroll from the hospital (five if you walked briskly), the location was ideal and Ellie was ecstatic when her offer was accepted. Equally delighted were the owners of the house who, burgeoning an ambition to retire to Cyprus and escape from the British weather, were keen to proceed as quickly as possible, the result being that Ellie became the proud owner of her own house just a week before she was due to start her new job.

'Thanks for the coffee. How's it going in the kitchen?' Ellie inquired, reaching for the proffered biscuits and taking two.

'I've unpacked everything, but it needs you to decide where you want things to be put. Nothing, miraculously, has broken.'

Ellie raised her eyebrows.

'Now that is amazing! I think I might come and do the kitchen now then. What time is it?'

'Just after four.'

'That's loads of time. I'm meeting Mum and Dad for dinner tonight. They're treating me to a meal at the Clockhouse restaurant.'

'Oh, very nice,' murmured Nigel.

'Well, it is their wedding anniversary but we're combining that with celebrating my moving in – or rather my moving all my possessions out of their house!'

Nigel laughed.

'I can stay for another couple of hours. We could get the kitchen just about done in that time.'

'Nigel, that'd be great. Thank you so much.'

Nigel blew her a kiss. Ellie got up and picked her way carefully out of the lounge and the two of them stood at the entrance to the kitchen while they finished their drinks.

Standing on a chair, wiping out the top cupboards, Ellie glanced over her shoulder at Nigel who was busy washing and drying wine glasses and plates.

'What did you say you were doing this evening?'

'I'm taking Emily out. We wanted to go to the theatre in Leeds but couldn't get tickets, so I expect we'll go for a drink and then a bite to eat.'

'When I'm settled, you'll have to bring her here for a meal,' Ellie suggested.

'Try and stop us,' Nigel accepted instantly, well aware of what an excellent cook Ellie was, having inherited this skill from her mother.

'I'm going to have lots of select little dinner parties,' Ellie went on. 'But you will be at my first. Oh, it is just so exciting having my own home.'

They looked at each other and smiled.

Ellie and Nigel had been friends since the first day at medical school, finding that they were sitting next to each other as their surnames, Woods and Worcester, respectively, followed on alphabetically. This meant that they were destined to share laboratory work and anatomy dissection for the first two years. Nigel's easygoing manner and acute sense of humour, coupled with a determination to do well, made him an attractive work colleague and the relationship soon metamorphosed into a solid and lasting friendship. Though they each had their own circle of friends and tended to drift apart geographically as their respective careers led them down different routes, a week never passed without them at the very least talking on the telephone, catching up with each other's news. Theirs was a mutually supportive bond. When the going got tough for Ellie, who was struggling with end-of-year exams and a broken heart, Nigel came round, coaxed her with her revision and offered her a non-judgemental shoulder to cry on. Reciprocally, when Nigel's father had died after a frighteningly short and one-sided battle with cancer, Ellie was the friend who helped him most; the one who was still there for him months later, aware that the pain and confusion of loss took years to come into perspective. Despite their closeness (and the best attempts of Ellie's mother) there had never been any romance between them. Ellie, if she was honest, had never really considered it, content with their special friendship and the trust and stability that came with it.

Nigel had been working in Harrogate for a year, striving to become a surgeon. Hearing about the vacancy, he had sent Ellie details of the job she had then applied and been accepted for. They were delighted to think that they would be working in the same hospital again and have more opportunities to see each other rather than rely on phone calls and occasional fleeting meetings.

Wiping her forehead, Ellie opened the fridge and brought out a bottle of white wine.

'Time for a glass before you go? I think we've just about finished. I can't thank you enough for all your help. Doesn't it look great?'

Nigel wrung out the dishcloth and arranged it tidily. He glanced at his watch.

'Go on then. Emily won't mind. She knows I'm helping you. Plus her shift only finishes at six, so she'll want some time to make herself look irresistible...'

Ellie leant forward, picked up the dishcloth and threw it at him.

He dodged, laughing.

'Get some glasses, Nigel, please,' Ellie spoke through clenched teeth as she wrestled with the bottle before the cork surrendered with a satisfying pop.

Nigel put his arm around her shoulders in a companionable way while Ellie filled the glasses and then turned to face him.

'To Ellie,' he announced. 'Wishing you every happiness in your new home and don't forget to ask me round for dinner!'

They chinked their glasses together and drank the chilled wine appreciatively, Ellie assuring him that he was welcome any time. It was good to sit and start to relax. Ellie decided that she too would stop working for the day; there was little point in starting again once Nigel had left as she had promised to meet her parents at half past seven. Draining his glass, Nigel put it in the sink, kissed Ellie on each cheek and she hugged him back.

'Have a good evening,' he told her. 'Give my love to your parents.'

'I will. You have a good time too. And thanks again.'

Ellie saw her friend to the front door, watched him jog down the path and turn to wave for a final time at the gate. She closed the door, turned and leant against it, smiling and laughing with delight and excitement that she was alone in her own house.

Performing an elaborate balancing act, Ellie negotiated a path between boxes of books that had been left on the bottom few stairs. A similar sight met her on the landing. Suitcases, bags and more boxes were waiting for her attention. Thanking providence that she had at least had the foresight to make up her bed, she sat on the edge of it while she rummaged through her large leather overnight bag and found soap, shampoo and her make up. In the bathroom, she turned the bath taps full on and added a very generous helping of scented gel which erupted into a furious froth on contact with the water. As she slipped between the bubbles, she felt every muscle sigh with relief after her long, hardworking day. Lying back, she gazed critically around her, imagining what colour to paint the walls, whether a few more shelves might not be useful and what species of houseplant might flourish in a steamy environment. Unable to resist the relaxing, almost hypnotic effect of the warmth, Ellie closed her eyes, aware that she could drift off to sleep with little problem. She allowed herself to ooze to the very verge of somnolence before suddenly immersing her head under the water to soak her hair and then sit up to apply shampoo.

Towel wrapped elegantly around her head, Ellie dried her slim body and managed to find clean underwear, a short-sleeved, lacy white blouse and a pair of smart dark blue trousers. She knew there was no hope of her unearthing her hair dryer, so she mopped up as much moisture as she could and then combed out her long, naturally wavy auburn hair. More excavating in her bag produced her jewellery box and she chose a choker of tiny pearls that her parents had given her for her twenty-first birthday and some matching pearl studs for her ears. Finally, after skilfully applying a minimum of make up, concentrating on making her eyes looks even more huge and green, Ellie stood back and surveyed the finished result, turned sideways to look at her profile, nodded her approval and then grabbed a jersey before running downstairs to look for her handbag.

Minutes later she was carefully locking her front door behind her and walking down the path to the waiting taxi.

The Clockhouse restaurant was situated in one of the larger hotels on the outskirts of the town, well reviewed by the sternest of critics for its opulence and exquisite cuisine. It was the place they always went when there was something to celebrate – birthdays, exam results, episodes of exceeding good fortune and, as was the case today, anniversaries. Invisible from the road, there was nothing other than a large sign to indicate that this was where to turn and then there was over a mile of gravelly drive to negotiate before arriving at the front of the hotel, which boasted mullioned windows, a turret and a dense coating of ivy. Ellie spotted her parents' car in the car park as she got out and paid the driver. Struggling a little with the gravel in her sandals, she finally reached the front door, entered the building and headed for the bar, where she knew they would be waiting. It was fairly busy in there, despite the fact that it was still quite early in the evening. The bar itself was surrounded by people queuing to order drinks and Ellie had to stand on tip toe to peer over and to either side of them before she spotted her parents sitting proprietorially at a table in one of the bay windows. As she approached them, weaving her way between other customers, Ellie noticed, before they saw her, that all was not as it should be. Normally, on evenings such as these, Ellie's mother, Diana, would be looking as if she were about to burst with excitement, chatting non-stop to her husband, whilst gazing around at all the other people to see what they were wearing and if there was anyone she knew, even if only to nod to. But tonight, they were sitting in silence, almost like mirror images across the table to each other, hands holding their drinks, heads both turned towards the gardens.

Puzzled, Ellie joined them, pulling a chair out and throwing herself onto it.

'Hello, you two!'

Her parents jerked their heads around and, after the merest hesitation, smiled broadly at her. Diana put her hand over Ellie's and gave it a squeeze. Keith, getting up, kissed Ellie on the cheek and asked her what she would like to drink.

'I'd love a dry white wine please, Dad,' Ellie told him.

'Another one for you, my dear?' Keith addressed Diana.

'No, I'm fine at the moment, thank you.'

'Right then, I'll not be a minute.'

Keith left them, pausing only to pick up his own glass, which he intended to have refilled.

Ellie watched him go and then turned to her mother.

'So,' started Diana, with slightly stilted cheeriness, 'how's the house coming along?'

'Mum, it's just brilliant. I love it so much already.'

Diana was unable not to enjoy her daughter's delight.

'Tell me what you've been doing today. Are you all unpacked?'

'As if, Mum,' Ellie retorted. 'But, I have made a good start. Nigel's been great, helping out all day and the kitchen is just about sorted. The lounge is getting there very slowly and my bed's made but the rest is still in turmoil. Not that I mind,' she added quickly, 'I knew it would take time and it's worth taking that time to get it right. Will you come round tomorrow and have a look. I can manage tea and biscuits...'

'Of course we will, Ellie. Is there anything we can bring you?'

'No, I'm fine. Oh, thanks, Dad.' Keith, having had more luck at the bar than a lot of other customers, put down a glass of wine in front of Ellie. He spilt it slightly and swore quietly before sitting down with his refreshed gin and tonic.

'We're just talking about Ellie's house, Keith.'

'It's great to be in, Dad. Mum says you'll both come round tomorrow and visit. But before I forget...' Ellie opened her handbag and brought out an envelope that she placed on the table between her parents. 'Happy Anniversary!'

'Thank you, darling.'

'Open it then,' laughed Ellie.

Keith pushed the envelope towards Diana, who took this correctly as a sign that she should do the honours. From inside, she produced a card which, when opened up, contained a voucher for a weekend away for two.

'How marvellous!' Keith exclaimed, reaching over again to kiss his daughter.

'Ellie, you shouldn't have,' Diana started. 'That is so very generous of you. You should be watching your money now that you have a mortgage, not spending it on us.'

'I wanted to get you something very special,' Ellie explained. 'You've been so much help to me over the last few months, house-hunting, letting me clog up your spare room with all my things. It's the least I can do. You make sure you have a good time.'

They sat chatting happily and Ellie noticed that her parents seemed to have thawed considerably, much to her relief. A waiter appeared with menus, greeting them warmly, if formally, recognising them from the last time they had been there. Ellie realised how hungry she was. She and Nigel had barely eaten all day. Although they had promised each other a break at lunchtime, during which Nigel was to go and get fish and chips, they had never quite got round to doing that, being so intent on their work, so the only sustenance they had actually had was tea, coffee and biscuits. Looking at the choices that evening, Ellie found it difficult to choose whether to play safe and go for one of her favourites or try something completely different.

'What's it to be, then, Ellie?' asked Keith, who had decided what he wanted before the menu had even arrived.

'Mmmm, it's so hard,' muttered Ellie, sipping on her wine.

'Would you like a little more time?' asked the waiter, tactfully. Ellie shook her head.

'No, take my parents' orders first and I'll have decided by then.'

Decisions made, they had time to finish their drinks before being summoned to their table.

'Just look at that beautiful centre piece,' commented Diana, enjoying a small, but exquisitely arranged bowl of flowers.

'Are they real?' Keith suggested, receiving a withering look from his wife.

'Of course they are.'

Keith extended his hand to touch one of the petals and knocked over an empty wine glass as he did.

Diana sighed and Ellie quickly picked it up.

'No harm done,' she reassured them, trying to make light of the situation.

'I wish the same could be said of my crystal vase,' Diana grumbled.

Keith, Ellie noticed was paying overly close attention to a bread roll on his plate.

'What's going on?' she asked.

Diana looked at Keith with some exasperation, raised her eyebrows and turned to Ellie.

'He bought me the most stunning vase for our anniversary. I'd seen it in Bowkers, in Leeds, when we went there a fortnight ago. I unwrapped it and then put it carefully on the worktop to wash before I decided where to keep it permanently. Then along comes your Dad, to wash up the breakfast things and knocks it onto the floor. It's now in a million pieces.'

'It was wet and slippery,' apologised Keith.

'I'm so upset. It was really expensive.'

'Oh, Mum,' commiserated Ellie. 'What an awful thing to happen. Still, it was just an accident, wasn't it?'

Diana sniffed and glared at Keith, who returned his attention to the buttering of his bread roll and Ellie realised why there had been an atmosphere between them when she arrived. Fortunately, the arrival of their starters meant that they could focus on their food.

'These prawns are just delicious,' said Keith. 'Try one, Diana.'

Hesitating for a moment, Diana smiled and picked one off Keith's proffered plate.

'Lovely. I wonder what they put in that dressing. How's yours, Ellie?'

Ellie, who had been hungrily mopping up garlic mushrooms and dipping her bread in the residual butter, had to be content with making appreciative noises as her mouth was full. She nodded in acceptance when the wine waiter hovered at her shoulder.

Their plates removed, they sat back.

'So, Ellie love, when does the new job start?' Diana asked.

'The day after tomorrow.'

'Looking forward to it?'

'Yes, I think so,' Ellie replied, rather doubtfully.

'You don't sound that convincing,' Keith commented.

'Well,' Ellie started, 'I'm looking forward to learning about care of the elderly. But the consultant I'm going to be working for has a bit of a reputation.'

'What sort of reputation?' Keith quizzed her.

'He's very strict. He likes his ward to be run like a military procedure, I'm told he doesn't tolerate ignorance or laziness, mistakes or mess. Nigel's been telling me all about him. Some of his previous junior staff have been reduced to tears or even to resignation. It's going to be very hard work and there is quite a lot of on call as well.'

'Even better then that you've got your own home to go to. It'll be good for you to get right away from the hospital when you're not working,' decided Diana.

'Plus, if the going gets too tough,' added Keith, 'you just come round and see us. It's so good to have you back nearer home again.'

Ellie looked gratefully at the two of them, secure in their support of all she did.

By the end of the main course – Ellie opted for the chicken, Diana for the duck and Keith, his favourite rump steak – and several glasses of wine, the three of them were laughing and joking and enjoying themselves thoroughly. Though full, they all had dessert and even Diana roared with laughter when Keith, who had a selection of ice creams served elegantly in a tall, thin glass – not entirely dissimilar to the vase that had fallen to its demise earlier in the day – kept missing the glass completely with his spoon.

'How much have you had to drink, Dad?'

'Oh, you know, quite a bit. Your Mum promised she would drive home. Oops, I can't even shpeak now!'

Diana tut-tutted in a half-hearted way. 'Coffee, I think for all of us, particularly you.' She glared at Keith.

'Let's go through into the lounge and look out at the gardens again.' Ellie got up and wisely decided that it would be a good idea to take her father's arm and walk with him.

'Thank you for a beautiful meal,' she said when they were sitting down again, tiny cups of coffee in front of them along with a plate of homemade petits fours.

Too full to talk much, they watched the sun setting behind the trees in the distance, casting long shadows across the lawn and flowerbeds. Ellie, replete and exhausted, looked forward to her bed and her first night in her new home. The grandfather clock in the corner of the room chimed.

'Ten o'clock. My taxi will be here any minute.'

Ellie reached down for her handbag and then stood up. Her parents did likewise. Ellie shook her head vigorously.

'There's no need for you to go. I'm exhausted. You two stay a while and enjoy what's left of your anniversary. It's been absolutely lovely here, as usual.'

She hugged her parents in turn.

'Don't forget you're coming to visit tomorrow.'

'What time would be best?' inquired Diana.

'Any time, although probably afternoon is best. That'll give me more time to get the place looking more like home before you see it. See you then.'

So saying, she walked away from them across to the door. Looking back, she was delighted to see her father take her mother's hand and kiss it gently before holding it on his knee.

2

Ellie was dreaming. Weird, vivid dreams that made no sense. Exhausted by the previous day's work and three acute admissions during the evening which had taken her until after midnight to deal with to her satisfaction, she had returned to her on-call room, torn off her clothes and abandoned them in an unruly heap by the side of the bed before falling under the duvet without even pausing to wash or brush her teeth.

She was out shopping, bizarrely wearing her white coat, the pockets crammed to bursting point with books on diagnosis and prescribing. Her stethoscope was draped around her neck and she had her best handbag over her shoulder. No one seemed to be giving her a second glance, a fact she found strange but was pleased about as she happily browsed amongst the rails of clothes, searching for something to wear. A slinky little dress fell off its hanger and she bent down to pick it up, never having been able to abide people who simply left clothes to be trampled on. As she did so, pens cascaded out of her top pocket, dozens of them, never seeming to stop until she was upright again. It was only then that she realised, to her horror, that she was completely naked under her coat. Fumbling, she tried to do up the buttons but her fingers were slippery and the button holes too small so she made little progress. Embarrassed, she fled from the shop, trying to wrap the coat, which now seemed to be two sizes too small, around her, hoping that no one had noticed.

Out in the street, she hurried towards the pelican crossing and waited impatiently for the traffic to stop. Hearing the bleeping signal to cross, she ran to the opposite pavement and down the next road that led to the car park. She couldn't understand why the crossing was still bleeping, persistently, more loudly, though she was getting further away from it.

Slowly, the fogginess of sleep clearing, it began to dawn on Ellie that her pager was going off, summoning her rudely back to reality and work. She groaned loudly, reaching automatically for the telephone which was by the bed, without needing to open her eyes.

'Dr Woods,' she mumbled as the cheery voice from switchboard answered.

'Good morning, love! Sorry to disturb you. It's Whitby Ward that wants you. Hang on and I'll put you through.'

'What time is it?' Ellie's words were groggy.

'Just after three. Hold on.'

Ellie collapsed back onto the pillows. She felt terrible, dragged back from the deepest pit of unconsciousness. She doubted that she would be able to force herself out of bed and over to the ward.

'Dr Woods? Staff Nurse Hepworth speaking. Can you come and see Mr O'Halloran please? He's suddenly become very breathless. He hasn't any pain but his pulse is fast and his blood pressure's quite low.'

'Okay, give me a couple of minutes. I'll be as quick as I can.'

'Thank you.' The telephone abruptly went dead.

The nurse sounded brisk and wide awake, a far cry from how Ellie felt. She rolled out of bed and shivered with the cold, empty feeling that she associated with that time of the night, sleep deprivation and hunger. Not caring what she looked like, she pulled on some jeans and a huge baggy, but cosy, jumper that her mother had knitted for her and pushed her feet into some sandals. Grabbing her white coat and keys, she let the door slam behind her, oblivious to the other sleeping resident doctors in the building. Ellie ran across the small courtyard from the doctors' residence to the main hospital, the skin on her face startled by the chill in the air, which hinted that autumn was well and truly established and winter not far away. Tying back her thick hair

15

as she scuttled down the corridor, she was more or less awake by the time she reached the ward entrance.

The sound of her shoes seemed amplified as she made her way to the nurses' station to find the nurse who had telephoned. Looking up from the notes she was writing, Caroline Hepworth smiled, half in welcome and half in amusement at Ellie's dishevelled state.

'Coffee?' she suggested.

Ellie accepted with a nod before asking, 'What's been happening?'

Efficiently Caroline summarised the problem.

'Mr O'Halloran appeared to be quite settled earlier on. Then one of the nurses found him sitting on the edge of his bed, gasping for breath, hardly able to talk. She's with him now. We're giving him some oxygen.'

'Right, that's great, thanks. Which bed is he in? Have you got his notes please?'

Though it was night, the ward was far from silent. Guttural coughs disturbed the peace along with the sound of restless bodies turning in their starchy sheets as Ellie made her way to the nearest bay of six beds, squinting to read her patient's notes as she went. She looked up and saw that there was an eerie glow emanating from behind the curtains which were pulled protectively around the middle bed, the lamp having been turned towards the wall so as not to disturb the other patients. Ellie could hear Mr O'Halloran panting, punctuated by the soft voice of the young nurse who was trying to reassure and calm him. Pulling the curtains open, Ellie joined them and sat on the bed next to her patient who has leaning forward, staring at the floor. Wisps of thin white hair stood up erratically from his scalp. His light blue pyjamas, which bore evidence of what he had had for supper, were ringing wet and clinging to his skin. His old, freckled hands gripped the bed covers, his shoulders were hunched, his whole body intent on working to help him breathe.

He turned his head to Ellie, his eyes pleading with her to help, his face contorted with a mixture of exhaustion, fear and distress. Sweat was pouring from his forehead and the unmistakable sound of fluid on his lungs was audible without Ellie having to use her stethoscope. Quickly and efficiently, Ellie managed to extract the briefest of histories and then conduct a thorough examination. She asked the nurse to rush and fetch a cocktail of drugs which she then slowly administered intravenously.

The results were gratifyingly rapid. Mr O'Halloran's breathing rate slowed, his colour returned and he visibly began to relax, letting go of the bedspread and pulling off the oxygen mask to that he could start to talk more, thank Ellie and the nurse and then, a few minutes later, urgently demand the commode as the full force of his diuretics took hold. Ellie re-examined him and, happy with his improved condition, felt that she could leave him to go and write up her notes.

A glance at the clock on the wall opposite informed her that it was four thirty, that no man's land of time when it was impossible to decide whether to go back to bed and risk feeling dreadful after a short but deep sleep or to stay up, get an early start to the day and feel shattered by lunchtime. Now wide awake, it seemed likely that she would choose the latter.

As Ellie sat down at the desk and reached into her pocket for a pen, Caroline came bustling back from the ward kitchen with a mug of piping hot coffee and some slices of fruitcake, left over from the previous day's afternoon tea.

'How is he?' she asked, concerned.

'Much better now. Acute left ventricular failure. He'll need an ECG and a chest x-ray but they can wait until morning. I'll be back to check on him before then. We'd better have everything sorted before the ward round.'

Carefully, she documented her findings and then the drugs she had given Mr O'Halloran, interspersed with gulps of her coffee and bites at a piece of cake. She had large, round, generous handwriting, clear and friendly to read, a mark of her extrovert nature. Finishing, she leant back and stretched, then got up and returned to her patient, who, improved even further, was also enjoying a hot drink, relaxed back onto his pillows and in a clean pair of pyjamas. He welcomed Ellie with a huge, edentulous smile. She perched on the bed side to examine him once more and then spent a few minutes chatting to him in whispers, which proved to be difficult on account of his poor hearing and the disapproving grunts from the occupants of the adjacent beds. Finally making one or two alterations to his drug chart which was hanging at the foot of his bed, she bade him farewell and went back to finish her coffee, which by this time was uninvitingly cool.

'He's fine now,' Ellie informed Caroline and the two other nurses who were sitting with her. 'I've written up his notes and made a list of what needs to be done before Dr Blake does his rounds. He'll need some bloods doing as well please, first thing.'

Caroline dutifully took the notes and scrutinised the requests that she would pass on to the day staff when they swapped shifts in three hours.

As if aware that the emergency had been dealt with, the rest of the ward seemed to be awake. Slippers shuffled across the floor, taking their owners to the toilets, chests were cleared and bells rang, demanding attention and, if possible, the first cup of tea of the day.

Ellie took her leave and made her way back to her room. The sun was just beginning to show signs of rising over the town but it was still very chilly. Only two months into the job, she had already learned a huge amount and gained irreplaceable experience but at the cost of long and arduous hours, frequently during the night.

Closing her door with decidedly more consideration than when she had left for the ward, Ellie hung up her white coat and sat on the end of her bed. From where she sat she could see her reflection in the mirror above the slightly chipped washbasin. A tired face gazed back at her. Sighing, she found her wash bag, grabbed a towel that was draped across the radiator and, kicking off her sandals, made her way into the little en suite shower room and turned the tap on full force. Leaving the water long enough to warm up, she discarded the rest of her clothes, stepped into the cubicle and stood with her eyes closed as the water drenched her and encouraged some life to return to her weary body. Slowly she washed her body and then her hair, enjoying the sensuous feel of the hot water against her skin. The water started to run cold, a sure sign that whoever was in one of the rooms on either side of hers had also decided to have a shower. With reluctance, she stepped out and dried herself quickly, before wrapping the towel around her head and walking naked back to the bedroom to find clean underwear, the charcoal grey trousers she had worn the day before and a tightly fitting aquamarine v-necked jumper.

Fighting with the tangles in her hair, she felt tired but fresher. She realised that she had forgotten her hair dryer and cursed before scraping her damp locks back from her face and tying them back up again. A little mascara, a touch of lipstick later and a rather more presentable sight looked back at her.

'It could be worse,' Ellie concluded critically and grabbed her coat.

She made her way back to the main hospital building which was gradually coming to life with the start of another day. The canteen was nearly empty, save for a few early risers who were reading newspapers while they drank their cups of tea before reporting to work. The fluorescent lighting cast an unnatural complexion around the room. Ellie's stomach protested as she walked past the hot counter where congealed fried eggs looked back at her like a row of deflated eyeballs and limp rashers of bacon were piled up against greasy fried bread which in turn rested against a bowl of luke-warm bloated tinned tomatoes. Playing safe, Ellie picked up a bowl of cereal and two pieces of toast. As she paid for her food, plus a giant mug of tea, she spotted Nigel, sitting alone and rather forlornly at a table in the corner. She made her way over to him and he looked up and grinned welcomingly.

'Ellie,' he greeted her warmly. 'I couldn't think of anyone I'd rather have breakfast with this morning. Bad night? Or just insomnia?'

Ellie placed her tray on the table and sat down opposite him. He too looked spent. An incipient beard cast a shadow over the lower half of his normally good-looking face.

'Late to bed then up since three with a chap with LVF,' Ellie explained, helping herself to a sachet of sugar, ripping it open and sprinkling the contents on her cereal. 'How about you?

'You look as bad as I feel.'

They laughed.

'You look beautiful, as always,' Nigel told her. 'We've been in theatre all night. A gangrenous bowel, then an appendix and we've just finished a ruptured aortic aneurysm. Fascinating stuff though. I got to do quite a lot, too.'

'That's great, Nige.'

Ellie scooped up a spoonful of flakes.

'Just remember, when you're a GP, you're to refer all your patients to me.'

'I can't think of anyone I'd rather entrust them to.'

They ate in silence for a while, Nigel munching his way through a huge, ungainly bacon and egg sandwich liberally anointed with brown sauce that was oozing from the edges and dripping mostly onto his plate but also onto the table.

'Got a busy day ahead?' he asked, wiping his mouth on the sleeve of his white coat and then trying to remove the resultant stain with a paper napkin, ignoring Ellie's disapproving look.

'Big ward round this morning with Dr Blake, then just sorting things out and clinic after lunch.'

'Want to meet up for a drink after work? I should be done by six.'

Ellie shook her head, mouth full of toast.

'Thanks, Nige, but not today. I'm worn out and so are you. Why don't you come round for supper tomorrow? My parents are coming. You've not seen them for ages. They've been brilliant, helping with the house, doing decorating for me. Bring Emily if you like. It'll only be pasta or something simple but Mum and Dad would love to see you.'

'Okay, you're on. I'll ask Emily but I've a feeling she said she was doing something with a mate. I'll ring you later and confirm. Bloody hell...'

This last comment was made as his pager went off. He got up, scraping his chair across the floor and walked over to the nearest telephone. Ellie smiled, watching him gesticulate wildly as he talked into the receiver. She was buttering her second piece of very cold and rubbery toast when her came back to join her.

'Can't stop long, I need to go and put a drip back up. The house officer has tried but can't do it. I just hope she hasn't used up all the best veins.'

He took a final, long drink from his cup and pulled a face.

'We used to have trouble too, Nige, when we first started doing drips,' Ellie reminded him.

'Oh I know, I guess I'm just tired out and had hoped for an hour's kip before I went back onto the ward. I'll never get away now.'

'Come on,' volunteered Ellie. 'I've finished now. I'll walk with you to the ward – it's on the way to Whitby Ward.'

They got up simultaneously, Nigel grabbing the half-slice of buttered toast that Ellie had left and walked companionably out of the canteen and down the corridor, chatting as they went.

'This is me,' sighed Nigel as they came to a halt outside Scarborough ward.

Ellie gave him a quick hug.

'Take care, Nige. Get some rest tonight and let me know about tomorrow.'

'Will do. Speak to you later.'

He blew her a kiss before he marched purposefully onto the ward, hands pushed deep into his trouser pockets, subconsciously perfecting the walk he would adopt when a consultant.

All the lights were now on in Whitby Ward and the cumbersome breakfast trolley blocked Ellie's way, forcing her to squeeze past it to gain access. The nursing staff had just swapped over to the early day shift and a feeling of prickly efficiency had replaced the nighttime quiet. Responsible for this transition was Sister Penelope Makepeace who positively bristled as she delegated tasks to her staff, barely pausing to acknowledge Ellie's arrival with a hint of a smile and a wave of her hand that was more like a salute. Ellie, knowing better than to interrupt, turned her attention to the notes trolley and began systematically to work her way through all the patients who were under the care of Dr Jeremy Blake, consultant physician. This task was obligatory before any of his rounds as he was a stickler for perfection and the manner in which he made his displeasure known was one best avoided at all costs. Ellie got out her notebook and made a list of jobs to be done. Blood and urine test results needed to be filed and x-ray and scan reports had to be chased as they seemed to have disappeared mysteriously on their journey from the radiology department to the ward. Efficiently, Ellie made several telephone calls with gratifying outcomes and then, seeing that Sister Makepeace had finished addressing her staff, went over to sit next to her.

As if blessed with the power of mind reading, Sister Makepeace announced that Mr O'Halloran would be going down for his chest x-ray in the next half hour and would be having his ECG on the way back to the ward. The night staff had already taken his bloods before they went off duty. Ellie thanked her and then worked her way around the patients, checking each one carefully but trying to keep one eye on the time. Mr O'Halloran was enjoying his breakfast, a sticky legacy of which was already clinging to his pyjama top. He looked well but tired, which Ellie could well empathise with, particularly when he emitted a huge yawn as she listened to his chest.

Her other admissions from the previous evening seemed to be stable and Ellie quite confidently sat down to put finishing touches to notes and await the arrival of Dr Blake. At nine twenty precisely, Ellie could barely conceal a smile when, predictably, Sister Makepeace made her customary disappearance to the staff toilets, only to emerge with freshly applied lipstick (the use of which she castigated her staff for) and in a haze of expensive perfume. With a certain amount of obvious discomfort, she persuaded her belt to fasten around her ample waist, smoothed her uniform over her very generously curved hips and patted her hair to make sure that there were no stray tendrils daring to make a bid for freedom from her chignon.

You'd think we were expecting royalty, thought Ellie, who had watched this performance three times a week for the last eight weeks, not just Jeremy Blake.

The double doors to the ward burst open, causing Sister Makepeace to leap to attention but it was simply a porter delivering some flowers for a patient and the day's post. Flustered, she accepted both, sent a nurse off with the flowers and threw the letters onto her desk to be attended to later, just in time to see Dr Blake turning into the ward.

'Good morning, Dr Blake,' she gushed, walking to meet him.

'Good morning, Sister Makepeace. Are we all ready? Then let's get on with it.'

Jeremy Blake glanced around him. He spotted Ellie and nodded curtly to her. In his early forties, he could have been a good-looking man had it not been for his inability to smile and consequently his rather haughty and unapproachable manner. The epitome of neatness, he wore a dark grey pinstriped suit, creaseless white shirt and a dark blue tie with the faintest of thin lighter blue stripes. His light brown hair was immaculately cut and his aftershave discrete but exotic.

'Dr Woods, come and join us.'

'I'm ready, Dr Blake. How are you today?'

'Well, thank you,' he replied, enunciating his words with care whilst with equal care avoiding actual eye contact with Ellie.

It was a curious procession that made its way to the first bay of patients. Dr Blake marched ahead, followed by Sister Makepeace, fighting to keep up, her tiny steps unable to keep pace with his purposeful strides. She kept turning to ensure that the following entourage was behaving in the prescribed manner; that her staff nurse was pushing the notes trolley, that Ellie was already fishing out the folder for the first patient to avoid any unnecessary delay that might be interpreted as disorganisation and that the two student nurses, who had been instructed to join the ward round, keep silent but be prepared to act as gophers, were bringing up the rear neatly and not whispering to each other or being silly. Earlier that morning she had caught one of them imitating her and the resultant scolding was not one for the faint hearted. Not for the first time, Ellie could not help but think that this performance was outdated and would have been more appropriate twenty years previously, rather than in the last decade of the twentieth century. She envied her colleagues whose ward rounds with their consultants were less formal affairs, everyone being positively encouraged to contribute, all ideas welcomed and discussed over coffee, nobody being made to feel inferior.

Even the patients, ill as they might be, seemed to sense the importance of the occasion and to Ellie's cynical eye, appeared to be sitting up to attention, their daily papers or paperbacks put tidily to one side, the earphones for the hospital radio hung neatly on the bed head.

Dutifully, once Sister Makepeace had introduced each patient, Ellie presented their medical details, a précis of their history and an account of their progress. This was followed by a hushed period while Dr Blake quizzed the patient himself, carried out any necessary examination, perused the drug chart and then barked a list of orders at Ellie who scribbled them all down as fast as she could, hoping that if she were to miss one, then Sister Makepeace would remember.

The staff nurse paled visible and looked on the brink of tears as Dr Blake left no one on the ward unaware of his anger when a chest x-ray was missing and she rushed off to try to find it, the sounds of Sister Makepeace's disapproving clucks in her ears as she went. Ellie bit her tongue, making a mental note to speak to the nurse later and make sure she was all right. In the meantime, she had to content herself with staying where she was on the opposite side of the patient's bed to her consultant, listening intently and nodding appreciatively when he shot pearls of wisdom over the bemused patient.

Thus, painstakingly slowly, or so it seemed, they progressed round the ward, dissecting the management of each patient and allowing one or two lucky ones to go home. When they came to Mr O'Halloran, Ellie recounted the events of the night and tried not to smile too much when he winked at her conspiratorially. She anticipated Dr Blake's requests by handing him the ECG and chest x-ray and was grateful for the most peremptory of nods from her boss as he patted Mr O'Halloran's shoulder before moving onto the next bed, unable to fault Ellie's management. Some two hours later, when Ellie's legs were weary from so much standing, the patients had all been seen and she, Dr Blake and Sister Makepeace were sitting in the doctors' room having a cup of coffee. The latter was doing her utmost, quite effectively, to monopolise the attention of Dr Blake, fluttering her eyelashes and giggling in a sickeningly girly way when he talked to her.

Ellie, coffee finished, asked to be excused on the premise of having many things to do on the ward. Jeremy looked her up and down.

'Off you go then, Dr Woods. What are you waiting for? Don't be late for clinic though. We'll be starting promptly at two.'

'I won't be,' promised Ellie, emitting a sigh of relief as she closed the door behind them and made her way back on to the ward. Her pager went off as she neared the nurses' station and she picked up the telephone to answer it.

'Ellie, it's Nige. Have you finished your mammoth round?'

'Hi, Nige. Yes, we're done.'

'How was it? Any better than usual? I rang the ward to see if you were free an hour ago but they said you were barely half way through.'

'Not really. He didn't shout quite as much as he can do. Penelope Makepeace was in her element of course. Reeking of French perfume and obviously wearing her new uplift bra!'

She heard Nigel guffaw.

'They make a right pair, those two. You know the gossip is that they're having some mad passionate affair behind his wife's back.'

Ellie was silent for a moment and looked round to see if anyone was listening.

'Anyway,' Nigel went on, 'I'd love to come round tomorrow. Emily's going out with some girlfriends to plan a hen party, so she's pleased to know that I'll be out of trouble!'

'That's wonderful. Mum and Dad will be thrilled to see you.'

'What time? About seven thirty?'

'Perfect. I'll have to go now, Nige, I've so much to do. Have a good night's sleep.'

'You too, Ellie. Take care.'

Ellie put the telephone down and started to plan what to cook. Her thoughts were rudely interrupted by the return of Penelope Makepeace, eager to ensure that all was shipshape on her ward and that no standards had even threatened to slip during her extremely brief absence. Ellie turned her attention to work and methodically began to plough through her list of Dr Blake's instructions. A conscientious and dedicated worker, Ellie relished in having things well organised. It, without a doubt, made both her life and the lives of her patients and those with whom she worked, infinitely sweeter; thus it was thanks to these enviable characteristics that Ellie found herself with time to sit down and have some lunch before the beginning of clinic.

One of the drawbacks however of sitting down was that she relaxed and by letting down her guard, exhaustion was allowed to creep to the surface. As she made her way down to the outpatient department, with leaden legs, Ellie could not stop herself from yawning. The prospect of a long afternoon was far from appealing. One look at the face of the nurse in charge of the clinic told her that the list of patients was even longer than usual. Despite having arrived with ten minutes to spare, Ellie was informed that Dr Blake was already in his consulting room and seeing the first gentleman. Wearily, Ellie accepted the set of notes that the nurse held out to her. Expectant faces looked up at her as she prepared to call out the name of the next patient. As the afternoon progressed, she could feel that she was decelerating rapidly and her eyelids felt as though they had been injected with quick-set concrete. She found that she needed to ask Dr Blake frequently for advice and each time this meant waiting until he was free, thereby prolonging things even more. He had been so incensed by her last question, which he perceived to be facile and unworthy of any doctor that was working for him, that he threw the folder of notes at her and told her to pull herself together.

Weakened by her fatigue, Ellie fought to hold back her tears. With as much dignity as she could muster, she simply picked up all the papers, apologised for having bothered him and made a hasty exit from his room. Taking a moment to collect herself, Ellie massaged her temples and briefly closed her eyes, extending her neck. The door to her consulting room flew open.

'Dr Woods!'

Ellie looked up alarmed and saw Jeremy Blake standing over her.

'You are no use to me in this state. Go home.'

Ellie stuttered but he continued.

'Go home. There are only a few more patients. I can manage. Just be sure this never happens again.'

Ellie sighed with a mixture of relief and despair.

'Thank you, Dr Blake. That's very kind of you. I'm so sorry.'

He had left the room by this time.

Resignedly but gratefully, Ellie gathered together her few possessions and left. The nurse watched her go, feeling wretched for her. Like most of her nursing colleagues, she liked Ellie and had a high regard for the calibre of her work. There had been no reason for Dr Blake to react that like that. But any further sympathy was not to be forthcoming as a bellow from within his room had her running back to see what he wanted. Working alone, it took Dr Blake rather longer to finish the clinic than he anticipated. But finally, he sat drinking a well-deserved cup of tea and waiting for his secretary Muriel to come down from her office to join him so that he could dictate his letters. Looking at his watch, he picked up the telephone and dialled.

'Hello, my darling. I've just got my letters to do and then I'll be with you.'

He laughed softly.

'About half an hour, I would imagine,' he went on. 'I can't wait any longer than that.'

The affection that had softened his face disappeared as if switched off when Muriel entered and sat down opposite him, taking out her notebook and pen as she did so.

3

Ellie, having bathed, wrapped her dressing-gown around her soft and perfumed body and ran downstairs. Her house was more or less just as she wanted now. Sure, with the passage of time, she might buy some new pieces of furniture to add to or replace what she already had but for now she was happy and content with the way it was. Thanks to her parents, it had been completely redecorated and the substitution of her well-chosen subtle shades for the ubiquitous magnolia had transformed each room to her satisfaction.

Opening the fridge door, she investigated the contents and reckoned that there was plenty there to create an interesting filling for a jacket potato plus a healthy side salad. She planned to prepare this and then take it into the lounge, eat it while curled up on the settee and flick through the television channels until she found something unchallenging but entertaining to watch. But first there was something much more important to attend to.

At that exact same moment, the front doorbell rang, three times in a row, two short rings and one long.

Eagerly, Ellie rushed from the kitchen, stopped to glance in the hall mirror and free her hair from its clasp and then opened the door.

'Hi,' she gasped, breathlessly, 'I thought you said thirty minutes.'

Jeremy Blake laughed, stepped inside and kissed her on the cheek, simultaneously producing a bottle of wine from inside his overcoat.

'Aren't I worth waiting for?' her asked, putting his arms around her and licking the side of her neck with the tip of his tongue, an action he knew was bound to make her squirm with desire.

'Oh,' breathed Ellie, trying half-heartedly to pull away, 'how long can you stay for?'

'Long enough, my darling. Let's open this bottle and take it upstairs.'

Ellie disappeared for a matter of seconds, returning with two glasses and a corkscrew.

'Here, let me take them.' Jeremy placed the glasses on the windowsill by the front door, where he had left the bottle while removing his coat.

Turning to face Ellie, he noticed lasciviously how very beautiful she was. Devoid of all her make-up, her clear complexion was adorable. Her auburn hair was half wet but still managed to create a tantalising effect and her eyes shone with excitement, despite the rather dark circles under them that gave away her tiredness. Slowly he reached out and undid the belt of her dressing-gown, opening it to gaze at her naked body.

'Christ, Ellie, you're so gorgeous.'

Ellie half smiled and fixed her eyes on him. She started to undo his tie, kissing him gently on the lips as she did so, aware of the effect she was having on him, enjoying the power that she felt. Deliberately, infuriatingly slowly, she unbuttoned and opened his shirt, caressing his chest, stimulating his nipples with her tongue. As she reached for his belt, he pushed her gently onto the stairs, before hurriedly discarding his trousers and underpants. They made love quickly and frantically. Ellie could feel the carpet almost burning her buttocks as Jeremy repeatedly thrust inside her but any discomfort paled into insignificance compared to the pleasure that she felt.

Mutually satisfied, they fell apart, laughing. Jeremy stood up, grabbed the glasses, corkscrew and wine and led Ellie by the hand up to her bedroom. Even though she had only thirty minutes' warning of his arrival, Ellie, with time to prepare, had lit candles which she had then placed strategically around the room. The duvet with its dark crimson cover was turned back and the resultant effect was one of a romantic, almost erotic glow. Ellie cuddled up to Jeremy causing him to open the wine in an unwieldy fashion. A few drops spilled onto her shoulder and he sucked them off before pouring them each a glassful and handing one to Ellie.

'I'll have to keep an eye on the time,' he announced, rather spoiling the moment.

Ellie tried hard not to sigh out loud. 'What time are you expected home?' she whispered.

'I rang and said I'd be a couple of hours. I had to leave a message on the answering machine as Helen wasn't in. Well, I suppose she could have been. She does have this excruciatingly annoying habit of not picking the phone up when it rings.'

Ellie winced a little at the sound of his wife's name. It was easier for her to pretend that this relationship was permissible when it was impersonal. She tried to change the subject.

'You know, the hospital gossip is that you're having an affair with Penelope Makepeace.'

Jeremy took a large gulp of his wine and roared.

'I expect she started the rumour herself,' he commented. 'No, she's not really my type at all. I prefer the more...delectable woman...' He ran one hand gently up Ellie's stomach and stroked her breast briefly before reaching out to refill his glass which he then drained in one further swallow.

'Careful,' Ellie could not resist saying. 'You've got to drive home.'

'I'm fine, my darling. Don't worry about me and let's not think about my going home just yet. There are a few things I'd like to do before I go.'

Ellie giggled and allowed him to draw her into his arms, where, as usual, the longing to be near him and wanted by him extinguished any conscience or guilt that she might have had.

They made love again, this time taking things more slowly and infinitely more gently. When they climaxed, Ellie clung to him, willing the moment to be prolonged as much as possible, only too aware of what his next words were going to be. Even as she did so, she was aware of his left arm moving and his head twisting so that he could see the time on his watch. She wanted to ask him to stay, to ring home and leave another message to say he had been delayed but she knew, from past experience, that this was not an idea he would receive well. She could feel the beginnings of tears prickling in her eyes, her usual self-control weakened by her fatigue.

Jeremy moved from beneath her and propped himself up on one elbow.

'I have to go, sweetheart.'

Ellie nodded miserably, trying not to look as she felt.

'I think your clothes are all at the bottom of the stairs,' she said, trying to sound light hearted, knowing that Jeremy hated sentimentality as he was going.

'I expect my bloody shirt's all creased now,' was the response, as he sat up, swung his legs out of bed and stood up.

He strode out of the room and Ellie ran after him, grabbing an over-sized jumper as she did so, suddenly embarrassed by her nakedness. She sat halfway down the stairs, elbows leaning on her knees, watching him dress, trying to reassure him that his shirt was fine. She descended the final few stairs as he reached for his coat.

'That was amazing, as always.' He kissed her on the cheek.

'Let's do it again, very soon,' suggested Ellie in a voice she hoped sounded both casual but alluring and did not reflect the pleading voice in her mind.

'Tomorrow, perhaps?'

Ellie shook her head.

'My parents are coming over for supper, plus a couple of friends. You could join us, you know, if you'd like...'

Jeremy shrugged dismissively.

'I don't think so. It'll have to be next week then. We'll sort something out. Maybe we could go out for dinner somewhere.'

'That'd be great, okay,' Ellie agreed excitedly and hugged him, craving for one last smell of him before he went.

'See you tomorrow, at work. I'll probably pop onto the ward later in the morning but I'll be in my office before that from about ten, if you need anything.'

Ellie nodded, transformed from the role of lover to junior doctor in an instant.

He opened the door and then surprised her by turning back and kissing her passionately.

'I need you, Ellie,' he breathed before giving her a final wave and disappearing into the dark, frosty evening.

When he was out of sight, Ellie closed the door, glad to shut out the cold. Exhaustion hit her head on, making her feel morose and lonely. No longer hungry, she crept back upstairs, picking up her dressing-gown as she went. She blew out the few candles that were still burning and then curled up under the duvet before falling asleep in seconds.

On Ellie's first day on Whitby Ward, some two months earlier, she was summoned to Jeremy's office, immediately. He was sitting behind his desk, which, like the rest of his office, was meticulously tidy. Neat piles of journals, all in chronological order, were arranged symmetrically on the top shelves. Rows of identical files filled the lower ones. A rather dull painting of some flowers was hung on one wall, perfectly straight. There was nothing to give away anything intimate about him, no photographs of laughing family, no gimmicky toys or ornaments, not even an old coffee mug. Ellie tried not to gaze around too much, fearing that it would be interpreted as impertinence rather than interest and sat down in the chair on the opposite side of the desk to him when he indicated that she should do so. She kept very still, feeling very nervous as he scrutinised her carefully.

'Dr Woods,' he stated.

'Ellie, please,' she replied, smiling, hoping to see some sort of crack in his façade.

'I am Jeremy Blake, consultant in medicine for the elderly. I am in charge of this ward where we have, at any time, up to twenty-four patients under my care. I am an excellent physician and my care of patients is exemplary. I expect my junior staff to work similarly. If you do so, I am sure we will get along well. However, I will not tolerate silly mistakes or sloppiness. If you don't know something, then ask. Here is the timetable for your week, including my ward rounds and my clinics, all of which I expect you to attend. You will learn a phenomenal amount from me if you work well. I appreciate that you are hoping to go into general practice, but you will of course realise that a huge amount of your workload in that speciality will revolve around the care of your more elderly patients. Thus what you learn from me will pay dividends when you join a practice. Please also note that I have allocated two one-hour periods each week during which time I will teach you on a topic which either you or I will have suggested beforehand, to allow you time to prepare. At the end of each of these tutorials, I will mark your performance and advise you on further reading. Do I make myself clear?'

Ellie swallowed hard.

'Yes, Dr Blake.'

'Good. Please also remember that every Tuesday I expect you to attend the lunchtime meeting that is held in the postgraduate centre. There is a programme of events on the notice board on the ward, next to the nurses' station.'

He looked at Ellie expectantly, waiting for her to speak.

'That's fine. Thank you. I'm looking forward to working with you,' she added, hoping to please him.

He nodded in a perfunctory fashion.

There was a knock on the door and Muriel came in, carrying a small tray from which she lifted a bone china cup and saucer and placed them with reverence on the desk in front of her boss.

'This is my secretary, Muriel. She will deal with all your letters. Muriel, my new SHO, Dr Woods.'

'Hello, it's lovely to meet you,' Ellie said warmly, holding out her hand.

'Shall I get another cup?' Muriel looked at Jeremy.

'No, she will be going back onto the ward in just a few moments.'

Muriel shrugged apologetically at Ellie and made her exit.

'Well, I think that's all. If you would like to go and introduce yourself to Sister Makepeace, I will join you shortly and we shall start with a ward round, so that you can get to know all the patients.'

He turned his attention to a pile of letters, leaving Ellie in no doubt that she had been dismissed. She got up, hesitantly.

'Thank you very much, Dr Blake.'

He continued with his work.

Relieved to be out of his office, Ellie made her way to the nurses' station where she had her first sighting of the formidable figure that was Sister Makepeace.

The first couple of weeks were harder than Ellie could have imagined. Only once did she make the mistake of not preparing properly for a tutorial, hoping that she would get away with it. The resultant soliloquy from Jeremy left her in no doubt that his wrath was not to be taken lightly. Since then, she had enlisted the help of Nigel, despite his protestations that the work was all about topics that he would never have to deal with as a surgeon, and with his encouragement she put in more effort than she had done for her final exams at university, often sitting up late into the night. Jeremy proved to be a fair man, however. He would acknowledge Ellie's preparation and contributions and so she found that she was looking forward to the teaching sessions. He had been correct; he did know an enormous amount and was also gifted in his ability to disseminate his knowledge. Ellie, sponge-like, absorbed it all and found her confidence growing. On one occasion she bravely attempted a joke and was rewarded by one of his rare smiles and a roar of laughter, his face changing completely, softening to become attractive. Any independent observer would have been aware, long before Ellie, that these interludes of humour and mutual enjoyment were becoming more frequent and longer lasting.

After a month, it had been a particularly long day and Ellie was just finishing on the ward when Jeremy strode down the corridor and asked her to step into his office. Frantically trying to think what she might have done wrong, Ellie followed him with trepidation. Muriel had left, so he stood in her empty office which led to his and looked at Ellie.

'It's been a difficult few days,' he announced. 'You've been working exceptionally hard and equally well.'

'Thank you,' stammered Ellie, unaccustomed to such praise.

'I wondered if you would like to come for a drink, if you've finished, before you go home.'

Ellie paused, but only fractionally.

'I'd love to.'

'Are you ready to go now?'

'I will be in about five to ten minutes. Shall I meet you in the doctors' mess?'

Jeremy shook his head.

'We're certainly not going there. It'll be far too busy and the beer's always warm and flat. Anyway I think it would do us good to get out of the hospital environment.'

Taken aback, Ellie heard herself agree.

'I'll wait here and sign some letters. Come and get me when you're ready.' He sat on the edge of Muriel's desk, picked up some papers and started sifting through them.

Ellie rushed back to the ward, afraid to keep him waiting. She hurriedly scribbled the last of her notes and glanced at some blood results which she decided could safely wait until morning. Then, rather like Sister Makepeace, she fled to the toilets to brush her hair and wipe the smudged mascara from under her eyes.

Jeremy took her to a small pub about five minutes' drive from the hospital. It was quiet inside, as it was still relatively early and only a handful of people were standing at the bar, gazing into their drinks like fortune tellers consulting their crystal balls or swapping stories of the day's events with friends. Jeremy pointed to a circular table in an alcove and Ellie, having requested a glass of red wine, went over there, took off her coat and sat watching him at the bar, thinking how different he already looked, out of his work context. She allowed herself to smile at him as he came over, carrying, to her surprise a bottle of wine, two glasses and a packet of peanuts.

'I thought you might be hungry,' he explained. 'And if you're not, I am.'

Ellie wrestled open the wrapper and placed the nuts equidistant between them.

They drank in silence. Ellie wondered what to say and was relieved when Jeremy broke the silence for her.

'That's better. Mmm, not bad at all,' he concluded, swirling the wine around in his glass expertly.

'Do you know a lot about wine?' asked Ellie.

'A little,' he conceded. 'I like fine wine and good food – who doesn't?'

'Certainly all doctors seem to,' agreed Ellie. 'I think it's probably because we have our fill of hospital food when we're at work, so we appreciate the finer points of good cuisine much more.'

'Do you cook?'

'I love cooking,' enthused Ellie, relaxing as she started to talk about one of her favourite topics. 'I don't do as much as I might at the moment but if I'm entertaining, then I love to spend time creating dishes. I used to do a lot of cooking at home, my mother taught me. Now, she's a brilliant cook.

'So whom do you cook for?' Jeremy enquired.

'Well, I live on my own. I bought a small house just before I started this job. Unlike some people, I actually like cooking for myself. I don't just make do with beans on toast or a bowl of cereal. I always make myself a meal in the evening – often only something quick and easy, but still a proper meal. How about you? Lots of men cook these days.'

'Yes, sometimes I cook,' Jeremy replied. 'Here, have another drink.'

They chatted about various things. Ellie heard herself telling him more about her house and also her previous jobs. Looking back on the evening, later, which she did on many occasions, she realised that, whilst she had revealed all manner of things about her life, she had learned very little about Jeremy's. But Ellie was enjoying herself. Away from the restrictions of the professional working relationship, Jeremy proved to be an amusing and charismatic companion. After rather more than half a bottle of red wine on an empty stomach, having left most of the peanuts for him, Ellie found that she was hoping that he might suggest dinner but was disappointed when he simply offered to give her a lift home.

Thanking him as she got out of his car as gracefully as she could, she hesitated before closing the door, suddenly feeling brave.

'If you'd like to, you'd be very welcome to come in and have supper.'

Expecting him to decline, she was taken aback when he politely accepted and found that she was trembling a little as she unlocked the front door.

'Make yourself at home,' she called, rushing around, switching on lights, and turning on the fire in the living room. 'Can I get you a drink?'

He followed her into the kitchen.

'Let me help you,' he suggested.

So Jeremy poured out more wine and sat at the kitchen table while Ellie chopped vegetables, cold chicken and weighed out rice, before conjuring up an exquisite risotto for them to eat.

Placing Jeremy's plate in front of him, she watched for his reaction as he took a mouthful.

'This is sensational,' he complimented her.

It was hard to believe that barely three hours before they had been on the wards, working hard and feeling (well, certainly Ellie had been) that they would never get away. Now, sitting together, laughing like good friends and content in each other's company, it felt as if the hospital was a hundred miles away. When Ellie offered cheese and fruit for pudding, Jeremy put his hand up to say no.

'I couldn't eat another thing,' he told her, 'but it was delicious.'

'You're welcome,' smiled Ellie. 'Coffee?'

He nodded.

'Let's go in the lounge. It'll be nice and warm in there now.'

They took their cups through. Jeremy sat in the armchair and Ellie, her legs curled up beneath her, settled on the sofa. He continued to ask her many questions, about the house, what decorating she had done, what she had left to do and where she had bought different pieces of furniture. Slightly more sober, Ellie looked at the clock on her mantelpiece and was amazed to see that it was nearly eleven.

Commenting on the time, Jeremy got up and apologised. 'I'm so sorry; I had no idea that it was that time. I've taken up all of your evening. I must be going.'

'I've really enjoyed it,' Ellie reassured him. 'I'd only have sat and watched television if I'd been on my own. It's been good to have such excellent company to say nothing of a good laugh.'

They collided as they moved to the door. Neither of them knew who made the first move so perhaps it was just mutual magnetism to blame for them ending up in each other's arms, kissing passionately with Ellie feeling that her stomach and legs had turned to jelly. Breathlessly, they broke apart and looked at each other, Jeremy alternately stroking her cheek or running his fingers through her hair.

Ellie broke the silence. 'Do you have to go?' she ventured.

'I ought to,' he whispered. Then, watching Ellie's face fall, 'But I don't think I can.'

Ellie moved to kiss him again. She felt her head swim, possibly from desire, perhaps from too much to drink.

Gauchely, she took his hand and they went upstairs, Ellie expecting him to resist and delighted when he didn't.

Some time later when they returned, exhausted by their lovemaking, Ellie suggested that he stay the night.

'I can't, I'm sorry. I have to get home. My wife will be wondering...'

Ellie felt as though he had just thrown her downstairs as pain shot through her with the same intensity as the passion that she had just revelled in.

'You're married?' she gasped.

'Yes, but it's not that simple. Ellie, you're beautiful. Everything about you is beautiful – the way you look, your face, your body, the way you think and converse and laugh. Even the way you cook. I can't get enough of you and I must see you again. I'll explain more next time. Just be patient with me and give me some time.'

Ellie did not know how to react. She knew what she should say but before she could, he kissed her sweetly on her lips and held her tight. She felt any resolve that she had to throw him out and slam the door evaporate. He stood, holding her, rocking her from side to side in a hypnotic fashion, and caressing her back. When he eventually felt her tension disappear, he cupped her face in his hands and smiled at her.

'I do have to go now, but you can bet your life I'll be back soon.'

Thus their relationship began. Ellie, lust cooled by her return to work the following morning, was determined to put the previous evening behind her and not tell anyone about it, including Nigel. In addition, she had somehow to manage to maintain a professional cool at work. As she walked to the hospital, she rehearsed in her mind what she was going to say to Jeremy when they met that morning for one of their tutorials.

He called her in when she knocked on the door to his office. Pushing open the door, the first words of her carefully prepared speech on her lips, she was momentarily floored by the fact that he was not sitting in his chair. Waiting behind the door, he closed it and then, when she spun round to face him, enveloped her in such a gloriously adoring bear hug that Ellie completely forgot what she had ever intended to say.

4

Nigel was in the kitchen with Ellie, keeping her amused, while she was cooking the supper, with descriptions of what he had been doing at work. He had arrived half an hour earlier bearing flowers that she strongly suspected he had bought at the last minute from the garage forecourt which was at the end of her road and two bottles of exceedingly good wine. He was helping himself to crisps, watching Ellie as she turned the heat down under pans and peered inside the oven. Despite the fact that she seemed to be juggling several tasks at once, she looked unflustered and happy.

'I thought you said you were doing something simple!' Nigel said, with his mouth full. 'I'm looking forward to seeing your Mum and Dad. When was the last time I saw them? It must be months. I must say, your Dad's done a great job with the decorating.'

Ellie agreed, glancing around at the brightly tiled kitchen.

'It's looking fantastic now, isn't it? Mum helped me with the curtains and some cushion covers. I'd never have got to this point without them. Dad's been here nearly every day, while I've been at work, slaving away, like the perfectionist he is. Oops, time to put the crumble on.'

She handed Nigel a paper bag.

'Here, chop these for me.'

Nigel dutifully reached for a knife and the wooden chopping board and set about his allotted task, wiping the mushrooms and then slicing them carefully.

'Oh, they're here,' cried Ellie, hearing her front door open and the sound of her parents' voices.

'We're in the kitchen,' she called out.

Keith and Diana appeared in the room arm in arm.

'Hello, Ellie! Nigel, it's so lovely to see you. You're looking well. How's life treating you?'

Nigel returned Diana's affectionate hug and shook Keith firmly by the hand.

'It couldn't be treating me more kindly.'

'Good, now let's open the bottle of wine that's in the fridge. Dad, if you wouldn't mind,' Ellie suggested, passing Keith the corkscrew.

Keith fumbled for a while, cursing what he called Ellie's new-fangled gadget.

'Here, let me.' Nigel took over and had the cork out within seconds. 'Glasses, Ellie?'

'Those ones there,' indicating with a nod of her head four glasses on the worktop that were gleaming after a vigorous polishing.

Keith, Nigel and Diana arranged themselves around the kitchen table which Ellie had set before Nigel arrived. Nigel complimented Keith on his work around the house and Diana on her good taste with the soft furnishings. Diana, who did most of the talking, asked Nigel about his work, how he was finding the job and how he thought Ellie was settling into hers. Thinking that Keith was uncharacteristically quiet, Nigel tried to involve him more, asking about his favourite football team and their chances in the league that season, well aware that he followed their progress avidly and usually liked to wax lyrical about their prowess but even then, most of his answers were monosyllabic and quietly spoken. Deciding that maybe he was tired, Nigel allowed Diana to take charge of t he conversation.

'And how's that girlfriend of yours, Nigel? Emily, isn't it?' Diana asked, once they had all started on their first course of smoked mackerel with a dressed green salad.

'She's fine, thanks, Diana. Things couldn't be better.'

'I asked her to come tonight,' butted in Ellie, 'but she's gone out with some girlfriends. What did you say they were doing, Nige? Planning a hen party?'

'That's right,' Nigel affirmed. 'Something about booking a weekend away at a health spa, being pampered.'

'Goodness,' commented Diana. 'Before I married Keith, I just had a few friends round to my mother's house and we spent the evening drinking sweet sherry and eating sandwiches which my mother had cut into triangles as she believed that to be the height of elegance!'

Nigel laughed. 'I think it's all a lot more involved and complicated, these days. Anyway it's important that they get it right, so she's glad that I'm safely accounted for, for the evening.'

'Which one of her friends is getting married?' enquired Ellie, munching. 'I forgot to ask you when you told me on the phone as I was too busy worrying about the ward round.'

Nigel cleared his throat.

'Well, actually, it's not one of her friends, it's Emily.'

'Nigel!'

Beaming, Nigel announced that he had proposed to Emily and been accepted.

Before he knew it, Ellie had thrown her arms around him and was kissing his cheek.

'That's such wonderful news, Nige.'

'Yes, congratulations, Nigel. I hope you'll be very happy,' Diana added.

Keith leant over and patted him on the shoulder.

'All the best,' he said, quietly.

'Champagne,' shrieked Ellie. 'We must celebrate. I've got a bottle in the fridge that I was saving for a special moment.'

She jumped up from her chair and extracted the said bottle which she then held over the sink while she opened it. In fact, she had bought it that day, thinking what a lovely surprise it would be for when Jeremy came round next and that maybe they could drink it while they were in the bath together. But never mind; it could easily be replaced and Nigel's fantastic news deserved to be feted appropriately.

She asked her father to pour out some for everyone, while she turned her attention to the sauce for the spaghetti, which she liked to make at the last moment, so that it was completely fresh.

'Cloth, Ellie, quickly,' Diana called.

Ellie turned and saw her dad and Nigel trying to mop up spilt champagne with their paper napkins.

'Oh dear, here you are. Shall I do it?'

'No, I'm fine,' her mother assured her. 'It's only a tiny bit, really. You concentrate on the food.'

Order had been restored to the table when Ellie passed over plates piled high with pasta which was being caressed by a rich sauce of chicken, mushrooms and onions with white wine and cream.

'Time for a toast, before we start,' suggested Ellie. 'Raise your glasses please,' she looked at her three guests, 'to Nigel and Emily, wishing them every happiness for the future and to the best parents in the world, with love and thanks for all their help.'

'And to Ellie, for being the best friend and hostess I could wish for,' added Nigel.

Laughing, they all drank simultaneously, enjoying the chill dryness of the sparkling (and if Ellie had dared to tell them, vintage) beverage.

'So, when's the wedding, Nigel?' Ellie wanted to know.

'We planning for Christmas,' he answered, messily winding spaghetti around his fork and shovelling it into his mouth. 'This is great, Ellie.'

'But that's only a couple of months away,' Diana criticised. 'There's so much to do when you're planning a wedding. Hasn't Emily realised that?'

'We've talked about it, of course. But we both want this so much that we don't want a long engagement. Plus Christmas is such a magical time; it just seemed like the perfect choice. There's going to be time enough to arrange what we want, I'm sure.'

'But what about Emily's parents? What has her mother got to say on the subject?' Diana continued, obviously convinced that no one could possibly organise a respectable wedding in that time.

'They're absolutely fine about it. I'm pleased to say they are quite overjoyed at the prospect of having me as a son-in-law.'

Ellie squeezed Nigel's hand.

'I bet they are. Has Emily got a big family?'

'Just an older brother Simon. He works abroad a lot but I'm sure he'd be back for the wedding. He's a nice guy. Not a bit like Emily – she's so small and cuddly; you'd not expect her to have a tall, slim brother.'

'And will you be getting married in church?' Diana quizzed him.

'Yes and, before you say anything, that is booked. There's a little church near where Emily's parents live and we're to be married there. Afterwards, we'll just have a dinner for relatives and special friends,' he paused to look at Ellie, 'and then we're off on honeymoon but only for ten days as I can't get any more time off. I've had to make all manner of swaps to manage that much.'

Diana and Ellie were full of questions which they alternately fired off at Nigel, trying to find out as much detail as possible, which was difficult as apart from the bare bones of the ceremony, little had been arranged definitely and Nigel certainly had no idea at all what colour Emily would be wearing and whether she would have any bridesmaids.

Suddenly, Keith, who had remained silent but attentive throughout, started to choke.

Ellie leapt up and started to pat him on the back, hard. Diana passed him some water and encouraged him to have a drink, even suggesting that perhaps champagne might be preferable as it was bubbly. Nigel, metamorphosed in a moment, rather like superman, from good friend to surgeon, primed himself to perform the Heimlich manoeuvre, but Keith, struggling to his feet, waved his arms about to fight off his would be helpers and lurched to the bathroom. Ellie, following him, found the door shut firmly in her face and had to suffer the angst of listening to him cough and cough repeatedly until he was finally sick. It went very quiet. Ellie, worried, banged on the door and was relieved to hear the taps running and noises suggesting that her father was splashing water on his face. When he finally appeared, after a few moments that

45

had felt like hours, he was pale but smiling.

'Sorry, love,' he muttered and allowed his daughter to help him downstairs and into the lounge, where she settled him in the big armchair and made him promise to stay put while she went to make him a cup of tea.

In the kitchen, Diana had started to wash up, having made the decision that the meal was over and was being helped by Nigel. They both looked up expectantly when Ellie walked in.

'He's fine now. I think a piece of chicken must have gone down the wrong way.'

Diana looked relieved.

'I thought everyone had about finished,' she told Ellie, to explain why the table was virtually clear. 'I'm sorry about that. It rather spoiled things. He really shouldn't eat so quickly. It happened last week as well when he was gobbling a sandwich.'

Putting the kettle on, Ellie shot a look at her mother, who was unconcernedly straightening the tea towel and hanging it back up on the oven door handle to dry. She then caught Nigel's eye, who shrugged his shoulders.

'Let's all go in the lounge and have coffee,' he suggested. 'Diana, you've done enough. Go and sit with Keith and Ellie and I will see to the rest. One thing though, Ellie, didn't I hear you say something about crumble?'

'Yes, blackberry and apple,' was the reply.

'One of my favourites,' hinted Nigel.

'I'll get you a dish. Could you just pop and ask Mum and Dad if they want any?'

Nigel returned in an instant, shaking his head.

'Diana says she couldn't eat another thing and you should know that pasta always fills her up. Your dad says thanks but no thanks and he could murder a cup of coffee. So... All the more for me.'

'Help yourself,' laughed Ellie. 'There's cream or ice cream in the fridge.'

'What about you?'

'Later, maybe, thanks.'

Ellie carried the coffee through, Nigel, following behind with an enormous helping of pudding, proceeded to tell them all what they were missing. Keith, a decidedly better colour than he had been, drank his cupful gratefully and accepted Ellie's offer of a small brandy. Chocolate mints were handed round and gradually they all relaxed back in their chairs, replete with food. Nigel, continuing where he had left off when Keith and Diana arrived, regaled them all with his antics in the operating theatre, which Ellie suspected were strongly embroidered by his imagination and sense of humour but nonetheless had everyone aching with mirth.

When her parents announced that they were leaving, Diana stood up first and Keith accepted her proffered hand.

'Thank you so much, Ellie, darling.' Diana kissed her daughter on both cheeks.

Keith emulated her moves.

'Take care, Dad,' whispered Ellie.

Ellie and Nigel watched them go down the path, arm in arm, saw them get safely into the car and drive off, Diana waving from the unwound window.

'More coffee?' Ellie suggested as they went back into the lounge.

'I'd rather have a glass of wine.'

'Me too.'

They settled in a companionable fashion on the settee. Ellie curled her legs up under her and Nigel lay down, his head resting on Ellie's knees. They drank in silence; the only sounds that could be heard the purring of the gas fire and the methodical ticking of the clock.

'Ellie,' began Nigel, extending his neck so that he could look up at her face, albeit upside down.

'Mmm?'

'What's up with your dad?'

'What do you mean?'

Nigel moved and sat up.

'I think you know what I mean. He was really quiet, which is not like him. When he did speak he spoke really softly and I'm sure his voice was all slurred. Then, your mother seemed to have to hold him up most of the time.'

Ellie thought about what he had said.

'I didn't really notice. He just seemed like Dad to me. I expect he's just really tired after all the work he's done for me in the house. I should remember he's not as young as he used to be.'

'Ellie,' Nigel countermanded, reproachfully, 'he's only in his early sixties. And for as long as I've known him, he's been as fit as a trout.'

'Yes, but...'

'Ellie, have you ever considered he might have an alcohol problem?'

'Oh my goodness!' Ellie was horrified.

'Think about it,' Nigel explained. 'He did have a lot to drink at supper, his gait, his speech, keeping quiet in the hopes that we wouldn't notice.'

'It's possible, I suppose,' agreed Ellie. 'It would all fit, wouldn't it?'

'I'm afraid so. What a terrible shame. What will you do, Ellie?'

'I haven't a clue,' answered a bewildered Ellie. 'Talk to Mum, I guess, first of all. See what she knows about all this. Why on earth hasn't she said something to me before?'

'You know what she's like. She wouldn't want to worry you. You know they've always tried to shield you from things, so that you can get on with your own life and job.'

Ellie was pensive for a moment or two.

'Nigel! I've just remembered. You know that day they took me to the Clockhouse for dinner to celebrate their anniversary?'

'Yes.'

'Well, when I arrived, they weren't speaking to each other and my Dad was drinking quite a lot. I thought it was because he had broken the vase he had given to Mum and that she was upset. His speech was slurred then, too, and his coordination was all over the place.'

Ellie felt tears trickling down her cheeks. Nigel instinctively reached out for her hand.

'Ellie, I'm so sorry. He's such a great guy. Don't feel you've got to deal with this on your own. You know that I'm always here for you.'

'I know,' Ellie gave him a watery smile. 'It's so good to know that. But you're going to be so busy, organising this wedding of yours.'

'I will always have time for you, I promise. Come on, let's have another glass of wine and make some plans.'

'Do you think we should?' Ellie sounded doubtful.

'Yes, of course I do,' Nigel rebuffed her. 'We don't have problems with alcohol. You know that as well as I do. Here, pass me your glass.'

Ellie did as she was told, secretly quite glad to have some more wine to steady her scrambled thoughts. They sat and deliberated for the best part of an hour and decided that Ellie's best first move was to talk to her mother, on her own, as soon as possible. Though she found the prospect quite daunting, Ellie knew that there was no way that she would be able to stop worrying, now that Nigel had put the first thoughts into her head. She felt numb with disbelief at how it had taken Nigel to notice that something was wrong when it should have been her, as her father's daughter, to pick up the very first hints that something was amiss. Admittedly, she had always been closer to her mother but that did not mean in any way that she did not adore her father, enjoy his company, respect his thoughts and ideas and welcome his advice. Perhaps one was simply blind to the subtle changes that came about when someone you loved very much was ill. Considering this theory, Ellie recalled vividly that, at the age of seven, when her mother had come down with mumps – never a simple illness in adulthood – she, Ellie, had been the only person who could not see the gross swellings around her mother's face and neck. She could still hear herself asking what was wrong and why was her mother in bed when everyone else was uttering consoling and soothing words.

After Nigel had left, Ellie's thoughts continued along a similar vein, while she finished the last of the tidying up and put the remains of the crumble in the fridge. With some guilt, she could not help but count the three empty wine bottles plus one champagne bottle that were waiting by the back door.

5

It was as much as Ellie could do to concentrate on the ward round the next morning. She had slept badly, waking frequently to worry about her father. She was now faced with a busy day, a night on call and another day's work before she would have any time to arrange to see her mother. She'd more or less decided to suggest meeting her mother on neutral territory, perhaps suggesting lunch in town, plus shopping, which was usually a temptation neither of them could resist. But a tiny voice kept telling her that this was not really fair to her father and maybe she should face the two of them together. The argument against this approach though was how silly she would look and feel if there, in fact, was no problem at all and that her father was simply suffering from exhaustion or had some worries of his own that were preoccupying him. As she vacillated from one idea to the next, she realised that someone was talking to her.

'Dr Woods!'

With a jolt, Ellie snapped back into the real world.

Jeremy was staring at her impatiently and Sister Makepeace, standing next to him, had a rather smug sneer on her face. William Brewer, an eighty-three-year-old diabetic with emphysema and angina, watched from his bed, feeling desperately sorry for the beautiful lady doctor who had been so kind to him.

'I'm sorry,' apologised Ellie. 'I really am. I was just thinking about something.'

'It was perfectly apparent that you were not listening to me,' complained Jeremy. 'How many times do I have to remind you that I will not tolerate this sort of shoddy behaviour on my rounds. You have the privilege of working with me and learning how the elderly should be cared for. Waste this opportunity and you can count on the fact that your reference from me, for any future jobs you might apply for, will not describe you in a favourable light.'

Ellie sighed and went rather red. Sister Makepeace continued to smirk. Mr Brewer cleared his throat and wondered if he dared to speak up for Ellie but, after one look at his consultant's face, thought the better of it.

'Keep up, Dr Woods. Tell me about this gentleman.'

Sister Makepeace handed her a set of notes and Ellie, after a rather stuttering start, managed to present a reasonably coherent and precise history with almost her usual aplomb, thereby exonerating herself to a degree. Jeremy nodded as she concluded and turned his attentions to Mr Brewer's blood results, before examining his chest and abdomen.

'You're doing well, Mr Brewer. I'm very pleased with your progress. I think we should have you home by the weekend, fingers crossed.'

'Thank you, Dr Blake. I'm sure it's all thanks to you and Dr Woods. She's been very attentive and good.'

Ellie smiled at her patient. Jeremy grunted and waved his entourage on towards the next bay of beds.

'Ah,' he said, 'the admission from clinic, yesterday. How are you, Mr Crowther?'

'Nicely thank you, Dr Blake.'

Jeremy introduced his team and Ellie looked down at the bucolic gentleman who was sitting, still fully clothed, on the top of the bed. His plethoric cheeks were the result of a mass of tiny broken blood vessels, the whites of his eyes yellowed by jaundice and his swollen abdomen protruded like a full-term pregnancy. His shirt buttons were stretched to their limit and his stained and smelly trousers were held up by an old elastic belt which was tied rather than fastened below his belly. Ellie could not help but notice the tremor of his hand as he reached into his trouser pocket for a large and well-used handkerchief, with which he then mopped his sweating brow.

'Mr Crowther has some problems with his liver,' explained Jeremy, before reeling off a list of tests that Ellie should arrange as soon as possible. They moved on, discussed the final patient and retired, as usual, for coffee.

'He used to be the landlord of the Dog and Gun public house,' Jeremy told Ellie, handing her the file of notes so that she could go and admit the patient formally. 'He still lives there, but his son has taken over now so he spends all his time propping up the bar instead. Being the most convivial of hosts, his alcohol intake has been way too much for years and now the complications are taking their toll. Nice chap, though. He's raised huge amounts of money for charity in his time with pub quizzes, karaoke evenings and the like. He still does, if he can. It's a shame he's come to this. What a waste. I don't know how much we'll be able to do for him if he doesn't stop drinking and I'm not sure just how motivated he is to do that. Still, from a purely educational point of view, Dr Woods, he will be an excellent learning opportunity and I suggest that we discuss the effects of chronic alcoholism in our tutorial tomorrow.'

Ellie wanted to suggest an alternative but knew better. She was aware of an uncomfortable churning in her stomach, thinking that this was rather too close to home for comfort. She couldn't bear to imagine her father in such a state, ending up in hospital, with no chance of recovery. Life was curious, she thought, whenever there was something in particular worrying you, the subject seemed to pop up everywhere. As soon as she had finished with Mr Crowther, she would ring her mother and make arrangements to meet.

Jeremy kept her longer than usual, talking at her while she hurriedly finished her coffee and was itching to get on with her work. Sister Makepeace sniffed audibly throughout, to make her disapproval felt. This was, by tacit agreement, her exclusive time with Dr Blake. Her mood was not improved when he said, 'I have some papers I think you'd be interested in, Dr Woods. Come with me to my office and I'll get them for you. Thank you for your time, Sister. I'm sure you have plenty to be getting on with.'

Ellie followed him to his office, giving Muriel a little wave as they passed her. She looked fraught, talking rapidly down the telephone, which was balanced precariously under her chin, while she sifted through a pile of papers, obviously searching for something. Jeremy closed the door behind them and put his hands on Ellie's shoulders.

'What is it, Ellie? I can tell there's something wrong. I hate having to shout at you.'

Despite her worries, Ellie felt a tingle run through her body at the lightest of his touches.

'I'm sorry, Jeremy. It's just that I've got some concerns about my father. I think he might have a drink problem. You know that they were coming round for a meal last night. Well, there were some problems; he kept spilling things, his speech was slurred and he drank quite a lot and vomited.'

'That could be anything, Ellie. Perhaps he's coming down with a virus or something. You must try to be objective. It's difficult when you're emotionally involved.'

'I know, I know, but it just all seems to fit.' She looked anxious.

'Come here.'

Jeremy pulled her towards him and ran his hands down her back and over her buttocks.

Ellie gasped and pressed against him. He kissed her gently for a long time.

'Better?'

'Much,' Ellie nodded, lifting her head to him so that he could kiss her again. 'Don't worry, I promise this won't interfere with my work. I'm going to have a chat with my mum and see what's happening.'

'Good. Keep me informed.'

'I will, and thank you.'

Ellie went to leave the room.

'Oh, and Ellie?'

'Yes?'

'Dinner tomorrow night?'

'That'd be lovely.' Ellie smiled, her whole face lighting up with excitement and love.

'I'll pick you up at eight. Don't forget these articles.'

He blew her a kiss and she returned, still smiling, to the ward, the worry about her father seeming to have diminished and come more into perspective.

Mr Crowther kept her busy for almost an hour. He insisted on embellishing all the answers to her questions with snippets from his life and as he proved to be an excellent raconteur, Ellie found it impossible to interrupt him or steer him in the direction she wished to go. He had her laughing out loud several times and the two of them giggled like guilty schoolchildren caught eating sweets after Sister Makepeace, still smarting from her dismissal at coffee time, thrust her head between the curtains and reminded them that there were sick people on the ward who needed peace and quiet. Ellie efficiently took blood samples and then explained that he would be going for an x-ray of his chest and an ultrasound scan of his abdomen in the first instance. She sat a little longer and asked if he had any worries, concerned that his humour was just a façade concealing his fear, but he assured her that he was fine. Ellie, arriving back at the nurses' station, cursed as she found that she had forgotten her stethoscope and hurried back to get it while she remembered. She was just in time to see Mr Crowther add a large measure of whisky to his cup of tea, from a bottle which he then stashed away under a pile of spare pyjamas and towels in his locker. After a moment's thought, Ellie walked towards him and retrieved her stethoscope which was still on the end of the bed. Mr Crowther beamed up at her and raised his teacup.

'Cheers!' he said.

'Mr Crowther, I saw you put alcohol in your drink. That's terrible. How can you ever hope to get better if you carry on drinking?'

Ellie burrowed in the locker, brought out the bottle and picked up his cup, marched to the sink and poured the contents of each down the plughole. Mr Crowther looked on with dismay and hung his head in shame.

'Have you any more of this?' asked Ellie.

'No.'

She glared at him.

'Honest, doc. Would I lie to you?'

Ellie gave him a look of disbelief, but all too aware of the duplicitous nature of alcoholics, she decided to give him the benefit of the doubt this once and returned to her work.

When he was as sure as he could be that she was out of sight, he glanced quickly around him and furtively fumbled under his pillow, whereupon he produced a large hip flask, chuckled and took a long drink.

The morning passed quickly as it invariably did when there was so much to do. There was no time for anything more than a rushed sandwich for lunch, eaten while she was writing and making telephone calls about patients. An attempt to contact her parents was unsuccessful as there was no reply when she rang, so she made a mental note to try again in the evening if she had a free moment. More ward work occupied her for the afternoon and then, from six, she was responsible for seeing all the new emergency admissions that were sent in either from GPs or via Accident and Emergency. She dealt with an old lady, wheezing badly from her asthma, and then a slightly younger lady, deeply unconscious after a massive stroke. By eight, she had things under control to her satisfaction and had even had time to sit down in the dining room and eat fish and chips followed by sponge and custard, justifying the calorific value of this meal by telling herself that if she had a really bad night and was up working most of it, then it was better to be prepared and have lots of energy to burn. With nothing pending, she wandered back to her on call room and was about to pick up the telephone to ring her parents when, predictably, her pager went off.

To her surprise, the ever-cheery woman manning the switchboard informed her that it was a personal call.

'Hello, Ellie love. How are you? Are you on call? Is it busy?'

'Hi, Mum,' Ellie began. 'Fine, yes and no, not too bad at the moment but the night, as they say, is still young. I was just about to ring you.'

'Thanks for last night, we did enjoy it. The meal was super and it was lovely to see Nigel again. Fancy him getting married!'

'I know, it's wonderful news. We had quite a talk after you'd gone. He seems really happy. Mum, how's Dad?'

Was there a momentary pause, or did she just imagine it?

'He's fine today. I think he must have picked up a bit of a tummy bug and he is so very sorry to have upset everyone last night.'

'Can I have a word with him?'

'Not at the moment, dear. He's just ...er...gone down the road to post some letters.'

'Oh, okay. Mum, I was wondering if you'd like to go out shopping this weekend. You know, have lunch, make a day of it. It seems ages since we've done anything like that as we've spent all our time working in the house. I thought it would make a nice change for us both.'

'I'm sorry, Ellie, I can't. Your Dad and I have decided to go away for a holiday.'

'What? You never breathed a word about this last night.'

'Well, events rather overtook us, didn't they? First, Nigel's news, then your dad. I know it seems short notice,' Diana tried to placate her daughter, 'but, we both felt a bit down, your dad's very tired from all the work he's been doing and it just seemed like a good idea to get right away, be pampered for a while and recharge our batteries.'

'Where are you going?'

'On a cruise. You know we've always wanted to try one. Well, this seemed like the ideal opportunity. We fly to Athens and then meander around the Mediterranean for a month. We can hardly wait.'

'A month?' Ellie was incredulous, as her mother described the itinerary in detail.

'We only booked last minute, so we had to take what we could get. As it was, we got a really good deal on this holiday and it seemed much more appealing than anything else we saw.'

'Well, that's great,' Ellie managed to say, recovering from the shock. 'Wouldn't you like to go shopping on Saturday and pick up a few new clothes?'

'We fly early that morning. We're off tomorrow, down to London so that we can stay near Heathrow for the night.'

'Wow, it sounds incredible. I have to say I was a bit worried about Dad and so was Nigel.'

'I'm sure a rest will do him the power of good,' Diana reassured her.

'Oh, I do hope so. Are you all packed then?'

'More or less. Just the usual last-minute bits and bobs to put in the hand luggage.'

Ellie's pager bleeped irritatingly from her pocket.

'Oh, damn, that's my bleep. I'll not get to see you before you set off by the sound of it, so have a fantastic time. Send postcards if you get the chance but most of all just concentrate on enjoying yourselves.'

'We will, I promise. Don't you worry about anything. Just think, when we get back it'll only be three weeks or so off Christmas.'

'Lots of love to Dad.' Ellie tried to turn off her pager which was bleeping again, insistently.

'Sounds as if you're needed, love. Take care and we'll see you soon.'

'Bye, Mum, have a great time...'

Ellie sat back and replayed the conversation over again in her mind. Though unexpected, this sounded like a good idea and would be helpful to both her parents. Her mother had sounded happy and excited, which was good, plus she had admitted that Ellie's dad had not been well and offered a plausible reason for why. In view of their imminent departure there was nothing more she could do for now; she had to be content with her mother's reassurances and put her trust in the fact that a good rest would be the simple solution that her father needed.

She picked up the receiver and rang switchboard who put her through to Accident and Emergency. Emily, Nigel's new fiancée, greeted her rather wearily.

'Hi, Ellie. Can you take a patient please?'

'Yes, sure. We've still two empty beds on Whitby. What's the problem?'

'Eighty-year-old lady with haematemesis. She's quite stable at the moment.'

'Send her up. By the way, congratulations. Are you ok? You sound exhausted.'

Emily thanked her and confirmed that this was the case.

'It's been bedlam all my shift and we've never stopped for a break. Luckily I'm off in an hour and I can't wait. Oh, by the way, don't make any plans for a fortnight on Saturday, that's my hen party and I'd hate for you to miss it. I'll ring you with more details later.'

'Thanks, Emily, I'd love to join you.'

'Better go, here comes yet another ambulance with a flashing blue light.'

Ellie took a few moments to unpack the few items that were in her overnight bag before setting off back to the ward where she arrived coincidentally with the lady from A&E. Lying on a trolley, clutching a grey cardboard dish, in case of more vomiting of blood, she looked as pale and wrinkled as the sheets that were covering her. Ellie allowed the nurses to settle her into bed, catching up with some blood results that had been phoned through to the ward with regard to Mr Crowther. No surprises there, then, thought Ellie, looking at his wildly deranged liver function tests, together with abnormal blood count and renal function. The said patient waved to her as she passed on her way to the latest admission. Swiftly Ellie went to work, asking questions, conducting a thorough examination, putting up a drip and arranging a few extra tests that had not been done in A&E. She organised a blood transfusion and an endoscopy, though the latter would have to wait until her patient was stable, probably the next morning. Following this she had to review one of the other patients who had developed abdominal pain which turned out to be due to constipation and appease two others who, thinking they would take advantage of the fact that she

59

was on the ward, asked her to look in their ears and at their toenails.

She had a final check round the ward shortly before midnight and was pleased to find that her admissions were either a little better than they had been or certainly no worse and then wandered back to her room, hoping for at least a few hours' sleep. An hour later, she was back, writing up some night sedation as a fastidious nurse refused to take a verbal order over the telephone. Three hours later she was back again, certifying the death of the lady who had had the dense stroke, consoling the relatives in her soothing compassionate tones, feeling tears welling up in her own eyes as she watched them weep.

Sleep eluded her thereafter until, inevitably, half an hour before she was due to get up, and so when Ellie did shudder back to reality as her alarm clock announced the start of a new day, she felt sick and as though she had been drugged. The recuperative powers of the shower failed to work, mainly because there was no hot water left and breakfast landed in her stomach with a thud and threatened to linger there for as long as possible. Arriving on Whitby Ward to look round the patients before her tutorial (which she felt badly prepared for) Ellie was pleased to find that it was not Sister Makepeace on duty but one of her staff nurses, who, taking one look at Ellie, went and made her a strong cup of coffee. To her amazement, she finished her ward work quite quickly and had time to sit and read the papers that Jeremy had given her yesterday. He was, of course, precisely on time. Ellie had to smile as she saw him walk arrogantly down the corridor, looking forward to their evening date and wondering where he would be taking her. He nodded curtly to her and then she took him round the patients who had been admitted overnight. They then adjourned to the doctors' room and began to discuss alcoholism. Ellie had brought Mr Crowther's results with her. It always helped her to learn if she could relate to real-life. She told Jeremy about the bottle of whisky in the locker and he shook his head sadly. Though perhaps not quite up to her usual standards, Ellie thought that she managed to acquit herself well. Jeremy's failure to find fault seemed to concur with Ellie's belief, but she was still relieved when the tutorial came to a rather abrupt end as Muriel interrupted to tell him that there was a professor from Chicago on the phone.

6

Just as he had done for the tutorial, Jeremy arrived at Ellie's house exactly on time. She had taken a long time to get ready, eager to please and delight him. Actually going out somewhere with Jeremy was a rarity. Their relationship usually only existed in Ellie's house, apart from the occasional brief kiss and cuddle in his office. Having persuaded a colleague who was on call for the weekend to let her go at four, Ellie had hurtled into town to a favourite boutique and found an elegant little dress in grape hyacinth blue and some shoes with perilously high heels that made her legs look long and svelte. She'd then managed to have a nap for an hour, bathe, do her hair and spend an undue amount of time on her make-up. By seven forty-five, she was ready and knew that she had rarely looked better. Her hair shone, the dress could not have been a better fit if it had been bespoke and so long as she did not have to walk too far in the shoes, then she ought to be fine. Her mother had rung briefly from the hotel near Heathrow, just to reassure Ellie one last time before they left the country. Ellie, excited about the evening and possibly the night ahead, had barely given her father any thought at all.

She ran downstairs carrying her shoes and stopped to examine the unopened post which lay on the table. She carefully scrutinised the writing on the envelopes, not wanting to risk scuffing her nail varnish. She took the only one that looked interesting into the kitchen and opened it with a knife. Inside was the invitation to Nigel and Emily's wedding. Clearly, Emily's mother had bounced into action as wedding planner. The prospect of a Christmas Eve wedding was the ultimate in romance. Ellie gazed wistfully at the invitation card and then took it through to the lounge, placing it in the centre of the mantelpiece, in pride of place for when Nigel next came round.

The doorbell rang.

Jeremy stood in the doorway, sheltering under an umbrella as the rain was lashing down, bouncing off the path and doorstep.

'Ready?'

Ellie took his outstretched hand, pulled the door to and ran, or rather tottered, after him to the waiting taxi. Inside, she perched on the seat and shook the raindrops from her head.

'What a dreadful evening,' she moaned as they drove off.

It took over half an hour to get to their destination, which turned out to be a country restaurant some twenty miles north of Harrogate. The outside suggested that the original building dated back several centuries but inside the décor was simply but fashionably done, with walls painted in a warm ochre, elegant modern paintings and an abundance of green plants. Soft jazz music wafted through the air as they made their way to the bar area where, at the merest of signals from Jeremy, the barman produced a bottle of champagne that he had waiting in an ice bucket. Jeremy took Ellie's coat and made suitably appreciative noises about her appearance, gently moving her hair from her cheek to kiss her.

Weirdly, Ellie felt nervous. They had never been anywhere this stylish before. There had been a few hurried pub meals in the evening but nothing like this. She sipped her champagne and looked at Jeremy, who seemed entirely relaxed and at ease. He was wearing a smart, well-fitting suit, which she suspected was made of silk, another creaseless shirt (Ellie had to force herself not to wonder who had ironed it) and a dark purple tie. A glance in the mirror on the opposite wall told her that they were easily the most attractive pair in the room and Ellie wondered just how obvious it was to the other customers that they were having an affair.

Jeremy was at his most charming. He was complimentary and attentive. Ellie could not help but feel at ease with him as they sat with their drinks, his hand holding hers under the table, his thumb rhythmically caressing her skin.

A waiter arrived with menus and indicated a blackboard on which the specials of the day were written. They deliberated over their choices, before deciding on starters and main courses and then sat back to chat while they waited to be summoned to their table. The champagne slipped down beautifully and Ellie told him about Nigel's wedding and her parents' sudden announcement of their holiday.

'So does that make you feel better?' Jeremy asked her.

'Yes, it does. I'm sure that Mum wouldn't even consider a holiday if she was concerned about Dad. She made me feel really guilty though, saying how worn out he was after all the work he'd done in my house. Still, at least he's finished now.'

'And you've stopped imagining him ending up like Mr Crowther?'

Ellie laughed, acknowledged that she had and, feeling a little foolish, sought to change the subject.

'This place is wonderful, Jeremy. How did you find out about it?'

'A group of consultants came up to Ripon on an interviewing skills updating course and we came out here one evening. I thought it was rather special then and so when I'd promised to take you out, I couldn't think of anywhere better to bring you.'

Ellie squeezed his arm and leant forward to kiss him but stopped half way as a courteous cough behind her announced the arrival of the waiter to tell them that their first courses were ready and waiting. They walked into the dining area side by side, Ellie deliciously aware of Jeremy's hand on her left buttock. Jeremy pulled out Ellie's chair for her and then sat opposite. The solitary candle on the table cast a flattering light and made a hundred different colours stand out in Ellie's hair.

'You are so beautiful, Ellie,' he told her, gazing at her.

'Thank you.'

Everything is perfect, Ellie thought, as she tasted her seafood pancake which was delectable.

Oblivious to all the other diners, they continued to chat as they dawdled over their food, neither wanting the evening to come to an end. By the end of the main course, Ellie had slipped off both of her impossibly uncomfortable shoes and was running one foot up Jeremy's leg, not caring whether anyone could tell what she was doing.

'Dessert, sir and madam?' asked the attentive waiter.

Jeremy raised an eyebrow.

'Oh yes please,' replied Ellie, looking at the choices. 'The raspberry soufflé please.'

'And I'll have the chocolate mousse. Thank you.'

The waiter hurried off.

'Would you like coffee here, or back at home?'

'At home, I think, don't you? Will you be able to stay long?'

Jeremy smiled.

'Quite a while, don't worry.' He signalled for a waiter and asked him to arrange a taxi.

Ellie looked relieved. She drew patterns on the tablecloth with her spoon.

'Where does Helen think you are tonight?'

She could have bitten her tongue as soon as the words came out. When they first began their relationship, Ellie had sworn to herself that she would be different from any other woman. She would not mention his wife at all, she would not badger him for details of his home life or try to compete in any way for him. Behaving like that, she reckoned, if they were to end up together then it would simply be further proof, if any was needed, that they were meant to be with each other and even if other people were critical and accusatory, she would know in her own mind that she had played her part honestly and decently.

'I really don't know. I simply told her that I was going to be very late.'

'Doesn't she want to know more, though?'

'No. I've told you, she's not interested in me. We live virtually separate lives.'

'She must suspect something though, Jeremy. Sometimes you don't leave my house until two in the morning.'

Jeremy shrugged.

'She's never asked. She sometimes makes a disparaging comment about me never talking to her but we really have nothing in common any longer, so, what is there to talk about?'

'Does she just sit at home and wait for you?' Ellie found that now she had started it was difficult to stop asking questions, her curiosity aroused and prowling.

'She goes out a lot with her own friends. She's busy with her own work and research as well of course.'

'What is it she does?'

'She's a neurologist in Leeds. Just waiting for a consultant's post to come up. Do we have to talk about her tonight? Can't we just concentrate on you and me?'

So saying, he let go of Ellie's hand which he had been holding on the table and produced a thin rectangular box from his inside pocket.

'I got you this. To thank you for being so wonderful.'

Trembling, Ellie took it from him and opened it. Inside was a truly stunning gold bracelet, quite simple in design but studded with tiny diamonds which made it gleam and sparkle in the light from what remained of the candle.

'I'm speechless, Jeremy. I really am. It's amazing. I'll never be able to thank you enough.'

'Here, let me put it on for you.'

Ellie extended her arm and waited while he fumbled a little with the clasp and then admired her gift from as many angles as she could. She had never been given such a beautiful, or expensive, gift.

'Oh, thank you a million times. Just look at it, it's exquisite.'

'Just like you,' Jeremy agreed, softly. 'Shall we go?'

Ellie scooped up the last couple of spoonfuls of her raspberry soufflé, which was far too delicious to leave and allowed Jeremy to lead her back to the bar area.

They sat very close to each other on the way home in the taxi, talking in whispers, stifling laughs in case the driver could overhear them. Jeremy rotated the bracelet on Ellie's wrist so that she could admire it even more and let his hand slip onto her knee and between her thighs. The journey seemed to take a long time. The driver, for reasons known only to himself, decided to take a different, less direct route and as a result they had to wait at temporary traffic lights and also the level crossing. Weather-wise, things had not improved. The monotonous scraping of the windscreen wipers and the splashing of water as they drove through puddles extending across the width of the drainless country lanes made Ellie cuddle up closer to Jeremy, rest her head on his shoulder and close her eyes. She was actually just dozing off when the car drew up outside her house and she was nudged awake as Jeremy leant forward to pay. Gallantly, he leapt out of his side of the car and rushed round to open Ellie's door, holding the umbrella protectively over her as she tried to maintain her poise as she got out. Shouting goodnight, they made a run for the front door and let themselves in. The door slammed shut behind them as Jeremy engulfed her in a huge hug and started to kiss her with a mixture of passion and tenderness before she had even had a chance to put on the light.

Afterwards, when they were lying in bed together, Ellie rested her head on his chest and listened to the reassuring throb of his heart, while inhaling his smell, a mixture of after-shave and sweat that she found so alluring. He seemed to be asleep, exhausted by their love making but she felt she could not rest as any moment he was bound to say that it was time for him to go. Maybe if she just stayed very still, he would sleep on until the morning and if that was to be the case, she was determined to savour every minute of it.

'What time is it?' he asked sleepily.

Ellie wondered whether it was worth lying but decided against doing so.

'You ought to be asleep,' he commented.

'I'm just enjoying having you here,' she replied.

'Then I'd better stay the whole night. Sweet dreams.'

With that he kissed her on her forehead, her nose and finally on her lips, closed his eyes and was dead to the world in seconds. Ellie, deliriously happy, made sure that as much of her body as possible was touching his and allowed sleep to get the better of her.

They woke in the night, made love drowsily and fell asleep again, arms and legs entangled. By the morning they had, inevitably, moved apart. Ellie, first to wake, lay quietly, watching him until he started to stir and then got out of bed and ran downstairs to prepare breakfast, which she then carried back up for the two of them. Fresh orange juice, hot coffee, toast, butter and marmalade. Heedless of where the crumbs landed, they ate ravenously, Ellie having to go and make more supplies of toast as the first slices ran out. She brought the paper up for Jeremy who pretended to try to read it, while Ellie stroked, nibbled and excited him. Somehow, they managed to squeeze into Ellie's tiny shower but despite their best contortions had to admit defeat and take turns to wash. Once dressed and downstairs, having another coffee at the kitchen table, Ellie began to dread the moment he left. She found her conversation was stilted.

'Thanks for the best night ever, Jeremy.'

He nodded and yawned without putting his hand over his mouth, showing Ellie some excellent and expensive dental work.

'What do you think Helen will say when you get home?'

'I don't really care.'

'Will she be cross? Will she be suspicious?'

'Who knows?'

Overtired, Ellie found his flippancy irritating.

'I need to know, Jeremy. When we're together everything seems too good to be true. But then when I'm on my own again I can't help but wonder what's going to happen to us?'

He leant forward to stroke her cheek.

'You have to trust me on this one, Ellie. Believe me when I promise you that we will be fine. But you have to be patient.'

Ellie looked down at the table.

'I know. It's just that I've never been in a relationship like this before. All my previous boyfriends were really just a bit of fun, they were all unattached, apart from being attached to me, that is. I could ring them when I wanted to and see them when I wanted to. I've always been able to call the shots, as it were. But now it's weird having to wait and fit in. I know we've only been seeing each other a few weeks but I just know that this is something very special. I don't want to lose you but I'm not sure if I'm cut out to play second fiddle.'

She stopped abruptly, afraid she had said too much and ruined a wonderful evening and night.

'Ellie,' Jeremy began, 'you are the best thing that has ever happened to me. I love you. I'm going to leave Helen as soon as I can. But it's not that simple. I can't just walk out on her. I need a few weeks to sort some things out.

Elli had heard nothing after the three words she had been hoping against hope to hear. She jumped up, climbed on his knee and threw her arms around him as tight as she could.

'I love you too, Jeremy, so much.'

Laughing, he unpeeled her arms from around his neck.

'You're amazing. Look, I'm going to have to go now but just remember what I've told you. Enjoy your weekend, I'll try to phone if I can, but I'm not promising anything.'

'Shall I call a taxi for you?'

'No, it'll do me good to walk to the hospital and pick up my car. I'll see you on Monday.'

'Bye, I love you!' Ellie called confidently after him and he turned, waved and blew her a kiss.

7

Ellie floated through the next few days. There was something delicious about having a secret of such magnitude. Ellie felt beautiful, desired and invincible.

She seemed to have developed the Midas touch. Nothing was too much trouble. Work seemed straightforward and she made a couple of astute but rare diagnoses. At home she received the first postcard from her mother, sent immediately before their flight from Heathrow, in which she mentioned that Keith was already looking better. Though Jeremy continued to be brusque and inflexible in the hospital, Ellie knew that their relationship had moved onto a new and higher level, one that afforded her more security. There was simply no way that he would have told her that he loved her if he did not mean it. In her experience of affairs, which amounted to no more than reading novels and one friend whom she had not seen for a couple of years, the married man would rarely commit by expressing his emotions to such a degree. It was far more usual for him to shower his mistress with compliments and gifts (well, yes, she had been given that amazing bracelet) yet be economical with admissions about his feelings. Jeremy had proved he was different. Though, admittedly, Ellie still knew next to nothing about his marriage, his home life or Helen, it was now clear that there was no need for her to know these things. Ignoring the small voice that told her she was thinking in clichés, Ellie was convinced that her feelings for Jeremy and his for her were strong enough to overcome any obstacle that came between them. She did shudder a little at the prospect of the comments that would ricochet round at work when the truth came out but again, they could ride that storm too. As with most items of news that rocked the constantly humming hospital grapevine, notorious for its ability to take the old party game of Chinese whispers to a new dimension, it would be an overnight phenomenon only. It would be hard, working together. The image of Sister Makepeace's face when she found out was not altogether an attractive one but at the end of January, Ellie would be moving to a different job and that would make life easier for the two of them for the next six months after which she would be back out in general practice again and away from the hospital.

Jeremy was away for a few days at a conference in Lisbon. It would have been wonderful if Ellie could have gone too but, as her holiday allocation had already been booked, there was no conceivable way that she could change it, plus, she was needed to look after the ward in his absence. He had only left that morning and she was already missing him desperately.

Sister Makepeace, assuming control in her consultant's absence, had gone on a ward round with Ellie and been heard to mutter under her breath at certain decisions that Ellie took that Dr Blake would never have done such a thing. Ellie, ever the peacemaker, had tried to involve her diplomatically and suggested they have coffee together at the end. This turned out to be an excruciating experience. Whilst Ellie tried to direct the conversation exclusively to the patients, Sister Makepeace had other ideas and used the time to eulogise about Jeremy's most wonderful traits and the close relationship that they had.

Ellie was glad to be able to escape to the lunchtime meeting in the postgraduate centre. The subject of the day, 'Bones, moans and abdominal groans – disorders of calcium metabolism' promised to be interesting and relevant to her everyday work. Having managed to complete her ward round decidedly more quickly than Jeremy did his, Ellie was one of the first to arrive for the meeting and took advantage of this by allowing herself to indulge in the buffet lunch that was on offer. With a plate stacked high with sandwiches, a vegetable samosa, pieces of pork pie and scotch egg, she poured a glass of fresh orange juice and went into the lecture theatre. Nigel was sitting at the back and waved to attract her attention.

'Come and sit with me, Ellie,' he called, mouth half full, as ever.

'Hi, Nigel, how's things?'

'Fine, thanks. And you?'

Ellie beamed.

'Couldn't be better.'

Nigel gave her a long hard stare, narrowing his eyes, trying to tap into her thoughts, a phenomenon he had always had an uncanny ability to do. Ellie, recognising the signs, decided it would be safer to divert his attentions away from her with as much speed as possible.

'How are the wedding plans coming on?'

'I feel like I'm on a runaway train,' he replied, looking perfectly happy about the situation. 'Between them, Emily and her mother are like a couple of whirlwinds. The reception's booked, you'll know the invitations have gone out, there's a poor soul somewhere with very sore fingers sewing sequins and pearls on Emily's dress and they've persuaded me to wear morning dress. I ask you!'

'I thought this was going to be a rather low key affair,' mused Ellie.

Nigel affirmed that she was correct.

'Yes, it was. But, you should know what women are like when they get the bit between their teeth. Unstoppable. We now have a service, a reception for family and close friends,' he nudged Ellie at this point, 'and also a winter-themed evening party. There's going to be white decorations, Carol singers, twinkling lights, a disco, artificial snow and an appearance by Father Christmas, would you believe?'

Ellie roared with laughter.

'This is certainly going to be a day you will never forget, Nigel.'

'Nor will anyone else, by the sound of it,' Nigel pretended to grumble.

'But it all sounds so romantic,' breathed Ellie, enviously.

'It's not really my cup of tea. It's all far too over the top, if you ask me. But, if Em wants it, then that's what she shall have. I just want to marry her and would be quite happy to pop along to the register office one afternoon but you can imagine what sort of response that suggestion got. I'd sort of hoped that there wasn't enough time to organise all of these things but Emily's mother is one of those people with a huge network of friends that she can call upon when she wants something. She seems to have been on the telephone twenty-four hours a day; she is indefatigable. Every time I see Emily, her mother's conjured up something else that, according to her, will help to make our day complete.'

He shook his head sadly but failed to fool Ellie.

'You're loving every minute of it,' she told him, quite correctly. 'Make the most of it; it'll pass in a trice.'

Nigel was just about to embark on a description of the menus when the speaker coughed loudly and announced his intention to begin.

'I'll tell you more, later,' he whispered.

It was proving to be an excellent talk, with a speaker who was entertaining and informative but, to her annoyance, Ellie was obliged to leave halfway through to see to a patient on the ward. Hurriedly, she arranged to see Nigel in the doctors' mess after work and when she arrived there only ten minutes late, he was relaxing in a chair, tie loosened at the neck, top shirt button undone, a pint of beer in one hand and a tabloid newspaper in the other. Only a few other people were in there. One of the urology consultants was treating all his team to a drink and a couple of weary-looking registrars were deep in conversation about their chances of success in some fast approaching interviews for jobs on the next level of the hierarchy. Nigel pointed to a glass of lager that he had bought for Ellie. Taking off her white coat as she walked over to him, Ellie felt that it had been a very long day, for no other reason than she had not seen Jeremy and there was still almost a week until he returned.

'Is Emily working this evening?' she asked as she sat down.

'Yes, she's been on nights this week, so I don't like to disturb her sleep. We manage to catch up each morning at breakfast as she finishes her shifts. It's her last night tonight and of course, it's her hen party this weekend.'

'How could I forget that? We're off to the Nidd Gorge Manor hotel to be cosseted.'

'Enjoy yourselves. Me and the boys are off go-karting and paint balling.'

'Oh, I'd quite fancy that, as well.'

'I'd gladly have you along as one of the boys, Ellie. You've been the best friend to me and don't think that's going to change when I'm married. Don't ever feel that you can't ring me up or that we can't sit down like this and talk. I'm always here for you, Ellie, good times and bad, okay?'

Ellie reached out and stroked his arm.

'I know that, Nigel. I want to be careful though. I'd never forgive myself if I upset Emily.'

'No chance of that,' Nigel assured her emphatically. 'She under-stands totally. Another drink?'

'Please.'

'Tell you what, let's have a quick one here and then go for a pizza. Come on, it'll be our own personal hen/stag party. You've nothing else planned have you?'

'No, that'd be great. I'm starving.'

The second drink was followed by a third as three of Nigel's surgical colleagues came in and had no hesitation in sitting down with them. Interesting cases were discussed initially and then the conversation deteriorated into the swapping of jokes that became progressively more and more risqué until Ellie, whose sense of humour was able to cope with most things but there was a point where she drew the line, raised her eyebrows at Nigel. Well versed in the interpretation of this sign, he stood up and made their excuses, so that they could take their leave. They walked into town, arm in arm. The night was frosty and dry, the sky bespeckled with millions of tiny stars. At their favourite pizzeria, the owner welcomed them warmly and led them to a small table in the corner of the room. Within seconds a carafe of house white was placed in front of them and huge menus were offered. But they were both familiar enough with the choice to wave them away and order garlic bread and two pizzas, marguerita for Ellie and inferno with extra pepperoni for Nigel.

Left alone for a few minutes while Nigel went to the toilet, three pints of beer having taken their toll on his bladder, Ellie watched a family on the next table, the parents eating large bowls of steaming lasagne and their two little girls, kneeling up on their chairs, colouring in pictures in the books they had brought with them, occasionally pausing to have a token bite of their dinner, hoping that they would still be allowed ice cream for dessert.

As they tucked into their garlic bread, Nigel continued where he had left off filling Ellie in with all the details of his wedding day.

'The guy who's doing the disco is threatening to play nothing but Christmas songs. Have you any idea how many dreadful Christmas records there have been over the years?' he asked her.

'There are some nice ones,' she commiserated.

'Not a lot. At least not that we've come across so far. Anyway, enough of that, what are you going to wear?'

Taking the last piece of bread and licking her fingers, Ellie shrugged.

'I haven't really thought about it yet. From what you tell me, I think perhaps a snowman outfit might go down quite well!'

'Don't even suggest it in fun. At least not to Emily's mother. Here, have some more wine and let's talk about something else.'

'Name your subject,' Ellie offered.

Nigel thought for a moment or two.

'I know what I wanted to ask you. This lunchtime, you were looking decidedly pleased with yourself. I think I deserve, as your best friend, to know what that was all about.'

'Oh, nothing,' Ellie tried to sound nonchalant and then spoiled the whole effect by giggling.

'Well, now I know there's something for definite. So, you might as well tell me.'

Ellie, who was bursting to tell him, pondered for the briefest of seconds about whether she should or not. Any remaining defences had been removed by the alcohol.

'I've been seeing someone.'

'That's fantastic,' Nigel encouraged her.

'For a few weeks now. I didn't say anything earlier as it was all a bit clandestine and I didn't know if it was going to go anywhere or just be an overnight wonder.'

'Okay, keep going. So now you think it's more than that?'

'Oh definitely,' Ellie said. 'I know it sounds really trite, but he told me he loved me a few days ago and that's definitely how I feel about him.'

'Wonderful. You look really happy. How did you meet him?'

'At the hospital.'

Nigel's eyes widened.

'Does that mean I know him?'

'Yes, a little,' Ellie replied evasively.

'Is he a doctor?'

She nodded.

'Oh, come on, Ellie, just tell me. I'm too tired for twenty questions.'

Ellie leant forwards, beckoning Nigel to do the same.

'This is all very secretive,' he commented. 'Is this really necessary?'

'I have to talk quietly. You never know who might be listening. But I'm seeing Jeremy.'

Nigel, bewildered, looked at her.

'Jeremy? Jeremy who?'

'Jeremy Blake,' hissed Ellie, lowering her voice.

It took a moment for Nigel to register who this was. His mouth dropped open. He mouthed the name and Ellie nodded, excitedly now that she had shared her secret.

'But you can't...'

He broke off as their pizzas arrived, vast in size, overlapping the plates' circumference, cheese still bubbling on the top. The waiter fussed over them, bringing black pepper, topping up their glasses, asking with urgency if their food was to their satisfaction. Nigel was uncharacteristically short with him, waving him away, desperate to get back to his conversation with Ellie, his mind alive with a thousand questions that he wanted to ask.

'Ellie,' he carried on, 'when exactly did this start?'

'In September.'

'But you're always telling me how rude he is to you on ward rounds and what a stickler he is to work for. You say you feel humiliated by him.'

'Yes, he's all of those things but that's just so no one finds out what's happening between us. When we're alone together, he's a completely different person. He's gentle, really funny, loving.'

'But Ellie, he's married.'

'Yes, I know, he has told me that. But he's not happy in his marriage, he hates being at home. He's promised me that he's going to leave her and be with me.'

Nigel, exasperated, slapped his knife and fork on his pizza.

'Don't tell me you've fallen for all that pathetic patter. I really thought you'd be above all that.'

'Nigel, this is different. I'm genuinely sure that it is. He really loves me. We're so good together. He's bought me an amazing bracelet.'

'A bracelet?'

'Yes, gold, with diamonds in it. It must have been terribly expensive.'

'What has price got to do with anything?'

'It shows how much he cares,' smiled Ellie.

Nigel rubbed his face with his hands.

'Oh Ellie, what have you got yourself into?'

'Nige, don't worry. I'm going to be fine. I just know it. This is different. He's promised me and I believe him. He just needs a few weeks to sort things out. Even though he doesn't get on with Helen, his wife, he can't just pack his bags and leave, can he? He's far too responsible to behave like that. I expect he thinks she at least deserves an explanation of where he's going and why.'

'Ellie, just stop a moment and listen to yourself. You're talking like some love-struck heroine in some extremely bad film.'

Ellie wound some cheese from the top of her pizza around her fork and nibbled at it. In the background the strains of a well-known Italian aria played, loud enough to be recognised but not to be intrusive. The children at the adjacent table had abandoned their colouring and were shrieking with delight as large ice creams decorated with fizzing sparklers were placed in front of them. Ellie glanced at Nigel, who was piling up the pieces of pepperoni from his pizza, one on top the other, unable to look at her while he thought. She cleared her throat and took a sip of wine.

'I love him, Nigel. I've never felt like this about anyone before.'

Nigel cocked his head to one side and raised his eyebrows, unconvinced.

'You know what it's like to be in love,' argued Ellie. 'You've got Emily.'

'I accept that,' Nigel concurred. 'But that is where the similarity stops. Can I just remind you that Emily is not married. We've been going out for over a year and she does not treat me like some sort of lesser mortal when we're in the company of others.'

'Okay, but as I've said, that's just so people don't start to suspect anything. He'll be completely different when it's all out in the open. Anyway, we've got to maintain a professional working relationship as well, haven't we?'

'It's hardly professional, the way he treats you on the wards,' Nigel muttered.

Ellie rose above what she considered to be a cheap jibe and continued.

'The bottom line is that we love each other. That's all that matters. His marriage was clearly a mistake from the beginning...'

'You know all about that do you? What did he tell you?'

'Well, not a lot,' admitted Ellie. 'But just look at the statistics, one in three marriages these days end in divorce. So, clearly, theirs is one of those that went wrong. It's better that they break up and move on then Helen stands a chance of being happy as well. I had no idea that this was going to happen when I went to work for him. I didn't feel attracted to him and try to seduce him, or him me...'

Nigel emitted something approximating to a grunt.

'...it was just completely natural and inevitable. One of those things you would never have predicted. That's what makes it all the more special and exciting and right.'

Ellie sat back, triumphant.

'Rubbish,' Nigel's sympathetic approach was running out fast, being replaced by plain irritation.

'His reputation precedes him. He's supposed to be seeing Penelope Makepeace at the moment as well. Plus if you were to ask around, I'm sure that you would hear plenty that you wouldn't particularly like about what's gone on in the past.'

Ellie burst out laughing.

'That's ridiculous. It's just idle hospital gossip. As for Penelope, he wouldn't go near her. He has to keep her sweet as she runs his ward for him and let's face it, she does do a pretty good job.'

'Ellie,' Nigel's voice was serious. 'Get real. You're making this up as you go along, refusing to see any negatives about this man. I can't believe this is you talking. One of the things I've always loved and admired about you is your commonsense and level-headedness. If it was me saying all these things, you'd be at my throat in an instant.'

A concerned waiter was hovering a few feet from the table, anxious that their food was barely touched yet simultaneously aware from their body language that a highly charged discussion was going on. Taking advantage of the pause, he coughed politely and took a step forward.

'Is everything all right?'

'Yes, yes, fine. Thank you.' Ellie tried to smile reassuringly at him and he backed away, years of practice in his job having taught him when to keep well out of the way of customers.

Ellie tentatively reached across the table for Nigel's hand.

'Don't let's fall out over this. I know it's all a bit sensational and you've been shocked but look at me – can't you see how happy I am?'

'Yes, I can. That's what bothers me. It'll never work out, Ellie.'

'Well, that's just where I shall prove you wrong. I'd love for you to meet him socially. Perhaps we could make up a foursome one evening.'

'Sorry,' Nigel replied immediately. 'Em and I are far too busy with the wedding preparations to do anything like that for the next few weeks.'

Ellie felt as though she had been slapped in the face.

'The least you can do is give him a chance,' Ellie retorted.

Nigel pulled his hand away from under Ellie's.

'I really don't want anything to do with this, Ellie. All I can say is, that when this does all come crashing down around you and believe me, it will, then I'll be there to help put you back together again. Having said that I would still implore you to think seriously now about it all and try to extract yourself from this doomed predicament before it goes any further and you run the risk of being hurt even more.'

Dismissively, he sat back in his chair with nothing more to say on the subject. Ellie, who wanted to say a lot more, realised that there was no hope of convincing him that evening. To emphasise his point, he studiously gazed anywhere in the room except at Ellie, who desperately wanted to get the evening back on an even keel, hating even the slightest antagonism between them. They had been friends too long and too close to be rent apart by this. In an attempt to lighten the atmosphere she called over the waiter, asked him to remove their plates and ordered a portion of tiramisu and two spoons plus two espresso coffees.

Diplomatically waiting for the arrival of these, she passed one of the spoons to Nigel and said, 'I'm really looking forward to this weekend. There are all sorts of treatments on offer. I think I'll have a facial and a whole body massage, get my nails done and then make the most of the swimming pool. I think I'll give the colonic irrigation a miss though!'

She studied Nigel's face, hoping for some sign of his normal reactions. It would be unlike him not to come out with some quip about colons. The corners of his mouth twitched and she felt a wave of relief start to wash over her.

'Actually, Ellie,' Nigel began, with a wry smile on his face, 'if I were you, I would put the colonic irrigation at the top of my list of requirements. You've said so much crap tonight that it might just help.'

Ignoring the horrified look on her face, Nigel handed her the spoon, got up, put on his coat and, having thrown a twenty-pound note on the table, walked out of the restaurant, leaving her open mouthed. Ellie wondered whether to run after him but as several of the other diners were already watching avidly, awaiting her next move, she sat playing dismally with her uneaten dessert and tried not to think over all that had been said. After what she considered to be a decent interval, Ellie paid the bill, thanked the owner as he opened the door for her and wearily started to trudge home.

Inevitably she replayed in her mind all of Nigel's comments. He had really hurt her with his final words yet rather than feel angry with him, she just wanted him to understand how she felt about Jeremy so that he could feel happy for her. Despite his admonitions, she was still sure, wasn't she, that her relationship with Jeremy, though awkward due to the fact that there was an extra player involved by the name of Helen, was genuine and unique. It was going to be messy and possibly unpleasant, mostly for Jeremy, but Ellie's constancy by his side would help pull him through. If the worst came to the worst, they could move away and start again somewhere new. Jeremy was gifted and supremely intelligent; he could pick up a consultant post wherever he chose and once Ellie had completed her GP training, then they could move anywhere, even abroad.

Ellie allowed herself some delirious moments imagining her and Jeremy house hunting, decorating together, shopping in the super-market and generally sharing domesticity. Then of course they would have children, two, maybe three. As many as Jeremy wanted. She would do anything for him. At that moment a little dark shadow did cross her thoughts. Did Jeremy have a family already? Was that why he needed so much time to sort things out? Not that it made any difference to how she felt, though it would complicate matters. Who would the children want to live with? What if it was their father? Ellie was suddenly unsure whether she was ready for instant motherhood. She gave herself a good telling off. It was stupid to let her imagination run away like this. Surely Jeremy, who had been so open with her about Helen – well, he had told her of Helen's existence, which must count for something – would also have mentioned any children. As if to apportion more weight to this argument, Ellie recalled his minimalist office at work. Any doting father would have photos on his desk. The doubt, however, refused to be totally erased and Ellie, with a sigh, decided that when Jeremy returned from his meeting, she would ask him.

By the time she reached her house, Ellie was tired out. Her brain ached from so much mental argument and she was miserable about Nigel's premature departure. She half hoped that there would be a message from him on her answering machine but was disappointed to find none, not even one from Jeremy which might have gone a long way towards cheering her up. She made herself hot chocolate and turned on the television and tried to turn her attentions to a rather crackly old black and white thriller that was just starting.

8

Ellie heard from neither Nigel nor Jeremy over the next couple of days. She was frantically busy on the wards, as well as trying to hold together the outpatient clinic and staggering through one day after an impossibly busy night on call that left her feeling physically sick and dizzy and fit, in all honesty, for nothing but sleep. The one time she'd tried to contact Nigel, an anonymous voice on the other end of the telephone had told her that he was scrubbed up in theatre. Whether this was true or not, Ellie would never find out as before she could even contemplate trying to get in touch again, work swamped her and even meals turned into hurried bars of chocolate bought from the trolley that came round to the patients selling papers, bottles of squash and sweets. One good thing about being so busy was that it meant that time flew by and before she knew it the weekend had arrived.

She was surprised and more than a little hurt by the fact that Nigel had not been trying to ring her. When she had enough time to give the matter some thought, she realised that he must feel very strongly about her situation to be behaving like this. The silence from Jeremy only compounded the feeling of unease that she was trying her very best to ignore.

When she got home on the Friday evening before Emily's hen party, Ellie felt uncharacteristically low. She threw her overnight bag across the hall floor and went and poured herself a drink before flopping onto the settee, tossing her shoes off as she did so. She felt shattered, dirty and rather smelly. She missed Jeremy more than she could say and could not understand that he had not been in touch at all since he had left. But, she acknowledged reluctantly, possibly more than she missed her lover, she missed Nigel, her friend and steadfast ally, the one she would have contacted for support and help about any other matter in her life. But by now, he and his mates would be on their way to Northumberland on the first stage of their raucous weekend away, starting off as they meant to continue, laughing and having fun.

The prospect of trying to do the same with Emily and her friends did nothing to entice Ellie out of her slough of despair. Usually Ellie had no qualms about joining in with groups of people she did not know very well, her gregarious nature making this second nature to her but on this occasion, she really felt that the last thing she wanted to do was chat, drink and possibly behave ridiculously.

Every time she had had a moment to relax and switch off from work, Ellie's brain had merely swapped from juggling thyroid function tests, CT scans and urine outputs to the ongoing dissection of her night out with Nigel. Jeremy's silence did not help. If only she had spoken to him, then the belief that they had a future together would have been reinforced. Instead Nigel's words had conjured up an embryo of realism, much to her annoyance. If she were honest with herself, she knew next to nothing about Jeremy, as Nigel had pointed out, having been blinded by his charisma, to say nothing of the terrific sex.

Hungry for some proper food, Ellie concocted a large omelette, stuffed with cheese, tomatoes and chopped peppers. She toasted some bread, buttered it generously and sat watching television while she ate. With room for a pudding, she found a small individual strawberry cheesecake in the fridge and was just on her way back to the lounge with this when the telephone rang.

'Hello?'

'Ellie, it's me, Nigel. I just wanted to apologise.'

The line was very crackly and she could barely hear him.

'Nigel! I'm so glad you've called.'

'I should never have said half of those things. It really is none of my business. But I just care about you.'

'I know, it's okay. Anyway, I'm just beginning to wonder if you're right.'

'You are? Oh, thank goodness. Look, I've got to go. The guys are getting the drinks in. They think I've gone to the toilet. I just knew there was no way I'd enjoy this weekend if I didn't speak to you.'

'Me neither. Listen – we'll always be friends. You have a fantastic time but come back in one piece, preferably with both eyebrows as well!'

She heard him laugh as he put the telephone down.

Much happier, Ellie finished her supper, had a bath and then settled into bed with a new novel that she'd been longing to start for several weeks. Only minutes later, she accepted that she was too tired to read as she found that she was trying to make sense of page five for the umpteenth time. She put out the light and snuggled down, luxuriating in that wonderful feeling of being warm, relaxed and deliriously woozy as sleep fast approached. Before she was able to surrender entirely to the beckoning arms of Morpheus, Ellie heard the telephone ringing again. Stumbling, trying to find her slippers, she inelegantly fled downstairs, only to find that the she had missed the call.

'Damn.'

As she turned to go back upstairs, she spotted that the answering machine was winking at her. Switching it on she waited for the message.

'Hello, Ellie. It's Jeremy. I'd hoped to catch you. I hope everything's fine at your end and that you're managing the ward with no problems. I'll be back next week as planned. I miss you.'

The answering machine clicked off. Ellie ruminated on the message. It wasn't quite the admission of undying love that she'd been expecting but he had said that he missed her and it was only natural that he was concerned about work. Possibly mollified a little, she went back to bed and pulled the covers up tight.

In the morning, after nine hours' uninterrupted sleep, Ellie felt infinitely better. She willingly repacked her overnight bag, though was unsure what to take as presumably she would not need many changes of clothes. As well as her swimwear, to be on the safe side, she threw in a spare pair of jeans, some shorts, a couple of tops which, depending on what you teamed with them could pass as either casual or smart and as an afterthought, a dress. They had arranged to meet at the spa, which was actually an offshoot of the hotel, only a short drive from the town but nestling resplendently in its own grounds with attached golf course. Lunch was the first thing on the agenda and anticipating twenty-four hours where food was a priority, Ellie played things cautiously and only had fresh fruit for breakfast.

She occupied what remained of the morning with housework, dusting that was long overdue, changing the bed linen and giving the bathroom a good clean.

The Nidd Gorge Manor Hotel boasted four stars in its own right and two award-winning rosettes for its restaurants, one Thai, one French. An indisputable fact about living in a town that boasted a huge conference centre which attracted a plethora of conventions and exhibitions was that as a consequence there were all manner of places to eat, stay, indulge in one's hobbies or simply relax. According to Nigel, as Emily's hen party was only encompassing one night away (unlike his), she had vetoed any undue travelling, quite naturally wanting to capitalise on the time spent with her closest friends. She'd drawn up a short list of likely venues but when she had been to visit them, there had been no contest.

Arriving at the hotel, in the nondescript gloom of the late November Saturday, Ellie parked her car in the nearly full car park and, feeling rather out of place as she had no golf bag over her shoulder, made her way to reception. Emily was checking in. Standing by her was a woman whose looks, despite the rather more mature skin, left Ellie in no doubt that this was Emily's mother, obviously taking a break from the wedding preparations. They had the same laughing, happy faces with rosy cheeks and masses of freckles, identical curly blond hair and blue eyes that crinkled in the corners, a legacy of much smiling.

'Ellie, hi. I'm so glad you could come. This is my mum Jean, chief hen-party planner.'

Ellie shook hands.

'It's lovely to meet you.'

'Isn't this exciting? I've got all sorts of treats lined up for us all. We'll be so relaxed after this weekend we'll probably fall over backwards when we try to stand up! Get checked in and then we're all meeting by the pool. I think everyone is here now – there'll just be the five of us. It's going to be great!'

Ellie was well impressed by her room, which she surveyed with awe. Expensive-looking curtains in heavy material of gold and yellow fell elegantly from behind the matching pelmets. The bedspread complemented the colour scheme as did the chaise longue, matching armchair and the thick pile carpet. She had never slept in a four-poster bed before. Child like, she sat on the edge of the bed and bounced tentatively before lying back and experimenting with a remote control panel which she discovered opened and closed the curtains, turned on the TV and radio and offered many different degrees of lighting. Aware of the time, she stood up, changed quickly into T-shirt and shorts, deciding to carry her swimsuit for now. A huge fluffy cream dressing-gown was laid out for her on the bed. She half expected the hotel's logo to be embroidered on the left chest area but it proved to be quite plain, so she wrapped this around her, slipped into some flip-flops and made her way down to meet the others.

The pool was situated in a huge room, crowned with a domed ceiling made entirely of glass, like an inflated conservatory. Adding to the opulent feel, ferns and palms of assorted sizes grew in chubby, wicker-covered planters, arranged carefully around the periphery of the room. The temperature must have been bordering on tropical and hit Ellie in the face as she entered. A couple of women were in the pool, lazily meandering from one end to the other, doing a form of front crawl that allowed their perfectly coiffured hair to remain unspoilt.

Ellie looked around the room and saw Emily waving frantically to attract her attention.

'Over here, Ellie,' she shouted, her voice echoing around the room.

They were all sitting around a small table, made of elaborately patterned cast iron and they were all clad in identical dressing-gowns. As she neared them, Ellie saw that the dressing-gowns were indeed embroidered after all, on the back, in bright red with 'Emily's chicks'. Ellie wondered if anyone had noticed and hoped not. Smiling cheerfully, she pulled up a chair.

Jean poured her a drink.

'Bucks fizz,' she announced. 'Let's start as we mean to go on. Help yourself to canapés.'

'Lovely, thank you,' said Ellie graciously.

'Now then,' Jean called for unanimous attention, leaning on the table with her elbows in a conspiratorial way. 'Let's get started. First, does everyone know each other?'

They all glanced around and nodded. Ellie recognised the other two members of the party as nurses who also worked in Accident and Emergency, Gaynor and Jackie.

'Enjoy your drinks and help yourselves to more food while I fill you in on what I've got in store for you. We've a busy afternoon ahead. I've booked us all massages or seaweed wraps, plus manicures, pedicures and facials. Then we'll swim and relax before dinner. This evening, we've been invited to a party. The daughter of some friends of mine – you know, Emily, Samantha Jesmond – gets married today and then has her reception and evening party here. So lots to eat, lots to drink, lots of chatting! I've bought three albums of great photos of Emily as a baby and growing up, so you can all see what a very special girl she is. Now, drink up, here's to Emily.'

Accordingly, they all raised their glasses and Ellie could not stop herself from looking at Emily to see how she was taking all this. Fortunately, rather than cringing with embarrassment, she appeared to be radiantly happy.

The bucks fizz was delicious. Ellie felt she might prefer just to sit by the pool for the whole afternoon, drinking. That, mixed with an occasional dip in the water, sounded exceedingly tempting but clearly that would not go down well with Jean. Wondering which treatment was to kick off the proceedings, Ellie put down her empty glass and looked expectantly at her hostess who was gathering her things together.

'Everyone finished? Right – let's go to the aerobics class! They've agreed to put one on especially for us. We'll appreciate our treatments so much more after we've burned off some energy. Plus, we'll work up an appetite for our dinner. Come with me.'

An amusing sight left the pool area, a group of women in identical gowns, the leader of which was a rather roly-poly lady whose booming voice was reminiscent of an enthusiastic lacrosse teacher. Gaynor giggled with Ellie and Jackie as they followed on obediently.

Ellie had her doubts about the wisdom of aerobics after three glasses of a fizzy drink. Sure enough, after some gentle limbering up, the young woman leading them, who was wearing an impossibly tight leotard which looked as though it might bisect her vertically, launched into a more energetic routine. As the tempo picked up, so did the aerated activity in Ellie's stomach, resulting in some uncomfortably large belches. Deep down, Ellie had always considered that she was probably quite fit. There must be considerable cardiovascular benefit to be gained by rushing around the hospital every day, racing against time. But as the third piece of strident pop music with booming bass began to blare out, Ellie had to confess that she was deluding herself and looked with admiration at Jackie, who was having no problems keeping up whatsoever. Gaynor was flat on her back laughing and puffing with Emily and Jean was making her own routine up as she went along, which involved a lot of arm waving and hip gyrating together with an occasional jump.

Thankfully the second half of the class was floor work, which meant that at least they were all either sitting or lying down. Very quickly, Ellie's abdominal muscles informed her that they had no intention of doing repeated crunches or press ups, so she sat with the others watching Jackie and the instructor who had begun to vie for who was the fitter. By the end of the class, they were all startlingly red in the face and too out of breath to complete a sentence, but Jean, tireless, coaxed them to their feet and introduced them to the first of their treatments.

Ellie enjoyed the rest of the afternoon. The massage left her feeling blissfully de-stressed and it was a treat to have her hands and feet rubbed and moisturised and her nails shaped and varnished. Jean had arranged afternoon tea for them that started with tiny triangular sandwiches, devoid of crusts, filled with either cucumber or egg and cress. There then followed a three-tiered cake stand which dared them to resist scones, still warm from the oven and smothered in blackcurrant jam, bite-size iced fancies and chocolate éclairs.

Their last treatment completed, at Jean's behest they lounged in reclining chairs by the pool for the final part of the afternoon, talking and laughing at the photos that were produced for them to see. With an arrangement to meet for pre-dinner drinks in the lounge bar, Jean and Emily went up to their rooms, but the other three preferred to stay and then swim or float in the enticingly warm water. They lingered longer than they'd anticipated and ended up having to hurry up to their rooms to get ready for dinner. Lying on Ellie's bed this time was a dress covered with yellow feathers, a matching fascinator, a pair of red tights and some yellow pumps. After showering, it was with a sinking heart that she dressed and, on looking into the mirror, saw a ridiculous chicken eyeing her warily. The pumps were nipping her toes menacingly.

It came as no surprise to find Jean dressed similarly, ensconced on a high stool, chatting up the uniformed barman, challenging him to create cocktail for their party, which he duly did.

'This is called Emily's Ecstasy!' decided Jean handing round glasses full of a luminous green mixture, topped off by a twist of lime and a cherry.

Warily, Ellie sipped. The back of her throat recoiled at the power of the liquid that hit it, making her eyes water.

'Wow!' she exclaimed. 'That's got some kick to it. But it is delicious,' she added, quick to disperse the beginnings of disappointment that were appearing in Jean's face.

'We all look gorgeous,' Jean declared, gulping her own drink and smacking her lips appreciatively. The other three chickens concentrated on their drinks, unable to speak. Emily's outfit was rather grander, with multi-coloured feathers.

'I wonder what Nigel's doing,' Emily said. 'I hope he hasn't hurt himself go-karting.'

'He'll be fine, Emily. There's no need to worry about him. Let's just concentrate on ourselves. Who's for another drink? Same again all round?'

'I feel decidedly drunk already,' confessed Ellie in a whisper to Jackie, who nodded in agreement but still accepted another full glass.

Despite Jean's rather dictatorial streak, she proved to be a very amusing hostess and over dinner, admittedly with the assistance of copious volumes of red wine, she had them all in stitches with her accounts of not just Emily as a child, but also the plans for the wedding. Judging by the meticulous planning that had gone into the afternoon, Ellie correctly anticipated that the wedding would be equally well organised and just as outrageous.

Replete after huge three-course dinners, Jean refused to allow them to rest. She led them into the party which was being held in one of the large, ornate private rooms. The relentless disco music was already blaring out. Regardless of their protestations that they needed a little time for digestion, she frogmarched them all onto the dance floor and had them emulate her every sinuous move.

'Where does your mum get all her energy from?' asked Ellie, out of breath and dancing nearer to Emily to make herself heard over the loud music.

'Oh, she's always like this. She constantly wears me out. I know, let's go and sit back in the bar. I'll just tell her where we're going.'

Ellie nodded and beckoned to Gaynor and Jackie, the latter of whom was eyeing up a good- looking young man, dancing eccentrically on his own. She looked unhappy to be dragged away.

'Phew, that's a relief,' puffed Gaynor, flopping into a chair in the corner of the room. .'I don't know about you lot, but I'm worn out. I'm spitting feathers – literally.'

'It's been a great day, Emily, thank you.' Jackie looked up as Emily came towards them.

'I've told Mum that we'll be in here for a bit. She's found loads of friends in there so she's going to stop a while and chat. Anyone want a drink?'

Without waiting for an answer, Emily went to the bar and returned with two bottles of white wine and four glasses. She poured them all a drink and handed them round.

'Your mum is amazing – she never stops!' Gaynor reached across the table, pulled a glass dish of salted snacks towards her and started to eat them, regardless of the fact that she was already full.

'She is,' agreed Emily. 'It's been like a dream come true for her, having to organise my wedding in next to no time. I offered to do it all but she refused and I must say that I would never have come up with any of the ideas she has, let alone been able to arrange them.'

'You're lucky, really lucky, Emily,' Gaynor continued. 'There is just no way on this earth that you could have worked all your shifts, plus those extra ones you've been doing and got your wedding off the ground.'

'No, I'd never had been able to do it,' Emily agreed, whole-heartedly. 'If it had been left to me and Nigel, we'd be getting married in a register office and then sloping off for fish and chips.'

They laughed together and drank. Jackie got up, excused herself and headed off rather unsteadily in what she hoped was the direction of the toilets. Gaynor topped up everyone's glasses, offered round the snacks and then, when everyone had shown more restraint and declined, continued to munch her way through them, pausing only to lick the salty tips of her fingers.

'Why have you been doing extra shifts, Emily?' asked Ellie.

'Partly to earn a bit of extra cash and partly...'

'Here comes the real reason,' interjected Gaynor.

Emily glowered at her.

'...Okay then, mostly to try to create a good impression. You know they've taken on a new consultant – an additional one. Well, there's to be a new junior Sister's post too and I'd really like to apply for it. It'd be the icing on the cake if I got it.'

'You'll get it,' Ellie and Gaynor spoke in unison and burst out laughing again, before Gaynor continued.

'Never mind the Sister's job – have you seen the new consultant? Simon Moody? He is just gorgeous. Tall, obviously works out, brown curly hair and a smile that makes your bones turn to blancmange. And single!'

Ellie shook her head and tried to look suitably impressed and interested. Emily nodded in agreement.

'Yes, he is very sexy. He just started last week. Next time my shift coincides with one of his, I'll think of an excuse to call you down to A&E, Ellie. He might be just your type.'

Jackie returned to the table and sat down with a thump, before drinking half a glass of wine in one gulp.

'What are you talking about?' she hiccupped.

'The new A&E consultant,' Emily filled her in. 'Ellie's not seen him yet.'

Jackie pretended to swoon.

'He is adorable. But you'll have to join the queue and I'm first in it. It is merely a matter of time before he becomes aware of my womanly charms.'

'Huh,' grunted Gaynor, 'in your dreams.'

Jackie was long practised in the art of ignoring her friend.

'Can I just remind you of some of my more notable conquests?'

'Such as? The porter from radiology?'

Emily sniggered as Gaynor winked at her and Ellie.

'Well, okay, perhaps there were some mistakes along the way but we all make them and they just make you appreciate the high spots more, don't they?'

'Go on, we're waiting with baited breath,' Emily pretended to yawn.

Jackie motioned to them all to lean forward.

'There was Jim Pearson, the urology registrar. We were together for almost a month.'

'True,' Emily accepted, 'but I could never tell what you saw in him.'

'Wouldn't you like to know. Then, I had a brief but passionate fling with Bob Gourlay from pathology.'

'Really?' Gaynor raised her eyebrows. 'Get away!'

Jackie nodded, enjoying her captive audience.

'Then there was Finlay Forster, the gynae SHO. I had a couple of dates with him but he always smelled of rubber gloves and reminded me of cervical smears.' She wrinkled her nose. 'After him, there were a couple more SHOs who've now moved on and left the hospital, Tony Laurence, the radiologist – but he said he could see straight through me...'

The others groaned loudly, suspecting she was making things up as she went along.

'And of course there was nearly Jeremy Blake, the Med Elderly consultant.'

If Jackie was hoping to shock, she certainly succeeded with one member of the group. Ellie felt her world stand still and go cold.

'Oh very funny,' Gaynor articulated each word with care, to emphasise her sarcasm. 'What do you mean by nearly?'

Jackie turned to her, her blood shot eyes, edged with blotchy mascara opened wide.

'Well, nothing actually happened because we were interrupted but I'll get him next time.'

'I don't believe you. That man is impenetrable.'

'That was part of the challenge.'

'When was this?' Ellie heard her voice ask; she hoped that it sounded calm but curious rather than frantic.

'At the party in the doctors' mess at Halloween,' Jackie told them.

'Why didn't you tell me at the time?' Gaynor sounded peeved.

'I was going to but you know how critical you are about my sex life.'

'But he's married,' Emily was aghast.

'So?' Jackie's lack of respect was clear.

'But not happily, so rumour has it,' Ellie heard herself contribute.

Three faces turned to look at her, eager for gossip.

'Oh, do tell us more,' Gaynor was agog. 'You know his wife's just come to do a locum in Harrogate, don't you?'

Ellie felt her mouth go dry.

'Has she?' she managed to say.

'Pour some more wine, Gaynor,' Emily ordered, nodding, 'and then get another couple of bottles. Yes, she's covering for Will Swindlehurst, while he's off sick.'

'What's wrong with Will?' asked Ellie.

'Colon cancer, I'm afraid. He'll be off for three months at least. He was admitted acutely last week with an obstructed bowel.'

'Oh, I'm sorry to hear that. I hardly knew him but he seemed a really nice man whenever he came onto Whitby to give an opinion.'

Emily and Jackie nodded in agreement.

'Anyway, to go back to what I was saying, there was a really bad accident on the Wetherby Road the day before yesterday. The driver had horrific head injuries and we had to ask for a neurologist to come and give an opinion before we could send the patient to Leeds. We were expecting Will but Dr Blake turned up instead.'

'What's she like?' asked Ellie, unable to curb her curiosity.

Gaynor returned and they all downed more wine.

'Huge!' roared Jackie. 'Absolutely vast. Great big fat legs as well! And a terrible complexion.'

'Really?'

'Yes, I kid you not. She could barely get through the door into resus.'

Ellie felt reassured but felt ashamed to admit that it was important to her that she should compare favourably with Helen.

'Hang on,' Emily felt obliged to explain and dribbled wine down her chin. 'That's a bit unfair.'

'I don't see why,' argued Jackie.

'Yoo hoo!'

Jean swayed across the room to them waving as she did so. Some of her feathers had come off, creating a semi-plucked look.

'Come back to the party all of you. There's bacon sandwiches and champagne. The music's great – all sixties and seventies hits.'

She grabbed her daughter by the hand, who in turn reached for Ellie. Wondering if she could possibly make her excuses and go to bed, Ellie quickly realised that there was no way she could do so. She felt more confused having learned things that she would have preferred not to know. Not for the first time, she wished that she was paintballing with Nigel and his friends.

Jackie and Gaynor stumbled after them, each carrying a half-full wine bottle. The noise of the disco was ear shattering, even louder than earlier. Jean steered them into a small gap on the dance floor, flapped her arms (or rather wings) and encouraged them to join in. Jean's dance bore an uncanny resemblance to her aerobics technique and the others, inhibitions totally obliterated by so much alcohol, had no hesitation in starting to imitate her, which delighted her. Jackie was keeping an eye open for the man she had spotted earlier. Seeing him by the bar, she deftly danced away from the group and made her way over to join him. In no time at all, Ellie saw the two of them, with a bottle of champagne, go and sit at a table in a very dark corner of the room.

Emily, who was watching too, shouted to Ellie.

'She's incorrigible.'

Ellie nodded in agreement, silently grateful that Jeremy had not fallen foul of her attempts to seduce him. As the record ended, Jean briefly paused to mop her cheeks with a small white handkerchief. She took Ellie's arm.

'Come with me a moment. I'll get us some drinks.'

Somewhat lightheaded, Ellie really did not want or need any more alcohol and wondered if Jean would be offended if she asked for an orange juice or mineral water. Before she could speak, though, a flute of champagne was pressed into her hand.

'Look, there's a couple of chairs. Quick – I could do with a sit down. I must talk to you about the wedding.'

They sat and Ellie felt her feet breathe a sigh of relief. Without thinking she slipped her pumps off and then realised that she would never get them back on. But before Jean could divulge exactly what it was she wanted to discuss, a mature-looking woman who would have been unusually tall had it not been for her marked dowager's hump, swooped down on them and with an apology whisked Jean away. Ellie, secretly pleased, rested back in her chair, surveyed her surroundings and found she was unable to resist taking a sip of the champagne that proved to be delicious. She ran her fingers through her hair and removed her feathery crown. As she stretched her legs and feet, she realised just how tired she was, wondered what time it was and how much longer she might be expected to stay up. There were certainly no signs at all of this party drawing to a close.

Only a few were dancing. The music was slow and romantic, inviting intimate body swaying and subtle foot shuffling. Jackie and her newfound friend were optimising this opportunity; his hands were caressing her buttocks in an over-familiar way while she nuzzled his neck. There was no sign of Emily or Gaynor and rather than go looking for them, Ellie decided that she deserved a rest and her absence would not be noticed for a while.

'Bacon sandwich?' asked a voice. 'Or do chickens not eat meat?'

Ellie looked up. Holding out a plate, on which there were two bread rolls, filled with crispy bacon, was a friendly-looking man in his early thirties, with well-cut dark hair and fashionable frames to his spectacle. He grinned at Ellie and motioned to the empty seat next to her.

'Of course, please sit down. I'll have to pass on the bacon sandwich though. Not because I'm supposed to be a chicken but because I've eaten so much already today. I don't think I'll need to eat again before Christmas.'

He laughed.

'Let me introduce myself. Ian Bonnington.'

Seriously he held out his hand, which Ellie duly shook.

'Nice to meet you. I'm Ellie Woods.'

'I didn't see you earlier,' he commented, taking a big bite out of one of the sandwiches. 'I think I might have noticed the outfit.'

Ellie explained about the hen party and pointed out Jean, who was still deep in conversation.

'Ah,' Ian said, knowingly. 'That answers quite a lot of my questions. Jean's my mother's best friend, so I know her very well and Emily too of course.'

'Then you'll understand without any more explanation. She's given us a fantastic day but she's more stamina that the rest of us put together. Is that your mother that she's talking to now?'

'No,' replied Ian. 'My parents called it a day about half an hour ago. They thought they'd done pretty well to make it as far as midnight. They were planning to sneak off when the happy couple left at ten, but I persuaded them to stay on a bit.'

'I envy your parents,' Ellie confessed.

He chuckled.

'So, tell me what you do when you're not a chicken.'

Ellie could not help but smile.

'I'm a doctor at Harrogate District. What about you?'

'A chartered surveyor.'

'Do you work in Harrogate?'

'Occasionally. My office is in Leeds. I'm lucky as I get to travel quite a bit. How long have you been a doctor?'

'A few years now. I'm training to be a GP but at the moment I'm working with the elderly.'

'You'll be very busy then.'

Ellie looked at him, impressed by his empathy.

'Yes,' she admitted, 'it is a very busy job, one of the hardest I've done. That's probably why I'm struggling to keep up today – I'd have been better off sleeping all weekend.'

'Do you get much free time?' Ian asked.

'Not a huge amount at the moment. I start a new job in Paediatrics in just under two months' time. It should be a lot less frantic, plus the on-call is much easier.'

There was a pause in their conversation. Ellie wondered if Ian was working his way round to asking her out and so was taken aback when he spoke again.

'If you really don't want that bacon sandwich, would you mind if I had it?'

'I'm quite sure. Go ahead. They look delicious. Any other time and I'd have eaten it by now.'

'Thanks. Shame there's no brown sauce though.'

With no warning, the loud music resumed and the energetic leapt to their feet and returned to the dance floor. Conversation with any meaningful content was impossible. Ian mimed having a drink and pointed to the door and Ellie nodded her agreement. Outside in the bar, Emily and Gaynor were slumped at a table, looking decidedly the worse for wear. Ian made no comment when Ellie asked for a large mineral water with lots of ice and the two of them joined their mutual friend.

'Hi, Ian,' Emily sounded weary. 'I see you've met Ellie. This is Gaynor.'

Gaynor hiccupped and put her hand over her mouth.

'Where's Jackie?' asked Ellie, knowing the answer before Gaynor told her.

'Taken that bloke up to her room. Need I say more? Oh, I feel so sick.'

'Perhaps, we should wind things up,' suggested Emily. 'I think Mum's got plans for us in the morning.'

Gaynor put her head in her hands and groaned.

'Only breakfast and a walk.' Emily tried to console her.

'I'll not be fit for anything.'

'I'm not sure any of us will,' agreed Ellie.

They sat quietly, too lazy to move, listening to Gaynor's repeated assurances that she was going to vomit. Sensing a good moment to make a move, Ellie offered to take Gaynor up to her room and took the proffered outstretched hand as a sign of acceptance.

'I think I'll go to bed too, Emily,' Ellie said. 'Thanks for a wonderful day. Ian, it was lovely to meet you. Please excuse us. See you in the morning, Emily.'

Ian stood up as they left and watched the rear view of two chickens, one holding the other one up, until they disappeared into the lift. Upstairs, Ellie made Gaynor drink a whole glass of water and then helped her into bed. She refilled the glass and left it on the bedside table. Unnecessarily, she tiptoed to the door; Gaynor was already flat on her back, snoring noisily. Back in her own room Ellie made a decaffeinated coffee and sat up in bed sipping at the hot drink while she thought about Jeremy.

9

Back on the wards, immersed in the daily routine plus all the unexpected that cropped up, the hen party seemed many moons away.
Ellie had been the first down to breakfast on the Sunday, only to be
joined a few moments later by Gaynor. They had greeted each other
sympathetically, each suffering from the effects of an over-indulgent
night out and a poor night's sleep. Reciprocally accepting the other's
need for silence, they'd sat nursing glasses of freshly squeezed orange
juice, consciously averting their eyes from the centre of the dining
room, where a long, attractively decorated table groaned under the
weight of every conceivable constituent of a continental breakfast.

Emily had arrived, looking pale and rather green around the lips,
clutching a box of ibuprofen which she offered to the others. Hot
on her heels had been the exuberant Jean, an advertisement for the
benefits of a good night's sleep – eyes sparkling, mouth watering
in anticipation of the next meal. She had wasted no time at all in
ordering fried bread, sausage, bacon, tomatoes and scrambled egg. Of
Jackie, there had been no sign at all. Indeed, she had failed to put in
an appearance before Ellie left. Fortunately, it transpired that Emily
had had a word with her mother and the morning's group activities
had been cancelled. Instead, they had lounged by the pool, dozing,
drinking coffee, only Ellie having the strength to float on the water
and gaze at the magnificent roof.

Thanking her hostess profusely, Ellie had got away just after lunch.
She'd been relieved to get home. After two hours sleep in her own bed,
she had been relieved to find that her head had stopped thumping and
that a full recovery was looking more likely.

Jeremy had returned from his conference. He looked well and fit, Ellie thought. His first ward round had been interminable as he sought to catch up with all the patients who had been admitted in his absence. Sister Makepeace had been positively radiant with joy and had even gone so far as to praise Ellie for all her hard work. Jeremy had absorbed this information without so much as a flicker of interest but when his round was finally over, he had called Ellie into his office, shut the door behind them and his subsequent actions had left her in no doubt whatsoever that he had missed her more than words could say.

Ellie was sorting through a pile of recently discharged patients' notes, dictating letters to go out to their general practitioners. Since his return, Jeremy seemed determined to make up for what he perceived to be lost time and was admitting twice as many patients from his clinics. Outside, winter had truly set in. Frost draped the branches and decorated the grass and fallen leaves. The few hours of daylight seemed precious. Predictably, winter illnesses were taking their toll on the older people and Ellie's on-call nights were fully occupied with cases of pneumonia, wheezing bronchitics and even a couple with hypothermia. Trying to save on their heating bills so that they could afford their council tax had resulted in them becoming colder and colder, almost to the point of stupor. Ellie's heart wept for them as she clerked them in. She made a mental note never, ever, to let anything like that happen to her parents.

Diana and Keith had returned from their cruise. Ellie's mantelpiece was a testament to the first week of their itinerary, the postcards having taken such an inordinate length of time to arrive that the rest were still in transit. She had spoken briefly to her mother the previous evening but had been called away urgently to a cardiac arrest which meant that the call had to be prematurely truncated. What little she did glean was that they were both fine and had had a wonderful time.

Finishing the last of the letters, Ellie took the Dictaphone through to Muriel. As a reward, she was given another pile of notes, somewhat bigger than the first and asked if she would mind doing her clinic letters too, as Dr Blake had commented that she seemed to be falling behind with them. Ellie begrudgingly took them and returned to the doctors' room on the ward. She hurried downstairs to the snack bar and bought a tuna mayonnaise baguette, a can of lemonade and, after a moment's prevarication, a bar of milk chocolate with a gooey caramel centre. Thus suitably equipped, she was ready to set to work when she remembered the previous evening and telephoned her mother.

'Hi, Mum.'

'Ellie, darling. How are you? You sounded dreadful last night. Did you get any sleep at all?'

Ellie marvelled how her mother was so intuitive that she could detect every vocal nuance when she spoke to her daughter.

'I'm fine, Mum. Sorry I had to rush off like that yesterday.'

'Don't worry, darling, I understand.'

'So how was the cruise? I'm longing to hear all the details.'

'Then why don't you come round and see us? We've so much to tell you. Not tonight though, I insist, as what you need is a good night's sleep. Much as your dad and I would love to see you, you must rest and look after yourself. How about tomorrow?'

'That'd be perfect.'

'Come after work. I'll cook supper. Any requests?'

'Anything you make is the best, Mum.'

'Right then, we'll see you tomorrow. Sleep tight, won't you. Perhaps that consultant of yours will let you go early today, eh? Why don't you ask him?'

'Perhaps,' repeated Ellie, holding out no hope for what sounded, in theory, like a very good idea.

Her call over, Ellie turned her attention to lunch and her letters. Hoping that Muriel would have no trouble deciphering the parts she dictated with her mouth full, Ellie worked her way assiduously through the task and then saw fit to award herself two squares of chocolate. Inevitably, in no time, she had eaten the whole bar.

'Oh well,' she sighed out loud, throwing the wrapper into the bin, 'I think I've more than earned it.'

That evening, Jeremy surprised her by turning up at her front door. Momentarily, Ellie experienced a conflict of emotions. Thrilled though she was to see him, she had been thoroughly looking forward to a relaxing bath, an hour or so of mindless television and an early night. She even considered trying to explain this to him but, as usual, when he started to stroke and explore her body, the familiar stirrings of wanting him badly took over. He made love to her twice, in the lounge and then again in bed. As he heaved his body off hers, it was more than Ellie could do to stop her eyelids from closing and sleep getting the better of her. The last waking thought she had was of Jeremy climbing into his clothes and then cursing as he stubbed his toe on the bed while he leant over to kiss her on the cheek. She heard him run downstairs and slam the front door behind him.

After a deep, dreamless sleep, Ellie was back on the ward again, catching up with overnight events and seeing to her patients. The rest had made her feel better but not totally restored her customary joie de vivre, so, aware that she was not quite firing on all cylinders, Ellie took her time over her ward work, checking each of her decisions even more meticulously and not worrying if it made her run late. Thankfully, there was no ward round. She saw Nigel briefly at lunchtime – long enough for a cup of tea, but he was racing back to theatre and so their chat was superficial and light. By six, she was in her car, driving to her parents' house. It was a foggy night and it took all her concentration to navigate safely along the dark, spookily lit roads.

She rang the doorbell and tried the door handle, her usual routine when she visited her parents. Surprised to find the door was locked, Ellie waited, hopping from one foot to the other in the cold for her mother to come and let her in. They hugged each other tightly.

'How marvellous to see you, Ellie. I've missed you loads.' Diana sounded fraught and on the verge of tears.

'It's great to see you, Mum, but it's only been a month.'

'No, but it seems so much longer.'

'Let me look at you,' Ellie perused her mother's face from arm's length. 'You've not got much of a tan, but I don't suppose it was that hot, was it?'

'Come on in, darling. Your father's in the lounge. The supper's cooking nicely. It'll be about thirty minutes – is that all right?'

'Fine. What did you decide on in the end?'

'I've done your favourite, toad-in-the-hole, mashed potato and Brussels sprouts. Lots of gravy. How does that sound?'

'I'm famished,' Ellie admitted. 'So it sounds incredible.'

'Come into the kitchen with me and talk while I peel the potatoes,' Diana suggested.

'Where's Dad?'

'Oh, he's just busy with some paperwork. He'll be finished in a few minutes and then we'll all have a sherry. Your dad developed quite a taste for it on the cruise. Now, let's leave him to it and you tell me about work and Emily's hen party.'

Alarm bells started to ring in Ellie's mind as she leant against the worktop. Trying to put them to the back of her mind she told her mother in detail about some of the more amusing incidents at work and skated over some of the sad moments. Diana threw her head back and hooted with laughter at her daughter's description of Emily's chicks and what they had got up to.

'Mind you, Ellie, you've got the legs for red tights,' was one of her comments. 'Even if yellow isn't your best colour.'

'I loved the foot and hand massage. It was so soothing and my nails looked just terrific afterwards. I tell you what, why don't you and I go there one day in the New Year – my treat?'

'That sounds good to me, Ellie. My hands are in a terrible state. So dry and wrinkled. I expect my feet are even worse but I just don't bother to look any more. Too much effort!'

Emily laughed and promised to arrange a day for them and then continued with her impressions of the hotel and Emily's mother Jean.

'I wish I had a fraction of her energy,' said, Diana, with feeling, opening the oven door to pour batter around the sausages, which were spitting raucously in the hot fat. 'There now, that's as much as we can do. Let's go and find your father. Keith!' she yelled, 'we're coming for our sherry!'

'Dad, hi!' cried Ellie, opening the door into the lounge.

Keith was sitting in what he considered to be his armchair, to one side of the fireplace and in prime position for watching the television. Ellie was completely taken aback by his appearance. He seemed to have shrunk. There was a smaller version of her father sitting huddled in clothes that were far too big for him. His collar gaped around his neck despite the top button being fastened and Ellie could see the outline of his scrawny legs under his trousers. His face was pinched, his cheekbones standing proud, creating an illusion of his eyes having sunk even further into his skull.

'Dad?'

Before she could say any more, Keith unsteadily got to his feet, after several false starts. He reached behind the chair and produced a walking stick. Relying heavily on this, he made his wobbly way towards the drinks cabinet on top of the sideboard. Ellie watched him, speechless. Diana rushed over to her husband as he reached out for the sherry bottle.

'Let me help you, love. A glass for you, Ellie?'

Not waiting for her reply, Diana helped her husband pour the drinks. She paid no attention to the fact that quite a lot of the pale liquid ended up spilt on the tray and that the glasses were all filled to different levels, one being so full that it splashed over as she carried it. Keith manoeuvred his way back to his chair and sat down with a thud.

'Lovely to see you, Ellie. Cheers!'

His speech was undeniably slurred. Ellie, well used to his voice, could make out what he was saying – just. A stranger would have had difficulty.

'Dad! Whatever's going on?'

Ellie accepted a glass from her mother, not taking her eyes off her father for a second. She watched while her mother decanted a measure of sherry into a plastic beaker and handed this to Keith. He held it with two hands, like a baby, and with enormous concentration raised it to his lips to taste. Almost immediately, he started to cough and Diana jumped up, took the beaker from him and placed it on the table. She rubbed his back soothingly until he had finished coughing and then sat on the arm of his chair, her own arm protectively around his shoulders.

Ellie stared at the two of them. Without thinking, she took a sip of her sherry, only a tiny drop but enough to make her shudder and recall that unless incorporated into a trifle, it was a drink she had no particular fondness for.

'Mum? Dad?'

'Ellie, love, we need to talk to you. This is going to be hard for all of us.'

Ellie strained to catch her father's words. Diana kissed the top of Keith's head and he looked up at her, adoringly. Ellie could see that they were both struggling to keep control of their tears.

'Shall I tell her?' Diana asked and Keith nodded.

'We'll do it together, my darling, like we do everything.'

Growing impatient, Ellie fought to keep the exasperation out of her voice.

'I really think it's about time you told me what's going on.'

Diana took a large gulp of sherry.

'There's no way on this earth that we can make this easy for you, Ellie. We've tried to keep it from you for some months, but, as things are now getting so much worse, it's time for you to know.'

'Know what? Please tell me.'

She looked at each parent in turn, imploringly. It was her father who spoke, softly but strangely clearly.

'I have motor neurone disease.'

Diana started to sob and clutched Keith's shoulder more tightly.

'Motor neurone disease?' echoed Ellie. 'Oh no! Oh, Dad, Mum. I can't believe it. I thought you'd got an alcohol problem.'

'I wish it were that simple,' Keith replied.

'I'm sorry, Ellie, but it's true.' Diana wept.

Ellie, now with tears streaming down her own face, went over and hugged her parents in turn and then they all hugged each other, clinging to one another for safety. None of them spoke, they just held on, bound together by their fear. Eventually, Diana broke away, dabbed at her eyes with a piece of paper towel that she extracted from the sleeve of her jumper and blew her nose.

Pulling herself together, she said, 'That's enough for now. Plenty of time for tears. Let's talk. But let me just go and check in the kitchen first.'

'I'm not sure what to say,' started Ellie, when Diana returned. 'How long have you known? Why didn't you tell me sooner? I might have been able to help.'

'I'll try to explain everything.' Diana glanced at Keith who nodded almost imperceptibly. He smiled a diluted smile at Ellie. She had to smile back. She loved him so much and even at a time like this she could still detect the faintest of twinkles in his blue eyes. Ellie sat back on her heels, leaning against her father's legs and holding one of his hands.

'We first noticed a problem just before you came to Harrogate. While we were house-hunting for you, Dad was starting to stumble and have trouble walking. We just put it down to his arthritis and we used to laugh about getting one of those stair lifts that are always being advertised on afternoon TV. Then he started dropping things and having problems with his coordination. Remember the anniversary present? Remember how he couldn't get his spoon into his ice-cream glass? We were worried in case you'd spotted something and that you might start asking questions.'

Ellie felt guilt creeping through her bones. Diana read her mind.

'Don't feel like that. We didn't want you to know. There you were, so many good things going on in your life. You were so excited about your new house and the job that there was just no way we could spoil that for you. Plus, at that time, we hadn't a clue what was wrong. Mind you, we knew something was and we went along to the GP, you know that nice Dr Urquhart – poor man, his patients never pronounce his name correctly – and he referred us immediately to the hospital where we saw Dr Swindlehurst.'

'Oh, Will,' Ellie muttered.

'Lovely man, so kind. I wouldn't want his job for a million pounds. He told us that he suspected the diagnosis that day, said he was almost one hundred per cent sure. Dad had a scan and some tests on his nerves to see if they were working properly and then there was no doubt at all. It was hard waiting for the scan but luckily we had your decorating to keep us busy. Dad painted all the big areas and I did round the edges! We make a great team.'

Diana attempted a laugh and kissed Keith again, this time on the cheek before continuing.

'We knew when we came for supper with you that evening Nigel was there. We reckoned that if we took things very gently and just said that Dad was worn out, that again, you wouldn't notice. I can't tell you how glad I was when Nigel told us he was getting married. It gave us all something to focus on, rather than your Dad. Despite the spotlight being on Nigel, there was still that awful choking bout.'

'My swallowing's buggered,' admitted Keith.

'Language, Keith,' admonished Diana.

Ellie's hand left her father's and flew to her mouth.

'Oh my goodness. After you'd gone that evening Nigel and I did stay up and discuss you. We'd both noticed. We wondered if you were drinking too much. How wrong could we have been? I'm so sorry, Dad.'

Keith, understanding, patted her forearm.

'We needed time to think, both of us, together and independently. Dr Swindlehurst had told us that there was no treatment. He did mention some tablets that might help a bit but you felt terrible with those, didn't you? So they were stopped after a week.'

'I couldn't cope with feeling like that. They stopped me from thinking clearly,' Keith recalled.

'So you went away on a cruise,' deduced Ellie. 'I thought it was really odd the way you went at such short notice and for so long. But of course I never imagined for a moment that it was because of this...'

'I went into the travel agents to see what was on offer. Cruising seemed perfect. Everything on tap. Lots of help, some warmer weather and plenty of time, just the two of us.'

'I wish you'd told me before,' Ellie said.

'There was no way we could tell you until we were ready to, until we'd sorted out our own minds. That way we knew that we'd be able to help you,' Diana explained.

'Mum,' Ellie objected, 'I am not ten years old. I'm an adult and a doctor.'

'All the more reason. You see too much illness on a daily basis. I've seen how emotionally involved you get with your patients sometimes. I was afraid to imagine how you'd be when it was your own father that was dying.'

'Dying? Who said anything about dying? Some patients, I mean people, live with motor neurone disease for years. Dad might be one of those. We must be positive.'

'Of course, dear, but sadly Dr Swindlehurst has warned us that the outlook for Dad is not good. His condition has deteriorated very quickly. We appreciated his honesty, even though it was the last news we wanted to hear, didn't we, Keith?'

More nodding.

'Now,' Diana sat up tall, 'we've to make the best of the time we have. Dad wants life to be as normal as possible so we can make a good start and have our dinner. I'll just be a moment or two. Ellie, if you could help Dad to the table, I'll serve up in the kitchen.'

Diana disappeared and could be heard dishing up the dinner. Ellie looked at her father.

'I just don't know what to say, Dad. I wish I could make it all better for you. I feel so helpless but you know I'll do whatever I can.'

Keith leant forward and clumsily tried to hug her.

'I know, Ellie love. Try not to worry about me,' he whispered.

'But you're my Dad. There's no way I can't worry.'

He settled for stroking her cheek.

'We have to try to make the best of it. No one said it was going to be easy though. I don't want any fuss.'

'I wish I had yours and Mum's courage,' Ellie started to cry again.

'Your mum is amazing. I could never do this without her. Please, Ellie, try not to cry any more.'

'I'm sorry, I just can't help it.'

All her attempts to stop just seemed to make more tears flow. Head resting on her father's knee, Ellie could smell the fabric conditioner in his trousers, the brand that her mother had used for years and that never failed to remind her of home. Keith said nothing but rhythmically continued to caress his daughter's hair, the way he had done all her life when she had needed to be consoled. Eventually calming down, she managed to look up at him and he did his best to smile reassuringly and winked one eye.

'Tea's ready. Let's get to the table. We don't want to upset your mum.'

Ellie dragged herself to her feet. She bent over to take Keith's arm but was dismissed immediately.

'Just pass me my stick. I must try to manage for as long as I can. Remember – no fuss.'

Reluctantly accepting his determination, Ellie let him walk the short distance unaided. She followed close behind, ready to lend a supporting hand at a second's notice and was relieved when he landed safely, if untidily, on his chair.

'I'll just pop and wash my hands and face,' Ellie said. 'Will you be okay?'

'I don't need to be wrapped in cotton wool,' Keith retorted.

In the bathroom, Ellie splashed cold water repeatedly on her face. She sat on the edge of the bath, trying desperately to make some sense of what was happening but failing miserably. Why had this happened and why to her father? Of all the illnesses he could have developed why did it have to be motor neurone disease, the most devastating and humiliating of conditions? He'd always been a fit man, perhaps not overly sporty but that counted for nothing. She could remember him having a hernia repair when she was at school and a week off work with food poisoning but he had never smoked and had never been much of a drinker. A mirthless laugh escaped from her lips. Fancy thinking that his problem was alcohol related. She could not have been more stupid. Why on earth had she not spotted the signs and made the diagnosis?

'Ellie?' Diana's voice accompanied a knock on the door. 'Dinner's on the table.'

'Coming.'

Ellie dried her face, checked in the mirror of the door of the cabinet and grimaced. Resigned to the fact that she could do nothing about her appearance, she took some deep breaths and returned to join her parents. Sitting down, she eyed the plate in front of her on which was a large portion of toad-in-the-hole – three sausages nestling in perfectly cooked Yorkshire pudding, a pile of fluffy, buttery mash, which contrasted with the vivid green of the Brussels sprouts. Diana passed her the gravy.

'Help yourself and then pass it on.'

Ellie poured some of the rich, aromatic liquid onto her sausages before offering it to Keith. Her mouth dropped open. On his plate there was nothing more than a large dollop of thick brown paste. There was no other word to describe it – disgusting.

Seeing the look on her face, Diana tried to make light of the situation.

'I popped your dad's meal into the liquidiser. The hospital suggested that. He's having just the same as us but it's easier for him to swallow.'

'Oh Dad! It doesn't look very appetising.'

Keith patted his so-called dinner with the back of his spoon.

'No, it doesn't does it? It tastes as bad as it looks.'

'Now then, Keith. You just get it down you. It's all home made, apart from the sausages, so it's full of goodness. We've got sponge and custard for afters. You know how you like that and I thought that Ellie could do with a bit of feeding up. Now, come on, tuck in everyone, before it gets any colder. Let's tell Ellie about the cruise, shall we? When we're finished, we'll get out the photos.'

Ellie could hardly believe her mother's enforced cheerfulness. It was rare that her appetite failed her but tackling this meal was fast proving to be one of the hardest things she had ever done. Diana kept chatting on, seemingly oblivious to Ellie's difficulties, determined to try to keep life as normal as she could. She recounted details of the boat they had been on, the facilities it boasted, the never-ending food and even the captain's cocktail party to which they had managed to wangle an invitation. Without even pausing for breath, she told Ellie about the places they had seen, the people they'd met and the weather they had experienced. Ellie tried to live up to her mother's expectations and listen intently, ask pertinent questions and make apposite remarks. But in the end Diana got up and without comment picked up all three plates of barely touched food. As the sound of the liquidiser was heard coming from the kitchen, Ellie shuddered internally. Keith shrugged his shoulders when she glanced at him. A dish containing a slice of marbled chocolate and orange sponge with chocolate custard was presented to Ellie. Keith also received a dish. Looking at the contents, one could have been forgiven for thinking that they were a second helping of the main course, such was the similarity. They all picked, disinterestedly at their dessert.

'Thanks, Mum, that was lovely. Sorry I couldn't eat much,' Ellie apologised as she helped to clear the table and carry dishes through to the kitchen.

'I understand. We were all a bit too upset tonight. You wash, I'll dry but first I must just check that Dad's got back to his armchair safely.'

Ellie scraped the plates and looked at the resultant mess in the bin.

Poor Dad, she mused, condemned to eating food pulverised beyond recognition for the rest of his life.

Diana returned and chivvied Ellie into action.

'How do you keep going, Mum?'

For a moment, Diana paused, half way through drying a handful of cutlery.

'I suppose it's my way of coping,' she decided, before, as if switched back on, she returned to her task with vigour. 'If I keep busy, I've less time to think about the future.'

Ellie understood. 'Do you need more help?'

'Not at the present time. I'm just going to take each day as it comes – and so should you. We want you to carry on normally, to do well at work, become a GP, enjoy your house. Just imagine how it feels for Dad. He's the one who's ill. He's getting a little worse physically each day but mentally he's completely normal and very aware. How terrifying can that be?'

'I can't begin to imagine,' agreed Ellie, sadly. 'I've spoken to patients with motor neurone disease and their relatives but nothing can ever prepare you for it happening to you.'

'Ellie, I don't envy you. But your experiences and knowledge will perhaps help you in a way you don't expect. Put the kettle on for a cup of tea, please.'

'I could move back home, if you like. It would be easy to rent my house out for a while.'

'We wouldn't hear of it. We're so happy that you've moved back to Harrogate. You can some and see us often and I promise I'll contact you immediately if there's any need. We had a long, long talk while we were sitting on the pool deck one day and one of the many things that we agreed on was that we'd like to preserve as much normality in life as possible. Your dad would never forgive himself if you moved back in with us. And don't look like that...'

Ellie had opened her mouth to disagree but shut it again smartly.

'...Yes we are horribly aware that far sooner than we would like, it's going to become very difficult indeed. Come here, darling.'

Diana enveloped Ellie in her arms, just as she had done a million and more times over the years. They stood there, not speaking, just holding each other. Ellie felt the beat of her mother's heart. It sounded strong and regular. Dependable. She felt tears starting to well in her eyes again.

The kettle switching off broke the spell and they moved apart, Diana keeping her hands cupped around Ellie's upper arms.

'Be strong, Ellie. We need you to be.'

As promised, the photographs were produced as they drank their tea and sucked wafer-thin chocolate mints. At least Keith's were spared the indignity of meeting with the liquidiser. Although the views were often spectacular, Ellie found it hard to keep up a conversation and yet again admired Diana's ability to provide a continuous commentary.

Just after nine, it was clear that Keith, who was looking increasingly jaded, needed to go to bed. Ellie started to offer her help but was silenced by a look from her mother.

'You get off now, Ellie. I'll see your dad to bed and then I'll tidy up these last few things and read my book for a while. It might still be foggy out there so drive very, very carefully and give me a quick ring when you get back home to say you've arrived safely.'

Ellie, feeling awkward about leaving, suggested she stay if only to keep her mother company. Diana dismissed this, with thanks and so, after kissing her parents tenderly and promising to see them very soon, she took her leave. Back home, she dutifully called her mother, who assured her that her dad was snugly tucked up in his bed and already asleep.

She made a hot chocolate and then rang the hospital, knowing that Nigel was on call. For once, he was not in theatre.

'Nigel, my dad, he's got MND.'

She heard Nigel's involuntary gasp.

'Oh Ellie. That's just dreadful. How is he?'

'I can't believe the change in him. He's deteriorated so quickly.'

'That's dreadful,' Nigel repeated, feeling his words were hopelessly inadequate but not having a clue what to say that might actually be helpful. 'Do you want to come up to the hospital and talk? I'm not back in theatre until midnight and there's nothing pending at the moment.'

'I'm tempted to,' admitted Ellie, 'but I won't. You know what it's like when you're on call. You'll probably be bleeped before I even get there. Can we meet up tomorrow?'

'Of course, how about lunch? I'll make sure I'm free. Give me a buzz when you're ready.'

'That'd be good. Thanks, Nigel.'

'Try to get some sleep, Ellie. But if you can't, remember you can always ring me, any time.'

Ellie finished the call. Her drink was stone cold. Not bothering to wash up the mug, she crawled up to bed and lay thinking in the darkness, her father's image going round and round in her head.

10

Penelope Makepeace emerged from the nurses' changing room after her predictable pre-ward round disappearance at exactly the moment Jeremy strode onto the ward. She became positively flushed when he commented on how well she was looking. Conversely Ellie, Jeremy considered after the briefest of glances, was looking a mess. She had dark circles under her eyes and her usually gorgeous skin looked matt and oily in patches. Uncharacteristically for someone who loved colour as she did, she was all in black – polo-necked jumper, skirt, tights and flat shoes. Her hair, which she had washed quickly that morning, was pulled back from her face and clumped together in an elastic band and far too much of it had escaped. She looked haunted and as if she hadn't slept for a week. Rather than greeting him with her dazzling smile, she sighed and as if it was the most Herculean of tasks, stood up from her chair and came to join the entourage.

'Let's get started. I have a meeting to go to when we're finished.'

These few words filled Ellie with dismay. She had been hoping to have a word with him in private once they were done, to tell him about Keith, sure that Jeremy would sympathise and swear to look after her through the next few months, or better still, for all time.

'Dr Blake, I was wondering if I could just have a few moments of your time today sometime,' Ellie tried. This ploy had worked before, in fact it was almost their own secret code. It sounded formal and sufficiently business-like not to arouse suspicion. Jeremy would acquiesce and usher her past Muriel into his room, where, with the door firmly closed behind them, he would proceed to delight her in many different ways.

'Not possible, I'm afraid. My meeting will last all day.'

If Ellie had been more alert she would have noticed Penelope Makepeace assume a triumphant expression on her face, which was erased instantaneously when Jeremy continued, 'I don't even have time for coffee. Now, please can we get started. We've wasted time unnecessarily already.'

Not waiting for a reply, he marched off with Penelope to the first patient; Ellie following, trundling the trolley, two junior nurses reluctantly bringing up the rear.

'Tell me about this patient,' Jeremy barked.

Ellie took up her allotted position on the opposite side of the bed and thanked the nurse who passed her the appropriate notes.

'This is Mrs Lucy Geelan, aged eighty-seven years. She was admitted by her GP yesterday having "gone off her legs".'

'That is such a ridiculous expression,' fumed Jeremy, interrupting.

Unfazed, Ellie continued.

'She has a background history of ischaemic heart disease and hypertension. Her presenting complaint is one of several weeks' duration. She has noticed dyspnoea on minimal exertion – for example bending to stroke her cat and that she cannot get her feet into anything other than her late husband's large slippers because her feet have been so oedematous. The GP has done bloods, which show that Mrs Geelan is profoundly anaemic, with a haemoglobin of only six. The blood film suggests iron deficiency.'

Ellie's presentation, though efficient, was delivered with little feeling. She had gone into automaton mode and her only desire was to get through the ward round as speedily as possible. Any hopes she might have nurtured that Jeremy would be less critical in view of his pressing appointment were short lived. He was clearly hell bent on being the opposite. Such being the case, Ellie had to endure snide comments, cynicism and lambasting. Patients cowered beneath their sheets, the two nurses looked on in disbelief but Sister Makepeace made no attempt to conceal the fact that she was thoroughly enjoying his every word.

118

'Dr Woods, tell me all the causes of bloody diarrhoea.'

They were at the foot of an empty bed. Sitting in the chair beside it was Mr O'Connor, gaunt, wiry, and angular with a goatee beard that made his chin seem even longer than it really was.

'There's no need to be offensive, Dr Blake. Just because I've got my pyjamas on, it doesn't mean I'm not a person,' he bridled.

There was a hush that spread through the ward like the calm before the storm. Nobody dared to cough. A tap dripping in the sluice was all that could be heard. Sister Makepeace hurriedly sent a nurse off to deal with it.

Jeremy, nonplussed, smiled his most disarming smile, rather reminiscent of a leopard about to eat its prey.

'Mr O'Connor, I think you misunderstand me. Bloody diarrhoea refers to the fact that there is blood mixed in with your faeces.'

Ellie stifled a laugh. She would thank Mr O'Connor later for the unintentional light relief that he had provided.

Jeremy focused on Ellie.

'Well?'

Somehow, Ellie managed to recite a commendable number of differential diagnoses that were associated with the symptom in question, perhaps not all of them but enough to satisfy her self-appointed examiner.

'And which of that bloody lot have I got?' asked Mr O'Connor, incredulous.

'That's for us to find out. Dr Woods, we need a full blood count, inflammatory markers, liver function tests, stool sample for culture and sensitivity and book him for a barium enema. Also, pencil in a sigmoidoscopy and colonoscopy.'

'Bloody hell,' whistled Mr O'Connor, 'I was feeling quite well up 'til now.'

'Don't worry, I'll come back later and explain everything,' promised Ellie, patting him on the arm.

'Thanks, lass. Good job someone around here has some manners.'

'Dr Woods?' Jeremy bellowed from the next bay of beds.

'I'd better go. Coming!' Ellie called, scurrying off to join the others.

Miraculously, Walter Musgrove's recalcitrant leg ulcers were finally showing the first but incontrovertible signs of healing, Sarah Fennerty's histology result turned up in the internal mail delivery and the last three patients to be seen were all sufficiently on the road to recovery to be discharged. Finishing on this high note appeased Jeremy slightly and he had the grace to thank the individual members of his team for their hard work and support. As he was leaving, having refused Sister Makepeace's last-minute try to tempt him with coffee, he called out over his shoulder.

'Dr Woods, if I have a free moment, I will ring you later.'

Ellie's heart throbbed with hope.

'Thank you very much,' she shouted after him but he had already turned the corner into the corridor and was out of sight.

'Coffee, Dr Woods?' It was a rhetorical question. Bracing herself, but feeling a fraction happier, Ellie joined Sister Makepeace in the doctors' room. They studiously kept the conversation to clinical matters only, aware that they had no other common bond. Reluctantly, Penelope offered Ellie one of the chocolate biscuits that evidently she had bought in for Jeremy. She accepted gratefully mentioning that she had not felt much like breakfast that morning. Together they went through each patient on the ward, one by one, drawing up an intimidatingly long list of things that needed to be done.

'So,' Penelope finished, 'that leaves us with three empty beds. That is perfect as it nicely fits the admissions that are expected this afternoon.'

'What?' Ellie gasped, horrified, as she had been hoping for a quiet day.

'Dr Blake saw them in clinic this week. At least he saw two of them.' She reached over and opened a large diary. 'There's a Clive Young, for investigation of loss of balance and Cissie Beckwith with diabetes and renal failure. The third one is a Stanley Godwin. He has pancytopoenia and so will be under the care of the haematologists primarily but you'll still have to clerk him in. Their notes are on Muriel's desk if you want to go and get them. You can familiarise yourself with their details over lunch.'

'Thank you,' Ellie replied, mentally adamant that nothing would stop her meeting Nigel. All visions of an early finish were vanishing like water mirages on a hot road.

Ellie returned to the ward and busied herself. Her mother was right; it was the only way to be as it did help one cope. By lunchtime, she had achieved so much that she fully felt that a lunch break was deserved and not one spent reading patients' notes. She rang Nigel, who was already in the canteen, arranging to see him in a few minutes. As she was on the verge of leaving the ward, Sister Makepeace called her back to write up some drug sheets and then Muriel waylaid her and asked her to sign some letters that Jeremy had omitted to do before he left. Consequently, it was nearly a quarter of an hour later that she pondered over the menu of the day before choosing chicken pie, peas, chips and a glass of grapefruit juice. Nigel was on the far side of the room but Ellie was downcast to see that he was not alone. He seemed deep in conversation with someone whose back was towards Ellie.

Picking up a knife and fork, Ellie then wound a serpentine path around the other tables which were nearly all full to join her friend. Nigel waved as he saw her coming. Ellie laid her tray on the table and tried to pull out the chair. She pretended to scowl as Nigel pinched one of her chips.

'Hang on a minute, I'll move up. Gosh, this is getting harder and harder.'

Nigel chuckled with his companion, who stood up, revealing her heavily gravid abdomen and moved her chair to make a space for Ellie. She was a pleasant-looking woman with kind, dark brown eyes that reminded Ellie of a Labrador. Her face was framed by a neat, spiky haircut and her complexion was heightened by the chloasma of pregnancy. Her clothes were smart. A crisp white blouse under a plum-coloured pinafore dress. Around her neck was a double string of pearls but she wore no rings, her fingers too bloated by fluid retention.

'Hello,' Ellie greeted them. 'Thanks for moving. Goodness, how many weeks have you got left to go?'

'All being well, a month but I doubt I'll make it that far.' She patted her belly protectively. 'There's two of them in here, but I think the scan must have been mistaken, because it feels like four. They're never still!'

'Gosh, twins. How exciting!' Ellie enthused. 'That's like having your whole family all at once.'

'We've already got twin boys at home. They're four and just about to start school. We never dreamt it would happen again.'

Nigel was finishing his dinner, watching the two women while he ate.

'I am so sorry,' he interjected. 'I 'm forgetting my manners, you two haven't met, have you? Helen, this is Ellie Woods, your husband's SHO; Ellie, this is Helen Blake. She's doing a neurology locum.'

It was as much as Ellie could do not to drop her cutlery and choke on her food. Nigel watched her with an innocent look on his face.

Helen, oblivious, was naturally chatty; just like Ellie in fact, and continued.

'So you're Ellie. How lovely to meet you. You poor thing working for Jeremy. Is he still as rigid as ever on his ward rounds? I used to dread them.'

Correctly identifying that Ellie was incapable of speech, Nigel thoughtfully kept on talking.

'Oh, you once worked for him, did you?'

'Yes, that's how we met. Seven years ago. Now look at me!'

She laughed, happily. Nigel kicked Ellie under the table, making her jolt back to reality.

'Er, he's a very good teacher. I've learnt a huge amount in this job.'

'Yes, he is, isn't he? Is that fearsome sister still in charge? I can't remember her name.'

'Who, Penelope Makepeace?'

'That's it! She made my life a misery for six months.'

'Oh, she's still there. She's very efficient but it doesn't do to get on the wrong side of her. How long are you doing a locum for?' Ellie felt she wanted to steer the subject away from matters that they might have in common.

'They wanted someone for a few months. Needless to say, that's not going to be me. But I promised to try to do four weeks if I could, while they advertised for someone else. I've managed nearly two, so far and I'm just crossing my fingers that my blood pressure doesn't go up and I have to go off sick.'

'That must be quite a risk, with twins,' Ellie commented, slightly unkindly.

'I sailed through my first pregnancy and, touch wood,' Helen looked around and then tapped her head, 'it's been the same this time.'

She glanced at her watch.

'Anyway, I must make a move. It takes me twice as long as normal to get anywhere. It was so nice to meet you, Ellie. Perhaps you can escape from the ward one day soon and we can catch up again. I'd like that.'

Ellie smiled in what she hoped would be interpreted as agreement. She stood up to let Helen manoeuvre her way out from the table and sat back down again pretending to eat but in truth secretly watching Helen waddle towards the exit.

Nigel watched her with a mixture of concern and amusement.

'I'm sorry about that, Ellie. She'd come onto the ward to give us a neuro opinion about a patient. We got chatting and agreed to come for lunch. She seems really nice, doesn't she?'

Ellie pushed away her plate, thankful that she no longer had to feign hunger. Nigel wasted no time and pounced on her uneaten chips.

'I can hardly speak. My mouth's gone dry and my heart's pounding,' she confessed.

'Twins, eh? In a month. And twins at home aged four. That's quite a family,' Nigel mused. He scrutinised Ellie's face, noting her reactions. 'Just going to get some pudding. They've got crumble today. Want some?'

Ellie shook her head and then rested it in her hands, letting her loose hair fall over her face. Engulfed by shame, she could not bring herself to look at anyone. Her stupidity knew no bounds. It had suited her to imagine that Helen was some sort of behemoth, vile tongued and devoid of feeling. But, naturally, she was none of these things. She was attractive, pleasant and worst of all pregnant and had even provided that extra bit of information that there was a family at home already. Ellie heard Nigel sit down opposite her.

'I've brought you a coffee,' he told her, adding diplomatically, 'I thought you might need it.'

'Nigel, what have I done?'

Ellie looked up and Nigel's heart went out to her as he saw the tears streaming down her face. He took her hand and squeezed it.

'I'm here for you. I'm not even going to say I told you so.'

'You can if you want. I deserve it.'

Nigel spooned up some crumble and custard, deliciously stodgy and sweet.

'I'll have to tell Jeremy that I'm not going to see him any more. I can't be responsible for hurting his family. I just hope that Helen never finds out.'

'Good for you, Ellie. That's more like it.'

'Nigel, it's all such a mess. I wish this horrible job was over. I've got another four weeks to work for him. It'll be excruciating.'

'Four weeks isn't long, Ellie. Christmas and New Year will pass in a flash, they always do and then you've got some holiday in January so before you know it, you'll have moved to paediatrics and you need never see him again.' Nigel hoped that he was sounding reassuring.

'I suppose you're right but I still wish it was all over.'

'You'll get though it, Ellie. The main thing though is that you finish whatever it is you think you have going with him. And don't have any second thoughts. If you feel the merest inkling of one coming on then, for God's sake, picture those twins at home and the ones about to arrive.'

'I've been a complete fool, Nigel.'

'We're all fools at times. The most important thing is that we recognise when we are being fools and do something about it. That's hard but you'll be a better and nicer person when you've done it.'

He winked at Ellie who had to smile. He waited a moment before speaking again.

'Now, tell me about your dad. I've not been able to stop thinking about what you told me.'

Ellie massaged her temples with her fingers.

'I'm still reeling from that. Half the time I think it's all a dream.'

'How bad is he?'

'Grim,' Ellie replied. 'You'll be so upset when you see him. He can hardly walk, talk or swallow but mentally he's completely unscathed. Mum's liquidising his meals.' She shuddered at the memory and Nigel, familiar with the off-putting appearance of said meals after a job on the thoracic surgery ward, grimaced.

'MND is the most ruthless of diseases.'

Ellie nodded in tacit agreement.

'What about your mum?'

'She's being amazing, as ever. Pretending she's got it all under control. Running herself ragged to keep it as normal as she can for Dad. I offered to go back home to live and help but they refused. I wish I could do more for them but I just don't know what to suggest.'

'Just be there for them, Ellie. Respect their wishes to carry on as best they can but visit when you're able, let your mum have some time off, even if it's just for a couple of hours. I hate to say this as there is a certain finality about it, but make the most of the time you've got left with your dad. That way, you'll be left with no regrets. Believe me, I've been there.'

'I don't think he'll live more than a few months.' Ellie clapped her hand to her mouth, aghast at what she had just said.

Nigel scraped up the last of his custard.

'Poor Ellie. What a lot you've got on your plate at the moment. I wish I wasn't all tied up with the wedding and honeymoon, and then I could be more help.'

'No, no, no,' repeated Ellie emphatically. 'You must not worry about me, Concentrate on Emily and your celebrations. It's going to be such a happy time for you both. She's a great girl and she is so lucky to be marrying someone like you.'

'We've a rehearsal this weekend but I should be able to pop in and see your parents. Do you think that would be okay?'

'Of course it would, but only if you have the time. Don't go rearranging things just for us. They know life's hectic for you at the moment and would be mortified to find out that you'd gone out of your way to visit, in the same way that they don't want me to miss work or move in.'

'It's no trouble, Ellie. I look on your parents as close friends. They've been so good to me since we were at medical school. I could take Emily with me, they'd like that, wouldn't they?'

'I'm sure that they'd love it,' Ellie answered with sincerity.

Her pager squawked insistently from her pocket. It meant that not only was there work to be done but also that it was time to get new batteries.

'I bet that's the lovely Sister Makepeace after me. I've been away from the ward for longer that she approves of. Nigel, thanks for being there, as always.'

'For you,' he replied, gallantly, 'any thing and any time. Take care, keep being brave and speak to me soon to tell me what's happening. Promise?'

Ellie blew him a kiss as she made her way to the telephone, which was now free. Her premonitions proved to be correct and she was summoned back to the ward to see the first of her admissions.

11

None of the new arrivals on Whitby Ward noticed that the attractive doctor who came to talk to them, examine them and then extract varying quantities of blood from them did not have her mind entirely on the job in hand. While they, at great length, provided her with blow-by-blow accounts of their symptoms, relishing the fact that some of them had started as far back as the late 1940s and continued to date, Ellie's mind was largely rehearsing what she was going to say to Jeremy the next time they were alone. Theoretically, it was quite straightforward. She would simply stand her ground and accuse him of failing to tell her about his family commitments and then inform him, in no uncertain terms, that she had no intention of being a home-wrecker. This would be followed up by the final blow which was to tell him that she regretted ever have fallen for his attentions in the first place. Somehow, she knew that, when she was saying this to his face that it would be very much harder. She dreaded the prospect.

Sarah Fennerty loved to talk. Ellie, she told her, reminded her of one of her grandchildren, the one who worked for the building society and was doing very nicely for herself. She had eight grandchildren and another one of them had put together an album for her, stuffed full of photos of them all. Proudly, she navigated her way through this book, which she had on her bedside locker, telling Ellie the names of everyone and what they were doing with their lives, interspersed with her own opinions, most of which were quite forthright. By the end of the afternoon, Ellie felt as though she had met them all individually and wandered back to the nurses' station with a head that was dizzy from all the personal details she had been privy to.

Finishing more or less on time, Ellie rang her mother and asked if there was anything she could do for her that evening. Diana, bright and breezy on the other end of the line, assured her that they were fine but perhaps Ellie could help out with the big shop at the weekend. Ellie was relieved to be given something to do. It made her feel more useful and less like a spare part. Before ringing off, she remembered to tell her mother that Nigel might be calling round, possibly with Emily. Diana sounded delighted and started muttering about whether she had the necessary ingredients to make a cake. She uttered noises of disgust when Ellie suggested that she buy one when she was doing the rest of the shopping.

As she put on her coat and scarf, it occurred to Ellie that Jeremy had never rung her. Perhaps this was just as well, now that events had taken such an unexpected turn and he had no idea of what lay in store for him. Outside it was freezing cold. Gritting lorries had been out in force, salting the roads and the hospital car park and the sky was a mass of heavy, black clouds promising snow. Ellie walked as quickly as she could, stopping briefly to buy milk, eggs and cheese as she planned to make a soufflé for supper. The heating in her house had come on about an hour earlier and it was a comforting welcome after the bitter evening air. Hungry as a result of missing lunch, or more accurately being unable to eat lunch, Ellie went straight to the kitchen, switched on the oven and took great pleasure in creating her meal. Pouring a glass of wine, she sat and watched the news while the soufflé obligingly rose to statuesque heights that could have graced the pages of any cookery book. It tasted as good as it looked. Ellie enjoyed an enormous portion with some generously buttered toast and a second glass of wine. She felt revived and opened the day's post, mostly Christmas cards, wrote out some cheques to pay bills and then settled down to watch a documentary on wildlife on the Orkney Islands. This had just finished and Ellie was washing up when the doorbell rang.

'Hello, gorgeous.'

For the first time, Ellie was not happy to see Jeremy standing there.

She wished that he did not look so delectable, with snowflakes settling on his hair and the shoulders of his long, dark blue overcoat. She'd hoped for more time to prepare herself for this encounter.

'Hello,' she replied.

'Can I come in? It's perishing out here.' He rubbed his hands together vigorously to emphasise his point.

Ellie stood to one side to let him in. He stamped his feet on the doormat and removed his coat.

'Put the kettle on. I could murder a hot drink.'

'It's quite late. I was just about to go to bed,' Ellie informed him, primly.

'Good. I'll come with you. Come here, I need a hug.'

Reluctantly Ellie went towards him.

'Oh you're so cold. Your hands and face are like ice.'

Using this as a convenient excuse, she broke away from him, trying to sound light hearted and made a big fuss of filling the kettle and getting out mugs and teabags. Internally, Ellie could feel her heart thumping and racing. I need to keep calm and try to stay as formal as possible. I must not give in. I must remember what Nigel said.

Repeating her self-invented mantra in her mind, she placed two mugs of tea on the kitchen table and decided not to offer Jeremy any biscuits. He sat down and she pointedly took the chair opposite him, rather than next to him.

'So, what did you want to talk to me about? Or was that just a ruse to get me to come round?'

Ellie cleared her throat. She pulled her hand away when he reached for it.

'I did have something I wanted to talk to you about but, as it happens, another more important matter needs to be dealt with.'

'This sounds very formal,' he tried to lighten the atmosphere but Ellie refused to be drawn.

'Jeremy, I met Helen today.' Ellie's steady voice surprised her.

'Ah.' He looked down and studied the contents of his mug. 'I see.'

'What am I supposed to think? She's pregnant with twins and due any day. What's more, there are four-year-old twins at home.'

'Yes, that's right,' he stated, simply.

'Did it never occur to you to tell me about any of this?'

'There was no need for you to know. You knew that I was married. That was enough. It doesn't make any difference to the way I feel about you.'

'How can you say that? Yes, I knew you were married but you said you weren't happy. You led me to believe that you and Helen were only living under the same roof for the sake of convenience. You told me things that made me hope that we had a future, that you would leave Helen and we could be together.'

'That's all true, Ellie. I swear.'

'How can it be? What about when the babies arrive? There's no way you're going to walk out on her then, is there?'

'I told you it was complicated. I can sort it all out, I promise you.'

Ellie was enraged.

'What are you talking about? I can't cope with the guilt of breaking up a family. It was bad enough that you were married, albeit unhappily but somehow I managed to rationalise that by convincing myself you had genuinely made a mistake. But I've just been fooling myself, haven't I?'

Jeremy banged his fists on the table.

'No, of course you haven't. I meant every word. Helen and I, well, I don't know how to explain. My home life is difficult... you are the one I want to be with.'

Ellie gasped, disbelievingly.

'Helen seemed perfectly happy to me. She was so excited about the new twins and spoke so proudly of the sons you already have.'

'Ah, well, that's different.'

'Jeremy, you are talking utter nonsense.'

'Let's go to bed, Ellie. I can explain better when you're close to me. You are so beautiful that I really can't resist you. Please...'

He stared at her intently and moved to the chair next to her. Slowly he began to run one finger down her cheek and neck. Ellie pulled away, appalled by his audacity.

'Jeremy, leave me alone. This cannot go on. Go home to your family. They must be wondering where you are. Go and read your sons a bedtime story and be a proper husband and father.'

'But Ellie, I need you so much. You feel the same, I know it. You've told me over and over. Think how phenomenal it is when we make love. It's wild, exciting, passionate and fulfilling. Each time is different but it's never anything short of amazing. You know it is. You can't get enough of me.'

'Jeremy, a relationship is more than sex. It should be built on trust and honesty. I can't believe you're saying these things. I'm serious, we must finish this now.'

'You don't mean that,' Jeremy whined, his hand this time running up the inside of her thigh, under her skirt. He moved closer, sucked on her ear lobe and was gratified to feel her tremble. 'Come on, Ellie. You know you don't really want this to end. Helen need never know about us.'

Ellie jumped to her feet, aware that if she stayed in that position a second longer, she would cave in to his wheedling charms. Facing him, she summoned up as much courage as she could.

'It's over, Jeremy. Your family need you. I do not. My father has been diagnosed with motor neurone disease, which is what I originally planned to speak to you about and I must spend all my free time with him and my mother.'

Jeremy stood up too.

'Ellie, that's such terrible news. You must be overwhelmed. No wonder you looked so pale and unwell this morning. I am so, so sorry.'

He edged towards her. He could see Ellie was shaking, trying desperately to keep her emotions in check. Tentatively, he put his arms gently around her, ignoring the initial resistance and pulled her closer. As he whispered in her ear, Ellie heard words of comfort, endearment and desire and started to cry. More confident of her compliance, he tightened his hold and started to kiss her cheeks. Feeling no rebuttal he let his lips lightly touch hers. Ellie, defences shattered, kissed him back with a ferocious passion, after which it seemed only natural to allow him to lead her upstairs, undress her and make love to her with tantalising tenderness.

Post-coitally, she watched him get dressed and then rolled away, ashamed at what had happened and at her weakness. She was unable to bear the sight of him but then again, she did not want him to go. She felt the bed give as he sat beside her and kissed her shoulder.

'I was right, wasn't I, Ellie? We're in this too deep to stop now. So long as we're here, hidden inside this house, no one else need exist. Never forget how I feel about you.'

He kissed her again and slipped his hand under the duvet to stimulate her nipple, but she pushed him away, feeling violated. Without saying another word, he left. Ellie lay where she was, waited to hear the front door close and then rushed down to secure all the locks. Back upstairs, she showered for longer than was necessary and put on a clean nightdress. On the verge of getting back into bed, she felt an irresistible compulsion to strip off all the bedding, banish it to the laundry basket and remake the bed with fresh, clean replacements, untainted by the smell of Jeremy.

12

There were just three days left to Christmas, two to Nigel's wedding. The cold infuriatingly had passed, leaving in many ways more miserable weather, unseasonably mild and wet. The snow that had come had lingered for a while and then turned to slush overnight which in its turn froze with the result that the Accident and Emergency department had had an influx of adults and children with broken bones, bumps and bruises. Despite work going on as usual, there was generally a feeling of excitement and anticipation at the hospital.

Ellie was holding a step ladder steady while one of the nurses, balanced halfway up, attached decorations in golden and green foil to the wall under the strict guidance of Sister Makepeace, who had decreed that the time had come for Whitby Ward to look festive. Chinese lanterns that had not seen the light of day for eleven and a half months had been dusted off and now dangled gaily, with a profusion of paper chains and plastic holly. Near the door to the ward the artificial tree had been resurrected for yet another year and was covered with a selection of the least battered baubles. Around the base was a selection of exciting-looking parcels which in reality were cardboard urinals wrapped up in colourful paper. With a show of uncharacteristic frivolity, Sister Makepeace had allowed her nursing team to adorn their hats with tinsel and had provided Ellie with a glittery robin badge which flashed rather hysterically when it was switched on. She had another badge for Jeremy, which she would present at the start of his ward round. His of course was far superior in all respects, being bigger in size and shinier – a laughing Santa head with eyes that moved from side to side and a hat that was bespattered with sequins. Ellie, ruefully, doubted that Jeremy would even consider wearing his as she subserviently pinned hers on her coat.

The patients seemed to appreciate the efforts that were taking place. Most of them would be going home, well enough either to be discharged finally or at least be granted a few hours' leave. Only a few were too ill to go anywhere and a further few had nowhere to go. It was unlikely that there would be any planned admissions from clinic, there being little point as investigations would be limited to emergencies only and apart from the very lonely, nobody wanted to volunteer to be in hospital for Christmas. The lull did not fool Ellie. She knew that after Christmas Day life on the ward would crank up again with an alarming acceleration. For her own part, she looked forward to having Christmas Eve and Day off. For once, the way the on-call rota had been planned worked in her favour. She was quite content to be on call on Boxing Day and New Year's Eve after which she was determined to cross off the days until the end of the job.

Her lack of self-control had meant that she had continued to be hypnotised by Jeremy's attractions and persuasive guile. Since the night when she had tried to end their affair, she was ashamed to admit that they had gone on seeing each other, three or four times a week, after work, at her house, inevitably ending up in bed. He had repeatedly told her that they needed each other and if the sex was anything to go by then they definitely had something in common. Ellie felt extremely uncomfortable with the situation and each time he left, she told herself that that was the last time it would happen but before she knew it, she had succumbed yet again. There had been no further mention of Helen or the children. Without actually discussing it, Ellie and Jeremy had come to a tacit agreement that they would only talk about themselves, or, nearer the truth, only about Ellie who had a lot to get off her chest and needed to feel supported. Not wanting to contact Nigel and depend on him as she would do under normal circumstances, she had used Jeremy as a substitute. She could not deny that he had helped her no end on the subject of her father. Whilst not a neurologist, he had a greater acquaintance with Keith's condition than Ellie and slowly talked her through what was likely to happen to him. On more than one occasion, Ellie was taken aback with just how much he did know and tortured herself for some hours wondering if he had been asking Helen for advice. None of his information made for easy listening but Jeremy proved to be a solid shoulder to cry on and held Ellie tightly while she grieved. He made no mention of Christmas, or his plans and where, if anywhere, Ellie might fit into them and she refrained from asking him. She was glad that she had the wedding to occupy her on Christmas Eve and then, naturally, she would be with her parents. These arrangements provided her with a ready-made excuse not to see Jeremy and thus avoid any guilt that she might feel if he was to spend time with her, rather than his family.

Ellie had seen only passing glimpses of Nigel. He was busy doing some extra nights on call, the swaps that he had had to make to free up time for his honeymoon. They spoke only briefly, mostly on the telephone and Ellie had managed to keep the conversation on the wedding and well away from Jeremy. Nigel, if he knew, would feel incredibly let down. Ellie hated to think about it. She knew the relationship was wrong and that Nigel was right but it was all proving to be so difficult as her emotions refused to see things in such a black and white fashion. She had vowed to herself that by the time he returned from his honeymoon she would be able to look him in the eye and genuinely tell him that she had finished with Jeremy and survived to tell the tale.

In the meantime the days were going to be hectic, starting off with the ward Christmas outing, a cause for great excitement amongst the nursing staff but hardly a romantic rendezvous for Ellie and Jeremy, though both had promised to go. Sister Makepeace had been planning it for some weeks, evolving a rota that allowed her best nurses time off to attend, leaving her less favoured staff to work the late shifts on the day of the party and the early shifts the day after, thus ensuring that they declined their invitations to attend. There was to be a meal followed by a disco and about twelve of them were going. Ellie was not looking forward to it. Eleven women, Penelope Makepeace and Jeremy – the prospect did not thrill Ellie. Hopefully, she would be able to sit with some of the nurses she had made friends with and have a laugh, as it went without saying that Jeremy would be monopolised by his ward sister.

Ironically, just when Ellie would have been quite happy to stay late and see new admissions or deal with problems and thus have a cast-iron excuse why she was not able to go to the party, she finished early, at least by her standards. At home, she bathed and prevaricated about what to wear before settling for some tight jeans and a multicoloured silk shirt. Leaving her hair down, she put on some make-up, specifically chose Jeremy's favourite perfume and then spent a few minutes phoning her mother and checking that all was as well as it could be. She promised to do a big supermarket shop for her the next day in the evening and hoped that it would be less frantic to tackle this task at that time. The list that Diana dictated to her was two pages long and Ellie felt like reminding her that there were only going to be the three of them but knew from many years of experience that she would be totally ignored. Quite why it was that boxes of sticky dates and crystallised fruits were required when none of them actually liked them would forever be a mystery but Ellie had considerable sympathy for her mother's desire to preserve tradition, particularly when it was probably going to be their last as a family, though neither of them dared to mention this out loud.

Ellie's taxi arrived and she jumped in and settled back in the seat to be patient while the driver took a circuitous route and picked up three of the nurses from their residence. They were dressed to kill and had obviously decided to start the party while they were getting ready, as there were unmistakable signs that they were slightly tipsy. The venue was packed and they had to fight their way to the bar to get drinks. Tables were set out around the perimeter of a huge dining room, which was playing host to a number of office parties that evening. The noise was deafening and it was nigh on impossible to chat to anyone. Attempts to shout soon were discarded and mostly people resorted to smiling, laughing and drinking.

Jeremy arrived with Penelope, having offered her a lift as they had coffee after the ward round. He was dressed casually in taupe trousers and a dark green shirt. Penelope eclipsed everyone. She was wearing a black leather bustier, though to be honest her ample curves were doing a good job of trying to escape from it and a tight, short black skirt of a shiny material, black fish-net stockings or tights on her extremely shapely legs and stiletto heels. She looked absolutely terrific. Although a large woman, she had no problem in enjoying her size and knew how to show herself off to great advantage. Her hair too had been left down with the result that she looked considerably younger than when on the ward and her make-up was flattering. Covetously, she had her arm through Jeremy's as they wended their way through the crowd to join the others at their table. To Ellie's amazement, Penelope kissed her on either cheek, greeting her like some special friend and even referred to her by her Christian name and suggested that, as it was a social occasion, Ellie should do the same. Jeremy bought everyone drinks and announced, to a roar of approval, that he would pay for the drinks all night.

Moving to their table, Ellie managed to sit away from Jeremy and next to two of the staff nurses whom she liked a lot. Penelope sat next to Jeremy. No one in the party dared to try to separate them. First courses of prawn cocktail arrived. Limp ribbons of lettuce, two slices of tomato and a spoonful of prawns in a pallid sauce were placed in front of them all, followed by a basket of bread rolls and foil-wrapped portions of butter. Bottles of wine arrived and Jeremy, appointed by Penelope as host for the evening, ensured that everyone's glasses were full. The food was insipid and tasteless. Ellie and several of the others left most of theirs and Ellie dreaded what might come next. They had to wait for everyone in the room to be served and eat before the plate clearing commenced. There then followed a long hiatus during which Ellie decided to fill up with another bread roll and butter and was on the point of considering a third when the main course arrived. It was supposed to be Christmas dinner. The pieces of turkey looked suspiciously circular and plastic. Each person had been allotted two roast potatoes and a mound of mash, carrots which had gone cold and waterlogged Brussels sprouts. There was also an unidentifiable object on the plate that was black and charred. Dissection and discussion led to the unanimous agreement that this had once been a sausage. The thick and unappealing skin that had formed on the gravy had to be held back with a fork while the viscous liquid was coaxed from the container. The room went quieter while over a hundred people tucked into their dinner. Occasional raucous laughter overwhelmed the munching noises and those less enamoured with their food let off party poppers and pulled their crackers.

'This is the worst Christmas dinner I've ever had,' shouted Caroline, who was sitting next to Ellie.

'I couldn't agree more. I don't think I'll be able to eat much more. Other people seem to be managing though.' Ellie tried hiding her vegetables under the slices of turkey roll.

'It's always the same at these parties – all mass produced. For some reason, Penelope likes it here, so we come every year. We tried suggesting that we went somewhere completely different, you know, like a curry or pasta, but she was having none of it.'

'Shame,' Ellie replied with feeling. 'Doesn't she look amazing though? I can hardly believe it's the same person. And she kissed me!'

'She certainly knows how to dress. Mind you, quite how she gets away with those clothes, I really don't know but somehow she does, so all credit to her.'

'Do you think it's all for a certain person's benefit?' Ellie asked casually.

Caroline nodded.

'Without a doubt. Note how she's clinging onto his every word and leaning rather too close all the time.'

'I've been watching,' admitted Ellie, refraining from adding that it had not been without a twinge of jealousy that she had done her best to quash as soon as she felt it rumble.

Tables were cleared and again there was a timed pause before dishes arrived, containing small symmetrical squares of Christmas pudding covered with a gelatinous white substance. Ellie tried very hard not to think what it reminded her of but even then found it impossible to eat. She passed the time chatting to Caroline and a girl called Dawn, who was on her other side, all the while trying not to look at Jeremy who seemed totally oblivious of everyone except Penelope.

Strangely enough, the mince pies that were placed on the table as a finale were warm, tasty and the pastry light. The rest of the crackers were pulled and most dutifully bedecked their heads with the paper crowns, read out jokes that everyone knew the punch lines to and wrestled with little puzzles.

'I hate crackers,' Ellie volunteered to no one in particular.

The disco started up and Penelope dragged Jeremy onto the dance floor, which encouraged others from around the room to join them. Ellie, who had never seen Jeremy dance before, was rather pleased to find that he was not good at it, being unable to keep in time with the beat and also fond of some ridiculous-looking arm movements. Close beside him, Penelope wriggled sexily. Ellie hoped that the music did not get more up-tempo, as she feared that Penelope's breasts, which were wobbling precariously, might succeed in their bid for freedom from their fragile captivity. She sat, trying to concentrate on her conversation with Caroline and Dawn.

A young man from another table, his jacket off and tie dangling around his neck, came and asked Ellie if she would like to dance. When she declined, politely, he asked Dawn, who accepted and the two of them disappeared into the crowd that was now dancing.

'Do you think we should show willing and go and join them?' yelled Caroline.

'No!' answered Ellie. 'Would you like another glass of wine?'
She refilled both glasses.

'How long does this go on for?'

Caroline half emptied her glass in one gulp.

'Usually until about midnight. Penelope likes us to stay until the bitter end. I tried to leave early last year, on the pretext that I had to get home to my husband and kids but she was having none of it. She had us all doing the hokey cokey or whatever it's called. It makes me cringe now to think about it, but I expect history will repeat itself before the evening's out.'

She emptied her glass in one further gulp. Ellie looked at Caroline and they laughed.

'Pour me another glass of wine, knock back one yourself and then we might feel like toeing the party line.'

Contemplating this for a moment, Ellie obliged and they drank together like two conspirators synchronising their watches. Ellie led the way into the heaving throng, arms waving above her head, hips swaying to the music, Caroline emulating her moves while following in her wake. The music at least was good dance music, thoughtfully designed to keep as many people as possible active in order to whip up the party frenzy and the excitement. Ellie had a succession of partners, who stayed for one dance before moving on to the next available female. She was just about to propose sitting down for a drink when she felt a hand on either side of her waist. Amazed by his familiarity in front of so many, Ellie turned around only to find that it was not Jeremy at all but Penelope, who was doing her best to round everyone from the ward up to dance together. Jeremy was still seemingly glued to her side. Beads of sweat were trickling down Penelope's neck and cleavage but her cheeks were glowing and her eyes shining. Without speaking, she used her best organisational skills and turned her party into a human caterpillar, which she led, like a proud figurehead of a ship, bouncing unsteadily around the room. It grew longer and more unwieldy as others linked on to the end. Somehow she managed to

140

preserve her snake until the final cords of the song at which point loud cheers and whoops filled the room. Balloons were released from a net attached to the ceiling and the revellers pushed and shoved in their attempts to catch or burst them.

As the evening grew to a close, the music became soft and smoochy, helping dissipate the feeling of madness that was exhausting everyone. A mass exodus from the dance floor took place, save for a few couples determined to stick it out to the bitter end. Ellie and Caroline drank water thirstily and finished off some mince pies that had been left on the adjacent table to theirs. Caroline nudged Ellie.

'Look at that.'

Ellie followed her gaze. Jeremy and Penelope were still dancing, locked in a close embrace. Penelope's head was resting on his shoulder, her eyes closed and a contented smile on her face. Jeremy's hands were on her naked back.

'Make a nice couple, don't they?' Caroline added and Ellie tried to laugh.

The music had stopped. People were leaving. The room looked devastated, the floor covered with paper streamers, screwed-up hats and napkins plus a few squashed mince pies. Jeremy had paid no attention whatsoever to Ellie for the entire duration. He had barely acknowledged her presence when he arrived, had not spoken to her at dinner, even when pouring her wine and had spent the remainder of the party moving (it could hardly be described as dancing, Ellie thought) on the dance floor. It was yet another indication that any relationship was wholly inadvisable and undoubtedly doomed to end in tears, but not his.

Miserably, Ellie finished off somebody's glass of wine. She did not care whose it was in the slightest. Looking round, she was unable to spot the three nurses with whom she was supposed to be sharing a taxi home. There was no sign of them and she presumed, correctly it turned out, that they had left without her. She declined a lift with Caroline, whose husband was coming to pick her up but who lived in completely the opposite direction, rang for a taxi and prepared herself for a twenty-minute wait. She went to the toilet and stood patiently waiting her turn, which helped pass the time. Finally coming out, she found her coat and went to wait in the foyer of the restaurant. Eventually, Ellie heard a car horn and, pulling up the collar of her coat, ran out to the waiting cab. There was a queue of traffic waiting behind a car that was trying to turn right out of the car park onto the main road and thus holding everyone else up. Sitting in the warm, Ellie gazed out through the window. She stiffened as she recognised Jeremy's car, surprised to see it still there. The sound of giggling and squealing made her look around and there were Jeremy and Penelope, running through the rain, hand in hand. Jeremy opened the passenger door. Penelope clambered in, inelegantly but not before she had stood on tiptoe and kissed him on the lips.

The following morning, Ellie looked dreadful. Partly hung over, partly shattered from not having had enough sleep, she felt mortified and humiliated. When summoned into Jeremy's office, she almost did not go. If he felt tired, there was no sign of it. As usual, he was smart and precise in his dress, shoes polished, shirt creaseless.

'You wanted to see me?' Ellie enquired.

'Yes, close the door.'

He was sitting at his desk, writing, head down. When Ellie had obeyed his instruction and turned back to him, he had moved and was perched on the edge of his desk.

'I owe you an apology,' he started.

Ellie said nothing but waited.

'Last night. We hardly had a chance to talk.'

'Actually,' Ellie replied pointedly, 'we didn't talk at all.'

'I know, I know. Believe me, I wanted to so much. You looked amazing. So beautiful. I'd have loved to sit next to you and danced with you. But you know it would've been impossible, don't you?'

'No, I don't, as it happens.'

'You know I have to flatter Penelope. She's a brilliant ward sister. If

I keep her sweet, she'll go on running the ward superbly and I need someone like that on my team. But I also need someone like you...'

'There was no need for you to devote the entire evening to her, Jeremy,' Ellie raised her voice. 'It was, if I'm not mistaken, supposed to be the ward outing. You should have danced with all of us, not just her.'

Jeremy shrugged and then smiled.

'Never mind, Ellie, my darling. That's all over for another year, thank goodness. Now come over here.'

'Jeremy, this is not a good idea,' argued Ellie, wishing desperately that she could be more assertive and find him less attractive.

He got up and closed in on her. Ellie's feet seemed to have been cemented to the floor. He lightly ran his hands over her breasts. Pressing himself against her, he teased her face and neck with little licks before parting her lips with his tongue. He kissed her with a certain amount of aggression before breaking away, leaving her breathless. Patting her on the buttocks, rather in the manner that a farmer might pat his favourite cow, he walked out of the office, his parting words being,

'I'll see you later. Have a good Christmas.'

13

Nigel and Emily's wedding day arrived with only one further incident. Arriving home the evening before, her arms aching from carrying heavy bags of shopping and her legs protesting from marching endlessly around the supermarket, Ellie found that a card and small parcel had been pushed through her letterbox. Relinquishing the shopping to the kitchen, she opened the card to find that it simply was signed with 'From J, with my love' and three kisses. Inside the box was a necklace, a diamond solitaire twinkling on a gold chain, dazzling her. Without removing it, Ellie put the lid firmly back on the box and placed it on the table, with the card. It could wait.

The next morning, she allowed herself the luxury of a lie in. She had the wonderful prospect of two days off work and intended to make the most of it. Mid-morning, she went downstairs, made coffee and cereal and decadently retreated to bed to read a glossy magazine, full of tips on how to make this Christmas the best ever.

Stretching out under the duvet, she finished the last page and reluctantly decided it was time to make a move. The service was at two and it would only take about an hour to drive there. As she bathed, Ellie wondered how Nigel was feeling; whether he was nervous or just excited. For a moment she thought how she might feel, were it her own wedding, which she had planned in her mind to be the most joyous of days, full of friends, happiness and laughter. She tried to imagine walking up the aisle, hearing the sharp intakes of breath from the congregation as they marvelled at her dress. Would it be Jeremy waiting for her at the altar? Much as part of her might want this, she knew in her heart that it could never happen. Ellie smiled as she pictured relatives standing in the pews but stopped abruptly as her bubble was burst by the realisation that her mother would be standing there alone.

Hastily, she climbed out of the bath and dried off the worst of the wet before combing out her sodden hair. Taking extra special care, she set about making herself look her very best, nothing less being good enough for her friend Nigel. She slipped on a short-sleeved dress of moss green. It had a low square-cut neckline and a pencil skirt. There was a short matching jacket with a black velvet collar and she had decided on black accessories in the form of very high-heeled sandals, a small clutch bag and gloves. It took some time to balance the pillbox hat that completed her ensemble on her head as she wanted to wear her hair up but the end result was more than satisfactory. Ellie chose plain gold hexagonal earrings and was about to pick up a chain made of similarly shaped links when she remembered what was waiting for her in the kitchen and mused that if Jeremy could not be there in person, then at least she would have something to remind her of him.

The roads were busy; people driving badly and madly, intent on getting away for Christmas or making for the shops for one last spend. It took Ellie longer than she had expected to get out of Harrogate and then found that she was stuck in a long slow-moving trail of traffic heading for the Yorkshire Dales. She passed the time listening to a Christmas Carol concert that she found on the car radio. Getting out of the car at the church, Ellie had to keep one hand on her hat as she scuttled under the lych-gate and up the narrow path to the door. Nigel's ushers, two of his best friends, greeted her warmly and showed her where to sit. Nigel, almost unrecognisable in his frock coat and pinstriped trousers, came over to welcome her, enveloping her in his usual bear-like hug. Spotting Nigel's mother, Barbara, Ellie crept up and sat behind her. She looked so happy and proud, thought Ellie. A complete contrast to Barbara, who was wearing a gown of the palest apricot, was Emily's mother, a fanfare in reds and gold with a hat of such width that the gentleman sitting next to her had to lean slightly to his left at all times to avoid disturbing it. Ellie nodded and smiled to a variety of other people, including a good-looking young man, who looked familiar but she could not recall why.

A change in the organ music from pastoral fugue to resounding flourish heralded the arrival of the bride. The congregation rose as one to its feet and all turned to watch Emily make her entrance, smiling from ear to ear and looking glorious in a long, red cloak trimmed with white fur. Gaynor and Jackie were her bridesmaids. They had long red dresses on and short white fur capes. On reaching the altar, Emily handed her bouquet of Christmas roses, holly and pinecones mixed cleverly to make a most unusual but showy arrangement, to Jackie and then slipped off her cloak which Gaynor caught as it fell from her shoulders. Her dress was unique. Strapless satin, the bodice was studded with seed pearls and the full skirt trimmed with red sequins. Ellie watched as Nigel adoringly took her hand and whispered in her ear. She felt a lump rising in her throat.

The service was beautiful. Emily had chosen a selection of well-known hymns all sung to their traditional tunes, so that barely anyone had an excuse not to join in. As the couple exchanged their vows, there was a rustling as handbags were raided for tissues to wipe away tears. Nobody, thought Ellie, as Nigel led his wife back down the aisle, could look happier than these two.

Outside the church, the throwing of confetti was prohibited but Jean, in a loud voice, promised everyone that there would be an opportunity for this later. Emily, Ellie was pleased to see, had put her red cloak back on for the photographs outside where it was now not only gusty but also unpleasantly cold. Ellie stood watching, hopping from foot to foot, trying not to look as uncomfortable as she felt and hoping that they would soon be able to move on to the reception.

'Hello again.'

The good-looking young man appeared at Ellie's side.

'Hello,' she greeted him, suddenly remembering where she had met him before. 'It's Ian, isn't it?'

He looked pleased that she had used his name.

'That's right. It's lovely to see you again, Ellie.'

'You too.'

He studied her critically for a second.

'I must say, I think you look much better in today's outfit than the one you were wearing last time we met.'

Ellie was puzzled and then laughed.

'Oh, the chicken costume! Well, it was tempting to wear it today but, fond of it as I am, I was afraid that with this wind, all the feathers might blow off and I didn't want to upstage the bride.'

'Emily is far too ecstatic to notice anything like that. They make a good couple, don't they?' Ian commented.

Ellie agreed, whole-heartedly.

'I think they'll be really happy together.'

She rubbed her arms, trying to promote some warmth.

'Look here,' said Ian, 'it's perishingly cold out here. Are you warm enough? I could get you my coat from the car.'

'That's kind of you,' Ellie thanked him,' but I'm hoping that this bit won't take much longer.'

'Ian, Ellie, come and be in this next set of photos!' called Nigel, not letting go of Emily's hand.

They did as they were asked, Ellie not only flattered that she had been included but delighted to find out that once these had been taken, the rest of the wedding photos would be taken indoors at the reception.

'Can I give you a lift?' Ian asked her, reappearing at her side as she made her way down the path at some speed.

'Thanks,' Ellie answered, 'but that's my car over there. Oh, just look at that!'

In the little car park stood a gleaming carriage, festooned with flowers and ivy. Two impatient palomino horses were mouthing on their bits, tossing their heads and stamping their hooves. Nigel had opened the door for Emily, who was having difficulty negotiating the step with her voluminous skirt and had to rely on a rather inelegant shove on the bottom from her husband, which caused much mirth.

'Follow me, if you like,' Ian offered. 'I know the quickest route. It'll only take us about ten minutes. Mind you, looking at those horses, I suspect the bride and groom might arrive in five.'

Ellie jumped into her car, turned the heater on full blast and sat shivering until it was her turn to drive off behind Ian, who was ferrying his parents. In no time at all, certainly not enough for the car to have warmed up to any significant degree, she saw Ian turning off the road to a hotel and followed suit.

Chivalrously Ian waited for her and threw his heavy tweed coat around her.

'You still look frozen. Come on, let's get in and find a hot drink. The photos will take an age, they always do.'

Only about forty guests had been invited to the meal; the rest of the guests would turn up later for the party. Most were shivering like Ellie and a lateral-thinking hotel manager had arranged for tea and coffee to be served as well as champagne.

'Plenty of time for the bubbly stuff later,' announced Ian, fetching two cups of coffee for his parents and then asking Ellie to join them.

Clive and Christina Bonnington were charming and made Ellie feel at home immediately. Christina admired Ellie's dress and envied the fact that she could wear shoes like that and survive. Clive asked her about work and had some intelligent, if not very complimentary, comments about the National Health Service. Ian joined them and forbade talk of work for the rest of the holiday period.

'Are you working, Ellie?' asked Christina.

'Just Boxing Day,' she replied. 'I'm spending tomorrow with my parents. My father isn't too well at the moment, so we're just going to have a quiet day at home.'

'Oh, I'm sorry to hear that,' commiserated Christina.

'I'm starting to feel decidedly warmer,' Ian sounded relieved. 'Which is just as well as it looks to me as though we're about to be invited in to eat and I'm starving.'

Dr and Mrs Worcester were waiting at the door to welcome their guests. Jean was rushing around in her inimitable style and Emily's father Rupert was trying to hover close behind.

'Congratulations, you two. I just know that you'll be so happy together.' Ellie kissed Emily and Nigel and meant every word she said. 'Emily, you look fantastic and even you scrub up quite well, Nigel.'

Inside the dining room there was one long table and four tables for eight. Ellie sat in her allotted place and found that she was rather pleased when Ian and his parents joined her, along with Emily's aunt and uncle, her brother Simon and a very pale, monosyllabic woman with long, straight hair who turned out to be his girlfriend, Natasha. Introductions were made all round and they then settled down to enjoy a delicious lobster bisque, served with melba toast.

It was a far cry from the ward Christmas outing. The room was tastefully decorated with clusters of gold and silver decorations and in the corner there was a real tree, the scent of which enriched the room. There was no sign of crackers, party poppers or tired paper hats. Ellie kept looking up at Nigel who was sitting with his arm protectively round his wife. The first course dishes vanished as if by magic and hot plates were put down onto which accomplished waiters served roast pheasant, game chips and all the trimmings, leaving bowls of steaming vegetables and the smoothest of creamed potatoes for the guests to help themselves to. Glasses were filled with a robust red wine and, with delight, everyone tucked in.

'This is so scrumptious,' Ellie almost moaned, savouring each mouthful.

Doubtless due to Jean's carefully planned seating arrangements, Ellie could not have been happier with her companions. Clive and Christina were witty and astute. Simon told them fascinating stories about his travels and even Natasha, relaxed by a couple of glasses of good wine, turned out to have a hilarious side to her and be possessed of a huge arsenal of funny jokes.

Chocolate bombe appeared for dessert, cleverly topped with angelica cut to look like holly, so that the overall appearance was that of a small Christmas pudding. As Ellie broke through the crisp covering with her spoon, she discovered the best coffee ice cream she had ever tasted. Clive revealed that he was diabetic and gave his dessert to his son who, having noticed Ellie's evident delight when eating hers, divided it in half and shared with her.

Coffee was served and they sat back, full and content, to listen to the speeches. Nigel's speech had Ellie almost in tears. His open proclamation of love for Emily and his gratitude to her parents and his own mother was so touching and genuine that Ellie had to pretend she was looking for something in her bag until he had finished. Looking around, she could see that she was not the only one who had been so moved. Christina was blowing her nose and sniffing and Jean and Barbara were wiping their eyes.

This is just such a perfect day, Ellie thought. Everyone is so happy for Nigel and Emily. The generosity of Emily's family is amazing and all these people are so friendly and united in their love for the two of them. This is just how it should be – sharing your happiness with others, laughing together, being honest and frank. Ellie considered her relationship with Jeremy ruefully. There was no comparison and what was more, there was no way in a million years that it could ever develop into anything even vaguely resembling what Nigel and Emily had. This was what she wanted, not some tawdry and tacky affair, conducted behind closed doors, relying on sex to keep it afloat when all the while guilt and shame were doing their best to sink it. Her hand went to her necklace and she wished that she had not put it on. Suddenly she realised that the rest of the table were cheering and applauding, things that she should be doing too. She caught Ian's eye who smiled reassuringly at her.

Nigel and Emily were making their way to cut the wedding cake. Jokingly, Nigel produced a scalpel which Emily discarded immediately as there was no way it could do justice to four tiers of fudge cake covered with roses made of dark, white and milk chocolate.

'Oh good,' chuckled Ian. 'I'm never very keen on dried-up fruitcake. This looks infinitely better.'

Despite the fact that she was convinced that she was full, Ellie tasted the cake which was so soft and light that she had no problem in finishing off her slice and scraping up the last of the chocolate with her fork.

'That was wonderful,' Christina sighed happily.

Speeches over, guests began to move around the room, swapping places to chat and introduce themselves. Ellie had a quick trip to the powder room where, when she had washed her hands, she removed the necklace and put it carefully in her purse to take home. Returning to the room and her table, she was joined by Emily and Nigel, who were circulating as best they could, trying to spend time with each person.

'It's been fantastic, thank you so much,' Ellie enthused.

'There's still the party to go,' Emily reminded her, 'and wait until you see what Mum has arranged.'

Ellie looked at Nigel who simply said, 'I did warn you.'

Doors at the far side of the room were flung open to reveal what could only be described as a winter grotto. In the warm, subdued lighting, everything was white. Tables had white cloths, chairs furry white covers. Icicles hung from the ceiling and lopsided artificial snowmen had been deposited at various sites. Stroboscopic lights on the far wall looked like snowflakes falling. On cue, a swing band, composed of men and women all dressed in white, started to play and everyone moved through, making appropriately stunned remarks. Jean had quickly been out to change. Gone were the vibrant colours she had been wearing earlier. From the crystal crown she had on her head down to the translucent slippers on her feet, she was the epitome of the ice queen, welcoming everyone, including all those who had been invited to the party only.

The drinks were white – cocktails and champagne – and so was the food – little cakes covered with fondant icing, sugared almonds, peppermint creams and marshmallows to dip into a fountain of white chocolate. There, in the corner of the room, was Father Christmas, who came round to speak to everyone, presenting small gifts. The music, far from being hackneyed Christmas pop songs, varied from light jazz to Glenn Millar and Ellie was tired out by all the dancing she did. She proved to be much in demand on the dance floor and partnered Rupert, Clive, Simon and each of Nigel's friends. When she finally managed to sit down and have a glass of sparkling water, Ian bowed before her and asked if she would have the next dance.

'Just give me a moment, please,' gasped Ellie. 'I must have a drink first.'

Ian, unlike Jeremy, was a good dancer and Ellie enjoyed the experience. It felt so good to be out, being entirely natural and having such a good time, with such delightful people. Nigel and Emily had made their escape some time ago, heading for the airport and a flight at some ungodly hour which would whisk then away to heat, sunshine and some well-deserved relaxation on a sizzlingly hot sandy beach. Ellie had watched them go rather wistfully, standing to the back as others crowded around them and threw the confetti. Natasha had caught Emily's bouquet. She had looked suggestively at Simon who had blushed, shook his head and steered her back onto the dance floor.

'I ought to be going,' Ellie told Ian. 'It's really late and I'm dead beat.'

'I think we all are. I haven't danced so much for years. Still the music was so good, it was impossible not to. Much better than the usual booming disco.'

He looked at his watch.

'Hey, it's Christmas Day. Happy Christmas, Ellie.'

He hesitated and then kissed her on the cheek. She returned the compliment.

'Are you sure you can't stay any longer?' he asked.

'I'd love to, but I must get back.'

He walked her to her car. It was a frosty night with a clear sky studded by a myriad of stars.

'I hope to see you again,' Ian said, holding the car door open for Ellie as she got in.

Ellie looked up at his honest, friendly face.

'That would be really nice,' she answered, sincerely, winding the window down so that she could wave as she drove off.

14

Ellie felt a rush of childish excitement when she woke on Christmas Day – her first in her own house. She had slept deeply and felt refreshed, apart from legs that were still complaining about all the unaccustomed dancing. She loitered over a cup of tea, putting the finishing touches to her parents' presents. What to get her father had been a real trial. Having settled on the boring but safe option of a sweater, Ellie had noticed one of the patients on the ward listening to talking books on a personal stereo and this had provided the perfect solution. Her father had always been an avid reader, from newspapers to encyclopaedic tomes and so, after rooting around the bookshops, Ellie had purchased a variety of fiction and non-fiction, which she felt sure he would enjoy.

She gave a passing thought to Nigel and Emily and smiled to herself at the reminiscence of the white grotto, looking forward to sharing all the details with her parents. She also thought about Ian and his parents, hoping that she would see them again but hadn't a clue when that would be, especially as they had not exchanged contact details. Only when she was loading the car with all the shopping, did it occur to Ellie that she had not given a thought to Jeremy and she strictly forbade any consideration of what he might be doing.

Compared to the day before, it was like driving through a ghost town. Everyone must be behind closed doors; those without children enjoying a lazy start to the day, those with, yawning from an early awakening and watching the delight as wrapping paper was ripped off and discarded to reveal the much-longed-for contents.

Diana opened the door as Ellie staggered up the drive, bags in either hand.

'Happy Christmas, darling!' she called. 'Can I help with anything?'

'There's a couple more bags on the back seat, Mum. Happy Christmas!' Ellie kissed her mother.

'You look tired, Mum. Are you ok?'

'I'm just fine. We've had a rather bad night but it's all sorted now, so let's get this lot in. I've got the coffee on and there are shortbread biscuits about to come out of the oven.'

Keith was in his chair by the fire, slumped to one side, his head tending to loll forwards in what looked like an uncomfortable way.

'Hello, Dad. Happy Christmas! How are you?'

The deterioration in his speech was unmistakable. It was virtually unintelligible but Ellie nobly pretended to understand and hugged him warmly. Diana entered, bearing cups, best china for her and Ellie, a plastic beaker for Keith.

The Christmas tree was up in its traditional place near the window, the lights on, despite it being daytime, flashing randomly and all the old familiar decorations were adorning the branches. There was the tiny sheep that Ellie had made at school from cotton wool (which was looking somewhat dirty), a spotted, wooden rocking horse, the paint badly faded and the fairy on the top, which had originally been a doll in a foreign costume but had been redressed by Diana at the last minute one year when its predecessor had been found with no head. Ellie added her gifts to the small pile that were already underneath.

'So what was the problem last night?' she asked, turning back to her parents and getting comfortable in one of the armchairs.

'Dad fell,' Diana started to explain looking at Keith. 'He was trying to get into bed and I was helping but we misjudged how far onto the mattress you were, didn't we?'

'Are either of you hurt?' Ellie was instantly concerned.

Keith shook his head and mumbled.

'Just bruised,' Diana interpreted.

'This is really worrying, Mum. Perhaps we should see about getting some more help in. You can't be expected to do all this on your own.

Even if someone just came in twice a day, in the morning to make sure Dad got up safely and then last thing to help him at bedtime.'

Diana was quickly dismissive of this suggestion.

'Oh, we don't need anybody coming in to help. We can manage just fine between us. Last night was just a hiccup. I was rather tired and so I didn't concentrate quite as much as I should have done. We had a bit of a laugh about it afterwards anyway, so no harm done.'

'But how on earth did you manage to get Dad up off the floor?'

'Well, we did and that's all that matters. Ellie, we're coping fine. We don't want any strangers coming into the house, nosing around.

'Mum,' Ellie felt frustrated, 'these are people who are professional helpers. They don't poke their noses in, they just come to help.'

'Dr Urquhart drops in most weeks to see how we are. He keeps offering us all manner of help but I tell him what I've just told you.'

Ellie was somewhat reassured to know this.

'What else has he suggested?' she asked.

'Lots of things. A district nurse has been round, so has someone from the Motor Neurone Disease Association. A speech therapist has been and so has a dietician. We feel very grateful but we're still adamant that we're able to manage. It's nice to know these people are there, just in case.'

'I think I should move back home,' Ellie announced. 'I could postpone my next job for six months then I could just be here all the time to help.'

Keith made some unintelligible but clearly disapproving noises, shaking his head all the while, becoming quite worked up. Diana went to him and stroked his head.

'It's all right, Keith, I'll sort this. Ellie, we love you dearly and we know you love us. Remember what I said before – your Dad and I, well we want to try and keep things as near to normal as we can, for as long as we can. We could not bear it if you missed out on part of your training, even if it was just a postponement. We look forward to you coming round, telling us about your day, what's been good, what's been horrible. The stories you tell us enthral us and make us constantly proud of you. Don't change that. If you were here all the while, we'd be snapping at each other in no time and that would simply make all three of us miserable. Can't you see that?'

Ellie buried her face in her hands and thought before she spoke, reluctant to accept her mother's opinion.

'I just feel so desperately that I want to help,' she pleaded.

'But you are doing by being the daughter we've always known. I promise you that if either your dad or I even so much as suspect that we need some extra help then we'll ask for it. Does that make you feel better?'

Ellie felt that she had to concur, though she was not entirely convinced.

'Good,' continued Diana. 'Now then, if I'm not mistaken it's Christmas Day, so let's enjoy it. Ellie, come and help me get things started for dinner. Keith, shall I put some music on?'

The latter seemed to be a rhetorical question as Diana marched over to the tape recorder and switched it on, filling the room with classical music.

In the kitchen, Diana, in her customary efficient mode, instructed Ellie to empty the shopping bags while she put the contents away.

'Something smells good already,' commented Ellie.

'It's a large chicken,' Diana informed her. 'I thought a turkey might just be too much for three. I made the stuffing last night. Have you got the sausages there? Now, where did I put that knife?'

Ellie obligingly did all she was told, happy to be kept busy and of course enjoying the fact that she was cooking. She offered in vain to take sole charge so that her mother could rest and enjoy being waited on for once.

'After all, Mum, I've had the best possible teacher.'

If Ellie hoped that this compliment would persuade Diana to acquiesce then she was to be disappointed for her offer was tossed to one side by a waft of a hand and a meaningful look.

'There's a lot to be done. Sheila and Gordon are coming round for drinks so I want you to start on some canapés. Do some stuffed dates – you see, it was a good job you bought some and some smoked salmon and cream cheese on crackers. Everybody likes those.' They worked in silence for a little, each intent on their own work, enjoying listening to the music that filled the air.

'How do you think Dad is?' Ellie plucked up courage to ask.

Diana halted in the middle of her carrot peeling.

'I can't lie to you, Ellie. He's getting poorer each week, I'm afraid. I try not to think about it too much as the speed at which he is getting worse is frightening. You'll have noticed already how much harder it is to understand what he says.'

'Yes, I have. It's only a few days since I popped in last and I can see a change just in that time. What about his swallowing, is that worse as well?'

'Pretty dreadful. He chokes even on liquidised stuff, plus he loathes it but who can blame him. He despises this loss of dignity, you know. I try my best, but I can't imagine how he must feel or what thoughts must go through his head.'

'There are other ways of giving him food, Mum.'

Diana agreed. 'Dr Swindlehurst told us about tubes and things. So did the dietician. It was one of the big discussions we had on the cruise. We went round and round in circles because I was all for it and your dad was absolutely determined that he did not want that sort of thing.'

'Why?' Ellie was exasperated.

Diana turned to her and leant back on the worktop.

'I think I understand now, but at times I still wonder, so it's going to be hard for you. I'll try to explain. When we first got the diagnosis, neither of us had the least idea what motor neurone disease was nor what lay in store for us. As we found out more, the less we liked what we learned. Then, as your dad realised that he was getting worse, he decided that what life he has left, he wants to be of good quality. He doesn't want to be in and out of hospital. He wants to be at home with me. He desperately does not want his life to be prolonged if he's in a miserable state, just for the sake of it. We have to accept that, Ellie. We know he's dying and he and I are lucky in that we have had time to discuss the situation, take decisions and make plans. Far too many couples don't have that luxury. In some ways though, I hate living like this because there is a very selfish streak in me that just wants to have your father with me for as long as humanly possible. I could cheerfully go against some of his wishes but I would be doing so for me and that would be a terrible mistake. When I married your dad, I promised to love and look after him in sickness and in health. I've abided by that to this day and that is what I shall continue to do.'

'Oh Mum.'

Ellie went and hugged her, marvelling at her devotion and strength.

'Thank you, darling. Now then, that's enough sentimentality for one day. How many times do I have to remind you that it's Christmas? So let's see how that chicken's doing.'

She opened the oven door and peered inside.

'Mmm, perfect.'

'Potatoes next, I think, and the sprouts. How are you getting on with your job? Come on, Gordon and Sheila from across the road will be here soon and I need to tidy myself up a bit before they get here.'

Ellie complied with her mother's desires and arranged canapés on glass plates, put crisps and nuts into wooden bowls and after a small dispute agreed to put out cubes of cheese and pineapple onto cocktails sticks but refused to arrange them in half a grapefruit. While Diana went to freshen up, Ellie carried things through to the lounge but felt rather mean putting them where Keith could see them and so left them on the sideboard which was behind his chair. He looked up as she came in and smiled. Remembering his request, she went and sat with him.

'Things are coming on nicely in the kitchen as I expect you can tell by the smell. Sheila and Gordon are expected at any moment so I think I'll pour us a drink, so we can get started, shall I?'

He acknowledged by putting his thumb up and Ellie fetched him a

159

whisky and soda, together with a glass of wine for herself.

'Cheers,' Ellie thought he said as she chinked her glass against his. She had to help him.

'Perhaps I should get that beaker from the kitchen,' she started but then saw the hurt look in his eyes and backtracked rapidly. 'It's waiting to be washed up, though, so you'll just have to make do with this glass.'

Diana returned, now clad in a figure-hugging dark brown jersey dress, her hair tidily brushed, a little make-up on her face.

'You look great, Mum,' said Ellie, genuinely. 'Have you been losing weight?'

'I don't think so. I've got a new foundation garment though that's supposed to flatter one's shape.'

'That's pretty impressive,' Ellie agreed as the doorbell rang.

Sheila and Gordon were long-standing friends. Gordon, a retired plumber and joiner, was in his mid-seventies and since a mild stroke a couple of years earlier had been forced to take life at a slightly calmer pace that would have been his choice. He had cut back on his hobbies of squash, tennis and cycling and replaced them with walking and swimming. Sheila, an extrovert, cuddly lady with widespread arthritis, having been excluded from her husband's more energetic pursuits, was able to join in with at least the swimming and in the past they had persuaded Diana and Keith to go along to the baths with them. Now, over the past months, they had proved themselves to be more than fair-weather friends. Scarcely a day passed without one or the other of them popping in, offering to shop, do any little jobs around the house or just stop and chat for a while. Keith and Gordon had a particular affinity with their interest in sport. They were addicted to any form of sport, from athletics to horse racing, darts to rugby league and for the first time, Diana was grateful that there was so much of it for them to watch on television. While the two of them were wrapped up in the intricacies of a football match, she could put her feet up for ninety minutes and more often than not, she would be fast asleep before she knew it.

They exchanged Christmas greetings and kisses. Gordon produced a bottle of wine and a bunch of mistletoe, Sheila chocolates and bottled fruits. Their arrival proved to be something of a blessing. They chattered away non-stop and Ellie was more than happy to take a back seat and listen. Gordon gave Keith a video of some football highlights and promised to come round the next day to watch it with him. Ellie was pleased to see the animated look on her father's face as Gordon talked to him and noticed that her mother also seemed to have relaxed in the company of Sheila. A much happier and less tense atmosphere prevailed and Ellie actually felt that at last it was a little bit like Christmas.

Sheila, ever the extrovert, sought to include Ellie in her conversation and enquired about her work, what her next job was to be and, with a mischievous twinkle in her eye, whether she had a boyfriend at the moment. Ellie regretted that she had to disappoint her, saying, what with work and studying, she really didn't have much time for one. She recounted some of the details from the previous day and Sheila suggested that maybe it would not be too long until it was Ellie's turn to get married.

Diana all the while kept popping out to the kitchen, juggling the minutiae of perfecting a festive feat with entertaining her guests. By the time that Sheila and Gordon reluctantly took their leave, she was looking hot and flustered. She put up no protest when Ellie took over, set the table and began to drain the vegetables. The starter was simple, a cocktail of diced melon, pineapple and orange. Ellie, about to prepare Keith's, threw caution to the wind and liquidised the whole lot, the result being a thick juice which she decanted into three tumblers and took to the table.

It took the two of them to help Keith to the table. Ellie learned that he had accepted the offer of a wheelchair loan but would only use this outside the house. Inside, he still tried desperately to manage by hanging on to his wife, or his walking frame and the furniture. Despite being a lean man and indeed much lighter than he used to be, he was heavy to assist, the way that people inevitably are when they cannot do much for themselves. The effort it took the three of them to get Keith into his chair had Ellie incredulous at the thought of her mother trying to do this of her own.

The meal was difficult. Nobody ate very much. Keith did his best with his revolting–looking portion, Ellie had no appetite and Diana was insistent in trying to instil a feeling of levity and jollity into the proceedings. Ellie wracked her brain to think of more stories from the wedding plus what had been going on at work. In desperation she even told them that Dr Blake and his wife were expecting twins any day.

'Will he be off on leave then,' asked Diana. 'You'd think his wife would need some help.'

'I'd not thought of that,' agreed Ellie, thinking that this might be a good thing. 'He's got twin boys at home and his wife is a doctor as well, so I expect they have a nanny.'

'That's no substitute for a father,' mused Diana, handing out colossal portions of Christmas pudding. 'Help yourself to rum sauce.'

Ellie was relieved when they had all finished; Keith was safely ensconced in his armchair and Diana sitting on the settee next to him with a cup of coffee and a small liqueur. She left the two of them, cleared the table and washed up, putting the unwanted roast potatoes out for the birds and the remainder of the leftovers in an array of small plastic tubs. After wiping down the worktops and the washing-up bowl, she poured a mug of coffee for herself and went to join her parents.

'Presents!' cried Diana. 'Ellie, be a dear and pass them round.'

Keith appeared genuinely delighted with his talking books and Diana went into raptures over the cashmere cardigan that Ellie had chosen for her. For her own part, Ellie was equally pleased with her own gifts, which included a cookery book, some garden tokens and a small silver brooch, so it was a contented threesome who eventually settled down to watch the best of the Christmas offerings on television, dipping into a box of chocolates and allowing the words and music to substitute the need for any conversation.

15

Boxing Day started quietly. Ellie arrived on the ward just before eight, ready to take over the responsibilities for the day. Thankfully, she found that Sister Makepeace had given herself the day off, so there was a generally more relaxed feel to the ward. Ellie did an impromptu ward round on her own, getting to know the admissions that had arrived in her two days off and catching up with the progress of the other patients. Christmas Day had, apparently, been quite quiet. There were only three new faces to meet, one of whom was so demented that forming any sort of rapport was beyond hope and one who, sadly, was unconscious and dying. So much for their Christmas, thought Ellie, watching the relatives around the bed, muttering to each other in hushed tones, holding their loved one's hands. She stopped to introduce herself to them, express her condolences and promise that everything would be done to ensure that any distressing symptoms could be dealt with.

Over a cup of tea with the nurses, Ellie reviewed any messages that had been left for her and test results that had come in. This job did not take long. As one of the days she had been off was a Bank holiday with only emergency services available, there was little waiting for her attention. Ward work done, the rest of the day stretched ahead with only the unknown of the emergency admissions to cope with. Taking the novel that she had brought with her, Ellie made her way to the doctors' mess in the hopes of some peace and quiet until her first call. There were a few of her colleagues already there, reading old newspapers and watching television. She made a coffee and went and joined them, answering their questions about Nigel's wedding and swapping stories of who had done what for Christmas. There was definitely the feeling of the morning after. Everyone seemed subdued and resigned to the fact that the holidays were over for another year. So much anticipation and then it was all gone in the blink of an eye.

No sooner had she opened her novel, Ellie's bleep went off, making everyone jump and check their own. While they breathed sighs of relief, Ellie groaned and made her way to the telephone, whereupon she learned that there was a patient on his way from Accident and Emergency to Whitby Ward. Ellie reckoned she would have time to finish her drink and the chapter she was halfway through before the nurses would have finished admitting the gentleman and so sank back in the old spongy chair and settled back to her book, only to be disturbed almost immediately by yet another call. This time it was a harassed-sounding GP, out doing calls, having what sounded like a very busy time. He wanted to admit a chronically confused old lady, found by her visiting relatives who had not seen her for a year and were now demanding that something be done, to absolve their own guilt for not having paid her enough attention. In the throes of taking down this patient's details, Ellie's bleep went off a third time and her next conversation was with another GP who had been called out to a breathless lady with chest and abdominal pain. Ellie slapped her book shut, waved good-bye to her friends, hoping to meet up with them later and plodded back to the ward. Why wasn't everyone still out there having fun?

Starting with the first patient, Ellie found herself face to face with Mr Crowther, the alcoholic, who had imbibed so much over the last few days while socialising with all his mates in the pub that his liver had finally called time on him. It was sad for Ellie to find the man who had entertained and joked with her in such a deplorable state. Tremulous, panting for breath and dehydrated, he looked close to death. Ellie revved into action and spent the best part of half an hour assessing him and instigating the necessary treatments and investigations, acutely aware that last time she had met him, she had barely been able to get a word in whereas now, he could hardly utter a syllable. Satisfied that he was more comfortable and that she had done all she could, she turned her attentions to the breathless lady who had not only arrived but walked on to the ward and looked far fitter than Ellie had been led to believe, followed by the confused lady who was repeatedly trying to get out of bed and leave. The morning passed in a rush. Two further admissions kept Ellie on her toes with no time to rest or think of anything other than work. Another stroke and then the final lady had so many pathologies, diabetes, heart disease, rheumatoid arthritis, peptic ulcer and incipient gangrene of her toes that Ellie hardly knew which to tackle first.

Finishing off her notes, Ellie went back and checked on each of them. Mr Crowther was at least peaceful and no longer distressed. There was an empty bed where the confused lady should have been and the other three were fine so, looking at her watch, Ellie informed the nurses that she was off to lunch.

Someone with either little imagination, or a warped sense of humour, had designed the menu for the day. The prospect of either turkey curry, turkey and ham pie or fricassee of turkey with rice did nothing to enthral Ellie who, after deliberating, chose the latter, took her plate to a corner of the room where there was an empty table and settled down to read. Much to her surprise, her meal was uninterrupted and she even had time for apple pie and ice cream before being called back to the ward to reassess Mr Crowther.

His agitation had returned and he was calling out, grabbing at hallucinations that were clearly bothering and scaring him. Ellie gave him an injection immediately and asked one of the nurses to set up a syringe driver so that he could continue to receive the drug in a slow, steady manner, obviating the need for more, possibly painful, injections. She spoke to the relatives, concerned to see that his son, now landlord of the pub, bore all the characteristic hallmarks of one who drinks too much, illustrating only too evidently the saying of 'like father, like son'.

As she made her way back to write up her notes, Ellie noticed that, sitting at the nurses' station, was a small fair-haired boy, his legs dangling from the high chair, a stethoscope around his neck, intent on some drawing he was doing on a piece of paper.

'Hello,' Ellie greeted him.

He looked up and smiled hesitantly.

'I'm Ellie. What's your name?'

'Jake,' he replied seriously. 'Do you like my drawing?'

'It's great. I thought you must be a new doctor when I saw your stethoscope.'

He smiled broadly this time.

'I am. Are you a doctor?'

'Yes, but I don't think I can draw like you can. That's really good.'

'It's me and Mummy and Daddy and my brother Luke,' he pointed to each of four figures.

'What's that in the corner?' Ellie indicated something she could not identify.

'That's my babies.'

'Oh,' Ellie paused, her mind quickly working things out. 'What are the babies called?'

'Laura and Faith.'

'They look very little,' Ellie prompted him.

'They are. They only were born yesterday. We were opening our presents when Mummy had to go to the hospital. We're going to see them now.'

'How exciting,' Ellie told him.

'Hello,' said a voice that Ellie instantly recognised as Jeremy's.

'Congratulations,' she managed to say, looking up. 'Jake's just told me your wonderful news.'

Jeremy was standing with a facsimile of Jake who was holding his hand tightly.

'Hello, Daddy,' Jake greeted him. 'Look at my picture.' He held it up.

'That's rubbish,' pronounced the other little boy, trying to wrestle it from him.

'No, it's not,' argued Jake, pulling it away.

'Jake, Luke, please.'

Much to Ellie's surprise, the boys both instantly calmed down. Jake went and took hold of his father's other hand.

'We're just off to visit Helen now,' Jeremy explained. 'Luke was desperate to go to the toilet and Jake promised to be very good and wait here.'

'He has been very good,' Ellie assured him. 'We've had a nice chat. How are the twins and Helen getting on?'

'They're all doing fantastically, thank you. It was a rather unexpected Christmas present but a very happy outcome.'

'I'm really pleased for you all,' said Ellie, meaning it. 'Please give my congratulations to Helen when you see her.'

'I will. Are you busy here?'

'It's been quite a hectic morning. Mr Crowther is back in and dying, I'm afraid. But everything is under control. You're supposed to be on a day off, so don't worry.'

'I expect I shall be taking a few days off actually, but I'll let you know which consultant will be covering for me.'

'Okay,' Ellie answered lightly. 'That's fine. You take some time to enjoy your family.'

She put on a bright, neutral smile so that Jeremy, who possibly had been hoping for some sign of affection, would see that she was happy in her work and efficient enough to manage without him.

'Boys,' started Jeremy, 'I need to have a quick word with Dr Woods here. We'll just be in my office. Why don't you both do some drawing for a minute? Ellie, come with me.'

'Sorry, Jeremy, but I'm really busy and can't leave the ward. I have to go back and check on some of the patients, especially Mr Crowther.'

She got up and made a big show of gathering papers together, avoiding eye contact.

After a moment, Jeremy spoke.

'Right then, boys. Let's go and see Mummy.'

'And Laura,' cried Jake.

'And Faith,' added Luke. They hopped excitedly from one foot to the other.

'I'll call you, Ellie,' Jeremy whispered, as she passed by him.

'No thanks, Jeremy. I don't think we have anything left to say.'

With a dignity that she found both slightly frightening but eminently satisfying, Ellie stalked off down the ward, head held high, not entirely sure where she was going. But it created the effect that she wanted as when she looked back Jeremy and his sons were gone.

Ellie was taken aback by the strength of the emotion she felt and had to dive into the nurses' changing room to escape. She was glad that her realistic streak had conquered her passion but yet part of her still wanted to run after Jeremy, call out that she would expect his call later and spend the rest of the day in anticipation of their next liaison. She knew, without a shadow of a doubt, that this really was the end of their relationship. Meeting Helen had been bad enough, finding out that she was expecting had made things worse but seeing and talking to Luke and Jake, both innocent parties in this mess, was the final straw. The sight of Jeremy standing there, with his sons hanging onto his hands and smiling adoringly up at him, told Ellie incontrovertibly that there was no way that he would ever leave his family and what was more, she no longer wanted him to.

Splashing cold water on her face, Ellie looked up and gazed into the mirror at the worried face looking back at her. Try as she might, she could not stop the tears from rolling down her cheeks as she replayed the highlights of her and Jeremy's time together in her mind. Sniffing, she dried her now-blotchy face and combed her hair, tying it back in a clasp. One of the nurses, who had noticed where she had gone, put her head around the door.

'Dr Woods, sorry but Mr Crowther has just died.'

'I'm coming. Just give me a moment.'

With a final resolute blow of her nose, Ellie went to confirm the death. As she consoled Mr Crowther's son and daughter in their grief, her own vulnerability caused the tears to well up in her own eyes. She felt foolish but unbeknown to Ellie, the relatives simply thought what a caring and sensitive doctor she was, exhibiting such empathy.

'Are you all right?' asked a nurse, concerned as she watched Ellie returning from Mr Crowther's single room.

Ellie tried hard to smile.

'I've just got a bit of a headache, that's all.'

She was touched when a cup of tea and two paracetamol were put down at her side. Her head was indeed thumping. Perhaps not the most conventional of headaches but in many ways far more painful. Before she had time to finish her drink, Ellie had to divert her attention to her unconscious stroke patient who died peacefully and a new arrival from Accident and Emergency with weakness and intractable diarrhoea.

The beauty of Ellie's job was that it demanded one hundred percent of her concentration; anything less was not a viable option. Fortunately there is nothing quite like the stench of faecal incontinence to focus the mind. Halfway through telling Ellie about her hysterectomy in 1979, Mrs McIver felt the rumbling warning of yet more intestinal activity. Excruciatingly embarrassed and not wanting to interrupt the doctor, one of a profession she had the greatest respect for, she clenched her buttocks as tightly as she could, a feat difficult to attain when ninety-one years old and worn out from two sleepless nights. The urgency, however, far outweighed the strength of her pelvic floor and with one horrifyingly undignified blast, she found herself sitting in a pool of foul-smelling brown fluid.

Ellie, who wanted to gag, rang for a nurse, reassured Mrs McIver that she was not to be upset and that it could have happened to anyone. Feeling that it was a bit unfair to leave the task of cleaning up to the nursing staff, Ellie nevertheless departed and waited until, clean and fresh, her patient was ready to resume where they had left off.

By teatime, when the nurses were dishing out the meals, Ellie's work had slackened off. She was able to make her way back to the mess and pass a pleasant couple of hours with her friends, watching television. Before they all went for supper together, Ellie took time to ring her mother. The telephone rang for a worryingly long time before it was answered and Diana was gasping as she spoke.

'Hu...hullo?'

Ellie, instantly alert, sensed trouble.

'Hi, Mum, it's me? What's going on? Is there a problem?'

'No, we're fine.'

Ellie felt initially relieved, then exasperated, wondering if her mother would ever admit that things were anything other than fine.

'Why are you out of breath? Why did it take you so long to answer the phone?'

'Stop worrying. I was just putting Dad to bed. He wanted an early night. I couldn't just drop him, could I?'

'No, of course not. Sorry, Mum. I was just ringing to see how you both were.'

'We've just had a quiet day. Gordon came over to watch that video with Dad and I went and sat with Sheila for a couple of hours. I fell asleep in her armchair! It was so restful; I'd no idea I was so tired.'

'Doesn't that make you think getting some help in might be a good idea after all?' Ellie seized the opportunity.

'I feel much better now for that nap, so we'll see. Anyway, how's your day been?'

Ellie skirted over the details.

'Not bad. Busy this morning and afternoon but calmer now. We're all just off to the canteen for supper.'

'I hope it stays quiet for you, love. See you soon. Must go now and check on Dad.'

They said their goodbyes and Ellie ran to catch up with the others who had started to make their way down the stairs.

Diana put down the receiver, went into the kitchen and switched the kettle on. It had been another totally exhausting day, despite the rest she had had after lunch when she had gone round to Sheila's. She had woken after another disturbed night. Try as she might, she could not settle to sleep. It was like having a baby again. She slept with one ear open the whole time, waking instinctively to the sounds of Keith moving or coughing in case he needed her. Generally speaking, he slept well but this afforded her little reassurance, certainly not enough for her to switch off her early warning system and get some quality rest. She would just make a hot drink and sit and watch something on the television for half an hour. That should give Keith time to get into a deep sleep, so that when she joined him, she would not disturb him.

Spooning cocoa powder into a mug, she realised that she should be heating up milk, not water and with a sigh, opened up the cupboard for a small pan and turned on a hotplate. As she reached into the fridge for the milk, she could not help but notice all the food that was left over. She had vastly overestimated what they would need. Keith had eaten next to nothing and come to think of it, neither she nor Ellie had done justice to the meal either. What would become of all the leftovers, she had no idea. She had no energy to start making stews, pies and curries with the remainder of the chicken, to stash away in the freezer ready for use at short notice. Talking of which, her freezer was the emptiest it had been for a long time – no loaves of home-made bread, no cakes and puddings, no vegetables from the pick-your-own farm on the way to Ripley. She had let things slide which was never a good thing. She resolved to do better in the New Year.

The sound of the milk coming to the boil jerked her back from her reveries and she stirred it into her mug, watching it turn muddy brown. Remembering that she had had no lunch, Diana opened up the biscuit tin and took out a piece of shortbread. It had been such an effort making that yesterday, she thought. They'd had that terrible night with Keith falling but she had so wanted everything to be as it usually was on Christmas morning for Ellie and shortbread was one of her favourites.

She made her way into the lounge and after puffing up the cushions, which looked flat and lifeless, sat down in Keith's chair. Nibbling at the biscuit, she found that it tasted horribly sweet. It was odd how she seemed to have lost her appetite. Normally food was very important to her. Cooking was second nature and part of the joy of cooking was savouring the end products. Ellie had been right when she'd asked her if she'd lost weight. When she'd put on that dress, Diana had been incredulous at how loose it was. Luckily, Ellie had seemed to believe her when she'd attributed her new figure to her underwear. The last thing she wanted was for Ellie to have to worry about her mother; it was bad enough what she had to cope with already.

Diana found the hot chocolate similarly distasteful and sickly. She forced herself to drink as much as possible, thinking that milk was a good foodstuff for someone who wasn't very hungry. If only she could get a few good nights' sleep then she suspected she would feel so much better.

The mornings started early, with Keith needing to go to the toilet. Fortunately, he had not developed any incontinence problems but he still needed help, even if it was just to get on the commode, which they had agreed to have by his side of the bed. The first time he had tried to use it, he had refused her help, pushed her away, determined to maintain some independence but he had fallen in an ungainly heap on the floor and burst into tears. Since that time, he had still tried to do as much as he could without assistance but Diana was unable to stop herself from wading in, offering two arms to support and guide him.

Once this call of nature was taken care of, there was little point in trying to sleep, so Diana would be up, wrapped in her candlewick dressing-gown and off to make the first cup of tea of the day. Thank goodness for central heating. Though the gas bill would be enormous, at least it meant that they could get up to a warm house and Keith was at no risk of getting cold when he was dressing, or rather, being dressed.

Tea on a tray, Diana returned to bed and helped Keith up onto his pillows and bolster. They sat companionably side by side, for all the world like a normal, contented couple until Diana would reach over to help Keith with his beaker before allowing any of her own drink to be taken. Then there was breakfast, Keith having his in bed after Diana had showered and dressed. The doctor and dietician had suggested some special formulated drinks for him which came under the guise of exotic flavours such as strawberry and mango, mocha, caramel and even wild mushroom but the taste usually turned out to be a far cry from these and Keith was not particularly enamoured of any of them.

When he had done his best with the liquid food, the two of them would somehow make their way to the bathroom. Locked in some wild embrace, they half danced, half staggered out of the bedroom and across the corridor, where, with any luck, Keith would land in one piece on the stool that had been fitted in the shower. The next step was easy, soaping him all over, washing it off, shampooing his hair and then taking great care to dry him well while he was still on his stool. Experience had taught them that trying to extract him from the shower while he was still wet was rather like wrestling with a slippery fish and more than once they had both ended up on the floor, arms and legs entangled but mercifully unhurt.

With Keith finally back in his armchair, Diana could relax a little. He was safe for the duration but she now needed to do the housework, the washing and ironing. Gordon and Sheila had been marvellous but she hated to ask too much of them. Just to have Gordon sit with Keith for a while was a blessing even if she and Sheila were just in the kitchen having a gossip. It broke the day up a little as well to see them and it was obvious that Keith enjoyed Gordon's company enormously. Sadly Gordon was not really strong enough to push the wheelchair and so take Keith out and there was no way that Sheila, with her arthritis-ridden hands, could do so either, so that was another task that fell to Diana. When Keith had first agreed to the wheelchair, it was like a godsend. Off they would go, well wrapped up against the cold (though Diana found that she was working up a sweat after a few minutes) and parade round the local roads, sometimes go the park or local corner shop, anything so long as it meant getting out.

Latterly though, Diana had been finding this increasingly difficult, worn out before they started and out of breath before the end of their road. She'd managed to come up with a good selection of excuses for why she couldn't take him, mostly related to the inclement weather. It was hard letting him down. She could see the disappointment in his eyes and demeanour.

Dr Urquhart had suggested a second commode in the lounge. Diana had had no compunction in refusing that point blank. One in the bedroom was just about tolerable, as no one else need know that it was there, but the lounge? Unfortunately this determination to maintain Diana's belief in decorum meant that, several times a day, she had to deal with Keith's requirements to go to the bathroom, each one sapping her of yet more strength until she found herself longing for it to be his bed time, so that she could have a few precious moments on her own.

Diana was dozing lightly, her mug of cocoa resting precariously on her lap. She had not got so far as switching on the television. Her chin was resting uncomfortably on her chest, which rose and fell slowly and rhythmically. The sudden noise of Keith calling jerked her awake, she spilt the cold cocoa all over her skirt and jumped up. Rushing into the bedroom, she found him yet again on the floor, another attempt to manage without her having ended in failure.

'Oh, Keith. Have you hurt yourself?' she wailed, going down on all fours to see to him. He was shaking his head and coughing, tenacious sputum rattling in his throat.

'Let's get you up and back in bed, love.'

He pointed to her skirt.

'I know, silly me! I fell asleep with my hot chocolate in my hand. Don't worry, it had gone quite cold, so I've not burned my legs. I'll change into my nightie once I've got you sorted.'

Gradually, she rearranged his limbs and manoeuvred Keith onto his knees. From there Diana, with intense concentration, put her arms under his and heaved him inelegantly onto the bed. They both lay there, panting.

'For all you don't eat much, you still weigh a ton!' Diana tried to joke as she stood up, lifted Keith's legs onto the bed and arranged the covers over him. He looked apologetic and tried to tell her so in words as well. This effort rekindled his cough. Diana gave him a little drink of water, on which he choked and the end result was him vomiting on the bedclothes.

'Oh Keith, those were clean on today.'

Wearily, she stripped the duvet cover off and left it next to the soiled duvet in a heap on the floor.

'I'll just get the one from the spare room, love. Don't worry. You couldn't help it.'

The spare duvet was lying on the bed, folded neatly. This necessitated a trip to the airing cupboard, the retrieval of a fresh cover and then the usual tussle of putting it on the duvet.

'Here we are, dear. I'll swear that job gets harder, not easier. Are you warm enough? Better not have another drink for a while. I'll just deal with these dirty things. Won't be a minute.'

Diana shoved the cover in the washing machine. The duvet she sponged down, hoping that this would be enough and hung it over the door to dry overnight. Her hands smelled hideously of vomit. Taking her nightclothes, she went and showered, sitting on Keith's stool and letting the water wash over her and soothe her aching muscles. Another crash from the bedroom had her racing back, dripping wet, towel draped around her body like a Roman toga. Keith, mercifully, was still in bed. He had, though, decided, that no matter what Diana had recommended, he was still thirsty, so had reached over, successfully got hold of his drink, at the expense of knocking over the bedside lamp and some books, rolled back and spilt it all down his pyjamas. He was wet through.

'What have you done now?' Diana raged at him. 'I've only just got things sorted.'

Distraught, spent to the point of confusion and furious, Diana slapped him across the cheek. She leapt back, alarmed at what she had done, staring at her hand as if it did not belong to her. One look at Keith told her that he was flabbergasted. His face was white apart from his left cheek which was red from the impact of her hand. Clapping her hand to her mouth, Diana fled from the room, back to the bathroom where she sat, shaking, on the edge of the bath, forcing herself to take deep breaths.

'I can't believe what just happened,' she said out loud. 'How could I have done such a terrible thing?'

Taking her time, she dried the remaining damp bits of her body, sprinkled some talcum powder here and there and slipped into her nightdress. She rubbed thick cream into her face, watching in the mirror as she massaged her skin. Finally she cleaned her teeth and washed out her mouth with cold water.

Opening up the airing cupboard again, she found clean pyjamas for Keith and a warm towel. Back in the bedroom, she caringly took off his damp clothes, patted him dry and settled him into his dry ones. The wet pyjamas and towel were thrown into the washing machine.

Diana went around the house, switching off the lights, locking the doors. Climbing into bed beside Keith, she wrapped her arms around him.

'I am so, so sorry. I never meant to hit you.'

She kissed his damp cheeks, damp from his tears, not his recent accident and started to weep as well.

'It's all getting a bit too much for me, my darling. Perhaps we should think about having a bit more help.'

Diana looked into Keith's eyes.

'I know you don't want anyone but me. I'll do my best. Let's ask the doctor to come in anyway and just have a chat.'

They lay together, silently cuddling, Diana still appalled by her actions, Keith trembling against her chest.

'Let's try to get some sleep, eh? Tomorrow's another day, we'll see how we feel then.'

Diana leant over and put out the bedside lamp. Gradually she felt Keith's breathing start to regulate as he fell asleep. Wide awake, she wished fervently that she could do so too.

16

Diana was sitting in a comfortable chair, waiting to see Dr Urquhart. She felt most uncomfortable, largely because Keith had no idea that she was there and she hated deceiving him.

The waiting area was pleasant enough, there was some nondescript music playing in the background and a selection of reasonably up-to-date magazines to read. The walls were a suitable neutral tone and decorated with a variety of posters admonishing smoking, imbibing alcohol and obesity. A few other people were also waiting. They had all been there when she arrived, so she was preparing for a long wait, pretending to read a glossy magazine about celebrities and the unreal lives that they led. The lady next to her coughed persistently, rarely covering her mouth with her hand and wiping her nose on the back of her sleeve. A couple of toddlers were building a tower of bricks and pushing a toy train with several carriages across the floor while their mother looked on disconsolately. One gentleman had his eyes closed, either in meditation, sleep or boredom; the remainder all had their noses buried in magazines. In the corner there was a fish tank in which tiny fish swam back and forth, oblivious of their calming effect on those who waited.

It was New Year's Eve. Tired decorations dangled from the ceiling, begging to be taken down and stored away until next Christmas. Although five days had passed since she had hit Keith, the event was still uppermost in her mind. Thinking about it made her cringe and she wondered if those around her could read her thoughts.

After a fashion, they had been managing. Keith had made it plainly clear that he did not want any other involvement in his care. When she had raised the topic, he had become blatantly upset, banging his fists on the arms of his chair, his face set in anger. Consequently she had promised, yet again, to try to cope. Perhaps she would be able to if she prioritised. Looking after Keith was the most important role in her life. Housework and ironing could take a back seat and if she asked, she was sure that Gordon and Sheila could be relied upon for the shopping and anyway, they needed very little these days. Regardless of these changes, she felt no better either physically or emotionally. Her exhaustion continued unabated, she felt breathless with the least exertion and what little appetite she had seemed to have deserted her completely. She really felt that she could not carry on any longer without talking to someone. Dr Urquhart had repeatedly told her that he was there to listen and help. Diana believed him. His visits to Keith were never complete without him asking her how she was, a gesture that she appreciated but never capitalised on, until now.

The coughing lady was called in, to the relief of everyone, glad of the silence. One of the other partners appeared, a Dr Jepson, if Diana remembered correctly and took away the young mother and the children, who had been waiting in the wrong place. It looked as though her wait was not going to be as long as she had anticipated.

Flipping idly through her magazine, Diana wondered how Keith was at the moment. Sheila was sitting with him, waiting for Gordon to return with the shopping. She had promised she wouldn't be long, making the excuse of a dental appointment which could not be changed as it had taken a long time to arrange. He should be fine until she returned. He had had what lunch he could manage, been to the bathroom and had been left with the television on as background noise, so that Sheila did not feel obliged to try to talk continuously.

'Mrs Woods?'

Dr Urquhart's voice made her look up.

'Would you like to come in now?'

He has such a kind face, thought Diana, as she picked up her bag and followed him into his surgery. In his mid-fifties, his face was lined but in a way that spoke of sensitivity and gentleness. His hair was still dark, though flecked with grey and he was dressed, unexpectedly, in a sleeveless Fair Isle jumper over a cream shirt and a pair of dark brown corduroy trousers.

'Have a seat, Diana,' he invited her, more familiar now that it was just the two of them.

'Hello, Dr Urquhart,' Diana replied graciously. 'Did you have a nice Christmas?'

'Very pleasant, thank you. How about you?'

'Quite nice, very quiet. Our daughter Ellie came over for the day.'

'She was lucky to have Christmas day off.'

'Yes, but she's been working hard since. She's on call again tonight, poor thing.'

'Not long now until she's a GP. A year is it?'

Diana nodded.

'Anyway, how can I help?'

'I'm not sure. It's just that…. Well, I don't really know how to put it.'

'Take your time.'

'You're very kind.'

Diana looked at her hands. She was curling her handkerchief round and round her fingers.

Dr Urquhart waited patiently, saying nothing.

'I'm not coping very well.' She blurted out the words in a rush. Tears sprang to her eyes. 'I feel such a failure. I should be able to do this.'

He passed her a box of tissues, anticipating her need.

'The last thing you are is a failure.'

'But I'm finding it so hard. It's so exhausting and he refuses to have any help in because he expects or wants me to do it all. He doesn't seem to be able to see that I'm on my knees. I never get a good night's sleep, I can't eat and lifting him is so, so hard.'

'You've been nothing short of miraculous, Diana. Lesser mortals would have fallen by the wayside long before this. Of course you can't be expected to do all this on your own. You desperately need some help.'

Diana blew her nose.

'What sort of help?'

'There's all sorts we can offer. I can get carers to come in during the day and a night sitter as well, if you'd like. That would at least give you the opportunity to have some proper rest. Alternatively, we could think of some respite at St Lambert's hospice.'

Diana looked curious. Dr Urquhart nodded.

'Yes, I know that traditionally the hospice is associated with cancer patients but, I am glad to say, they will help with other conditions. I am sure that if I had a word, they would take Keith for a couple of weeks' respite. He'd be wonderfully looked after, you'd have a complete break but be able to visit whenever you wanted. It might be no bad thing to get to know the staff there – he may need to go there later on.'

'He's always said he wants to stay at home, doctor,' Diana sniffed. 'And I promised him that he could.'

'Let me talk to him, Diana. Folk change their minds all the time. It's easy at the beginning of an illness to think you know what you want but as changes happen to you, your thinking alters as well. He may accept these offers much more readily now. He's bound to have noticed how you are having difficulties.'

'I wish I had your confidence,' Diana said warily.

'He'll take it differently if I make these suggestions. I'll come round,' he opened his diary and turned a couple of pages, 'the day after tomorrow. How would that be? Or do you want me to come after surgery today?'

'Oh no, a couple of days would be fine and I'd be so grateful if you would. Are you sure it's no trouble?'

'That's what I'm here for. I'm so glad you came to see me. You look tired out. How about you? Should be talking about you as well?'

Diana shook her head vehemently.

'I'm fine. If I can just get some help and a bit of time to myself, then that will make all the difference. Thank you so much. I feel better already.'

'I'll see you in two days then. About lunchtime, I guess, after morning surgery.'

Finally Diana managed a brief smile and plucked up courage to ask, 'He's getting worse quite quickly, isn't he, doctor?'

'I'm afraid he is. I'm sorry. It's no life for him, is it?'

'It's barely an existence. He hates it.'

'So would I.'

'I'd really like him to stay at home, if possible,' begged Diana.

'We'll do everything we can, Diana. But I have to look after you as well, you know.'

Diana picked up her bag and took a last tissue to wipe her eyes for a final time.

'Thank you again, Dr Urquhart. Happy New Year.'

They shook hands, Dr Urquhart warmly taking Diana's hand in both of his, squeezing slightly to emphasise his promise to help and saw her to the door. Closing it behind her, he shook his head sadly. She looked drawn and ill, completely washed out. Picking up the telephone, he dialled the number for the hospice to enquire about the bed status.

Diana strode out of the surgery feeling infinitely more positive. If anyone could persuade Keith to see things differently then it was likely to be the doctor. Part of her felt as if she had betrayed her husband though, going behind his back in this way. She ambled up the hill and into town, amazed at how long it took her as she had to keep stopping to look into shop windows while she got her breath back. The streets were already starting to quieten down as shops closed early for the party night ahead. A few early revellers were staggering across the road, arms round each other, party hats akimbo on their heads, on their way to the next pub. Diana went into a department store and found that the café was still open. Tempted by the thought of some more time to herself, she decided that they could manage at home without her a little longer. She picked up a tray and made her way along the self-service counter, not tempted at all by the cakes and pastries, settling for a pot of tea and a small scone which she took to one of the many empty tables. Even when smothered with butter and strawberry jam, the scone did not appeal to her and after two mouthfuls, she pushed the plate away. She thought with pride of her own scones, light, fluffy and generously scattered with sultanas. The hot, strong tea was welcome though and Diana wrapped her hands around the cup to warm them as she drank. She always felt cold these days, no matter how many layers of clothes she put on.

Of all the ideas that Dr Urquhart had mentioned, Diana was most attracted to the thought of Keith having some respite at the hospice. How wonderful it would be to be able to sleep undisturbed, have a lie in and do exactly what she wanted, all the while knowing that he was safe. But as soon as this vision entered her head she felt dreadful for even considering it and being so selfish. A tiny voice kept telling her that he had not much longer to live, so his wishes had to be paramount. Whatever it took, she could manage.

Having finished off the last drops of tea, Diana took her time walking back through the shop, stopping to look at bargains in the sale and picking out a pair of thick cotton pyjamas in a cosy bright red for Keith which were sure to come in useful. She then waited disconsolately for the bus, climbed on board and then stared out of the window, not seeing the familiar scenery passing by but all the while half dreading going home. Opening the front door, she was greeted in the hall by Sheila, rushing towards her, looking fraught.

'Thank goodness, Diana. We were so worried about you. You've been gone a lot longer than you said. Is everything all right?'

'Oh dear,' Diana sighed, 'I am so sorry. Has Keith had a problem?'

'No, only that he's been getting really agitated because you're not here. I'm sure he'll calm down now that you're back.'

Diana undid her coat, took it off and slowly hung it up in the cloakroom. On entering the lounge, she found Keith, looking angst ridden, shaking and sweating.

'There now, darling, here I am. I had a bit of a wait at the dentist. You know how slow he can be. Everyone seemed to want to see him, even though it's New Year's Eve.'

She went over and hugged him, not failing to notice not only how he was trembling but also how frail and thin he had become.

He mumbled at her, words incoherent to others, but words that she could understand. She kissed him repeatedly on his cheek and took his hand.

'You can get off now, Sheila,' Diana said, looking up at her friend. 'Thank you so much for sitting with him. Sorry again about being so long.'

'No harm done,' Sheila reassured her. 'Are you sure that you can manage?'

Diana smiled.

'We're just fine now. See you in a couple of days – oh that'll be next year, won't it!'

'Well, just ring if you want anything. I'll pop in when we get back. We're only staying with Gordon's sister for a couple of nights. I'll see myself out, you stay with Keith. Happy New Year.'

'Well, that's more like it,' Diana turned her attention to Keith. 'Just the two of us. What's that? No, no fillings today, so that was a relief. I hate the sound of that drill. Now, what shall we do, watch some telly? Are we going to stay up and see in the New Year or do you feel as tired out as I do?'

Happily, she snuggled into his shoulder and switched to a quiz programme for the two of them to watch.

At the hospital, Ellie was having a grim day. Foolishly thinking that perhaps it would be quiet as it was still part of the Christmas season, she found that she was inundated with work from first thing in the morning. A couple of days earlier, in a rash moment of generosity, she had volunteered to take the calls for one of her colleagues who was desperate to have the day off, an act she now bitterly regretted. Her routine ward work had to be put on hold as the first admission of

185

the day arrived and she was aware of Sister Makepeace's look of wrath burning a hole in her back as she scurried back and forth for blood bottles and x-ray forms. Ellie was then called to another ward where the exceedingly polite and charming Sister greeted her warmly and gratefully before accompanying her to see a patient who was insistent on taking his own discharge against medical advice so that he could first-foot his neighbour.

By lunchtime, which for Ellie was merely a time of day, rather than for anything to eat, she had oscillated between wards more times than she could remember. She had managed to appease Sister Makepeace to a degree by catching up with most of her work but then infuriated her by accepting a tiny, cachetic old lady who had been found huddled in her slum of a house when police, alerted by distant relatives who had called with a box of chocolates and a bottle of cheap sherry, had broken in. It was obviously a very long time since she had had any contact with soap and water. Her crumpled clothes were filthy and held together with string and her legs were swathed in grey, ragged pieces of torn-up sheet. These had to be soaked off, for they were densely adherent in places to multiple oozing ulcers. Once they were off, the foulest of stenches exploded into the atmosphere.

Spotting a teaching opportunity, Penelope summoned one of the student nurses and started to quiz her on the various dressing that they might be able to use. It was while she was leaning over the patient, measuring the size of one of the ulcers and commenting knowledgably on it, that Sister Makepeace realised that the patient was not alone. With horror, she spotted the incontrovertible evidence of infestation. Not just fleas but also scabies.

'Dr Woods,' she bellowed.

Ellie, busy reassuring someone that their chest x-ray was normal, sighed and went to find her. Before she knew it, she was on the receiving end of a tirade of abuse, the like of which she had never been subjected to before. Sister Makepeace even threatened to report her to Dr Blake for bringing infection onto the ward. Unwisely, Ellie tried to butt in, to explain that she was not in a position to be selective about admissions and that the old lady needed their help but her words were drowned by the nursing sister's ongoing ranting.

'And I'm telling you, that as soon as Dr Blake is back, you'll be in real trouble.'

'Back?' asked Ellie.

'He's rung in this morning. His wife is home today with those dear babies, so he's taking ten days off. You're to liaise with Dr Barnstaple if you've any problems. I'd have told you this morning, if you hadn't been so busy wasting time with other things rather than looking after this ward. Now, for goodness sake, get out of my way. This poor soul needs to be cleaned up thoroughly.'

Ellie did not need telling twice. She suddenly understood what had motivated Sister Makepeace's vehement outburst. The fact that Jeremy was going to be away, his attentions presumably and hopefully focused strictly on his family, whilst excellent news to Ellie, was entirely the opposite to his most adoring admirer.

'Let me know when she's ready for me to examine her, please.' Ellie turned on her heels and walked away, unable to miss hearing Sister Makepeace's purposefully loud mutterings about how disgraceful it was that this job had to be left to nurses while junior doctors swanned around doing nothing. Knowing that the nurses would be occupied for a considerable length of time, Ellie went to the office to catch up with some paperwork. Halfway through, her pager disturbed the peace and rather dreading the prospect of another admission she rang the switchboard.

'Dr Blake for you,' the operator informed her.

Ellie's heart plummeted somewhat.

'Hello?'

'Ah, Ellie, how are things on the ward?'

'Fine, thank you, we're having a very busy day, but everything's under control, I think.'

'Good, I know I can rely on you. Hang on a minute.'

Ellie could hear the sound of a door closing in the background.

'Helen's home with the twins,' Jeremy started.

'I know, Penelope told me. How are they?'

'Doing well, thanks. I'm going to have to take some time off to help.'

'Of course you are. Don't worry, we can manage fine. Penelope's passed on the message that Dr Barnstaple is covering for you. I won't hesitate to ring him if I've any questions.'

There was a pause during which Ellie could hear his breathing.

'Ellie, I miss you. Can we get together?' His voice was now more of a whisper.

Ellie closed her eyes and took some deep breaths.

'No, Jeremy. It would be totally wrong. I can't go on seeing you. Not now.'

'But we were so good together, you know we were.'

'Using the past tense is correct. It's over Jeremy.'

'Please. I could come round to your house tomorrow.'

'I'll be with my parents. Look, Jeremy, I have to go, there's an emergency on the ward. Enjoy your time off at home. Good-bye.'

With a firm finality, Ellie replaced the receiver. She was fuming. How dare he think that she would go on having an affair with him? Did he really think that she was that easy and desperate enough to be prepared to have a series of sordid clandestine liaisons whenever it suited him? The sooner this job was over, the better.

By the evening, Ellie had calmed down. Work was very therapeutic at times, demanding all her concentration. Penelope's shift was over and a more relaxed air settled on the ward. Even the patients seemed more cheerful. The nurses sat laughing and drinking tea with Ellie, sharing out chocolates that the ward had received at Christmas. Everyone had been admitted, assessed and their immediate needs seen to, including Lucy Parsons, the lady with the infestation. There was nothing pending at the moment and Ellie was glad of the break. She even managed a decent evening meal which, whilst quite tasty, left her feeling full and bloated as she had overeaten, thinking that she was making up for her missed lunch. Promising to meet up with some friends later on in the doctors' mess, Ellie returned to the ward to check that all was well only to be informed that another admission was on its way from Accident and Emergency.

Any hopes of a quiet evening disappeared as a porter arrived pushing a trolley on which a hugely obese man was half sitting, half lying and wheezing like a badly played accordion. Concerned relatives were on either side of him, carrying his possessions which had been hastily shoved into plastic carrier bags and chattering away to each other. They had to be asked repeatedly to go and wait in the lounge whilst the nurses settled him into bed so that Ellie could go and see to him. Her clinical impression was that he had had a massive heart attack and his ECG and blood tests confirmed this. His old notes appeared, revealing that Kenneth Dickson had had two previous heart attacks and had been warned time and time again to try to lose some weight and stop smoking. It took Ellie a considerable length of time before she felt that he was stable enough for her to leave for a while. She went and spoke to the relatives, gently warning them about the severity of his condition and saying that she would try to get him transferred to the coronary care unit, if possible. Seemingly though, the rest of the hospital had been having as busy a day as Ellie. There were no free beds currently on the unit, so Ellie, feeling a little out of her league, rang Dr Barnstaple to talk through her management with him.

Contrary to all her predictions, Mr Dickson seemed to improve and half an hour or so before midnight, Ellie felt that it was reasonable to leave the ward and go and join her friends. Imploring the nurses to ring her if they had the slightest concern, she rushed along the corridor and found the mess alive with on-call doctors, some of whom had persuaded their partners to come in from home to join them. She was greeted with a glass of lemonade, jazzed up with an umbrella and a maraschino cherry on the top. No sooner had she taken a sip, her pager went off, at double speed, indicating an emergency. Several other bleeps went off simultaneously. Knowing in her heart that it was going to be Mr Dickson, she fled to the telephone.

'Cardiac arrest on Whitby,' shouted someone, hurtling through the door with two other doctors in hot pursuit.

Ellie was right behind them, running for all she was worth, either hand holding on to her pockets to prevent the contents from spilling out. They burst in convoy onto the ward.

'That way,' a nurse pointed down the ward, surprising Ellie who was preparing to turn in the opposite direction. The curtains were pulled around Lucy Parsons' bed. Caroline, the night staff nurse was kneeling on the mattress performing cardiac massage. Another was positioning the arrest trolley.

'Is this lady one of yours, Ellie?' asked a tall, dark-skinned anaesthetist who had assumed control.

'Yes, Joe,' gasped Ellie, still fighting for her breath. 'She came in earlier today. The police had had to break into her house as she hadn't been seen for days. She was hypothermic and hypoglycaemic but both of those improved very quickly once she arrived on the ward. The only other thing that her investigations showed was mild hypothyroidism.'

'Okay. Any past history?'

Ellie shook her head.

'I don't think she's seen a doctor in years. She hasn't any hospital notes at all.'

They worked on Lucy steadfastly, watching for the slightest sign that she was responding to their ministrations but despite their best efforts, they were forced to abandon their attempt.

'Right, everyone,' called Joe. 'There's no more that we can do here. Sorry, Ellie. Thank you, everyone, for your help. Time of death – oh oh five. Happy New Year!'

Ellie sat with Joe while he wrote his notes in tiny, perfect italics. Thanking her again, an emotion which she reciprocated, he left and Ellie decided that the last thing that she felt like doing was returning to the party. She leant over the desk and rested in her head in her hands, acutely aware of her exhaustion. Her pager went off.

'Oh no,' she wailed, 'not again.'

'I'll get it for you,' offered Caroline, sympathetically.

'Thank you very much,' replied Ellie, waiting, dreading to hear what was going to happen next.

'It's an outside call, Ellie,' Caroline said softly, her hand over the mouthpiece. 'Some bloke wanting to wish you Happy New Year.'

Damn Jeremy, Ellie cursed inwardly. When will he start to leave me alone?

'Just tell him that I'm unavailable.'

'He sounds very nice,' Caroline tried but one look at Ellie made her do as she was told.

'He said, he'll catch you another time. He said he was called Ian.'

'Who?' Ellie jerked her head up.

Caroline repeated what she had said but had already put the phone down.

'Did he leave a number?'

'No, sorry, I never thought to ask.'

17

Ellie was late getting to her parents. She had been called three times in the night and each time she had fallen back into bed it had proved harder to get back to sleep. Wearily, she had done a ward round that morning, taken aback but pleased when Dr Barnstaple arrived, looking dapper in dark casual trousers and a golfing sweater and came with her to see all the patients. He was swift and efficient. He even managed to get a bed on the coronary care unit for Mr Dickson, which was a great relief to Ellie. Content with what he had seen, he congratulated Ellie on her hard work and excellence before returning to his own ward. After a quick résumé, Ellie passed on any relevant messages to the colleague that was covering for her that day and fled from the hospital before anything could hold her back.

At home, she fell asleep for three hours, woke feeling even more tired but a shower revitalised her. Diana and Keith were, as usual, sitting in the lounge. Keith, Ellie was pleased to see, was listening to one of his talking books and Diana, who had started to listen with him, had nodded off. Diana woke with a start.

'Hello, you two. Happy New Year! No, don't get up, Mum, I'll make us all a coffee.'

The kitchen was a mess. There were pots and plates in the sink and on the draining board. Some pans were resting on the cooker and a quick peep under the lids revealed the remnants of scrambled egg in one and congealed custard in another. Ellie grimaced and while she waited for the kettle to boil opened the fridge to reach for some milk. She was appalled to see the state of it. There was no fresh milk; what little there was had separated into two layers. A handful of green beans, now mostly brownish grey in colour, lay dry and curled up in the salad compartment and two half- empty cans of soup nestled side by side on one shelf. Keith's liquid feeds took up the whole of another shelf and apart from a crust of cheese and two eggs, there was nothing.

'Mum,' Ellie called. 'Is there any fresh milk?'

Diana came in, massaging her face, which felt squashed and wrinkled where it had been pressed against the wing of the chair.

'Is there none in there? I could have sworn that I got some yesterday.'

'It doesn't look as if you've been to the shops for days, Mum. Whatever have you been living off?'

'Oh, stuff from the freezer,' Diana answered vaguely.

Ellie, unconvinced, put her coat back on.

'I'll go and find a shop somewhere and get a few things.'

Ellie drove to a mini-mart that she had noticed was open on her journey over and parked erratically in a back street nearby. Apparently, a lot of other people had run out of basics as the shop was heaving. Patiently, she made her way round with a misshapen wire basket, picking up a variety of items that would see her parents through the next couple of days until she could do a proper shop for them.

Back at their house, she finally made the coffee before returning to tackle the mess in the kitchen, despite Diana's insistence that she would do it later. It was most unusual for her mother not to leave everything spotless. Much of the rest of Ellie's day was spent tidying up. She went into the bathroom and found a load of washing waiting to be done, so that was her next task. She changed the sheets on her parents' bed and found a pile of ironing hidden behind the cloakroom door.

'You really ought to get a cleaner, Mum,' Ellie announced as she neatly folded the newly ironed clothes.

'Maybe. Things have only slipped a little because it's been the holidays. I'll be back on track in no time once the week gets back to normal.'

'Talking of holidays, don't forget that in a couple of weeks I finish this job and then I'm off for the rest of the month. I'll be able to come in every day and give you both a hand.'

'But it's your time off, dear. You should go away for a bit – perhaps find some sunshine. Shouldn't she, Keith?'

Ellie glanced at her father who was nodding in a rather wobbly way.

'No, I couldn't possibly. If you both refuse to get some help in, then at least let me do my bit. It'll give you a break, Mum.'

Diana helped Ellie put away the clothes. Closing the bedroom door behind them, to ensure complete secrecy, she told her daughter about her visit to Dr Urquhart.

'He's coming in tomorrow. I really hope Dad will listen to him.'

'I think he will, Mum. Dad's not daft. I know he wants you to look after him but he must understand that you can't be expected to do it all the time. The hospice sounds a great option, if he'll agree to it.'

'Well, just keep your fingers crossed that Dad thinks the same.'

They spent the day quietly. Ellie took Keith out for a brief walk but the cold air forced them to return sooner than they had wanted. She made omelettes for lunch and a soft-boiled egg for her father. In the afternoon, Diana fell asleep again, so Ellie tried to do crosswords and puzzles with Keith but they ended up watching yet more banal television. She left early, having helped get him into bed, though Keith had drawn a line at being seen changing into his pyjamas by his daughter. Back home, Ellie had an early night with a favourite novel and a large mug of cocoa.

Work dragged the next day, as Ellie could not stop thinking about her parents and what the outcome of Dr Urquhart's visit had been. As soon as she had a moment later in the afternoon, she rang her mother.

'So how did it go with the doctor?' she asked as soon as she heard her mother's voice.

'Oh, Ellie, I am so relieved. He was wonderful.'

The tension had gone from her mother's tone and Ellie felt herself relax also.

'That's great, Mum. What did he say? How is Dad?'

'I left the two of them to it. I even turned the Hoover on as I didn't want Keith to think I was listening. After a while, Dr Urquhart called me in to join them. Your dad's agreed to go into the hospice as soon as there's a bed. Unfortunately, there isn't one at the moment, but we're on the waiting list so hopefully it won't be too long.'

'I am so glad to hear that, Mum. You sound better already.'

'Dad seems quite happy about it all, so I am too. While he's in there, I might just put an advert in the corner shop for a cleaner to come in a couple of times a week. So if you want to think about that holiday, you can do.'

'I'm not making any plans just yet, Mum. Not until I know that you two are okay.'

'We're fine now. Anyway, I must go as Dad wants to go to the bathroom again. We'll see you soon?'

'Tomorrow. I'm working tonight again. I've had to do a couple of swaps.'

'Take care, darling.'

'Bye, Mum.'

Ellie put down the phone, confident that her mother sounded better, unaware that Diana was still clutching her receiver and despairing just how long it would be before there was a bed for Keith.

The next few days flew past, probably because she knew that there was no danger of Jeremy appearing. Ellie managed the ward with her usual skill and Dr Barnstaple, who popped in each day, found nothing to complain about. She visited her parents on an almost daily basis, staying for as long as it took to make sure that they were both as comfy as possible. Her social life was zero as when she did finally get home, it was as much as she could do to tidy up her own house, have a bath and crawl into bed.

Nigel and Emily returned from their honeymoon looking tanned and happy. Emily received the good news that she had been successful in her application for the new Sister's post in A&E and Nigel announced that they would have a 'bit of a do' to celebrate this and the end of

Ellie's job. He had cornered her in the dining room one lunchtime and sat blocking her exit.

'So, have you finished with him?' he had asked bluntly.

'Yes,' Ellie had replied, with total honesty. 'Helen's had the twins. He's off on paternity leave at the moment. When he gets back, I've only four days to work with him so that shouldn't be too difficult to survive.'

'Good,' Nigel had congratulated her. 'You've done the right thing.'

'I know, Nige. I'm sorry that I upset you so much. I really didn't see what I was doing.'

'Hey, don't give it another thought. I bet you can't wait to finish.'

'No, I can't,' Ellie had agreed. 'It's been a good job in some ways. I've learned so much and it's been an amazing experience to have so much responsibility.'

'You only got that because you're so good at your job.'

Ellie had grinned at him and squeezed his arm.

'It's good to have you back, Nigel.'

As promised, Nigel and Emily threw a fish and chips and champagne party for a select group of friends. Ellie had sailed through her last day, euphoria carrying her high above all of the sarcastic comments from Sister Makepeace, who was clearly pleased to see her go. Jeremy had shaken her hand, holding it for perhaps a little longer than he should have, praised her for everything she had done and promised to write her a first-class reference. Ellie heard Penelope sniff loudly at this point but ignored her and thanked Jeremy sincerely for all his good teaching and wished him and his family well. She had left with a sense of release as she turned out of the ward for the final time.

With two weeks' vacation to look forward to, even if it was going to be hard work of a different kind, Ellie drove over to her parents, tidied up for her mother and made the two of them some supper. They seemed to be managing but Ellie was aware of a tension as they were still waiting to hear about the long-promised respite bed. When she told them what she was doing that evening, they appeared to be thrilled for

196

her, stressing how she needed some time off and how good it would be for her to spend some time with her friends. Diana was still trying to get Ellie to go away, reminding her that she could easily pick up a last-minute bargain, just as they had done with their cruise, but Ellie remained adamant that she was staying at home to help them.

She dressed in jeans and a cashmere jumper the colour of squashed raspberries, leaving her hair loose, but making a mental note that it needed a trim. A little make up, a dash of perfume and she was ready. Nigel had told her that it was to be casual and, knowing him, he would be in some baggy tracksuit bottoms and a rugby shirt.

He answered the door wearing exactly what she had predicted, gave her a hug and steered her into the living room where Emily was pouring champagne.

'Ellie, come in. Take this glass.'

'Thanks, Emily, that's lovely.'

Ellie looked round and saw a few faces she recognised from the hospital and went to join a small group who were standing by the fireplace beckoning her over. They chatted and laughed, mostly about work and colleagues at the hospital. Ellie felt full of fun in her excitement at having left Medicine for the Elderly firmly behind. Nigel, who was playing the role of host perfectly, refilled their glasses frequently and Emily could be heard in the kitchen getting out plates.

A ring at the doorbell caused Nigel to leave his role of wine waiter temporarily.

'This should be the fish and chips!' he announced, opening the door.

Ellie looked over towards the door, as did everyone else, expecting to see some sort of delivery but weighed down by large carrier bags there was Ian, wrapped up well against the cold, droplets of rain in his dark hair, starting to enter the house before the door was barely open.

'Make way,' he ordered, 'these are really hot.'

Emily took one of the bags from him, Nigel the others and they disappeared into the kitchen together but it was only a moment or two before they summoned the guests to come and eat. Delicious pieces of haddock covered in crispy batter, golden chips and garishly green mushy peas were on offer with enough of a variety of sauces to please them all. Ellie took her plate, added a vigorous shake of salt and vinegar and retreated to the living room where she perched on the edge of a chair and balanced her meal on her lap.

'We really ought to be eating this outside in the cold night air for the full effect,' suggested Nigel, breaking up his fish with his fingers having refused to use a knife and fork. His guests groaned in unison.

'Well, you're welcome to go out if you want,' Emily told him. 'But looking at the state Ian was in when he arrived, it looks as if it's pouring with rain. Why don't you just pour us all some more drinks. More peas anyone?'

Ian crossed the room and sat on the floor in an ungainly manner beside Ellie.

'Hi, how are you?'

Ellie smiled at him, indicating that her mouth was full. Swallowing she spoke. 'Fine. You?'

'Good thanks.'

'I think I owe you an apology,' started Ellie.

'Why's that?' Ian looked puzzled.

'You rang me on New Year's Eve, just after midnight and I couldn't come to the phone.'

'Don't worry. I knew it was potluck whether you'd be too busy to talk. I just wanted to wish you all the best.'

'That's really kind of you. It would have been nice to have a chat. I'd had the most awful day. It was so busy that I'd had no time to sit down until the evening. Then one of my patients collapsed. We'd been trying to resuscitate her when you rang.'

'Were you successful?'

Sadly, Ellie shook her head. Ian waited a little, concentrating on his chips.

'The newly-weds look well, don't they?' he commented, changing the subject tactfully.

Ellie laughed. 'Positively ecstatic, I would go so far as to say. It's great news about Emily's job, too. It'll mean far less night work for her, so she'll be able to tend to all Nigel's needs!'

'What about your job, Ellie? Did I hear someone mention that you've finished it?'

'Yes, thankfully. I've got two weeks' holiday ahead to look forward to and then I start on the paediatric ward, which should be not only fun but slightly less work.'

'So what are your plans? Are you going away somewhere?'

'No, I'm just going to stay at home.'

Ellie forked up the last of her meal.

'That was great. It's ages since I had fish and chips like that.'

'Let me take your plate,' offered Ian. 'Back in a minute.'

He returned with two helpings of strawberry cheesecake.

'I thought you might fancy some of this.'

'Gorgeous, thanks.'

'Ellie, I was wondering...'

'Yes?'

The cheesecake was delectable and Ellie was licking her spoon to make sure she did not miss any of it. She looked at Ian, wondering what he was going to say.

'I'm off to Scotland for a couple of weeks. My parents have a house up there. Would you like to come and spend a few days with us? They'd love to meet you again.'

Ellie was taken aback and did not know what to say. Ian was busy eating his pudding, concentrating on getting the last crumbs.

'It's a wonderful place to have a break. There's plenty of walking, fresh air and good food. If there's any snow, we could find somewhere to ski.'

Ellie recalled what her mother had said to her about a holiday. Though this wasn't quite the sun-kissed destination that her parents had been suggesting, it was none the less attractive. She liked Ian, with his honest face and eyes that twinkled with laughter and his parents had been engaging and welcoming. There was no getting away from the fact that, in an ideal world, she did need a complete change but unfortunately her situation at the current time was far from ideal.

'Ian, that's so kind of you. I would have loved to come but I promised my mother that I'd give her some help while I'm off. She really needs it at the moment.'

'That's a shame, Ellie, but maybe another time. Perhaps we could arrange to do something when I get back and you're settled into your new job.'

'I'd really like that,' Ellie assured him, sincerely.

They swapped contact details, Ian promising to ring her soon. Joined by Emily and Nigel, who were circulating round their guests, the conversation shifted to the honeymoon, Ellie keen to hear all the details and Emily more than happy to oblige her. When Emily opened up the photograph album, Ellie vaguely noticed that Nigel and Ian had started talking about football. Dismissing them, the women laughed and ignored them, Ellie a captive audience for all Emily's tales.

That was just what I needed, thought Ellie as she carefully drove home, looking forward to her warm, cosy bed and the promise of a lie in. It was a pity that she'd had to decline the invitation to Scotland but her parents had to come first, there were no two ways about it. Still, Ian had said he would get in touch with her and that was definitely something to look forward to. In many ways, life was looking up. She had erased Jeremy from her memory, at least she hoped she had, the perils of Whitby Ward already seemed far behind her and there was just a certain indefinable quality about Ian which caused a slight internal fluttering that was rather pleasant.

18

The first part of Ellie's so-called holiday passed before she knew it. Quickly, she settled into a routine. Each morning, after hastily tidying up and putting her own house in order, she would make her way to her parents' house, usually arriving by elevenses' time, unless she stopped to shop on the way. By this time, Keith would be up and dressed. He still refused point blank to let his daughter assist with any of his more personal needs. From her arrival, Ellie would take over. Diana needed little persuasion to sit in a chair with her feet up, though she offered token protestations but invariably gave in, secretly delighted to relinquish most of the work to Ellie.

To Ellie's mind, Keith's condition seemed to have plateaued. His speech, unintelligible to all but Diana, in the manner of a young child and its mother, never sounded to change. His swallowing was precarious with frequent choking outbursts and his breathing often laboured. Totally dependent now on help to transfer from bed to chair, or chair to toilet, he and Diana had developed a system which, despite its looking clumsy and ergonomically unsound, worked and latterly there had been far fewer falls to deal with. Emotionally he was flat and subversive, showing neither interest nor hedonism. The only time there was a flicker of animation on his face was when Diana or Ellie came into the room.

Ellie had always known that her parents were two of the lucky few who had a symbiotic relationship. Their mutual love had supported them through many years of marriage and it was evident now that it had never been stronger since Keith's diagnosis, a testing time for the most secure of couples. Both were acutely aware of the finite time that was left for them to be together, the bond between them was invincible and Ellie, observing them each day, was humbled by what she saw, understanding now why they did not wish to be separated or have their privacy invaded by outsiders.

Once the housework was out of the way, any washing done and a light lunch made and cleared away, the rest of the day stretched ahead with little to recommend it. Ellie chastised herself for feeling bored and a touch frustrated, finding it difficult to relax when her everyday lifestyle was carried out at a canter. Her offers to take Keith out in his wheelchair were either refused or stymied by the January weather. She tried urging her mother to go out, to have her hair done or rummage through the sales but Diana, privately thinking that any activity that required energy expenditure was anathema to her, declined politely explaining that she would much rather stay with Keith.

So Ellie sat with them, initially enjoying the unaccustomed luxury of uninterrupted time to read but soon starting to feel restless. As she curled up in the chair, supposedly engrossed in her book, she eyed her parents sneakily and, not for the first time, marvelled at her mother's fortitude and patience.

Dr Urquhart visited, jovial yet alert for problems.

'Great news,' he announced triumphantly as he curled up his stethoscope and put it back in his bag after listening to Keith's chest, 'there's a bed for you at St Lambert's tomorrow. I'll arrange some transport to pick you up. It'll just be for a fortnight but it's amazing how you can both recharge your batteries in that time.'

'That's terrific,' agreed Ellie.

'It's not giving us much notice,' worried Diana, slowly reaching for her husband's hand. Now that his transfer was imminent she was not sure if she wanted it to go ahead. 'Could we possibly postpone it for a week?'

'There's plenty of time to get ready,' contradicted Ellie.

'If it works out well, this could be a regular arrangement,' Dr Urquhart went on. 'Keith, you could have, say, four weeks at home and then one or two at the hospice. How does that sound?'

'Well...' Diana's voice was full of doubt but she did not want to appear ungrateful.

Dr Urquhart put his hand on her shoulder.

'Give it a try, Diana. Go into this with an open mind. I think it'll do you both good.'

'Yes, doctor. Keith, what do you think?'

Keith grimaced but looked resigned.

'Mum...' began Ellie, but Dr Urquhart stalled her.

'The ambulance will pick him up mid-morning. That leaves plenty of time to settle in. You can go in the ambulance with him, Diana, and stay as long as you like.'

'That's right, Mum. I can follow on in my car and bring you home. It's only on the other side of town.'

Their assurances did little to assuage Diana's indecision. Much as she wanted a rest from looking after Keith, she felt disloyal. While they were together, they were managing to jog along satisfactorily; a change such as this to their routine might rock the boat too much. Plus there was that unthinkable question starting to form in her mind, which she was trying hard to ignore and push away – would she want him back?

Ellie was upbeat and positive after Dr Urquhart had left. Diana tried to mirror her mood but in spite of her best efforts spent much of the rest of the day sitting silently very close to Keith, as if a countdown were ticking away and not wanting him out of her sight.

The next morning was brighter; even a pallid sun put in an appearance, low in the sky but enough to instil some cheer into the three of them. By the time Ellie arrived, earlier than usual by design, Keith was already sitting waiting, his coat on, his packed bag in the hallway. Diana was restless, marching up and down, checking the clock and peering out of the window, unable to settle. She fussed overprotectively when two ambulance men, who would not have been out of place on stage as a comedy duo, arrived to pick Keith up. Their witty badinage was infectious. Diana could not fail to laugh at some of their dreadful jokes and even Keith had to smile. Ellie waved them off, promising to meet up with them shortly.

'What a remarkable place,' Diana enthused as Ellie carefully negotiated her car up the long and winding drive to the road in the dark. It was nearly teatime and Diana had spent the whole afternoon at the hospice, ensuring that Keith was comfortably settled in, that the nurses knew of all his little foibles and that they had taken down the correct details of all his medications. She had been reluctant to leave even then, believing that no one would be able to care for him quite like she did.

Ellie had experienced the hospice ambience before and knew of the almost magical way in which anxieties and fears evaporated as soon as you entered through the front doors. She could see the change on her father's face, relief that he had come to such an attractive place with a charming bedroom of his own and relaxation that he had been taken out of the increasingly tense environment at home He had even managed to eat a small amount of lunch and Diana, encouraged by this hint of improvement, had eaten a piece of home-made cake with him. She had lovingly unpacked his bag and put his clothes in the chest of drawers and washing things in the little bathroom. Before she left, the nurses had settled him beautifully in bed and she could imagine him there now, with the colourful duvet over him, listening to the radio.

They had decided, or rather Ellie had and she had been backed up by the nurse, not to come back in the evening to visit. Keith was worn out and needed to rest and Diana had been advised to do likewise.

'Shall we go out for something to eat, Mum?' asked Ellie as they drew into the town centre.

'I don't think so, dear. What if they ring about your dad? I'd never forgive myself. Anyway, I'm not overly hungry, so I don't think I would do justice to a big meal. Another day perhaps?'

'Whatever you want, Mum. I'll make us something at home.'

The evening was spent exceedingly quietly. Ellie found that she was peeking at her watch more than once. When Diana announced that she was going to bed, Ellie offered to stay over. Diana refused. She was looking forward to some peace and tranquillity plus the lie in she had been promising herself for so long. As Ellie was leaving, Diana called after her.

'You could think about a holiday now, Ellie. Dad's fine and I will be as well.'

'Are you sure?'

'Yes, perfectly. As I say, we're sorted here now so it's your turn to have a bit of a treat. I hate to think of you spending all your time off looking after us.'

Ellie looked doubtful.

'Well, I don't know. But I'll think about it overnight. What time shall I come round in the morning?'

'Late, darling. Tell you what, I'll give you a call when I'm up. Let's both have a really good sleep.'

Ellie hugged her mother and ran to the car, waving as she drove off.

Back in her own house, she changed into her night things after a hot bath and settled on the sofa, curling up with a glass of wine and a packet of crisps. She thought about what her mother's parting words had been. It was tempting, she mused. Her father was safe in the hands of professionals, which meant of course that her mother could recuperate. Ian's invitation loomed large in her mind and after only the briefest of prevarications, she went to the telephone and dialled his number.

19

Ian met Ellie off the train at Inverness. He was wrapped up against the cold in a long striped scarf and a duffel coat that came down to his knees. Luckily he had forewarned Ellie about the temperature so she too was dressed in many layers. They gave each other a friendly hug and he led her to his car.

'Goodness,' Ellie blew on her gloved hands in an attempt to warm them. 'I thought it was cold at home but it's really freezing here. Have you had any snow?'

'Not yet,' Ian replied, turning the car heater on to its highest setting. 'The countryside looks stunning. Just wait until you see it.'

It was nearly an hour's drive to the house. They turned off main roads on to less populated ones and from there on to single-track lanes that wound their way higher into the hills. Ellie kept looking back over her shoulder, asking Ian to stop so she could give her full attention to the view. He obliged and she jumped out, drinking in the crystal-clear air while watching her smoky curling breath then leapt quickly back into the warm. Ian asked after her parents and was pleased to hear that the hospice was proving to be such a success.

'Dad is so happy there. They are just brilliant with him. There's a huge bath that he can wallow in as well as aromatherapy and massage. And as for mum, she's still tired but I think she's better than she was.'

'I suppose she's visiting him every day.'

Ellie nodded.

'Correct. I don't think that we'd ever be able to stop her doing that. But at least it's not as stressful as having to care for him single-handedly.'

'Here we are!'

Ian turned right up a small and bumpy track which meandered towards a large grey stone property surrounded by rhododendron bushes and pine trees.

'You should see this place in the early summer,' Ian advised Ellie. 'The colours are incredible. Come on in. Mum'll have the kettle on.'

'That'd be great. How often do you come up here, Ian?'

'Not as often as I'd like on account of work. My parents come up every six weeks or so. They love it here.'

Ellie looked around her. It was a very special place. Secluded from any other sign of civilisation, the view stretching for an eternity, and the only sound she could hear was that of birdsong. She felt a million miles from work and home.

Clive and Christina greeted Ellie warmly. They ushered her into a beautiful lounge where a log fire was crackling and spitting happily in the hearth. On the table in front of the fireplace was a pot of tea, some cups and a rich fruitcake. Ellie, who had resisted without difficulty any food available on the train, was ravenous and found it no hardship to eat a large slice that Christina cut and handed to her.

'I wish I could take the credit for this,' Christina apologised, 'but I have to confess that I bought it at the local village store. So it's definitely home made, but just not by me.'

'It's excellent, whoever made it,' Ellie replied diplomatically. 'I had no idea I was so hungry.'

'Dinner won't be until eight, so I thought we might need something to keep us going until then. When you've finished, Ian will show you to your room, so that you can unpack. Please just make yourself at home.'

'Thank you so much – you're very kind.'

It was impossible to find anything about the house to dislike. Her room, with a window looking out over the side of the house, was small but all the warmer for that. Apart from the bed and a huge, heavy wardrobe, there was still room for a cosy armchair by the window and a small table on which there was a selection of country magazines. Though not entirely sure that she was the slightest bit interested in hunting, shooting and fishing, Ellie felt sure that she would enjoy thumbing through them last thing at night.

The next few days were hugely enjoyable. After colossal cooked breakfasts, Ellie and Ian went out, steeling themselves against the cold weather that continued unabated. They spent one morning in Inverness, exploring the town and shops but the remainder of the time walked in the hills, or down by the nearby loch. Ian taught Ellie how to skim stones across the water and they had competitions to see who could do best. Ellie proved to be a quick learner and was soon able to equal her teacher. Lunch was either hearty sandwiches in floury rolls prepared by Christina or bowls of steaming hot soup in local hotels, accompanied by bread fresh from the oven, smothered with creamy butter. One afternoon they took two horses out from the local trekking centre. Sturdy highland ponies with long shaggy coats and faithful eyes carried them up into the hills and down again, their sure-footedness never failing as they picked their path along the stony tracks. Ellie was thrilled, not having ridden since her youth and Ian virtually had to drag her away from her pony, which she kept hugging and patting while feeding it carrots and ginger biscuits.

The fresh air generated large appetites, so they were more than ready for Christina's cooking in the evenings. Ellie tasted steaks so tender that her knife slid through them, wild salmon and even haggis. Clive provided a selection of excellent wines that perfectly complemented his wife's cooking and they sat around the table talking, discussing and laughing, all the while Ellie feeling completely at ease.

After Clive and Christina had bid them good night, Ellie and Ian retired to the lounge, sitting in front of the fire, sipping malt whisky or the remains of the wine, talking long into the night. Ian quickly proved to be a sensitive listener, knowing when to speak and when not to. Ellie, possibly because she was relaxed by good food and wine, but more probably because she simply felt so comfortable with him, told

Ian all about her parents, her sadness at her father's diagnosis and the horrifying acceleration of his decline. Reminiscing, she talked about him before he had become ill, how he had influenced her growing up, what an energetic and generous man he had been, living life to the full, taking each day as it came. Ian learned how Ellie's parents had met, bumping into each other as they simultaneously tried to board a bus, how their courtship had flourished as they arranged to synchronise their daily journeys to work and how they had married within the year, Ellie arriving almost precisely nine months later. Sensing permission to continue from Ian's non-verbal cues, Ellie went on to tell him stories of her own childhood, school, tennis matches, pets and ponies. Her confession that she had been something of a swat as an adolescent made Ellie cringe but Ian laugh so she assured him all that had changed when she went to university and discovered her new-found freedom. Without any further encouragement, she revealed brief details of her significant relationships and, before she knew it, was telling him about Jeremy. Openly, she told Ian how she had made a terrible and humiliating mistake that she could hardly bear to think about. Ian said nothing, knowing that his role was not to comment or judge, but flattered and pleased that Ellie was being so honest. He was enjoying finding out all about her, starting to understand how she thought and felt, hoping that he was helping her and wishing that he could ease the pain she felt about her father.

Ellie rang both her mother and the hospice daily. The latter calmly informed her that all was well and that her father was continuing to enjoy his stay, which they had managed to extend for a further week with his agreement. Her mother sounded bright and chirpy, asking Ellie for all the details of her stay, repeatedly changing the subject when Ellie tried to steer it back to her and at the end of each call, Ellie would take stock and conclude that she had learnt nothing at all about how her mother was.

The end of her visit was nearing too quickly. Ellie was due to return in three days and a large part of her already did not want to go. The next day she and Ian walked for miles in the morning. The tables were turned this time and she made a point of finding out all about Ian, feeling that she had rather monopolised their conversations previously. To her delight, she found they had a similar love of animals, books and food, though to be fair, Ian's interest was largely eating rather than cooking. His job often took him abroad but, whilst he enjoyed visiting foreign countries, he knew that he would never want to be based in any of them. As they marched, half jogged, down the hill back to the house, he took Ellie's hand and waited to see her reaction. Much to his relief, she did not pull away but looked at him and smiled.

At Ellie's request, they rode again in the afternoon taking the same ponies off in a different direction, cantering along the riverbank and splashing through the water. Although it was fun, Ellie felt that it was all tinged with sadness. Being away up here, far from everyone and everything had been such wonderful escapism and she guiltily felt that the last thing she wanted to do was go back to Harrogate.

Christina was busy in the kitchen, conjuring up yet another mouth-watering dish for dinner. Wonderful aromas met their noses as they arrived back and hung their coats up in the hall.

'Dinner will be about an hour,' a voice called. 'There's plenty of hot water for baths so help yourselves.'

'Thank you so much,' Ellie said, going into the kitchen to find Christina. 'Is there anything I can do to help?'

'No, nothing at all, but thank you for offering.' Christina stood back from the cooker and scrutinised Ellie. 'This break's doing you good. You look so much better than when you arrived.'

'I feel better,' agreed Ellie, 'I'm having the most wonderful time. I'm so glad I came.'

'You're welcome anytime. Just remember that.'

'I will, thank you.'

Upstairs in her bedroom, Ellie gazed out of the window. She could just make out the shape of the trees in the dark. How peaceful it all was. This time next week it would seem like a dream.

She bathed and dressed, putting on smart but casual clothes and a little make up. There was just time to make her telephone calls before a pre-prandial drink. The report from the hospice was much as she expected. Her father had spent the day quietly but had seen the consultant who had suggested some changes to his treatment that might help his more troublesome symptoms. But there was no reply when she rang her mother. Leaving the phone to ring and ring, in case her mother was in the bathroom, Ellie was still disappointed and presumed that her mother must be en route to or from the hospice. It was a little curious, however, as usually she did not like to go out after dark alone. Most likely, she had popped round to see Gordon and Sheila; that would be it. Oh well, thought Ellie, I'll try again after dinner.

Ian greeted her with a glass of white wine. He looked refreshed and attractive, Ellie decided, glad that she had made a little extra effort with her own appearance that evening. Clive joined them and they sat with their drinks, sharing details of their days. Ian brought out a map and they traced the ground they had covered that morning to show Clive, leaving Ellie surprised at how far they had been.

'The possibilities for walking are endless,' Clive showed them. 'Next time you come up, Ellie, you'll still have plenty of choice.'

Ellie's heart gave a little skip. It was so nice to be so accepted and welcome. Clive stood up to refill their glasses when they heard the telephone ring in the hall and Christina shout that she would answer it.

'Ellie?' Christina's head popped round the lounge door. 'It's for you. It's Nigel.'

'Nigel?' she echoed. 'I wonder what he wants. I expect he's just riddled with curiosity as to what I'm up to.'

Chuckling, she went and picked up the receiver.

'Hi, Nigel, checking up on me are you?'

'Ellie, oh Ellie. I'm sorry to ring but something terrible has happened.'

Ellie felt her knees turn to water. A feeling akin to an electric shock coursed through her chest as adrenaline surged through her body.

'Is it dad?'

'No, no. He's fine. I went to see him today actually. Ellie – it's your mum.'

'What's happened?'

'She was brought into A&E late this afternoon. She'd collapsed at home. Fortunately a neighbour was with her. I think you should come home as soon as possible.'

'Collapsed? What's wrong with her?'

'She's having some tests done. They're keeping her in for a few days. She's quite comfortable at the moment.'

'Don't insult me by talking to me like any old patient's relative, Nigel. What is going on?'

'Ellie, I've told you as much as I know. Emily was on duty in A&E when Diana came in, so she rang me, knowing that you were up in Scotland with Ian and gave me your number. You need to come home.'

'I'm coming, don't worry. I can set off now.'

'No, don't do that. Just come down tomorrow, in the daylight and don't rush.'

'I'm going to ring the hospital now, Nigel. Which ward is she on?'

'Bedale.'

'Which consultant is she under?'

'Dr Barnstaple.'

'Thank goodness for that. Oh, Nigel, I knew I shouldn't have come away. I could have prevented this. She was tired out and I didn't see just how bad she was.'

'Calm down, Ellie, and stop babbling. Ring the ward and then I'm sure you'll feel better.'

'Okay, I'm going to do that now. Thank you for ringing, Nigel. Would you go and see her for me this evening? Please?'

'Of course I will. Then I'll ring you back, I promise. Speak to you later.'

Ellie's hand was trembling so much that she could barely dial the hospital number. It seemed an eternity before the switchboard answered. She shivered as she waited to be put through to the ward, impatient for them to pick up at their end. Her prayers eventually answered, Ellie spoke to the staff nurse, who passed her on the registrar who, as luck would have it, was still on the ward. Ellie heard him tell her that her mum was settled, in no pain and having a bite to eat. She was due to have more tests in the morning and see the consultant. He knew little about the circumstances that had brought about her admission. At least Ellie felt some peace of mind from speaking to him, understanding that there was no immediacy about her return.

'I'll be down tomorrow. Will you pass that message on to her, please?'

'Of course, Ellie. Try not to worry. We'll take good care of her.'

Christina, emerging from the kitchen to summon the others to the table, found a trembling Ellie sitting on the bottom stair, hugging her knees.

'Ellie dear, what's wrong?'

Falteringly, Ellie explained and Christina squeezed in beside her and put her arm around her waist.

'You poor thing. What a dreadful shock.'

'I have to go in the morning, first thing.'

'Of course you do.'

'I'm so sorry if I'm causing any inconvenience. I've loved it here, every minute of it.'

'I can see you have, Ellie, and we've loved having you. Let's all look forward to your next visit. I've a feeling it won't be long before you're up here again. Come on, you're cold. Let's go and join the others then you can warm up by the fire and have a drink. Luckily dinner can wait a few minutes.'

Clive and Ian, on hearing Ellie's news, were equally sympathetic. They sat her in the chair nearest the fire and urged her to have some of her wine.

'I'll drive you down tomorrow,' Ian told her. 'There's no way that you're going to sit on a train, all on your own, worrying yourself to death.'

Ellie opened her mouth to protest but he silenced her with a look. There was no disputing the fact that his company would be immeasurably helpful.

Slowly, Ellie warmed up. Christina took Clive back into the kitchen, ostensibly to perform some task integral to the dinner preparations that he alone could do and Ian moved closer to Ellie.

'Is there anything I can do?' he asked.

'Not really, but thanks. I've just got to try and keep this into perspective. It sounds as though she was just tired out and fainted. I'll feel better when Nigel rings back because he will have seen her. I'm sorry that I've spoilt the evening.'

'Don't be daft,' Ian stroked her hair gently. 'If this had to happen, I'm glad it did when we were here to help.'

'That is so kind, thank you.'

Ellie was on edge, waiting for her call. Uncharacteristically, she toyed with her starter, hardly tasting the homemade pâté that had probably taken Christina most of the afternoon to make. Her mind was on Bedale Ward and not on the heated debate that Ian was having with his father about the current political situation. Likewise the casseroled venison in a rich red wine sauce served with dauphinoise potatoes and fresh vegetables she failed to finish, even though there was no denying the fact that it was delicious. As the others were finished, the phone rang and without waiting for anyone else, Ellie flew to the hall.

'Nigel?'

'Hi, Ellie. Calm down. I've just seen your mum. I knew you'd be in a state so I've come to the mess to ring you. She's okay. Very tired and a bit pale but chatting away as usual. She told me to tell you to stay where you are and come back when you'd planned but I warned her you'd be having none of that and that you'd see her tomorrow.'

'Did she say what happened?'

'She can't remember a lot. Apparently, she'd invited Sheila round for a coffee, was putting the kettle on and the next thing she knew was that she was having her blood pressure taken by a nurse in A&E.'

'That doesn't sound so bad, does it? I feel better now. Nigel, you're a star. Thank you for doing that for me.'

'You're still coming tomorrow, aren't you?'

'Definitely. Ian is going to drive me down. We'll set off after breakfast so we should be there in the afternoon.'

'I'll see you then, Ellie. I'm sure you can relax now and enjoy your evening.'

They said good-bye and Ellie, wiping a small tear of relief away, returned to the others and repeated the conversation. Feeling infinitely better, she ate two helpings of chocolate and ginger sponge with vanilla sauce and found that she was keen to join in with the others again. That evening though, she went up to bed early, to pack her things ready for an early start the next morning.

Sleep, however, was elusive. Her body was physically tired from walking and riding, but her mind was alert and refused to lie down. Waking frequently, she witnessed more or less every hour of the night on the bedside clock and when it was finally time to get up she felt rough and slightly hung over.

Christina was busy in the kitchen.

'I've just done you some toast. There's cereal if you want. I didn't think you'd feel much like a cooked breakfast today,' she said thoughtfully.

Ellie managed a large cup of tea and half a slice of toast. Ian, arriving shortly after Ellie, had no difficulty eating a large plate of kedgeree and three slices of toast. He ate quickly and efficiently, knowing that Ellie was fidgeting to be off and it was barely light when they left.

They talked little on the journey, spending more time listening to the radio and music. Ellie managed to doze a little, on and off, wishing that they could go faster and get there sooner. Ian drove heroically, as fast as he dared within the speed limits. They had to stop twice, once for petrol and once for refreshments, but he could see that Ellie was itching to get back on the road, suggesting that they buy sandwiches and cans of pop to eat and drink in the car rather than sit down in the café.

Reaching Harrogate mid afternoon was not the most opportune time to try to find a place in the hospital car park. Ian, worried that Ellie would just jump out and he would lose her, nipped into a space incurring the wrath of a harassed-looking woman who thought the gap was hers.

'What would you like me to do?' asked Ian, half running to keep up with Ellie as she made a beeline for the entrance.

'Come with me, please. I'd like you to meet my mum anyway and I know she would like to meet you.'

'If you're sure, I'd be honoured.'

Bedale Ward was at the far end of the hospital and they hurried down the long corridor, Ellie leading, occasionally saying hello to people who passed by. Diana was in a single room just inside the ward. Barely waiting for permission from the ward sister, Ellie tapped on the door and went in. Diana was lying back on the pillows. Ellie was shocked by how pale she looked with no make up on and how bony her shoulders looked in her thin nightdress.

'Mum!'

Diana reached out her arms to her daughter. Ian stood back, not wanting to intrude. Ellie perched on the side of the bed and motioned to Ian to come in.

'This is Ian.'

'How do you do, Mrs Woods. Ian Bonnington.'

He held out his hand and Diana grasped it in both of hers.

'How lovely to meet you. Ellie has told me quite a lot about you. I'm only sorry that I'm here in hospital when I meet you.'

'How are you feeling today? It sounds as if you had a bit of a scare yesterday,' he went on conversationally.

'Yes, Mum, tell us what happened. When are you going home?'

'Ellie, love, calm down. I've seen the consultant this morning and I'll be staying in a few days. I'm sure he'll have a word with you, I've told him he can. As to what happened, I really can't remember very clearly. I know I hadn't slept well and I didn't feel like breakfast. Sheila came round and persuaded me that I ought to try to have something, so for a treat we were going to have hot chocolate. I went into the kitchen but after that it's all very vague. The consultant says he thinks I fainted. Apparently I'm anaemic.'

'You do look very pale. I haven't seen you without your make up for ages.'

'Personally,' interrupted Ian, 'I think you look lovely. Pale, but lovely. I can see where your beautiful daughter gets her looks from.'

Despite her pallor, Diana blushed and Ellie groaned.

'Tell me about Scotland,' suggested Diana and Ellie did not need to be asked twice.

She was just describing the pony she had ridden when Dr Barnstaple's head appeared round the door.

'Hello, I thought I heard some laughing. You're looking better, Diana, for having some visitors.'

Ellie introduced Ian.

'How's Mum doing? Can she come home soon?'

'One thing at a time, Ellie. Can we have a word?'

Ellie looked at her mother, who nodded to her and Dr Barnstaple.

'Of course.'

'Let's go into my office.'

20

Ellie followed Tim Barnstaple past the nurses' station and into the small room that he used as an office. She could not help but compare it with Jeremy's spacious, airy office. But while Jeremy's was minimalist and impersonal, Tim's was crammed with books, papers, photos and paintings which had obviously been done by young children. He tried ineffectually to clear a chair for Ellie to sit on but ended up with a pile of things in both his hands that, not knowing what to do with, he balanced precariously on the top of another pile. Slowly, the whole tower slid sideways and he reached out to catch it and then, defeated, placed everything on the floor.

Ellie sat down and looked at him expectantly. He looked at her seriously. Suddenly she knew there was something very wrong. Why wasn't he smiling at her as he usually did? Why had he asked her into his office rather than talk in Diana's room? She started to feel sick and her mouth went dry.

'Ellie, we need to talk. I'm afraid that the news I have for you is not good.'

Ellie said nothing but swallowed hard.

'Yesterday, your mother came into A&E. She'd collapsed at home...'

'I know, she told me. She's been worn out looking after Dad, who has MND.'

'They did a few tests in A&E and found that she was very anaemic. Her haemoglobin is only five, less than half what it should be.'

'No wonder she's so pale,' Ellie contributed.

'When she came up to the ward we were able to get a better history from her. She told us that for a long time she's felt short of breath, had no appetite and been losing weight...'

'As I said, she's been busy looking after my Dad.'

'Let me finish, Ellie. Just after your father was diagnosed, she apparently found a lump in her breast.'

Ellie gasped.

'She did nothing, partly not wanting to accept that it was there and partly because she put her husband first. She showed us the lump. It's very large and obviously malignant.'

'Oh no!'

'I'm afraid what I have to say next is not easy for either of us. There are signs on your mother's chest x-ray that the tumour has spread to her lungs. In addition she has fluid on the right lung, which is not helping her breathing. This of course is very serious indeed. She also has signs that the tumour has spread to her liver and bones. In other words, it is widely disseminated.'

I don't think I'm really here, thought Ellie. This is the sort of thing that happens in books and on television. It's usually me breaking the bad news to other people. This is unreal.

'I don't know what to say,' Ellie muttered, then burst out with, 'why didn't she do something about it? She would have known what a lump meant.'

Tim Barnstaple said nothing.

'We're keeping her comfortable and she's due a blood transfusion in the morning. That'll make her feel a lot better, albeit temporarily. Then we can all sit down and talk about where we go from here.'

'What about some chemotherapy?' asked Ellie eagerly. 'That could slow the progression down, couldn't it? I'll persuade her to have some. Once she's had the blood transfusion, she'll have much more energy and a better appetite, so she'll feel more positive.'

'Let's wait and see, Ellie. We have to be honest here and not build up your hopes unfairly but it may well be that we are looking at palliative care only.'

'I'll speak to her, see what she says. There must be something we can offer her. I'll...' Ellie ran out of things to say.

'You need some time, Ellie. Just like your mother does. To come to terms with what I've told you. When do you start your next job?'

'Not until the middle of next week.'

'Good. Now I think you should go have a few moments here on your own. I'll speak to you again tomorrow, all right?'

Ellie nodded, dumbly.

'I'm so, so sorry.' Tim Barnstaple left the room after one of the worst moments of his working life.

Ellie, still feeling as though she was trapped in some hideous nightmare, sat gazing at all the different things in the office. Any moment she would wake up and find that she was in bed, at home, possibly in Scotland. Scotland? Was she really there only a few hours ago? Tears slowly started to creep down her cheeks and she put her hands to her face. She didn't hear the door open quietly and Ian come in. His heart wept for her as he saw her there, sobbing. He went over, knelt beside her and wrapped his strong arms around her, feeling her lean against his chest as if it was the most natural response in the world.

'Sshh, I'm here for you.'

They sat there for what was possibly an eternity. When Ellie finally felt that she could not cry any more, she lifted her blotchy, tear-bespattered face to him and he simply hugged her more.

'Do you know?' she whispered.

'Yes. Dr Barnstaple had a word with me. There's nothing I can say to ease things for you, Ellie. But I am always here for you.'

'I ought to go back and see Mum.'

'Are you sure?'

'Yes. Sorry,' Ellie wiped her nose inelegantly and sniffed loudly.

'Here,' Ian dug deep in his pocket and produced a handkerchief which Ellie took gratefully.

'I must look dreadful,' she decided.

'Do you want me to come with you to see your mother?' offered Ian.

'No, not just now. Do you mind?' Ellie looked at him.

He smiled. 'Of course not. I understand completely. Tell you what. I'll go for a wander, perhaps have a coffee, definitely find a toilet and then come back and pick you up.'

'Thank you so much.'

He kissed Ellie softly on the cheek and then on the back of her hand, rather in the manner of a chivalrous Prince Charming and backed out of the room. Ellie managed a noise approximating to a small laugh. Giving him a moment to leave the ward, she found her way back to her mother's room.

'Hello, darling. Come and sit with me.'

Tears fell anew as Ellie went and balanced on the bed beside Diana.

'Don't cry, please. You'll start me off.'

'Why, Mum?'

'I had to look after Dad,' she replied simply.

'But surely you knew when you found the lump in your breast that it could be serious.'

'Yes, I suppose I did but at the time we were still reeling from your dad's diagnosis and struggling to deal with that. I felt I couldn't introduce another problem into his life. He was relying on me to look after him. I couldn't have kept going for radiation treatment or chemotherapy or whatever it is they do. So the simplest thing was just to ignore it. It didn't seem to be getting any bigger.'

'But, Mum, you must have realised when you were getting short of breath and losing weight,' protested Ellie.

'Well, to be honest, I just thought I was tired out. I knew I wasn't eating well. I couldn't sit and eat a big plateful of food when Dad was just having liquids. It wouldn't have been fair. So I thought that was why I was losing weight. To start with I was quite pleased. All my clothes fitted really well and I was rather chuffed with my new shape. But of course, it didn't stop at that. I went on losing weight and by then I just didn't want to eat at all.'

'I should have noticed something was wrong,' Ellie admonished herself.

Diana took her daughter's hand.

'It would have made no difference at all, Ellie darling, if you had. I wouldn't have gone to the doctor's. I had to be there for Dad. I told you that when we went on the cruise, I promised him that I would be there for him and look after him and nothing would stop me. I had to keep my word.'

Ellie felt exasperated.

'Does Dad know about this?'

Diana turned away from Ellie and looked towards the window.

'No.'

'Does he know you're in hospital?'

'The nurses let me ring and speak to him yesterday. I just said I was having some tests. Will you be going to see him today?'

Ellie was momentarily bewildered. She had been so blown away by the revelations of the day that she had barely given a second thought to her father.

'Yes, of course,' she faltered. 'What shall I tell him?'

'Just tell him I'm fine, send him all my love and I'll see him very soon.'

'But what about your treatment here?''

'So many questions, Ellie. Let's just take this one day at a time. I'm sure they'll let me home soon.'

'Oh, Mum, I just can't believe all this is happening. It was bad enough with Dad being ill but now you as well...'

Tears welled in her eyes again and Diana rested Ellie's head on her shoulder.

'Hush, try not to cry. Tell me about this young man of yours. Isn't he something? He was quite delightful when he was left talking to me. He's very taken with you, that's for sure. Come on, tell me more.'

Between sniffs, Ellie told her mother how she had met Ian and how their relationship had started to develop. Diana made suitably impressed noises as she gently stroked Ellie's hair. Gradually the stroking became less frequent and finally stopped. Ellie could hear deep, rhythmic respirations and delicately extracted herself from her mother's arms. Diana was fast asleep, her face relaxed by the rest, making her look young and vulnerable. Ellie softly kissed her mother's cheek and crept from the room, after writing a note to say she would be back later.

Ellie paused on her way out to let the ward sister know that she would come back later. She found Ian sitting in the patients' day room, chatting to a lady in a threadbare, mauve dressing-gown, who was showing him her catheter bag, proudly. Impressed by the fact that he seemed to get on with everyone, Ellie watched the two of them for a few moments before coughing strategically when there was a hiatus in their conversation.

Ian drove her to the hospice and again asked for his instructions.

'I'd like you to come in. Mum doesn't want me to tell him any details and that's going to be really difficult for me, so if you didn't mind, it might be really helpful if you were there.'

'It would be my pleasure,' replied Ian, manoeuvring his car into a small space.

Unlike in the hospital, the floors were carpeted and they made their way noiselessly to Keith's room. He too was in bed, head lolling to one side, secretions rattling in his throat, possibly watching the television that was on at the other side of the room. Ellie hesitated in the doorway, not wanting to go in, not having a clue what she was going to say. Gently from behind, Ian pushed her in. She turned to look at him and he nodded, encouragingly, taking her hand.

'Dad, hello!' Ellie did her best to sound cheery.

He turned his eyes to her and coughed.

Ellie went over and kissed him then reached for a tissue to wipe the saliva that was trickling from the corner of his mouth. She noticed his gaze move from her to Ian and introduced them. They sat, one on either side of the bed, Ellie resting her hand on her father's arm as she tried to keep up a more or less constant monologue, repeating her report on Scotland almost word for word. As she found herself running out of things to say, Keith tried to make a noise but ended up coughing, causing Ellie to panic and ring for one of the nurses to come and help.

Once he was settled again, Ellie wondered what she could say next. Ian, reading her mind, solved the dilemma for her.

'We've just been to the hospital to see Diana.'

Ellie glared at him for mentioning the one topic she really wanted to avoid. Keith looked appealingly at her.

'She's, she's... er...missing you, Dad. She sends all her love and promises to see you soon.'

Keith struggled unsuccessfully to speak.

'I took Ian to meet her. They got on like a house on fire.'

'She's very comfortable,' Ian corroborated.

'Yes, she is,' Ellie agreed, glad of the prompt. 'She's had some tests and she has some more tomorrow. One of my colleagues, Dr Barnstaple, is looking after her; he's really good and very nice.'

'We're going back to see her this evening,' added Ian.

'Yes, just to let her know we've seen you. So we can give you more news tomorrow.'

Keith sighed loudly. His eyes were full of concern and bewilderment.

'Don't worry, Dad. Please,' begged Ellie.

Run out of things to say, they sat in silence, interrupted only by futile attempts by Ellie to tell her father snippets of news. But he seemed to have switched off, no longer showing any signs of interest. He had retreated into his own, secret and troubled world, where nobody knew what was going through his thoughts; his facial expressions so limited that they could give no clues.

Ian and Ellie left a short while after. They sat in Ian's car, in the car park.

'That was awful,' admitted Ellie.

'Poor man. What a despicable and undignified disease,' Ian said, voicing his thoughts and shuddering.

'I feel that I've let them both down. But I just don't know how to handle this. I'm so sorry to burden you with all of this, Ian. It's not fair on you at all.'

'I couldn't bear to contemplate you having to deal with this on your own, Ellie.'

Ellie smiled at him.

'Look,' decided Ian. 'I don't know about you but I'm pretty tired. We've driven hundreds of miles, your emotions have been put through a blender and we still have to go back and visit your mum. It's nearly seven now. Shall we go and get something to eat first. I think we're both hungrier than we realise. We could go and grab a bite somewhere in town and then go to the hospital. How does that sound?'

Ellie gave his suggestion some thought. Food was the last thing on her mind but she suspected that he was right and she was glad that she had someone with her who could think logically. She didn't have the strength not to go along with his plans.

'That sounds good,' she managed to say.

'Excellent. What do you fancy? Indian, Thai, Chinese?'

'You choose.'

'Right. Seatbelts on and off we go.'

After a glass of red wine, Ellie felt immeasurably calmer and was even looking forward to the seafood pasta that Ian had chosen for, insisting that she needed more than the small salad she originally chose. She had even started to nibble at one of the hunks of fresh bread that had been placed on the table to assuage their appetites while they waited. Ian tried hard to encourage Ellie to talk, believing that this would do her more good than ruminating on her worries. She looked exhausted, her usually cheerful and attractive face washed out, her hair lank and her posture drooping. At least she made a valiant effort with her bowl of pasta, finishing nearly all of it and looking as though she was enjoying it. He toyed with the idea of ordering coffee but seeing that the anxious look, temporarily removed, had returned to Ellie's face, he thought better of it and called for the bill.

225

In the hospital car park he made a decision.

'You go on in, Ellie. You need to spend some time with your mum. I'll wait here.'

Ellie fumbled in her bag.

'I can't have you hanging about. Here are my house keys. Why don't you go there? At least you can make yourself a coffee and watch TV or something. I can easily walk back.'

He raised one eyebrow. 'Sure?'

'Positive. If you bought some milk on the way – there's a garage at the end of the road that will be open, then that would be great. Ian, you've been wonderful.'

'I'll see you later then. Give my best wishes to your mum.'

'I will.'

'Ellie?'

She was halfway out of the car.

'Yes?'

'Where do you live?'

Ellie had to laugh. She gave him the address, closed the car door and waved as he drove off.

Diana was sitting out in the chair next to her bed. On the table in front of her was a half full cup of tea and an uneaten digestive biscuit, a box of tissues, a plastic jug of water with an orange lid and a bowl of grapes.

'Hi, Mum.'

'Hello, darling. How's Dad? Have you been?'

'Yes, we've been. He seems fine. I tried to reassure him about you.'

A pang of guilt ran through Ellie's heart as she knew full well she had not done the best of jobs.

'He seems to like it at the hospice,' Ellie started.

Diana agreed.

'It was just the best thing that could have happened to him. It's taken a huge weight off me, knowing that he's well looked after.'

'If I ask Dr Barnstaple, I might be able to take you to see him. Once you've had your blood transfusion, you're going to feel so much better. By this time tomorrow, you'll be brighter, less breathless. Ian would take you in his car; you could sit in a wheelchair if you don't want to walk...'

Diana laughed softly.

'Oh, Ellie, you are simply the best daughter anyone could have.'

'Well, I don't know about that.'

'Come here.'

Diana hugged her daughter, holding her as close as she could without it hurting. She felt that she could not speak, being on the verge of tears and did not want Ellie to know how upset she was.

'You're so thin, Mum,' gulped Ellie.

'Maybe I'll feel more like eating after the blood as well. Dr Barnstaple – he speaks very highly of you, Ellie – he was talking about some tablets that would make me feel more like eating.'

'Steroids probably. Yes, they do improve the appetite,' Ellie told her, suddenly feeling on surer ground. Diana smiled to herself as Ellie gave her an account of the pros and cons of oral steroids, confident of her facts as she swapped into her role of doctor.

'You know so much, Ellie. I'm so proud of you. We both are, your Dad as well. But you look tired. You've had a long, long day. We both have. Why don't you get off home and come back tomorrow. Try and get some sleep, eh?'

Diana shifted her position, groaning a little as she did so.

'Are you all right, Mum?' Ellie was suddenly concerned.

'I'm fine. Just a pain in my side but it's gone now.' Diana did her best to sound convincing.

'Are you sure? Shall I call for someone? I don't want to go while you feel unwell.'

'No, I'll be fine,' Diana announced, emphatically. 'I think you should go and get some rest. I'm tired too. Plus,' she whispered conspiratorially, 'I think I need to go to the toilet.'

'I can take a hint, Mum. I'll ask the nurse to come in as I go. Good night. Sleep well. See you in the morning.'

'Good night, my darling. You sleep well too.'

Ellie got up and went to the door. As she turned to say a final farewell, Diana spoke first.

'I do love you, Ellie. Look after yourself.'

'I love you too, Mum.'

Ellie fretted as she ambled home in the cold night air, going over the events of the last twenty-four hours, still unable to absorb all that had happened. There was some small consolation in knowing that Ian was waiting for her, as she did not particularly relish the thought of being on her own. Unlocking the front door, she went in, smelling freshly brewed coffee and hearing laughter from the television.

Ian came out to meet her.

'I've made myself at home. I hope that's not a problem. I love your house.'

'No, that's fine.'

'Coffee?'

'Thanks, but I think I'll have some cocoa. I don't want anything that might keep me awake.'

'Shall I do that for you?'

'No, it won't take a moment.'

'Could I just use your phone to ring my parents? I promised them that I would get in touch this evening.'

'Of course. Please pass on my thanks for everything and give them my love.'

'Will do.'

He was about to pick up the telephone when it rang. Knowing that Ellie was watching milk heat up he called out to her, offering to answer it and having been given the go ahead, did so.

'Ellie?'

She came out into the hall, carrying her mug of hot chocolate.

'It's for you. It's the ward... about your mum.'

Ellie knew before she heard anyone speak. Her mother had died.

21

'Ellie,' Dr Barnstaple began, 'there is no way that I can make this easier for you. When I promised to speak to you today, I had no idea it would be like this.'

It was the next morning. Ellie had rushed back to the hospital after receiving her call, aware that there was nothing that she could do but needing to see her mother. The door to her room was closed and the ward seemed incongruously noisy to Ellie who felt that everyone should be paying their last respects to the most wonderful woman she had ever known. She had slowly opened the door. Her mother was on the bed, sensitively laid out by the nurses, a small rose on her pillow beside her head. Somehow, she not only looked at peace but she also looked younger, carefree and there was just the hint of a smile at the corners of her lips. Ellie had seen this look before in the course of her work. It had made her stop and think. Were these people given a glimpse of the new life that awaited them? Was it a message to those left behind, the relatives, grief stricken and confused, to let them know that all was well and not to weep? Or maybe it was just Ellie's interpretation of the mask of death, a way to ease her own sorrow.

She spent only a short time with her mother. Weirdly, she felt awkward and did not know what to do. There seemed no point in talking to her for she could not reply. It was as though her mother was no longer there, her spirit gone, far away, the remaining body a mere vehicle, now discarded, no longer required.

Ian had taken her home, had brought her fresh cocoa and sat beside her until she fell asleep in bed, promising not to leave her. In the morning, when she woke, flabbergasted that she had slept solidly for almost eight hours, he was there, sitting on the bed, waiting for her to wake. He had then run her a bath and while she was busy with her ablutions, had made the breakfast, which he brought up to her, so that she could have a little more time cosseted under the duvet before she had to get dressed. She'd felt safe there. It had been easy to pretend that nothing had happened.

'I think the most likely thing is that your mother had a pulmonary embolism,' Ellie heard Tim Barnstaple continue. 'Talking to Sister Thomas, your mother had been complaining of some pain in the side of her chest earlier in the day.'

'She did when I was there,' Ellie agreed sadly. 'I never thought...'

'Unfortunately, she collapsed while she was on the commode. Quite a common mode of death, as you know. The patient strains to have their bowels open and clots break off from the pelvic veins. What I can assure you is that, whilst sudden, she died very quickly, with little pain.'

He was watching Ellie to gauge her response.

'If it's any consolation, her cancer was far too widely spread for there to have been any hope of treatment. Perhaps this is the best way. She obviously was a very proud lady.'

'She was. She never wanted to be a trouble to anyone. All she ever did was put herself last, after my dad and me.'

'I'm really sorry that this happened, Ellie. How are you today?'

'Well,' she sighed, 'at least I slept like a log so I feel better for that. I can see that this was perhaps best for Mum; she would have hated being a burden to anyone. But how I am going to tell Dad?'

Tim brushed his hair back with his hand.

'I'd been thinking about that. Would you like me to ask Graham Silverton, the medical director at the hospice, to tell your dad? Then you could just go over later, once he knows.'

'Don't you think that I'd be avoiding things?'

Tim shook his head.

'To be honest, Ellie, it might be the best thing. Graham's got to know your dad. He's good at communicating with him. I think it would be best if you let him do it.'

'It would be so much easier,' Ellie acknowledged. 'But I can't help but feel that I'm being selfish and not accepting my responsibilities.'

'Ellie, you're having to cope with your own grief. Let people help you.'

Ellie concurred.

'Good, I'll ring him immediately. What shall I say? That you'll be over to see him this afternoon? Don't go rushing off there. He needs time, just as you do.'

Ellie, relieved, thanked him for all his help. Tim shrugged, feeling impotent that there was nothing more he could offer her. She left his office and briefly slipped back onto the ward, to pass on her gratitude to the nursing staff and to pick up a plain white plastic bag into which her mother's things had been placed. She thought of trying to find Nigel but decided that there was nothing she wanted more than to get away from the hospital.

It was another cold day, but bright, with radiantly blue skies and no sign of a cloud. As Ellie walked home, lost in her own thoughts, she failed to see the clumps of snowdrops in her own garden, promising that spring was on its way.

Ian heard her key in the lock and switched on the kettle. Ellie deposited the carrier bag on a kitchen chair and peered inside at the sad mementoes she had brought home with her.

'Do that later,' Ian told her, mashing the tea. 'How was it at the hospital?'

'I don't know what to say. Part of me is glad that Mum didn't have to suffer the ignominy of her illness but most of me just wants her back. I've things I want to ask her and talk to her about and now I shall never be able to. Does that sound silly?'

'It sounds quite normal, if you ask me,' Ian replied.

'I just feel empty inside, as though part of me has died as well.'

'In a way, it has. But you are alive and you will survive this, even though it doesn't seem like it at the moment.'

'She was only sixty-one,' Ellie said morosely.

'No age at all.'

'It's not fair.'

'Tell me something about life that is.'

'You're right, I know you are. But just now it's hard to be rational.'

'It'll get easier, with time.'

They drank their tea, Ellie's swallows interspersed by heartfelt sighs.

'Do you think we should go to their house?' asked Ian. 'To check everything's all right?'

Ellie thought for a moment.

'That's probably wise. I'm not sure I really want to.'

'Maybe not, but it needs to be done. Let's go when we've had this.'

'Oh dear. I'd better ring the undertaker first. There are so many things that I have to do.'

'And what about your dad?'

Ellie explained. Ian, after listening carefully, took charge. He sent her off to make her telephone call while he washed the mugs. Continuing to deputise for the normally assertive Ellie, he held out his hand and took her to the car.

'Directions, please.' He started the engine.

Ellie entered her parents' house with trepidation, not sure what she was expecting to find. To her surprise it was exactly as she remembered it, if anything rather tidier than it had been for some weeks. There were no bloodstains on the walls or upended furniture. Indeed the kitchen was tidy, the lounge pristine and the hallway unsullied. The only sign that the paramedics had been in was a discarded rubber glove, obviously overlooked, as it lay in a corner of the hall by the bedroom door.

Ellie wandered disconsolately from room to room. One of her mother's nightdresses was hanging up to dry over the bath, the electric alarm clock by her parents' bed still showed the correct time and even the houseplants showed no sign of neglect. It was as though they had

232

gone on holiday and might return at any minute. How weird that life goes on regardless. Even though I know she won't, I keep expecting Mum to call from the kitchen, Ellie mused. The only thing missing was the smell of baking but even that had been absent for weeks.

There was a tentative knock on the front door and Ian went to investigate. Sheila and Gordon stood there, looking concerned and slightly baffled at being greeted by someone they did not recognise. Ellie, inviting them in, introduced Ian as she led everyone through to the lounge so that they could sit down.

'We just wanted to pass on our condolences,' started Gordon.

'She was such a remarkable woman,' continued Sheila.

'The way she cared for Keith,' Gordon added.

'Truly remarkable,' Sheila reiterated.

'Thank you so much for popping in,' Ellie began, taking advantage of a lull in the conversation and managing to stall the fresh tears that were prickling threateningly. 'And thank you for all you did to help Mum and Dad. I know it meant so much to them, especially Mum. I think she saw you as her main lifeline.'

'We were glad to help. They've been good friends to us over the years and have helped us with our own health upsets,' Sheila assured Ellie. 'I stayed and tidied up after the ambulance took your mum. I was hoping it would look nice for her when she came home...'

'Sheila, what actually happened?' inquired Ellie.

'I'd come across for a cup of tea, like I often did and we were just chatting. I thought to myself that your mum looked very washed out. I was asking her how Keith, I mean your father, was getting on and if it would be okay for me and Gordon to visit him later that afternoon. I was rabbiting on, like I can do, when I suddenly noticed she had gone as grey as could be and was holding her chest She started to say something about feeling faint but before she could finish she was just a heap on the floor. I rang Gordon, who dialled 999. It was quite frightening.'

'I'm sure it was, but thank goodness you were here with her.'

'Yes, absolutely, otherwise who knows what might have happened,' agreed Sheila, though Ellie personally preferred not to envisage any of these scenarios.

Gordon cleared his throat. 'What'll be happening to your father now?'

'I'm sorry?' Ellie did not understand.

'Well, I mean, can he stay at the hospice or will he have to move into a nursing home?'

Ellie looked at them blankly as they presented her with a conundrum that she had never even begun to try to solve. She had no idea what to say and helplessly turned to Ian.

'It's early days to be making any decisions,' he informed them. 'Obviously we will be trying to achieve an end result that pays attention to everyone's best interests.'

Grateful for his intervention, Ellie could not stop herself from thinking that he sounded like a company director being interviewed for the ten o'clock news, making her father sound more like some consumer commodity than a human being. Still, it would do for now until she had the strength to tackle answering a question of such enormous importance.

Remembering to be courteous, she offered Sheila and Gordon tea or coffee and hoped that her relief when they declined was not too apparent. They took their leave, offering their assistance if Ellie felt that they could help with anything at all.

The house seemed eerily quiet after they had left. Ellie started to wander again and Ian allowed her to do so for a short while before he stopped her.

'Are you ready to go? You can always come back later if you want to.'

'I don't really know what I want to do,' Ellie admitted honestly. 'The only thing I'm sure of it that I'm not ready to face Dad yet.'

'Right then, come with me.'

Ian drove out of Harrogate, turned off to the right and after a couple of miles parked in a small lay-by. He encouraged Ellie to get out of the car and then they walked across the fields, climbing upwards, gently at first and then gradually more steeply, having to stop and get their breath before the summit of Almscliff Crags. The air was sparkling and the wind whipped around their faces, giving them rosy cheeks. They had to shout to make themselves heard and even then most of their words were carried away by the wind. Ian sat on a boulder while Ellie stood, on the highest point she could find, arms out and eyes closed, leaning into the wind and letting it blow right through her. She then opened her eyes and stared out, at the miles and miles of countryside around her, at the well-defined horizon and the cloudless sky. Even though she knew that Ian was sitting not far behind her, the solitude she felt and the silence apart from the buffeting wind afforded Ellie a tranquillity she had not felt for almost forty-eight hours. Even her tiredness seemed to have been blown out of her. But it was bitterly cold and standing in the path of the oncoming icy wind put a severe constraint on the amount of time she was able to stay there. Reluctantly, she turned back to Ian and bellowed.

'This is great but freezing. Let's go!'

They walked speedily, half running, back to the car, jumped in and turned the heater on full. Finally feeling some sense of warmth returning into her bones, Ellie drew in a deep breath.

'I'm ready to go to the hospice now.'

Ian nodded and started the engine. Minutes later, he dropped her off.

'I'll come back in an hour.'

Leaving Ellie no opportunity to suggest otherwise, he drove off and Ellie was left watching him disappear down the drive. She turned and entered the building. As she reached the in-patient unit, Graham Silverton was writing up notes in the staff office. He glanced up.

'Ah, Ellie. Hello. Let me just finish this and I'll be with you.'

Ellie looked around the room. Nearly all the walls were covered with notice boards, displaying nurses' off duty rotas, pathways for symptom management and advertisements for forthcoming courses. One wall was devoted to letters and cards of thanks. She stood reading them, appreciating their sentiments and making a mental note to send one of her own.

Graham put down his pen and closed the file of notes with a slap. Taking this as a cue, Ellie rushed to speak.

'Have you told Dad? How is he?'

'Sit down, Ellie, please. Firstly, I was so sorry to hear about your mother. What a tragic situation. How are you?'

'All over the place but I can sort that.'

'Yes, then, I've told your father. We spent a long time together. I don't need to tell you that he is devastated to a degree I've rarely seen before. I've talked him through what happened but it's so difficult for him as he cannot voice his thoughts. We've tried everything to help him communicate while he's been with us, in an attempt to make his life have just a little better quality but he just refuses, time after time.'

'He always did when he was at home. I think he just wants Mum.'

Nodding, Graham went on.

'I know. When he was first admitted, I sat with both your parents, going through all their plans for his future care. It seems that as his disease has progressed he has become increasingly reticent to accept any help or support from anyone. I wondered if he was depressed. It would be understandable, if almost inevitable, bearing in mind the social isolation that comes from not being able to communicate but I could not find any evidence of this. I've tried again on several occasions when it's just been him and me but he has never even wavered from his original ideas.'

'I'm afraid that losing Mum might just make him give up altogether,' confessed Ellie, feeling a large lump loom in her throat.

'You may well be right. He has deteriorated physically in the short time he has been with us, quite significantly. I suspect that this latest development will have a profound effect on him emotionally.'

'This is just too awful to contemplate.' Ellie started to cry, quietly. 'I'm so mixed up about things and I've so much to sort out.'

'Try not to worry. Your father is safe here and very well cared for.'

'I know that, but for how long? Do I have to find a nursing home for him? Should I try to look after him at home and postpone my next job?'

'Ellie, he's due to stay a while longer anyway. I'm sure we can extend that in view of the circumstances, so let's just take our time over this one. What do you think your parents would want you to do?'

'Oh, they'd want me to be at work. I've no doubt about that.'

'Well, then, you've answered your own question.'

'I suppose so. It is so kind of you to say he can stay.' Ellie blew her nose. 'I'd better go and see him now. Thank you again.'

'It's the least we can do, Ellie. Come and have a word before you go, eh?'

Promising to do this, Ellie walked softly to her father's room. For once, the television was not on, nor was the radio or the talking book. The curtains were closed and the only light that was on was the small bedside lamp. Keith was in his wheelchair, half turned to the door. As she stood in the doorway, Ellie could hear the rattling of his breaths, mucus bubbling in his lungs, impossible to cough up. He must have sensed that she was there for he turned his head as best he could and emitted a pitiful howl like a tortured animal, which seared through Ellie like an electric shock.

'Oh, Dad,' she whispered, hugging him tight. 'I'm so sorry. Poor, wonderful Mum.'

As she clung to him, their tears mingling together, Ellie told him her version of what had happened. She promised him that the final moments of her life had been swift and pain free; even though she was not entirely convinced about this fact, there seemed no point in adding to her father's despair. Ellie made much of the kindness of the doctors and nurses who had been looking after Diana and how, despite her knowing how ill she was, her only concern had been for him.

'She literally loved you more than life itself, Dad.'

22

'The funeral's this Friday,' Ellie announced, returning to the kitchen where she had left Ian watching cheese bubble on toast under the grill, having just spoken to the undertakers.

Ian studied her carefully, trying to get a hint of how she was coping.

'Well, that's good. It's better to have made the arrangements.'

'Yes, it is. They've been wonderful at helping me and telling me what to do.'

'Just what you need at a time like this.'

Ellie grabbed the grill pan and rescued their lunch before it burned.

It was Monday, the clouds were low lying and threatening but at least it was dry.

'I have to get back to work tomorrow, Ellie,' Ian informed her, splashing brown sauce on his cheese.

Ellie paused, her piece of toast halfway to her mouth.

'Oh?' The disappointment in her voice was unmistakable.

'Yes, I'm sorry, but there are meetings coming up that I simply cannot afford to miss.'

Rallying, Ellie smiled at him.

'Of course. I understand. I've just lost track of time a little. My new job starts on Wednesday.'

'Will you be ready for that?'

Ellie nodded seriously.

'I think I should try. I've spoken to my consultant and she's been really understanding. Mum always used to say it was better to be busy, so I'm going to give it a go. She'd not want me to be moping at home.'

'Good for you.' He took another couple of mouthfuls. 'There's another thing, Ellie.'

She looked up from her lunch.

'What's that?'

'Some of these meetings are abroad. I'm going to be out of the country for a while.'

'Oh,' repeated Ellie, rather sadly.

'I'll not be too busy to keep in touch,' Ian tried to reassure her but Ellie was silent.

'Where are you going?' she finally asked.

'Milan, Geneva, Berlin.' Ian sounded almost apologetic.

'When do you leave?'

Ian wanted to reach for her hand but was unsure whether he ought to.

'I need to go back to my flat later today. There are a lot of bits and pieces that I need to sort out.'

Ellie tried hard to recover her usual cheerful façade.

'There must be. I quite understand.'

'You could come with me and stay over if you'd like. I have a small but quite pleasant spare room.'

'No, no. I'd just be in the way. Plus I'd better start reading up on some paediatrics, hadn't I?' Ellie tried a tentative laugh.

'You'll be wonderful. The children will adore you.'

There was another long pause, neither of them quite sure what to say.

'Coffee?' Ellie suggested, over brightly.

'Please and then it'd be best if I packed up and made a move.'

Ian's attempts at making meaningful conversation while they had their drinks failed miserably. Reluctantly, he gathered together his few possessions, promised to ring Ellie that night and after a brief hug, left, not being one for prolonged good-byes. As soon as the door closed behind him, Ellie was struck by the quiet in her house. She put the radio on quickly, letting loud music replace the silence and started to wash up the minimal amount of dishes. As one tune faded away, another began, a favourite of Diana's. The familiar sound of the melodic introduction was more than Ellie could bear. She sat down and wept, her shoulders heaving with her sobs, the tea towel that she had grabbed as the nearest object to serve as a handkerchief soon drenched by her tears.

She was exhausted from trying to maintain a dignified and controlled sorrow. For a while she had been able to assume a professional mask to shield her from her mother's death, pretending that she had been a patient and trying to step back from it in a dispassionate way. She had spent the weekend contacting relatives and friends, hating the prospect of each telephone call but knowing that it had to be done. Most of that morning had been spent at the undertakers, then with the vicar, being efficient again, making decisions on behalf of her parents about flowers and hymns and the wake. Now her strength was depleted allowing the real significance of her loss to spill over.

With no more energy to cry, she got up and trundled upstairs to wash her face, which was swollen, red and unpleasantly blotchy from the ravages of her despair. The cold water felt refreshing but made little inroad into improving her appearance. Sniffing, she made a token effort to tidy up. The little windowsill looked empty without Ian's wash bag, even though it had only been there for such a short time. Dutifully, but without giving the process much thought, Ellie went through the motions of cleaning the bath and washbasin, piling up the dirty towels to take down with the other washing and watering the plants. With an armful of laundry she made her way back downstairs, started up the machine and heard the front doorbell ring. She took a quick look at her reflection in the mirror in the hall and shook her head, dismayed by what looked back at her. Opening the door, she found herself enveloped in a strong pair of arms.

'Ellie, how are you?'

'Nigel, what are you doing here? Why aren't you at work?'

'I managed to get off a bit early. It is half past four.'

'Never!' Ellie was shocked. She had no idea that it was that time.

240

'You look terrible,' Nigel commented. 'You poor thing.'

Ellie burst into tears again.

'Don't be nice to me – it just makes me cry,' she wailed.

He waited until he could feel that her sobs were ebbing and then steered her into the lounge, where they sat close to each other on the sofa, Ellie's head still buried in his shoulder.

'Em sends her love,' he whispered.

'That's kind of her,' gulped Ellie, coming up for breath and to blow her nose. 'Goodness, I must have been crying for most of the afternoon, but I just miss her so much.'

'You cry as much as you need to. It's far better than bottling it all up. I can remember how I felt after Dad died. I wanted to cry for days. Trouble is, blokes aren't supposed to. You girls are lucky.'

'She didn't deserve this, did she?'

'No but, what you have to think about is that it was her choice. She wanted to devote all her energies to your dad. I expect she knew what was happening to her but she chose to put your dad first. How selfless is that?'

'It's incredible. I just wish she'd told me, then I could have done more. I cannot believe that I didn't see this coming. I thought she was tired out and I could understand that. I didn't notice that she wasn't eating and I didn't spot that she was wasting away before my eyes. How terrible a daughter am I?'

'You saw what you could. Being rational goes out of the window when you're emotionally involved. You cannot take two paces back to be objective. Keep telling yourself what a wonderful woman she was and how lucky she was to have experienced such love so deep and strong that it obliterated any thought for herself.'

'It's all such a muddle, Nigel.'

'But it will unravel with time, I promise.'

He held her tight.

'Thanks for that. I think it's helped. Oh, look at the time now – I've got to go up to the hospice. Dad'll be expecting me, waiting to hear about the funeral arrangements. Can you come round tomorrow for a bit?'

'I'll try, at the very least I'll phone. You go and tidy up a bit – I'll wait here.'

In spite of her best efforts, it was a pink, puffy-faced Ellie who arrived at the hospice and made her way to her father's room. She gently told him all that she had done that day, read him a few cards that had arrived and stroked his hand as he gazed at her with sad, rheumy eyes. When a passing nurse looked in and offered to make Ellie a cup of tea, she tried to persuade Keith to have one too but he shook his head. As she drank hers, Ellie racked her brains for things to talk about but rapidly ran out of ideas and finally resorting to inanities about the weather and what was on television.

She left with a good deal of relief and carefully drove home. There was a message on the answering machine from Ian, saying that he was thinking of her and would try her again soon.

Deciding that she was past hunger and in any case she needed to go shopping, Ellie had a long soak in a hot bath and then, wrapped up warmly in brushed cotton pyjamas, she curled up in bed where, to her surprise, she fell asleep almost instantly.

The funeral passed. Nature for once was in sympathy with Ellie, bestowing bright sunshine, which at the very least put a more positive feel on the day than if it been pouring with rain. Keith arrived from the hospice with one of the nurses. He looked old, shrivelled and like a stranger. His wheelchair was placed by Ellie in the church, right up near the altar, so that the aisle was free for the pallbearers to make their way. Not many people attended. Gordon and Sheila of course, Nigel and Emily; Graham Silverton was kind enough to come, as was Dr Urquhart. The few relatives that Ellie had, but rarely saw, were represented by two cousins, who stood smoking outside until the very last minute when they stubbed out their cigarettes on the flagstones and shuffled noisily into the back row. Ellie tried hard to sing the hymns. The swell of the organ brought a huge, immovable lump into her throat and she was afraid to utter a sound. Listening, she could hear Nigel's deep, tuneful voice leading the others, persuading them all to join in rather than hold back in shyness.

The service was short but poignant. At the crematorium, tiny yellow and purple crocuses were peeping out from the grass, ironically heralding new life, as they drove slowly up the long drive.

Ellie held on tight to her father's arm as, after a few words and a piece of music that Diana and Keith Woods had danced to at their wedding, the coffin disappeared inexorably.

The hospice, concerned for Keith's well being, had suggested that everyone go back there for drinks and a bite to eat. Ellie would have preferred to have entertained at her parents' home, believing that this would be much more fitting but she finally capitulated. She had spent the previous evening and the early part of that day baking, creating mouth-watering little pastries and buns, crunchy biscuits and bite-sized sandwiches, wanting her mother to be proud of her rather than take the easy way out and book a caterer. Inevitably there was a huge amount left over. Cooking for an unknown quantity is invariably impossible and, rather like Diana at Christmas, Ellie had over estimated spectacularly. Still, at least it could be left for the staff at the hospice and any patients who were well enough to eat it.

By the time the final guest had left, it was nearly dark. Ellie, a little light headed from a glass of sherry on an empty stomach, went for a final word with her father who had retreated to his room after only a short while. The room was in darkness. He was in bed, turned away from her, apparently asleep. She kissed him lightly on the cheek and crept away.

23

Graham Silverton had been a consultant in palliative care for over ten years and his experience of dying patients was vast. His prediction regarding Keith's prognosis was uncannily accurate. Keith died just a month after his wife, what little will he had left to live extinguished by his misery. Ellie did her best. She visited daily, sometimes having to cajole her colleagues into covering her duties for an hour while she dashed over to the hospice. At the same time as trying to cope with her own grief, she valiantly endeavoured to raise her father's spirits. She told him things at length, read to him, brought new talking books and sat quietly with him while they listened to music or watched television. As she did so, she became intimately acquainted with the number of flowers on the wallpaper, counting them over and over as she passed the time. Nothing she tried, however, resulted in a flicker of interest. Keith's sunken eyes were sad and dull, his movements minimal and his attempts to communicate increasingly rare.

'It's as though he's not there any more,' Ellie explained during one of her many conversations with Graham.

'You're right. We've tried everything we can think of, so have you, but he continues to blank us out. I'm afraid he wants to die.'

There was no alternative than to accept this, for Ellie could see that it was true. So she sat with him and watched as his life slipped away, trying to make the most of what time they had left together, still acutely aware of how her mother's sudden death had deprived her of the chance to say so many things.

Keith stopped eating, not that his appetite amounted to much, and then refused any fluids at all. No amount of coaxing from Ellie made any impression. She even got Nigel to come and try but he was equally unsuccessful. The secretions in Keith's chest became more thick, sticky and troublesome, harder to cough up and clear. His kidneys began to fail and drowsiness set in but he was spared any pain. Ellie spent her visits sitting beside him, his hand in hers, softly speaking to him, trusting that somewhere inside his shell of a body he could hear her and felt safe as he slipped into deeper unconsciousness.

Towards the very end, she stayed overnight, the kind staff putting up a camp bed in the room for her but sleep was elusive as she waited, appalled at times with herself for wishing that he would die quickly but in reality only wanting his torture to come to an end. He finally took his last rattling gasp in the early hours of one morning, Ellie, awake and by his side, confused by the relief and sadness she felt.

With a feeling of déjà vu, Ellie went through the motions of organis-ing another funeral. The same church, the same vicar and give or take a few, the same small congregation. Even the flowers were similar though the hymns were not, Keith having left very definite instructions as to what he wanted. This time, Ellie did hold the wake at her parents' house, even though Graham had again offered the facilities at the hospice. She went to just as much trouble with her baking but for a fleeting moment considered liquidising all that she had made so that the mourners could share in the horror of what her father had been forced to tolerate.

Perfecting the preparations kept her focused and busy. It was afterwards that she looked around her and saw an empty void. Ellie took a few days' compassionate leave; she was entitled to a week but cut this short after an incident in town which left her feeling shaken and bemused. Walking along one of the shopping precincts, she thought she saw her mother coming towards her, only to find, as their paths crossed, that the woman bore no resemblance to Diana whatsoever.

Perhaps foolishly, Ellie had decided that, as she knew the theory of bereavement, this was bound to help her. She quickly realised that she was wrong. Nothing could have prepared her for the plethora of different emotions she felt, oscillating with incredible speed from one to another. Sadness, anger, despair, loneliness and confusion all interweaved their effects from day to day. Then they would be followed by a good day, when she felt like herself again and laughed and joked with her friends at the hospital. But afterwards she was consumed with guilt for being happy when she felt that everyone expected her to be sad. She came across mixed reactions from her friends and colleagues, despite the fact that most of them were dealing with grieving people all the time. Some avoided her, giving her a wide berth in the corridor, not wanting to make eye contact, as they did not know what to say. Others greeted her as if nothing had happened, keen to chat about any subject other than her parents and looking awkward and embarrassed if Ellie broached the topic herself. But good friends, like Nigel and Emily, were there for her, particularly Nigel, whose personal experience of death in his own family meant that he could listen to Ellie or leave her alone when she needed isolation, but most of all he could repeatedly reassure her that the evolution that she was going through was normal.

Ian telephoned regularly and Ellie looked forward to hearing from him. He sent a variety of postcards, so that she could visualise where he was. The arrival of the first had her in tears as the last card she had received had been from her parents on their cruise. He was very busy, setting up a new company and working long hours. Tired but full of job satisfaction, he recounted all the details to her, keen for her approval and praise. He had been mortified that he had been unable to attend either funeral, work commitments totally forbidding this, as he had wanted to be there to help Ellie whom he knew would be putting on a brave face as much as she could. He was pleased that Ellie, even when speaking to him when he was hundreds of miles away, still felt comfortable enough to laugh and cry with him. He longed to be with her but felt that her emotions were raw enough without confusing her further by telling her how he was feeling.

Paediatrics was the greatest healer of all. Ellie loved the specialty, from her first glimpse of the ward. Her consultant, Beth Martin, in stark contrast to Jeremy, was relaxed, friendly and a joy to work with. Unanimously, the nursing staff, led by a cheery, freckled charge nurse, welcomed her and the two other new senior house officers on to the ward, helping them settle into their new roles and find their way around. The ward was bright with colourful paintings and posters. The beds had cheerful harlequin-patterned duvets and there were toys in abundance. Beth, aware of Ellie's domestic upheaval, was supportive and approachable, finding time to take Ellie to one side every now and then to check that all was well. Ellie's work, predictably, was excellent. She found the subject matter easy because she was enjoying it so much. Learning the basic skills was fun, even the paediatric resuscitation course, which was often viewed with some trepidation by her colleagues.

Ellie found that her patients were a far cry from the elderly on Whitby Ward. She spent time with babies, regularly being on call for the Labour ward to help with difficult deliveries and checking the newborn before they went home. The sick ones were placed on the neonatal unit where the work was hard and pressurised. The patients were so tiny and vulnerable that it was incredibly difficult to site intravenous lines and nasogastric tubes and Ellie watched, impressed as the nurses expertly carried out these delicate tasks. It was a highly emotionally charged unit, with anxious and distraught parents to look after in addition to their babies but the sense of satisfaction when they were finally well enough to be discharged home was immeasurable.

The turnover on Ripley, the ward for toddlers and children, was fast and furious, many children only staying for observation overnight, their clinical condition rapidly improving and relieving parental concerns. Within a few weeks, Ellie was confidently managing children with high temperatures, diarrhoea and vomiting or wheezy chests – an unlucky few having two or all of these – and loving every minute of it. It amused her how black and white the world seemed to be to children. They told her the details of their illnesses with such innocence and honesty and she wondered when it was in their lives, at what age, that this was lost.

Though it was a busy job, there were three of them to share the workload which meant that life in general was much more civilised and the on-call commitment kinder than her previous job. Lunch became a regular feature in Ellie's life rather than a rarity and she was grateful for the camaraderie that existed amongst the paediatric team and the way that she and the others were included in it.

Making her way to the canteen one day over halfway into the job, she spotted Jeremy Blake approaching her. Ellie, much to her annoyance, felt her stomach flip over. She hadn't seen him since the end of her last job, an arrangement that suited her very well and was usefully assisted by the geography of the hospital, Ripley and Whitby Wards being at opposite ends. She infrequently attended the lunchtime meetings as they clashed with departmental case presentations, so their paths had not had much of an opportunity to cross. As he neared, she was ambivalent about whether she wanted him to speak to her. Far the easiest option was for them to pass by and fail to acknowledge each other. He did look intent on his own thoughts and Ellie considered that there was just a chance that she might get away with it. Suddenly, it dawned on Jeremy who was coming towards him.

'Ellie,' he greeted her, sounding surprised but not displeased.

'Hi,' returned Ellie, trying to keep calm.

'How are you? Enjoying looking after all those kids?'

'Yes, thanks, it's great.'

'I was sorry to hear about your parents,' his voice softened as he commiserated.

'Thanks,' repeated Ellie, willing her bleep to go off, but needless to say, the one time she wanted it to, it failed to oblige.

'You're looking good.' He surveyed her up and down.

'How's Helen?' Ellie asked pointedly.

'I've left her.'

'What?' Ellie was astonished.

'I did tell you I was going to.'

'But what about your family?'

'I see them regularly. I miss the boys but the girls are too young to know any different. I say,' he looked at his watch, 'why don't we go and get some lunch?'

'I can't. I'm just on my way now to meet up with some friends.'

'That's a shame. Another time perhaps?'

'Maybe,' agreed Ellie, setting off purposefully in the direction of the canteen and feeling quite proud of herself as she managed to avoid the temptation to turn and look back at him.

Joining her friends, Ellie was disinterested in her food. Her mind kept returning to Jeremy, how handsome he had looked and the outrageous announcement he had made. She could not help but wonder what had happened and how it had all come about. Why had he left? What was the fall out of his actions? Was Helen hankering after him going back to them? And then a tiny, mischievous voice spoke up, had he left because he really did want to be with Ellie? Pushing her plate away, the food untouched, Ellie excused herself on the grounds of having left something unfinished on the ward and went out into the fresh air to try to think more clearly and logically.

She felt like one of those cartoons where a little devil and a little angel are hovering around someone's head offering conflicting advice. The former was beguiling her into finding out more –surely no harm would come from that; the latter, sorrowfully shaking its head, was admonishing her to steer well clear.

She sat out in one of the small courtyards, ostensibly for patients, which had become one of her preferred places when she needed solitude but had to be within paging distance. It was a sunny day in late May, warm enough for two ladies clad in their dressing-gowns and towelling slippers to come and join her. She smiled at them politely, a gesture that they reciprocated before burrowing in their large hand bags, bringing out their knitting and starting to chat loudly. Peace disturbed, Ellie left them to it and wandered down to out patients for the afternoon clinic. For a while she was able to forget about her dilemma as she learned more about a diverse selection of conditions such as type I diabetes, encopresis, growth problems and the psychological effect of bullying. The clinic was full but efficiently run, so that they finished with time to spare and Beth suggested to Ellie that she got off home a little early, having been on call the night before. Not needing to be asked twice, Ellie gathered her things from Ripley, checked that there was nothing else that she needed to do and rejoiced in the feeling of the sun on her face as she walked across the car park. Just before she reached the main road, she turned, ran back into the hospital and to the nearest internal telephone she could find that had a modicum of privacy. Trembling, she dialled Jeremy's office number, not even knowing if he would be in there. There was no answer. Frustrated but now determined to find him, she tried the switchboard operator to see if they knew where he was. After a nail-biting wait, which in reality was only a few seconds, she heard his voice at the other end of the line.

'Dr Blake.'

'Jeremy, it's me, Ellie. I wondered if you'd like to come round for supper this evening.'

Her words were delivered with a rush, as if she might change her mind before they were out.

'I'd love to. I'll see you at eight.'

Shaking even more, Ellie replaced the receiver, experiencing some emotion that she could not quite define but hoped might be excitement. The deed done, she hurried off home, jumped into the car and went shopping, planning all the while what she would make for the two of them. She wanted to keep things simple and casual, to make sure he did not think that she had gone to any special effort on his behalf. Settling for moussaka and a green salad, followed by pineapple upside-down cake, she threw her ingredients into a basket with alacrity, was round the supermarket in record time and off back home to start her preparations.

Letting herself in, she had bags in either hand and stepped over the two days' worth of post that lay on the mat. Dumping her purchases on the kitchen table, she emptied the bags and noticing that time was marching on started to fry mince and onions and slice the aubergines. Absorbed in her love of cooking, she perfected her two dishes, rustled up the salad so that it simply required the dressing adding at the last minute and then ran upstairs to shower and get ready. Ten outfits later, which ranged from a skimpy strapless top and skin-tight jeans to an evening dress with a plunging neckline and little, if any, back, Ellie got a grip and plumped for not quite such tight jeans and a mallard green sweater. Standing back, she did her usual routine of examining herself from as many angles as she could physically manage, then brushed her hair and returned downstairs to calm her nerves with a glass of wine. Definitely feeling better after two large gulps, she went to sit in the lounge to await Jeremy's imminent arrival, stopping to pick up the post on the way. Collapsing into the armchair, she flicked through the letters. Two bills, several medical journals (how did so many find their way to her?), some advertisements from drug companies and three postcards from Ian.

Delighted, she read each one carefully. She had not heard from him for a few days and had to admit that she had been concerned, so now she felt reassured. He sounded as busy as ever but there was a hint of loneliness in his words. There was a picture of the centre of Berlin, another was a German Shepherd dog with its puppies and the third a scenic view of mountains and a valley. On the back of the latter he had written, 'This reminds me of Scotland. I wish I was there now, with you.'

In a trice, Ellie was transported back to the end of January, her mind filled with memories of the cold, the congeniality of her hosts, the walks, the riding and the true friendship that she had forged with Ian. Looking at her mantelpiece, she saw the huge number of cards that he had sent her, amounting to at least two or three a week, all lined up for her to look at, re-read and enjoy, arriving, post permitting, with reliable frequency, regardless of how busy he was with his work. Next to them was the photo of her parents, smiling at her from happier times, before either was ill, the way she was determined to remember them.

Something was wrong. She felt uncomfortable and bewildered, scrabbling to make sense of the situation.

Suddenly she had no doubt what was happening.

The doorbell rang, loudly and insistently.

Taking one last swallow of wine, Ellie went to and opened the door. Jeremy was standing there, looking as attractive as always, dressed in a polo shirt and casual trousers, a bottle of wine clasped in each hand, a bouquet of flowers at his feet.

'Hello, my darling.' He leant forward to kiss her.

'Jeremy,' began Ellie, pulling back, 'there's been a terrible misunderstanding. Sorry, but I can't do this. Not now, or ever. Goodbye.'

She shut the door in his face, made sure all the locks were fastened and waited, listening for the sounds of his footsteps retreating down her path and his car driving away.

24

Jeremy, however, over the next few weeks, showed Ellie that he was not going to give in without a fight. He became a frequent caller at her house, at any time of the day, from early morning up to the late evening. His unpredictability was not limited to his timing. Sometimes he would knock, sometimes ring the bell, leaving Ellie feeling unnerved and in time rather like a prisoner in her own home as she started to ignore all intimations that there was someone at her front door.

If that were not enough he telephoned regularly, begging Ellie to spare him some time to talk about their relationship and refusing to be put off at all by the fact that she would slam down the receiver when he was in mid sentence. Then there were the cards and presents that arrived with monotonous regularity. Books, jewellery and items of clothing such as glamorous lingerie were fed through the letterbox only to be bagged up en masse and posted back to him via the internal mail at the hospital. The wording in the cards was all in a similar vein, professing his love for her and how he had left Helen to be with Ellie. In one, Ellie felt that he had really stooped about as low as he could as he wrote how he appreciated that she was grieving for her parents and thus could not see how she needed him. Bringing her parents into the equation so infuriated Ellie that she returned all further epistles unopened.

Even on the ward, Ellie was the embarrassed recipient of a gigantic bunch of roses (dark red, of course), mixed with lisianthus stems of white, pinks and purple. Her friends gaped with envy when this staggeringly attractive arrangement arrived and was presented to Ellie, whose heart was already sinking as she had guessed whom it was from.

Everyone, of course, quizzed and teased her, trying to find out who her admirer was and she was forced to lie and pretend that they were a thank you from a patient she had looked after in her previous job, which, she admitted to herself, sounded too far fetched for anyone to take seriously

One day in the canteen, Jeremy came and sat with Ellie, who was on her own, having just finished admitting a five year old with probable gastroenteritis and had thus missed lunch with her friends. Though the lunchtime rush was nearly over, it was still busy and Ellie had to share a table with a couple of physiotherapists that she knew vaguely. This turned out to be a blessing in disguise as it meant that Jeremy had to maintain his gruff professional front. He was tastefully polite, asking about her job mainly. Ellie spotted Nigel on the other side of the room, eating with his surgical colleagues and saw his eyebrows raised in curiosity. She rolled her eyes upwards back at him, hoping that he would interpret this sign correctly and then scooped up the last of her jam roly-poly, excused herself politely and hurried back to the ward. No sooner had she got there than her bleep went off. It was Nigel, wanting to know just what was going on.

'Nothing at all,' Ellie told him honestly. 'He just came and sat with me, was perfectly pleasant and then I had to go.'

There was no way that she was going to admit to the rest of the Jeremy debacle. Nigel would only want to know how it had come about and she really did not feel that she wanted to go into all that.

'Okay, then. But you just watch him. I don't trust him an inch. He's got a shifty-looking face, if you ask me!'

Ellie laughed and rang off. Nigel, without knowing it, had brought things back into perspective and she felt better. She enjoyed the afternoon, spending a lot of time talking and playing with her young patients, making the most of her time on Ripley Ward, which was fast coming to an end.

Much as she knew she would miss paediatrics, Ellie was looking forward to her final six months of training to be a general practitioner, in which she would be out in general practice, doing the job that she had chosen for her career. It would be wonderful to get back into the community and see real life again, with all the spectrum of problems it presented, from the sublime to the ridiculous, the emergency cases to the verrucae and warts.

She was particularly happy with her job, having applied and been accepted for six months at the Teviotdale Medical Centre in the small market town of Lambdale, some thirty miles north of Harrogate. After a visit up there to look round, she had been captivated by both the little town and the surrounding idyllic Yorkshire dales. Her trainer, John Britton, was avuncular and cheery, someone she knew, from the hour they spent together, she would be able to admire and work hard for. Ellie also met John's wife Faye, as she was taken to their house for lunch. Faye was equally welcoming and after a delicious meal of quiche and various salads, she gave Ellie a tin of home- made biscuits to take back with her. After they had eaten, Ellie was given a tour of the surgery. The premises were interesting, being in a listed building in the centre of the town, looking out onto the market square. While not the most ideal building, no one seemed to mind. The receptionists were as far removed from the archetypal dragons as was imaginable and even the patients, who were sitting waiting their turn, looked relatively happy.

Before she left, John told her that the job was hers if she wanted it and after thanking him effusively, it was a victorious Ellie who drove back home and immediately called Nigel and Emily, inviting them round to celebrate with coffee, wine and the biscuits she had been given. Nigel expressed his concern about the commute, but Ellie was prepared to accept this, happy to drive along listening to the car radio or to music. She did not want to leave her house and felt that she still had a considerable number of ties to the town, mainly her parents' house, which she had been dragging her feet about clearing out with a view to selling.

Her excuses, well rehearsed in her mind, were several. It was not a good time to sell, the place would benefit from some titivating before any estate agent came round to value it and she was too busy at work to set about what was required to be done. Actually, every time she went into the bungalow, ostensibly to make a start, she was so overwhelmed with sadness that she got no further than fingering ornaments that held so many happy memories and poring over photo albums, which transported her back through time.

Ellie was at home one evening at the beginning of July, the end of her paediatric job in sight before the welcome respite of nearly three weeks' vacation. She kept telling herself that she would use this time practically and by the end of it her parents' house would be on the market. She would work more productively with a deadline, she was confident. Whimsically, she hoped that genuinely good, friendly folk would be the next occupants, having bought because they loved the house and wanted to care for it.

Coming in from the garden, summoned by the sound of the telephone ringing, Ellie put her gardening gloves and trowel on the draining board, wiped her hands on her jeans and picked up the receiver, willing it to be anybody but Jeremy. To her delight, it was Ian.

'It's so good to hear from you,' she told him.

'Did you get my postcards from Paris?' he inquired.

'Yes, I did,' Ellie smiled down the phone, 'all five of them. My mantelpiece is protesting under the weight of all the cards you've sent. But,' she suddenly panicked that this might sound ungracious, 'I've loved getting every one.'

'Good. I haven't been able to speak to you as much as I'd have liked and I didn't want you to forget about me.'

'As if!' Ellie joked, but a tiny frisson of delight tickled her heart. 'I think the postman's wondering what's going on though! Anyway, how's work going?'

'Brilliantly. That's one of the reasons that I'm calling. I'll be back home in a fortnight.'

'Oh, that's fantastic news.'

Ellie felt ridiculously excited.

'I know. I can't wait to see you. Are you still as gorgeous as ever?'

'Certainly not at the moment,' Ellie replied ruefully. 'My hands are covered with mud, I expect my face is too and my hair needs washing badly.'

'That all sounds good to me.'

'Why else were you ringing? You said that telling me you were coming home was just one reason.'

'I just wanted you to know that I miss you.'

'That's so nice. Thank you.'

The doorbell rang.

'Oh, there's someone at the door, I'd better go. Ring soon, won't you?'

'Of course, plus I shall see you soon. The time will go very quickly,' he promised.

Thinking only of Ian, Ellie opened the door, saw Jeremy, fumed and shut it with a firmness that would have made a less substantially built house shudder. When the bell rang again some half an hour later, she was incandescent. Standing behind the door, she opened the letterbox, saw flowers and yelled 'go away and don't come back, ever', at the top of her voice. She then ran upstairs, shut herself in the bathroom and sat on the edge of the bath, totally unaware that a bewildered Ian was standing on her front path, having telephoned from the end of the road to check that she was in, all ready to surprise her with his return. His repeated attempts to summon Ellie's attention met with no response whatsoever, so he drove off in his car, having thrown his bouquet of flowers, which he had thought was a particularly touching gesture, on to the back seat and wondering what on earth was going on. By the time he reached his flat, he had devised what was, in his opinion, nothing short of a very cunning plan. But first he needed to make one more telephone call.

Ellie was performing a lumbar puncture, supervised by Beth, who was happy to let her junior doctor do almost any practical procedure.

Personally, she felt that it was a great shame that Ellie was going into general practice, as she showed such aptitude for paediatrics.

'Perfect,' she congratulated her. 'Very well done.'

Ellie sat back, her face flushed with concentration and achievement. She helped one of the nurses turn over their small patient and make sure that he was settled.

'You go and answer that, I can manage,' the nurse said, as Ellie's bleep reminded her of its existence in her pocket.

'Sure?'

Given an affirmative nod, Ellie did as she was told.

'Outside call for you, Dr Woods,' announced the switchboard operator.

Ellie's pulse quickened involuntarily, hoping that it might be Ian from whom she had not heard for a few days. That, taken in isolation, was not a particular concern as often he could not get away from work to ring, but more worryingly, the steady stream of postcards had dried up.

When she heard Christina, Ian's mother, on the line, Ellie felt a mixture of disappointment but some pleasure. She was in town for the afternoon, wondering if they might meet up for a chat. Due to finish shortly, Ellie arranged a time and set to, efficiently completing her work for the day. She had just enough time left to borrow Nigel's on-call room in the doctors' mess and make herself look presentable before heading off towards the town centre

They met up in a chic and fashionable café, where waitresses, neatly dressed in black with frilly starched white aprons, served them with old-fashioned decorum. Christina had arrived first and taken advantage of the teatime lull to secure a table by the window. She waved as she saw Ellie scouring the room for her. They kissed affectionately on each cheek before sitting down and making small talk in between studying the menu. Christina ordered cocktails and then leant back in her chair. She was an attractive woman, cleverly dressed to emphasise the assets of her figure and disguise the areas she was less proud of.

'It's lovely to see you, Christina. How come you're in Harrogate?' asked Ellie, sipping a rather lurid but delicious pink drink.

'I promised Ian I would come up and check his flat for him. So I thought how nice it would be to catch up with you at the same time. I was so sorry to hear about your parents. You obviously got my letter; there was no need to reply. It's always so difficult to know what to write, to express how you're feeling without sounding mawkish and trite.'

Ellie thought for a moment.

'Speaking as the one on the receiving end, it was just so touching to know that people cared. It was some consolation to read any words. It wasn't so much what they were, just that someone had taken the trouble to put them on paper.'

'That's kind of you. I'll remember that. Now tell me about your job. It must be fun working with children.'

Ellie, glad to be able to change the subject, has no hesitation in chatting about the work that was just finishing and what lay in store. She told Christina what she planned to do with her holidays.

'That sounds a bit dull, Ellie. I know it's got to be done but you deserve a bit of a break as well. When's the last time you had a proper holiday?'

'I suppose when I came up to your house in Scotland.'

Their food arrived, piping hot rosti with bacon and chives for Christina, macaroni cheese for Ellie. They ate for a while, giving the food the attention it warranted.

'I tell you what,' suggested Christina, wiping her mouth on her napkin and indicating to the waitress to refill their glasses, 'Clive and I are off to Scotland the day after tomorrow. Why don't you come and join us for the weekend?'

Ellie prevaricated. It was tempting for sure and she had nothing else planned but she felt a little awkward in accepting. Christina, sensing Ellie's hesitation, turned on the persuasion.

'Do come. You could fly up on Friday evening and there's a Sunday afternoon flight back. I know it's only a couple of days but I'd love you to see the house in the summer.'

Ellie, won over, agreed and Christina was delighted.

'Excellent. I'll organise your travel, you've enough to do at work. Now, shall we be naughty and have one of those irresistible-looking cakes?'

Having secured Ellie's promise to visit, Christina did not mention the trip again but instead chatted about shopping, clothes, holidays and Ian. He was due back in ten days, she told Ellie and he was working furiously to finish off all the odds and ends before he returned. She spoke proudly of his achievements as only a mother can.

A pianist began to play in the centre of the room. It was soothing, congenial background music, quiet enough not to be too intrusive and prevent conversation.

'That explains why he hasn't rung recently,' mused Ellie, looking towards the piano.

'Probably. He's looking forward to seeing you though, I know that for a fact.'

Ellie felt warm and wanted.

'The feeling's mutual. To be honest, I had no idea that I would miss him quite as much as I have done.'

'Then this weekend is the perfect way of helping the time pass more quickly,' commented Christina and Ellie laughed.

'I can see where he inherits his charm from!'

Christina refused to let Ellie pay for their meal and, gesticulating at a waitress, produced a credit card that was whisked away. They hugged briefly on the street before going their separate ways, Ellie wandering slowly back to her car, enjoying the warm summer evening.

As promised, Christina contacted Ellie the very next day, ringing her when she was in the clinic to confirm that her flights were booked and that she simply had to turn up at the checking-in desk at the airport.

'We'll meet you at the airport. Can't wait! Take care!'

Ellie bumped into Nigel at lunchtime and told him her plans.

'I'm not overly sure if I want to go,' she confessed.

'Why ever not?' Nigel asked, disbelievingly.

'Oh, I don't know. They're great people and I get on really well with them but it seems a long way to go for just two days. Plus it'll feel odd without Ian there. I'm afraid I'll feel a bit like the odd man out.'

'You'll have a great time. Take a good book to read − if you do that, the chances are you'll barely have time to open it. If it does turn out to be unbearable, which it won't, you'll no sooner have got there than it'll be time to come back.'

As usual, Nigel succeeded in making Ellie feel better and realising that he had done so, he then seized the opportunity to tell her about the hemicolectomy he had done that morning.

25

Friday dawned humid and cloudy with more than a threat of thunder in the air. Ellie did not relish the prospect of flying in a small plane in those conditions and uttered a silent prayer for the weather to improve as the day progressed. She overslept, having had a restless night. She had tossed and fought with the bedclothes as it was so hot and sticky but then fallen into a deep sleep just after dawn. Groggy and not in the best of humours, she rushed to shower and get dressed, threw a few items of clothing into a bag to take away with her but at least did remember to pick up the note with her ticket reference which she had left in a conspicuous place in the hall. She paused for a hurried look at the post but there was nothing of note and more to the point, nothing from Ian. There was of course a distinct possibility he might ring this weekend, for surely his parents would have told him that Ellie was spending the weekend with them.

Halfway to her car, she cursed, ran back to the house and rummaged through the wardrobe, suddenly fearful that Christina and Clive might suggest going out for dinner on Saturday evening. If this were the case then she would need something presentable and all that she had packed so far were casual clothes for walking and lounging about. Frantically aware of the time, she pulled out one coat hanger after another, giving each garment a cursory glance and then flinging it on the bed. She finally settled on a dress and realised she would have to think of shoes, tights (as it might not be warm enough to go bare legged) and a bag.

Back at the car, she shoved these extra items into her holdall, confident that there would be an iron to revive the dress if necessary.

There were temporary traffic lights that had sprung up overnight at the end of her road and it took even longer than usual to turn right into the main stream of traffic.

Ellie felt guilty arriving late on the ward, but no one else seemed to have noticed. She was greeted with the usual cheerful welcome by the nursing staff and her medical colleagues. Beth was on the ward, just about to start her round to review all the overnight admissions but was relaxing with a cup of coffee while she waited for Ellie.

Apologising profusely, Ellie hung up her jacket and hooked her stethoscope around her neck. She rarely wore her white coat on the paediatric ward, which was great and much better for the children, but did leave her with the dilemma of where to put her pens and equipment. Beth leisurely poured Ellie a coffee and told her to sit down and calm down, there being no particular rush that day to get started. Ellie could not help but spend a moment or two thinking how very different it would have been if she had still been on Whitby Ward.

The ward round went well. On the neonatal unit, the patients were progressing steadily, if slowly. Ellie gazed at their tiny bodies, overwhelmed by tubes and wires, their little heads protected and kept warm by white knitted caps. They were so utterly defenceless that it never failed to bring a lump into her throat. The Labour ward was quiet with no deliveries pending and the older children's ward was noisy and lively with yesterday's admissions who had made rapid recoveries overnight and were now getting out as many toys as possible while they waited to be given the official notice of discharge.

More coffee followed as plans were made for some of the sicker children. Ellie was left to write discharge letters to general practitioners, which took her until lunchtime, one of her peers being less scrupulous about getting these done promptly and having allowed a backlog to build up. Keen to get away smartly on time, or if possible a little sooner, Ellie gave lunch a miss to concentrate on her paperwork, which was arduous but important. She tried to put herself in the position of the GP receiving the letter (which she shortly would be) and imagine what information she would find useful.

The afternoon dragged by, with Ellie watching the clock every few minutes. As the clinic drew to a close, she asked to be excused and ran back to the ward, startling visitors who were ambling down the corridors. They stepped back in horror tinged with morbid intrigue, imagining that she was on her way to a medical emergency, the like of which they had only ever witnessed on television. Ellie grabbed her bag and shouted goodbye to everyone. She was touched when some of the children waved vigorously as she hurried from the ward and realised, not for the first time, how much she would miss them when this job was completed.

Time was of the essence. She had only half an hour to get to the airport, a trip that could take twenty minutes on a good day and immeasurably longer on a bad one. Today was neither one nor the other. It being the rush hour did not help, with many drivers on their way home for the weekend, content to chug along, obeying the speed limits, looking at the countryside, happy with the prospect of a brief respite from the daily commute. Ellie, contrary to her usual manner, drove close up behind them, bizarrely thinking that if she did so, they might read her mind and accelerate. There were few parts of the journey where overtaking was either permissible or conceivable and the amount of traffic coming in the opposite direction negated all these possibilities. Hitting her hand on the steering wheel, Ellie became increasingly wound up, knowing at the same time that it was achieving nothing at all apart from high blood pressure.

Finally she swung off to the left towards the airport and located the short stay car park that would be suitable for her brief holiday. The weather, she was pleased to notice, had improved. The skies were clearer and the stifling heat had eased leaving a refreshing breeze and good conditions for an aircraft taking off. Ellie fervently hoped that it would be just as suitable for landing at the other end.

The airport was teeming with people. Businessmen with shiny briefcases and rolled-up newspapers under their arms were waiting impatiently for their internal flights to take them home. Smartly dressed women were arguing into their mobile phones. Children with rucksacks on their backs were following their casually clad parents, clearly off to seek the sun for their holidays.

Ellie scanned the departures list and found where to check in. There were only a handful of other passengers on her flight and she was relieved to find that they were already being called through to a departure gate. In the duty-free shop, Ellie treated herself. She had got this far, admittedly cutting it a bit fine, but there was nothing left for her to do now apart from board the plane. Remembering Nigel's advice, she bought a fat paperback, a murder mystery by an author she had not experienced before but had read good reviews about, and then indulged in some gifts for her hosts.

The flight was delayed. Ellie fell into a chair in the small restaurant and watched the board for news of her flight. All that hurrying for nothing. She suddenly felt tired out, slightly smelly from all the sweat she had worked up rushing hither and thither and grimy from sitting in the airport lounge.

A gin and tonic plus a couple of chapters of her book later, she felt mellower. There was already a good selection of corpses who had met their ends in a variety of unlikely and gruesome ways. She was fascinated by the pathological details, though not quite so convinced by the heroine whose vocabulary consisted predominantly of a lot of coarse language.

Hearing her flight number called, Ellie waited while a handful of people stood up simultaneously and made their way across the room before following them. An apologetic steward, dressed all in tartan, welcomed them aboard and promised them a smooth flight that, winds permitting, might actually be rather shorter than planned. No sooner were they airborne than she reappeared, tartan jacket removed to reveal a more workmanlike short-sleeved shirt, offering free drinks to compensate for the delay and Ellie, determined to make the most of her trip, but already feeling a little woozy from a gin and tonic drunk quickly on an empty stomach, gratefully accepted a glass of wine and a small bag of crisps.

To Ellie, the flight seemed very smooth and uneventful. How much of this was due to her alcohol-induced relaxed frame of mind was debatable but the fact that the time passed easily was all she needed to be aware of. She was, in fact, so relaxed that as they began to descend, she was on the verge of nodding off but thanks to a small hiccup due to a patch of turbulence, she was jerked back to reality with a lurch.

By the time the plane had landed and taxied across the apron, Ellie was starting to feel a little apprehensive. Now that she had actually reached Scotland, the weekend had begun and there was no turning back until Sunday. Then she thought of Christina and Clive, how kind they were and what good company they were. She felt a little foolish for being so churlish as to doubt the fact that she might have a good time and remonstrated with herself as she was squashed in the aisle of the plane while everyone tried to access their bags from the overhead lockers at the same time. They filed out onto the tarmac. Fresh, wild air, mixed with the chemical smells of aircraft fuel hit her nostrils as she stared around her. Dutifully, she followed her fellow travellers to the main terminal building and stood in the orderly queue around the baggage carousel. She was unlucky. Suitcases of all descriptions appeared from the outside, the black plastic flaps snapping closed loudly until the next piece of baggage, until finally Ellie's small but functional weekend bag appeared, last of all.

Alone, she walked along the passage towards the door to the main arrivals lounge, wondering if Clive or Christina would be there, or maybe both of them. She hoped that they knew of the delay, otherwise they would have been waiting for some considerable time. The automatic doors slid open to let Ellie through. She looked around but there was no sign of either of them. Her heart sank. The last thing she wanted to do was get the weekend off to a bad start by her hosts being inconvenienced. She walked around, but still could see no one. The area was emptying quickly as passengers were collected or leapt into waiting taxis. Ellie looked on enviously as wives greeted their husbands lovingly and then led them away to the car park.

She sat down, unsure what to do next. She seemed to have planned for every other eventuality apart from this. Logically, the sensible thing to do would be telephone the house, but, remembering that it was over an hour's drive from the airport, she pondered on the wisdom of waiting a little longer in the hopes that either of them showed up. She looked up expectantly each time the doors to the terminal glided open, only to be disappointed. More times than not, the opening mechanism had merely been triggered by someone on the outside walking past.

'I'd better telephone,' she said out loud, rummaging in her handbag for her mobile. She was dismayed to find that the battery had run down and looked around for a public phone. Fortunately she spotted one not far away. Not wanting to leave her holdall unattended, she lugged it over to the phone booth. She found the house number in her notebook and fished out some loose change. She was just balancing the coins on the top of the machine before dialling when a voice behind her said,

'Taxi for Dr Woods.'

'Thank goodness,' she replied with a heartfelt sigh, putting her cash back into her pocket for speed and picking up her bag again.

She turned, expecting to see anyone apart from the person who was actually waiting for her.

'Ian!' she cried, dropping her bags and throwing herself into his open arms.

'Ellie!' he whispered, holding her very close, at that moment vowing inwardly that he would never let her go again.

The weekend was magical. As they drove back to the house, Ian confessed that Ellie was the innocent victim of his plan, which would not have been possible without the help of his mother.

'My first plan didn't work. I wanted to surprise you,' he explained. 'But it was me who got the surprise. There I was, turning up with flowers – which I though was a rather good idea and sure to please –

only to be shouted at and told to go away.'

Ellie was mortified as the penny dropped, remembering the occasion only too clearly.

'I knew that you didn't realise it was me. But I hadn't got a clue what was going on.' Ellie wondered what to say but fortunately he continued. 'So I rang Mum and together we concocted this plan, which I must say, is a far better idea.'

'It is,' Ellie endorsed. 'It's just wonderful. It is so good to see you, Ian. I just can't tell you how good.'

They drove along in silence apart from Ellie's gasps of rapture at becoming reacquainted with the countryside. The scenery which had been so splendid almost six months previously had become even more magnificent and Ellie found herself just as entranced by the views, even though she had seen them before. The house was just as she recalled but now the gardens surrounding it were awash with colour and the lawn neatly cut (Ian was quick to point out that he had done this job that afternoon before setting off for the airport). The car crunched to a halt at the bottom of the steps leading to the front door and Ian leapt out first so that he could open Ellie's door for her.

Touched by his chivalry, Ellie leant against him and he put one arm around her shoulders, picked up her holdall with his other hand and together they went indoors. Inside, it was refreshingly cool. Ian looked on with amusement while Ellie peeped into the downstairs rooms, excited at seeing them again.

'Where are your parents?' she asked, appearing from the kitchen.

'Back at home, I expect,' he replied. 'I trust you don't mind being here alone with me...'

'Not at all, it's even more perfect.'

Ellie, slightly ashamed of her griminess, went to shower and freshen up while Ian promised to start on their supper. On her return, she found him with two steaks, a pile of salad vegetables and a cookery book, looking out of his depth. She took the hint, gently guided him to a stool and took over. They talked continuously as she cooked, Ian whetting their appetites with a glass of excellent wine and watching her adoringly while she made cooking look easy. They stayed in the kitchen to eat, sitting up at the worktop, relaxed and at total ease with one another as if they did this every night.

'Delicious,' pronounced Ian. 'Leave the washing up. Let's go up onto the hills for a walk.'

Hand in hand they clambered up the slope behind the house, still chatting as they had so much to say. The actual content of their conversation was of little relevance, they simply needed to catch up with every little nuance that they might have missed. At the summit, they sat on lichen-clad rocks, staring out to the horizon, their shoulders just touching, their fingers entwined. The still-warm breeze blew Ellie's hair across her face and she loved the way that Ian tried to stroke it away from her eyes.

Sitting there in that remote spot, their conversation assumed greater depth. Ellie admitted what had happened the day he had called, describing how irritating and persistent Jeremy had been. She then spoke of her parents and her grief, telling Ian secrets of how she felt, emotions that she had not dared describe to anyone else, even Nigel. But as he held her, she felt so secure that she knew instinctively that telling him would help her and that he would understand. He said no words but uttered encouraging noises and hugged her tighter when she sobbed before kissing the tears off her cheeks and making her laugh again. She studied his face with incredulity. It did not matter what she said or did, whether she cried with sadness or mirth, his reaction was solid, dependable and appropriate, a phenomenon she had never experienced with anyone before.

They strolled back to the house, made up the fire in the sitting room and sat up late into the night, neither wanting to make the first move to go to bed and disturb the deliciousness of their reunion.

Ellie slept in the same room as she had done on her first visit. If she was surprised or disappointed when Ian showed her there, she concealed the fact admirably and rested well after some initial insomnia, waking full of excitement at the prospect of the day ahead. Hearing Ian moving about downstairs, she dressed quickly and ran down to join him and make his breakfast. He greeted her with a crushing hug.

'I'm so sorry about the weather.'

Ellie looked at the window, where rain was teeming down the glass panes. The magnificent view had disappeared and was replaced by mist and low cloud. Even the flowers in the garden seemed to be dispirited and lacking the exuberance they had exhibited the day before.

'Perhaps it'll clear up,' Ellie suggested optimistically but feeling downcast.

'It looks set for the day, I'm afraid.'

'Not to worry,' Ellie said, balancing sausages on the grill pan and putting it under the heat. She broke some eggs into a bowl and beat them confidently. 'Let's eat first and then review the situation.'

By the end of their meal, which they took as long as possible over, the weather, if anything, was even worse. They adjourned to the sofa in the sitting room and cuddled up on it.

'We could go for a drive,' Ellie kissed his cheek. 'Or be touristy and go on a boat trip. But it'd be very wet.'

'We could go into Inverness,' returned Ian, kissing her back, on the lips.

'Hmm, I'm not keen on that. Probably be really busy.'

'Yes, it would be.'

'We could look what's on at the cinema...'

'That's a possibility, I suppose...but we'd get soaked just getting there.'

He looked at her, raising one eyebrow. Understanding, she smiled and gazed into his eyes.

'I can think of something we could do here,' she suggested, a little timidly.

He returned the smile.

'Do you know, so can I.'

CHAPTER 25

He took her hand and led her upstairs.

26

Six months later, Ellie was moving house again. She stood in the hallway of her new home, surrounded by packing cases, house plants and boxes, even more excited than she had been when she had first moved into Swaledale Crescent. Outside she could hear Ian laughing with the removal men, telling them where to put various pieces of furniture and then the ominous sound of something being dropped.

'Don't worry,' she heard Ian call. 'It was just some books.'

When they had returned from Scotland, Ellie, buoyant with the energy that comes with falling in love, had literally rolled up her sleeves and cleared out her parents' home. With Ian popping in at regular intervals and insisting that she was as ruthless as she could be, the job, whilst not easy, got done. Local charity shops benefited, in particular the hospice shop. Many trips to the tip were mandatory. Ellie felt that she was not far off being on Christian-name terms with the rather surly, muscle-bound chap who seemed to be in charge and shouted at people for putting the wrong items in the incorrect skip when he wasn't sitting in his hut which seemed to be furnished with the best pickings of other people's rubbish.

One weekend, Nigel and Emily came round and the four of them brightened up the walls with a fresh, light paint after a thorough clean-up. They sat on the floor eating fish and chips, drinking warm white wine out of plastic picnic cups that Ellie had unearthed from the back of the hall cupboard, Nigel reminiscing about Diana and Keith, telling the others wonderful stories about them, making Ellie feel so proud that she joined in, for the first time concentrating on all the happy memories that were stored for all eternity in her mind and that no one could take away.

It went without saying that Nigel was over the moon about Ellie and Ian. Both he and Emily had been privy to the plan to get Ellie to Scotland making her understand instantly why he was so insistent that she should not renege on her invitation.

Ellie was rather saddened when her parents' property was put on the market. It was so final and the bungalow looked so forlorn with the estate agent's sign leaning to one side in the front hedge. Several offers came in almost instantaneously, which she found a little frightening but was glad at least that it was attracting a lot of attention. With Ian advising her, she avoided making the mistake of accepting the first offer and hung on, to be rewarded with a far better one slightly more than the asking price and the sale went through uneventfully. It felt decidedly odd when she closed the front door behind her for the very last time, as if that part of her life was gone but not forgotten. Ahead of her was an open car door, with Ian waiting inside to embark with her on the next chapter, which promised romance and excitement.

Ellie's job in general practice was as good as she hoped. She fitted in at the practice and quickly became popular with the doctors, staff and patients. John Britton turned out not just to be a trainer but a good friend and role model in addition and he and Faye regularly invited Ellie and Ian for meals and to stay for weekends. Shortly before Christmas, he called Ellie into his surgery just after she had seen her last patient. Worried that she had done something wrong, Ellie felt nervous as she waited outside his door and knocked. Hearing him shout for her to come in, she was taken aback to find the other three partners in with him. Now she was really scared.

'We'd like you to come and join us, Ellie, as a partner. If I'm not wrong, I think you've enjoyed your time with us as much as we've enjoyed having you and we can't think of anyone better for the job.'

Ellie could barely dial Ian's number, she was so euphoric and of course he was thrilled for her. He met her that evening, having booked a table for dinner and they drank champagne and toasted to her success as a principal in general practice.

It was a hard Christmas for Ellie as she could not help but compare it with the previous year. She and Ian spent the day with Clive and Christina and Ellie was flattered by their sensitivity and the way they handled her. With a certain guilt gnawing away her insides, she really enjoyed the day. They gave her presents, took her round to the neighbours for lunchtime drinks and then put on the most superb meal in the evening for eight, having invited Nigel and Emily and Emily's parents Jean and Rupert. Christina had pulled out just as many stops as Diana would have done and Ellie could not help but chuckle at the ubiquitous crystallised lemon and orange slices, sticky dates and sugared almonds, which, true to form, just about everyone avoided. Satiated by rich food, Ellie promised her stomach that she would not eat again for a fortnight. She rested her head in her cupped hands, elbows on the table and looked around at her generous and warm-hearted friends. Nigel was whispering to Ian, Jean was showing Emily how to crack walnuts without making a mess and Clive and Rupert were having a hot debate about cognac. Christina came in from the kitchen.

'I forgot to put the crackers out. Here, everyone.' She passed them round and the room was filled with startling bangs, ripping of paper and the predictable groans as jokes were read out.

'Ellie hasn't had one!' cried Ian.

'Don't worry,' Ellie begged him.

'No, you must have one. You stay where you are, Mum, I'll get one for her.'

He returned in an instant and held one end of the cracker towards her. Ellie took it politely and pulled, suddenly aware as she did so that the room had gone quite quiet. Something landed on her empty plate. She looked down.

'Open it,' urged Ian.

Ellie gave him a quick glance and carefully prised open the lid of the small velvet box. Winking up at her was the most glorious, scintillating diamond ring.

She opened her mouth but no sound came out.

'Ellie,' Ian began, dropping on to one knee by her side, 'will you marry me?'

'Yes, yes. Yes please.'

The other erupted into cheers and whoops of congratulation as Ellie and Ian kissed each other passionately, momentarily oblivious of all but themselves.

There was a lot to plan and Jean was immediately keen to get started on the wedding, thinking that an Easter theme could be workable, with eggs, chocolate and rabbits all to take on starring roles. Ellie shuddered inwardly at the thought of her chicken costume being resurrected but Ian was swift to point out that, had she not been wearing that precise outfit when they first met, he might not have fallen in love with her immediately. Gratefully but gently, Ian and Ellie tried to rein her in, determined to get Ellie settled in her new job and if possible find a house near Lambdale and move in before getting married. They did agree to set a provisional date for late June and promised to listen to Jean's innovative suggestions before making any final decisions.

Down a short lane, only a short drive from the surgery, they found a large, double-fronted property, with a well-stocked garden that encircled the house, useful outbuildings and a large adjoining paddock. It was in need of quite a lot of work and Ellie would have been put off, had it not been for Ian's ability to see the potential that was lurking there. They put in an offer, haggled a little, thought they had lost it and then after one nerve-racking telephone call, heard that it was theirs.

Ellie decided to rent out her house in Harrogate to some doctors who had come to join on the general practice training scheme and thus wanted a base for three years. She hoped that they would make reliable tenants – at least it gave her some time to concentrate on her new house.

They moved in on a spring day, daffodils waving a welcome as they arrived, tiny buds on the horse chestnut trees a promise of spring being just around the corner. By the time the removal men had left, both Ian and Ellie were shattered and could do no more than fall wearily on some comfy chairs.

'We've nothing to eat,' mourned Ellie.

'I'll ring for a pizza,' replied Ian, struggling to his feet to look for the telephone and the directory.

While he ordered, Ellie managed to find the correct box marked 'kitchen' and unwrapped two wine glasses. Thanks to the fact that they had had the foresight to do two things, one, put a bottle of wine in the fridge and two, make the bed, she felt she was able to put her feet up. Pouring two glasses, she presented one to Ian and sat on his knee.

'Here's to our new home,' he toasted. 'I think we're going to be very happy here, don't you?'

'It is going to be simply wonderful.'

And she was right.

THE END